Special thanks to Benjamin Moser for spearheading the retranslation program of all Clarice Lispector's fiction at New Directions, a fifteen-year campaign now completed with THE APPLE IN THE DARK.

◆

PRAISE FOR CLARICE LISPECTOR

"Sphinx, sorceress, sacred monster. The revival of the hypnotic Clarice Lispector has been one of the true literary events of the twenty-first century." —Parul Sehgal, *The New York Times*

"Lispector should be on the shelf with Kafka and Joyce." —*Los Angeles Times*

"One of the twentieth century's most mysterious writers in all her vibrant colors." —Orhan Pamuk

"Everything about Clarice Lispector was unlikely: her great beauty, her early fame, her unique voice, her status as an icon to Brazilians, her passions and masks, and her family history as the daughter of destitute Jews who barely escaped the murderous pogroms of their native Ukraine to settle in Recife. Perhaps as important to modern literature as Virginia Woolf." —Judith Thurman

"It's not enough to say that Lispector bends language or uses words in new ways. Plenty of modernists do that. No one else writes prose this rich." —Lily Meyer, NPR

"I love her because she writes whole novels where not one thing happens—she describes the air. I think she's such a great, great novelist." —John Waters

"Brilliant, demanding, tempestuous, relentless, exultant." —Martin Riker, *The New York Times*

The Apple in the Dark

THE APPLE IN THE DARK

Clarice Lispector

Translated from the Portuguese by Benjamin Moser

Afterword by Paulo Gurgel Valente

A NEW DIRECTIONS PAPERBOOK ORIGINAL

Published by arrangement with the Clarice Lispector estate and Agencia Literaria
Carmen Balcells, Barcelona. Originally titled *A maçã no escuro*

First published as New Directions Paperbook 1579 in 2023
Manufactured in the United States of America
Design by Erik Rieselbach

Library of Congress Cataloging-in-Publication Data
Names: Lispector, Clarice, author. | Moser, Benjamin, translator. |
Valente, Paulo Gurgel, writer of afterword.
Title: The apple in the dark / Clarice Lispector ; translated by Benjamin Moser ;
with an afterword by Paulo Gurgel Valente.
Other titles: Maçã no escuro. English
Description: New York, NY : New Directions Publishing Corporation, 2023. |
Originally published under the title A maçã no escuro.
Identifiers: LCCN 2023016474 | ISBN 9780811226752 (paperback ; acid-free paper) |
ISBN 9780811226769 (ebook)
Subjects: LCGFT: Novels.
Classification: LCC PQ9697.L575 M313 2023 | DDC 869.3/42—dc23/eng/20230410
LC record available at https://lccn.loc.gov/2023016474

10 9 8 7 6 5 4 3 2 1

New Directions Books are published for James Laughlin
by New Directions Publishing Corporation
80 Eighth Avenue, New York 10011

By creating all things, he entered into everything. By entering into all things, he became whatever has form and whatever is formless; he became whatever can be defined and whatever cannot be defined; he became whatever has support and whatever has no support; he became whatever is coarse and whatever is subtle. He became all manner of things: that is why the wise men call him the real one.

— Vedas (Upanishads)

Contents

First Part

HOW A MAN IS MADE

1

THIS STORY BEGINS ON A MARCH NIGHT AS DARK AS night gets while you sleep. The way that, peaceful, time was passing was the extremely high moon passing through the sky. Until much deeply later the moon disappeared too.

Nothing now would distinguish Martim's sleep from the slow and moonless garden: when a man was sleeping so in the depths he came to be nothing more than that tree over there or the leap of a toad in the dark.

Some of the trees had grown up there with rooted ease until reaching the top of their own crowns and the limit of their destiny. Others had already come out of the earth in sudden tufts. The flower beds had an order to them that was concentratedly trying to serve a symmetry. If that symmetry were discernible from the height of the balcony of the big hotel, a person standing even with the flower beds could not make out this order; amidst the beds the driveway was picked out in small chiseled stones.

Above all on one of the lanes the Ford had been parked for so long that it already belonged to the great interwoven garden and its silence.

Yet by day the landscape was different, and the crickets vibrating hollow and hard would leave the expanse entirely open, without a single shadow. Meanwhile the smell was the dry smell of exasperated stone that daytime has in the countryside. On that very same day Martim had stood on the balcony trying, with useless obedience, not to miss anything that was going on. But whatever was going on wasn't much: before the beginning of the road that wandered off in the suspended dust of the sun, just the no-more-than-contemplatable garden; comprehensible and symmetrical from up on the balcony; tangled when you belonged to it—and for two weeks the man had been keeping that memory in his feet with careful studiousness, stashing it for a possible use. No matter how much attention he paid, though, the day was unscalable; and like a dot drawn atop another dot, the voice of the cricket was the cricket's own body, and told you nothing. The only advantage of the day is that in the extreme light the car was becoming a little beetle that could easy reach the main road.

But while the man was sleeping the car would become enormous the way a halted machine is gigantic. And at night the garden was occupied by the secret weaving with which the dark sustains itself, in a work whose existence the fireflies unexpectedly bring; a certain moistness would also denounce the labor. And the night was an element in which life, because it became strange, was recognizable.

It was in that night that, reaching the empty and sleeping hotel, the car's motor gave a jolt. Slowly the dark had begun to move.

Instead of waking and hearing it directly, it was through an even deeper dream that Martim went to the other side of the darkness and heard the noise that the wheels made spitting out dry sand. Then his name was pronounced, clear and clean, somehow pleasant to the ear. The German was the one who had spoken. In his dream Martim savored the sound of his own name. Then the vehement cry of a bird, whose wings had been frightened in their immobility, the way fright resembles great joy.

When the silence remade itself inside of the silence, Martim slept even farther away. Though in the depths of his sleep some thing was echoing difficultly, trying to organize itself. Until, without any meaning and free of the inconvenience of having to be understood, the noise of the car remade itself in his memory with the details more finely picked out. The idea of the car awakened a soft warning that he didn't immediately understand. But that had already spread through the world a vague alarm, whose irradiating center was the man himself: "so, then, me," his body thought, feeling moved. He remained lying down, remotely basking.

Two weeks ago that man had come to the hotel, found in the middle of the night almost without surprise, so much did exhaustion make everything possible. It was an empty hotel, with just the German and the manservant, if he was a manservant. And for two weeks, while Martim was recovering his strength in an almost uninterrupted sleep, the car had remained halted along one of the lanes, its wheels buried in the sand. And so immobile, so resistant to the man's habit of incredulity and to his care in not letting himself be fooled, that Martim had finally ended up thinking of it as at his disposal.

But the truth is that already in that night of wobbling feet — when he'd finally let himself collapse half-dead into a real bed with real sheets — already in that instant the car had represented the guarantee of another escape, in case the two men should show themselves more curious about the identity of their guest. And he'd dropped into sleep confident as if nobody would ever manage to wrest from his firm claw, which was only holding the sheet, the imaginary steering wheel.

The German, however, had asked him nothing, and the manservant, if that's what he was, had hardly glanced at him. The reluctance with which they'd accepted him didn't come from mistrust, but from the fact that the hotel hadn't been a hotel for a long time — as much time as it had been uselessly for sale, the

German had explained to him, and, in order not to look suspicious, Martim had nodded with a smile. Until the new highway was built, this was where cars still had to pass, and the isolated plantation house couldn't be better located as a forced rest stop for people spending the night. When the new highway had been laid out and paved fifty kilometers away, creating a distant detour, the whole place had died and there was no more reason for anyone to need a hotel in the region that had now been left for dead. But despite the apparent indifference of the two men Martim's stubborn search for safety had been anchored in that car upon which spiders too, tranquilized by the varnished immobility, had carried out their ideal aerial labor.

This was the car that in the middle of the night had uprooted itself with a croak.

Within the once again intact silence, the man now looked stupidly at the invisible ceiling that in the dark was as tall as the sky. Tossed on his back in the bed, he tried in an effort of gratuitous pleasure to reconstruct the sound of the wheels, since as long as he didn't feel pain it was as a general rule pleasure that he'd feel. From the bed he couldn't see the garden. A bit of fog was entering through the open shutters, which revealed itself to the man with the smell of damp cotton and with a certain physical ken for happiness that mistiness gives. It had just been a dream, then. Skeptical, however, he got up.

In the shadows he couldn't see anything from the balcony, and he couldn't even guess at the symmetry of the flower beds. A few stains blacker even than blackness indicated the probable location of the trees. The garden was still no more than an effort of his memory, and the man looked quietly, asleep. The odd firefly was making the darkness even more vast.

Having forgotten the dream that had led him to the balcony, the body of the man thought it was nice to feel itself healthily standing: because the suspended air was hardly changing the dark position of the leaves. There, then, he let himself remain, docile, stupefied, with the line of empty rooms behind him. Without emotion those empty rooms were repeating him and repeating him until going out somewhere the man could no longer fathom. Martim sighed inside his long daydream. Without pushing too much, he tried to reach the notion of the final rooms as if he himself had become too big and scattered, and, for some reason he had already forgotten, needed obscurely to pull himself together in order perhaps to think or feel. But he couldn't, and it was quite delightful. That's how he stood there, with the courteous appearance of a man who'd been struck on the head. Until—the way a watch stops ticking and only then makes us realize that it was ticking in the first place—Martim noticed the silence and inside the silence his own presence. Now, through a very familiar incomprehension, the man started at last to be indistinctly himself.

Then things started to reorganize themselves from the starting point of himself: darknesses started being understood, branches started slowly to take shape beneath the balcony, shadows divided into still-irresolute flowers—with their limits hidden by the motionless lushness of the plants, the flower beds were marked out full, soft. The man grunted approvingly: with a certain difficulty he'd just recognized the garden that during these two weeks of sleep had constituted at intervals his irreducible vision.

It was at that moment that a faint moon crossed a cloud in great silence, in silence spilled over calm rocks, disappearing in silence in the darkness. The moonlit face of the man then looked toward the lane where the Ford ought to be immobile.

But the car had disappeared.

The man's whole body suddenly awakened. In a sly glance his eyes ran over the whole darkness of the garden—and, without a gesture of warning, he turned toward the room with a monkey's light leap.

Nothing however was moving in the hollow of the room that had become enormous because it was so dark. The man stood panting watchful and uselessly ferocious, with his hands held out for the attack. But the silence of the hotel was the same as that of the night. And without visible limits, the room was prolonging in the same exhalation the darkness of the garden. In order to wake up the man rubbed his eyes several times with the back of one of his hands while leaving the other free for defense. His new watchfulness was pointless: in the darkness his totally open eyes couldn't even see the walls.

It was as if they'd dumped him by himself in the middle of a field. And as if he'd finally awakened from a long dream in which had featured a hotel now dissolved onto an empty floor, a car merely imagined by desire, and above all else as if the reasons for a man to be all expectant in a place that was itself only expectation had disappeared.

All he had left of reality was the wisdom that had made him leap in order indistinctly to defend himself. The same wisdom that was now leading him to reason with unexpected lucidity that if the German had gone to turn him in it would be a while before he could go and come back with the police.

Which still left him temporarily free—unless the manservant had been asked to keep an eye on him. And in that case the manservant, if that's what he was, would be at this very moment at the door of that very room with his ears listening for the guest's slightest movement.

That's what he thought. And summing up his thinking, at which he'd arrived with the malleability with which an invertebrate makes himself smaller in order to slip away, Martim plunged back into the same previous absence of reasons and into the same obtuse impartiality, as if nothing had anything to do with him, and as if the species would take care of him. Without a backward glance, guided by a slick dexterity in his movements, he started to climb down from the balcony pressing his unexpectedly flexible feet onto the bumps of the bricks. In his watchful remoteness the man was sniffing close to his face the malevolent odor of the straggly ivy as if he'd never again forget it. His soul now simply alert couldn't tell what mattered and what didn't, and to the entire operation he gave the same scrupulous attention.

With a soft leap, which made the garden choke in a held-back sigh, he found himself right in the middle of a flower bed—which trembled all over and then closed back up again. With his body on the lookout the man waited for the message of his leap to be transmitted from one secret echo to the next until being transformed into a distant silence; his thud ended up spreading across the slopes of some mountain. Nobody had taught the man this connivance with whatever happens in the night, but a body knows.

He waited a bit longer. Until nothing happened. Only then did he tap his pocket with caution in search of his glasses: they were whole. He sighed with care and finally looked around. The night was of a great and dark delicacy.

2

THAT MAN WALKED MILES LEAVING THE PLANTATION house further and further behind. He tried to walk in a straight line and sometimes would freeze up for a moment grasping with wariness the air. Since he was walking in the darkness he couldn't even guess in what direction he'd left the hotel behind. The thing that led him in the dark was just his own intention to walk in a straight line. The man might as well have been black, so little use the lightness of his own skin was to him, and he only knew who he was because of the sensation inside himself of the movements that he himself was making.

With the meekness of a slave, he was fleeing. A certain sweetness had overtaken him, except that he was monitoring his own submission and was somehow directing it. Not a single thought was disturbing his constant and already numb march, except for every once in a while the unexplained idea that he might be walking in circles, with the disconcerting possibility of once more finding himself before the walls of the hotel.

Always, besides the ground that his steps were reaching, was the darkness. He'd already walked for hours, which he could calculate by his feet swollen with fatigue. He'd only discover where the horizon was traced when day broke and the fog dissolved.

Since the darkness was still so stuck to his uselessly open eyes, he ended up concluding that he hadn't escaped the hotel at dawn, but in the middle of the night. Having inside him the great empty space of a blind man, he was moving on.

Since he didn't need his eyes, he tried walking with his eyes closed, since as a generalized precaution he was trying to save his energies wherever he could. With his eyes closed it seemed to him that he was turning around on himself in a dizziness that wasn't at all unpleasant.

As he was walking the man was feeling in his nostrils that acute lack of odor that is the property of very pure air and that keeps itself apart from any other fragrance that you also might be able to smell—and this was leading him as if his only destiny were to encounter the finest part of the depth of the air. But his feet had the distrust of millennia of the possibility of stepping onto something that might move—his feet were feeling out the suspicious softness of things that take advantage of the darkness in order to exist. Through his feet he entered into contact with that way of giving in and being able to be shaped that is the way you enter into the worst part of the night: into its permission. He didn't know where he was stepping, though through the shoes that had become a means of communication, he was feeling the dubiousness of the earth.

The man couldn't do anything but wait for the first half-light to reveal a path to him. Meanwhile he could sleep on the ground that, distanced by the darkness, seemed unreachable to him. No longer prodded by danger, the wisdom that would now only be a hindrance to him had disappeared. And again the soft bru-talization was overtaking him. The ground was so far off that, abandoning his body, that body for an instant experienced the fall into the void. He'd however hardly touched the ground that retreated at his feet, and that ground instantly was disenchanted into something resistant, whose hard stable wrinkles seemed like those of the palate of a horse's mouth. The man stretched his legs and laid down his head. Now that he had immobilized himself, the air had sharpened and was hurting extremely cleanly. The man didn't feel like sleeping but in the dark he didn't know what to do with his great watchfulness. Anyway there was nothing to watch.

By now he'd already grown used to the strange music you hear at night and which is made of the possibility of something squawking and of the delicate friction of silence up against silence. It was a lament without sadness. The man was in the heart of Brazil. And the silence was savoring itself. But if mildness was the way you could hear the night, for the night mildness was its own sharp sword, and in mildness the whole night was contained. The man didn't let himself be bewitched by the delight he felt in the tenderness; he could guess that for miles around the darkness knew he was there. So he kept on the lookout, having under perfect control the night's means of communication.

Several times he tried to find a more comfortable position. He was taking an impersonal care of himself as if he were a package. But beneath was the definitive ground, above the only star, and the man was feeling awakened by the two things awake in the darkness. With each movement he made, his face or his hands would encounter something energetic that once pushed away would return with a slight slap at him. He groped around with wise fingers: it was a branch.

A moment more, however, and abruptly sleep assaulted him in the most unexpected position: with one of his hands protecting his eyes and the other pushing away the rough foliage.

The man slept watchfully for hours. Exactly the hours it took for a thought to shape, whatever thought it might be, since he could no longer reach himself except through the sharpness of sleep. From the moment he'd closed his eyes the vast inarticulable idea started to take shape—and everything worked so perfectly that the idea filled, without a break and without needing to go back a single time to correct itself, the sleep he was needing in order to sleep. While he was sleeping he wasn't feeding off the little he had become, but was taking from some thing like from his race of man, which was indistinct and satisfactory. Through that thing made of growling he was reaching a great deal: his mouth was thick with good and nutritive saliva. So, when the final step of his future was complete, Martim moved on the hardness of the ground. He hadn't yet opened his eyes but as he felt his own numbness he recognized himself, and with reluctance understood that he was awake.

In fact atop his thin eyelids he had already felt with pain the great weight of the day.

But in a mistrust without intelligible reason he apparently thought it was more prudent to communicate with the situation through touch: with his eyes closed, he slid gradual fingers across the earth that now, with a promising sign, which he didn't understand but approved, seemed less cold and less compact. With this primary guarantee, he finally opened his eyes.

And a rough brightness blinded him as if he'd received in the face a salty wave of sea.

Stunned, his mouth open, that man was childishly seated in the middle of a stretch of desert that extended out of sight on every side. It was a stupid and dry light. And he was sitting there like a doll dropped into the middle of that thing that was asserting itself.

The place where he found himself was far from being confused in the way in the dark his sleeping feet had imagined. Worried, his body didn't know if it should or shouldn't feel pleasure in this discovery. With caution he noted the few trees scattered by the distance. The infinite ground was dry and reddish. It wasn't a forest as he'd calculated by the branch that had hit him in the face. He'd happened to fall asleep near one of the rare bushes in the open field.

Seated, he was however looking around on the alert: because if silence is a natural part of darkness, he hadn't counted on the vehement muteness of the sun. He'd always experienced the sun with voices. He therefore remained motionless in order not to frighten whatever was there. It was a silence as if something were about to happen that a man doesn't notice, but the few trees were swaying and the animals had already disappeared.

Wisely keeping in mind his own limitation that was making him more defenseless than a rabbit, he then waited with his head uplifted as if a neutral pose would make him invisible. Nobody had taught him that either. But in two weeks he had learned how it is that a being doesn't think and doesn't move and nevertheless is entirely there. After, with the carefulness of prudence, he started to look almost without moving his head, merely tilting it imperceptibly backward, in order to enlarge his field of vision.

And what Martim saw was an extended plain vaguely rising. Far away a slight slope was beginning which, thanks to its lines, was promising to slide into a yet invisible valley. And at the end of the silence of the sun, there was that elevation sweetened by gold, barely discernible amidst mists or low clouds, or perhaps by the fact that the man hadn't dared put on his glasses. He didn't know if it was a mountain or just illuminated haze.

Reassured then by the vastness of the distance that was pushing off any extremities, the man started slowly bringing his gaze to everything around him in a more personal way.

In the calm expanse, the odd bush stuffed by the final immobility of the sun. Spaced far apart, a few rigid trees. The occasional boulder was arising perpetual.

Then the man undid the tension of his body: there was no danger. It was a calm and loyal expanse, entirely at the surface of itself. And without any traps—except the short and hard shadow that dug itself in next to every thing that had been placed there. But there was no danger. In fact you couldn't even imagine that that place had a name or had ever been seen by anyone. It was just the great empty and inexpressive space where, out of their own free will, stones and stones were arising. And that brightness of energy that had set him on edge was nothing more than the other side of the silence. Even so, with extreme frankness, the brightness as much as the silence were looking with exposed faces at the sky.

The sun's silence was so total that his ears, rendered useless, tried to divide it into imaginary stages as on a map in order to comprehend it gradually. But right after the first stage the man started to spin inside infinity, which startled him as a warning. His ears, rendered more modest, tried at least to calculate where the silence would end: in a house? in some forest? and what actually was that smear in the distance—a mountain or just the darkness that comes from the heaping up of distances? His body was hurting.

But by standing up the man unexpectedly retrieved all the stature of his own body. Which automatically gave him a certain superiority as if, by standing, he had inaugurated the desert. And despite his hunched shoulders, he felt himself dominating the expanse and ready to follow it. Though he was blinded by the light: there none of his senses were helping him, and that brightness was disorienting him more than the darkness of the night. Any direction was the same empty and illuminated route, and he didn't know which path would mean moving forward or going back. In truth, wherever the man tried to stand, he himself became the center of the great circle, and the merely arbitrary start of a path.

But ever since, two weeks ago, that man had experienced the power of an act, he had also seemed to have gone to allowing the stupid liberty in which he was finding himself. Without a thought of reply, then, he withstood motionless the fact that he was his own only point of departure.

Then, as if contemplating for the last time before departure the place where his house had been burned down, Martim looked at the great sunny emptiness. He saw it clearly. And seeing was what he could do. Which he did with a certain pride, his head held high. In two weeks he had recovered a natural pride and, like a person who doesn't think, had become self-sufficient.

Soon his even and repeated steps created a monotonous march. Thousands of rhythmic steps that addled him and brought him forward by themselves, benumbed, inflated by fatigue, now moving ahead with the look of a contented idiot. So much that, if he stopped, he'd fall. But he kept going and getting more and more powerful. As time went by, the sun was getting rounder and rounder.

It was in the direction of the sea that the man had intended to go, even before finding the hotel by a happy coincidence. But— without a map, knowledge, or compass—he'd threaded his way inland. Either because any path would necessarily end up in an open coast, which was a truth, but difficult to attain with feet; or since in reality he didn't have the slightest plan to go to any specific place. Later, with the flattening continuation of days and nights—and joining himself to the continuation, pasting his whole body onto it, had become the secret objective since he had fled—with the continuation of nights and days the man had ended up forgetting the reason why he'd wanted to find the sea. Maybe it wasn't for any practical reason. Perhaps it was just so that, when he finally reached the sea, in an instant of obscure beauty, that's where he would have arrived.

Whatever the reason might have been, he'd forgotten it. And walking without stopping, the man scratched his head violently with hard fingers: he had a naughty pleasure in having forgotten. Which didn't stop even now—if in the semiwatchfulness of his steps he'd close the eyes whose moisture the light had already dried—even now the vision of the former desire was being made concrete. When he closed his eyes he suddenly saw green water break against cliffs and salt his hot face. So he ran his hand across his face and smiled mysteriously as he felt his hard beard growing sharp, which also was some promising and satisfying thing; he smiled in a scowl of false modesty, and hurried his steps still more. He was being led along by the tenderness of the beast, the same that lends animals such a lovely pace.

But sometimes, to that body that his steps had rendered mechanical and light, a deserted sea no longer meant much. And searching inside himself, only God knows why, the contact with a more intense desire—he managed to see the sea full of the extreme height of masts and of the rattling of the gulls! gulls of intestines screaming their breath of salt, the fizzing sea of those who depart, the tide that leads further on. I love you, his gaze said to a stone, because the sudden sea of screams had profoundly disturbed his own intestines, and that's how he looked at the stone.

A kilometer later the man however had already forgotten that form of sea, whose effort of invention had in fact left him exhausted. And stumbling hurriedly on the pebbles, he stretched in a great appeal his arms toward the desire of a nocturnal sea, whose murmuring would unravel at last the thickness that exists in silence. His hollow ears were thirsty, and the primary murmuring of the sea would be the thing that least endangered the cautious way in which he had become just a walking man. Because he'd stretched out his arms abruptly, he lost his balance and almost fell—his heart thumped in fright several times. All his life that man had been afraid of one day falling over during a solemn occasion. Since it would have to be at that moment that, losing the guarantee with which a man stands on two feet, he ventured into the painful acrobatics of awkward flight. With his mouth wide open, he looked around because certain gestures become terrifying in solitude, with a final value in and of themselves. When a man collapses by himself in a field he doesn't know to whom to give his fall.

For the first time since he'd started walking, he stopped. He no longer even knew what he'd stretched out his arms to. In his heart he was feeling the misery that exists in suffering a fall.

He then started walking again. Limping was lending a dignity to his suffering.

But with the interruption he'd lost an essential speed for which he tried to compensate by substituting a kind of intimate violence. And since he needed to look forward to something awaiting him—once again the sea broke in fury against a cliff.

Reaching the sea someday was, however, something of which he only now was using the dream part. He didn't think for so much as a moment about acting in such a way that the happy vision would become a reality. Not even if he knew which steps would bring him to the sea, would he take them now—so much had he been slowly with instinctive wisdom shrugging off everything that could keep him fettered to a future, since future is a double-edged sword, and future molds the present. With the passing of the days other ideas too had gradually been left behind as if, the longer that time by not defining the danger was making it all the greater, the man was shaking off everything that weighed him down. And especially everything that could keep him stuck to the previous world.

Until now—without any desire, lighter and lighter, as if hunger and thirst were likewise a voluntary detachment in which he was slowly starting to take pride—until now he was moving ahead enormously in the countryside, looking around with an independence that went to his head with an uncouth pleasure, and started to make him dizzy with happiness. "It must be Sunday"—he even came to think with a certain glory, and Sunday would be the great crowning of his impartiality. It must be Sunday! he thought with sudden haughtiness as if his honor had been offended.

This was his first clear thought since leaving the hotel. In truth, ever since he'd fled, this was the first thought that didn't have the mere usefulness of defense. At first, moreover, Martim didn't even know what to do with it. He simply stirred at the novelty, and scratched himself voraciously without ceasing to walk. Then, approving of himself with ferocity and following the thought with a hoarse encouragement, he repeated: it must be Sunday.

Apparently it must have been more of an indirect acknowledgment of himself than of the day of the week, since, without halting his stride for a second, he completed the radiant and dry gaze that he'd just called "Sunday" with an awkward tap of his pockets. For no reason, except that of fatigue itself, he was walking faster and faster. In fact he could now hardly keep up with himself. And agitated in this competition with his own steps—he looked around with innocent bedazzlement, his head boiling with sun.

Without counting the days that had passed there was no reason to think it might be Sunday. Martim then stopped, a bit disconcerted by the need to be understood, of which he had not yet freed himself.

But the truth is that the countryside had a clean and foreign existence. Each thing was in its place. Like a man who closes the door and goes out, and it's Sunday. Besides, Sunday was a man's first day. Not even woman had yet been created. Sunday was a man's countryside. And thirst, freeing him, was giving him a power of choice that inebriated him: today is Sunday! he determined categorically.

Then he sat upon a stone and quite stiff looked out. His gaze met no obstacles and wandered in an intense and tranquil noon. Nothing was keeping him from transforming his escape into a great journey, and he was ready to enjoy it. He was looking.

But there is something in a stretch of countryside that makes a lone man feel alone. Seated on a stone, the final and irreducible fact—is that he was there. Then, with sudden tenderness, he lovingly tapped the dust from his jacket. In an obscure and perfect way he himself was the first thing set down on the Sunday. Which was making him as precious as a seed, he plucked a piece of lint from his jacket. On the ground his black and defined shadow was outlining without room for error the place he was. He himself was his first frame.

Although, besides trying to clean himself up as a simple matter of decency, the man didn't seem to have the slightest intention of doing anything with the fact of existing. What he was doing was sitting on the stone. Neither did he plan to have the slightest thought about the sun.

This then was where freedom ended up. His body squealed with pleasure, the woolen suit was making him itch in the heat. The limitless freedom had left him empty, every one of his gestures would echo back like handclaps in the distance: when he scratched himself, this gesture rolled directly toward God. The most dispassionately individual thing would happen when a person had freedom. At first you're a stupid man having as an advantage the greatest solitude. Then, a man who got whacked in the face and nevertheless smiles blessedly because at the same time the whack gave him as a gift a face he never suspected. Then, bit by bit, you start, slyly, to pull yourself together and to take the first immodest intimacies with freedom: the only reason you're not flying is because you don't want to, and when you sit on a stone that's because instead of flying you sat down. And then?

Then, like now, what seated Martim was experiencing was a mute orgy in which was the virginal desire to degrade everything that was degradable; and everything was degradable, and that degradation would be a way of loving. Being content was a way of loving; seated, Martim was very content.

And then? Well, really only whatever would happen then is what he'd say would happen then. For the time being the fugitive man remained seated on the stone because if he wanted to he could not sit on the stone. Which was giving him the eternity of a perched bird.

After which, Martim got up. And without questioning what he was doing, he knelt before a dry tree in order to examine its trunk: he no longer seemed to need to reason in order to make up his mind, he'd disburdened himself of that too. So he tore off a half-loose piece of bark, crumbled it between his fingers with a slightly affected attention, behaving as if he were in front of an audience. And this having been his study of the peculiar way in which whatever is unknown organizes itself, Martim stood as if in response to an order and continued his march.

It was further on that he halted in front of the first little bird.

Picked out in the great light was a little bird. Since Martim was free, that was the question: in the light the little bird. With the careful zeal to which he was growing accustomed, he set to work straightaway greedily with this fact.

The little black bird was perched on a low branch, at the level of his eyes. And prevented from flying by the man's rude gaze, it was moving more and more uncomfortably, trying not to face whatever was about to happen to it, shifting nervously the weight of its body from one foot to the other. That's how the two remained facing off. Until with a heavy and powerful hand the man picked it up without hurting it, with the physical goodness that a heavy hand has.

The bird was trembling all over inside the hand without daring to peep. The man looked with a harsh and indiscreet curiosity at the thing in his hand as if he had imprisoned a fistful of living feathers. Slowly the small dominated body stopped trembling and its tiny eyes closed with a female sweetness. Now, against the man's extremely auditive fingers, only the minute and quick beating of the heart indicated that the bird hadn't died and that comfort had resigned it to rest at last.

Startled by the automatic perfection of what was happening to him, the man snarled looking at the little animal—satisfaction made him laugh out loud, with his head tossed back, which made his face confront the great sun. Then he stopped laughing as if that had been a heresy. And absorbed by its task, the half-closed hand letting only the bird's hard and sharp head peek out, the man started walking again with lots of strength bearing his companion in mind. The only thing in him that was thinking was the sound of his own shoes echoing in the head that the sun was now tranquilly igniting.

And soon, with the sequence of his steps, once again the physical taste for walking began to overtake him, and also a barely discerned pleasure as if he had ingested an aphrodisiac drug that made him want not a woman, but to respond to the tremor of the sun. He'd never been so close to the sun, and he was walking faster and faster clasping before him the bird as if he had to bring it before the post office closed. The vague mission was inebriating him. The lightness that came from thirst suddenly overtook him in ecstasy:

—Yes, indeed! he said loud and meaningless, and he was looking more and more glorious as if about to drop dead.

He looked around at the perfect circle that, in a stunned horizon, the sky of lights was making as it joined an ever softer earth, ever softer, ever softer … The softness bothered the man with the pleasure of an itch, "yes, indeed!", and he free, freed by his own hands—for suddenly it seemed to him that had been what happened to him two weeks before.

Then he repeated with unexpected certainty: "yes, indeed!" Each time he'd say these words he was convinced that he was alluding to some thing. He even made a gesture of generosity of largesse with the hand that was holding the little bird, and thought magnanimously: "they don't know what I'm referring to."

Afterward—as if thinking had reduced itself to seeing, and the confusion of light had trembled inside him as inside water—it occurred to him in a confused refraction that he himself had forgotten whatever he was alluding to. But he was so stubbornly convinced that it was something of the greatest importance, though so vast that it was no longer discernible to him, who respected with haughtiness his own ignorance and allowed himself ferociously: "yes, indeed."

— You no longer know how to talk?!

The man halted with a wide-open mouth. As if he'd been thrown forward, he saw again the impatient face of a woman who had once cut him off only because he hadn't answered her. The first time the sentence had sounded like just another sentence—while trams were dragging themselves along and the unremitting radio was playing and the woman ceaselessly listening to the radio with a lack of ennui and hope, and he one day had broken the radio while the trams were dragging themselves along, and yet the radio and the woman had nothing to do with the meticulous rage of a man who probably already had inside himself the fact that one day he'd have to begin from the exact beginning, he who was now starting from Sunday.

But this time the simple irritated phrase, resounding in the red silence of the countryside, made him grind to a halt with such perplexity that the little bird awoke moving afflicted wings inside his hand. Stunned, Martim looked at it, astonished to have a bird in his hand. The drunkenness of the sun had been suddenly cut off.

Sober, he looked with modesty at the thing in his hand. Then he looked at the Sunday countryside with its silent stones. He'd been sleeping deeply while he'd walked and for the first time was waking up. And as if a new wave of sea were breaking against the rocks, the brightness settled in.

The man looked with docility at the little bird. Without a mind of their own, his now innocent and curious fingers let themselves obey the extremely living movements of the bird, and opened inert: the bird flew in a bolt of gold as if the man had launched it. And it perched worriedly on the highest stone. From there it was looking at the man, chirping without relent.

Paralyzed for a moment, Martim looked at it and looked at his own hands that, empty, were looking at him astonished. Pulling himself together, however, he ran furiously over to the little bird, and in that way chased it for a short while, his heart beating in rage, his impatient shoes stumbling over the pebbles, his hand getting scraped in a fall that made a little rock roll in several dry leaps until going mute …

The stillness that followed was so hollow that the man tried to hear one last thud of the stone in order to calculate the depth of the silence into which he had tossed it.

Until a wave of great light undid the tension of waiting, and Martim could look at his hand. It was burning, and thin blood was seeping out. Forgetting his chase, very interested now, his dry lips sucked at the scrape with a keenness of a caress like a person who is alone. At the same time that it awakened his thirst, the blood in his mouth gave him a warrior attitude that immediately passed.

When the man finally raised his eyes, the disturbed little bird was waiting for him as if it had only struggled because it planned to surrender. Martim held out his wounded hand and grabbed it with a firmness without effort. This time the bird flapped less and, recognizing its former shelter, made itself comfortable in order to sleep. With the light weight to carry, the man continued his march amidst stones.

—I no longer know how to speak, he then said to the little bird, avoiding looking at it out of a certain tactful modesty.

Only later did he seem to understand what he'd said, and then he looked straight at the sun. "I lost the language of others," he then repeated nice and slow as if the words were more obscure than they were, and somehow quite flattering. He was serenely proud, with bright and satisfied eyes.

Then the man sat on a rock, erect, solemn, empty, officially grasping the bird in his hand. Because some thing was happening to him. And it was some thing with a meaning.

Though there was no synonym for that thing that was happening.

A man was seated. And there was no synonym for any thing, and so the man was seated. That's how it was. The nice thing was that it was indisputable. And irreversible.

It's true that that thing that was happening to him had a weight that needed to be borne—he was well aware of the familiar weight. It was like the weight of himself. Though it was some matchless thing: that man looked as if he no longer had anything equivalent to put in the other pan of the scale. He was vaguely aware of that. In his former apartment sometimes he'd had this discomfort mixed with pleasure and awareness—which had always resulted in some decision that had nothing to do with the disconcerted feeling. He'd never felt it, it's true, with that final neatness of the desert. In which he was helped by his own shadow that was marking him off unmistakably on the ground.

That thing that he was feeling must be, in the final analysis, just he himself. Which had the taste that the tongue has in the mouth. And that lacked a name the same way that the taste the tongue has in the mouth lacks a name. It wasn't, then, anything more than that.

But, in the face of that thing, a person would grow a bit attentive; and growing attentive to that, was being. Thus, then, on his first Sunday, he was.

Which, however, started to get a bit intense. The man then moved uncomfortably on the rock, responding physically to the immateriality of his own tension, like a person who's disturbed. And if that's what he did that was because, though he didn't know himself, he was familiar enough to himself to know how to reply. That though wasn't enough. He then looked around, like someone seeking the counterpoint of a woman. But there wasn't so much as a synonym for a man seated with a bird in his hand.

So, patient and dignified, he waited for the thing to pass without so much as touching it.

Because that man had always had a tendency to fall into profundity, which one day could lead him to an abyss: that's why wisely he took the precaution of refraining. His restraint, on the easily breakable scab of profundity, gave him the pleasure of refraining. It had always been a difficult balance, that balance of his, not to fall into the voracity with which waves and waves were awaiting him. A whole past was just a step from the extreme caution with which that man was seeking to keep himself merely alive, and nothing more—the way an animal sparkles in its eyes alone, keeping behind it the vast untouched soul of an animal. Then, without touching it, he prepared to wait stolidly for the thing to pass.

Before it passed, he involuntarily recognized it. That—that was a man thinking ... Then with infinite distaste, physically clumsy, he recalled in his body what a thinking man is like. A thinking man was one that, when he saw something yellow, would say with a dazzled effort: this thing that is not blue. Not that Martim had quite reached the point of thinking—but he'd recognized it in the way you recognize in the shape of the legs the possible movement. And more than that he recognized: that thing in fact had been with him during his entire escape. It was only out of carelessness that he'd now almost let it spread.

Then, startled, as if in alarm he'd recognized the insidious return of an addiction, he was so repulsed by the fact of almost having thought that he pressed his teeth in a painful grimace of hunger and helplessness—he turned worriedly in every direction of the desert seeking amongst the stones a way of recovering his powerful previous stupidity that for him had become a source of pride and dominion.

But the man was disturbed: so a person couldn't take two free steps without falling into the same fatal error? since the old system of uselessly thinking, and of even savoring thinking, had tried to return: sitting on the rock with the little bird in his hand, out of negligence he'd even felt pleasure. And, if he neglected himself another minute, he'd recover in a single gush his previous existence: when thinking had been the useless action and pleasure simply shameful. Helpless, he moved on the hot rock: he seemed to be seeking an argument to protect him. He was needing to defend something that, with enormous courage, he'd conquered two weeks ago. With enormous courage, that man had finally stopped being intelligent.

Or had he ever really been intelligent? the happy doubt made him blink his eyes with great vivacity—since if he managed to prove to himself that he'd never been intelligent, then he would reveal as well that his own past had been something else, and would reveal that some thing in the depth of himself had always been whole and solid.

"The truth is," he then thought trying out with care this defensive stratagem, "the truth is I just imitated intelligence the way I could swim like a fish without being one!" The man stirred contented: imitated? but yes! Because, by imitating whatever it would mean to come in first in the statistics exam, he'd come in first in the statistics exam! The truth is, he then concluded very interested, he'd just imitated intelligence, with that essential lack of respect that makes a person imitate. And along with him, millions of men who were copying with great effort the idea that they had of a man, alongside the thousands of women who were copying attentively the idea they had of a woman and thousands of people of goodwill were copying with superhuman effort their own faces and the idea of existing; not to mention the anguished concentration with which they were imitating acts of good or evil—with a daily care not to slide into some act that was true, and yet incomparable, and yet inimitable, and yet disconcerting. And meanwhile, there was some old and poor thing in some unidentifiable place in the house, and people sleep worriedly, discomfort is the only warning that we're copying, and we listen to ourselves attentively beneath the sheets. But we are so distanced by imitation that whatever we hear comes to us so without sound as if it were a vision that were so invisible as if it were in the darkness that was so compact that hands are no use. Because even comprehension, the person was imitating. The comprehension that had never been made of anything but someone else's language and of words.

But there was still disobedience.

Then—through the great leap of a crime—two weeks ago he had risked not having any guarantee, and had started to not understand.

And beneath the yellow sun, sitting on a rock, without the slightest guarantee—the man was now rejoicing as if not understanding were a creation. That caution that a person has in transforming the thing into something comparable and thus approachable, and, only starting from this moment of security, looks and allows himself to see because luckily it will always be too late to not understand—that precaution Martim had lost. And not understanding was suddenly giving him the entire world.

Which was entirely empty, to tell you the truth. That man had rejected the language of others and didn't even have the beginning of a language of his own. And yet, hollow, mute, he was rejoicing. The thing was excellent.

Then, to kick off the conversation, the person was sitting on the Sunday rock.

And the man, with perverse enjoyment, was feeling so far from the language of others that, from a daring that came to him from security, he tried to use it again. And he found it odd, the way a man who soberly brushing his teeth doesn't recognize the drunk from the night before. In that way, as he fumbled around now with still cautious fascination in the dead language, he tried out of pure experience to give the formerly so familiar title of "crime" to that thing without a name that had happened to him.

But "crime"? The word echoed emptily through the desert, and the voice of the word wasn't his either. Then, finally convinced that he wouldn't be captured by the former language, he tried to go a bit further: had he by chance felt horror after his crime? The man felt around carefully in his memory. Horror? and yet that is what language would expect of him.

But horror too had become a word from before the great blind leap that he'd taken with his crime. The leap had been taken. And the jump had been so great that it had ended up transforming itself into the only event he could and wanted to deal with. And even the motives for his crime had lost their importance.

The truth is that the man with wisdom had abolished motives. And had abolished the crime itself. Having a certain experience with guilt, he knew how to live with it without being bothered. He'd already previously committed the crimes not proscribed by law, so that he probably considered it just bad luck having carried out two weeks ago exactly one that had been proscribed. A good civic education and long training in life had made him good at being guilty without giving himself away, it wouldn't be just any torture that would make his soul confess itself guilty, and much would be necessary in order to make a hero finally cry. And when this happens it's a depressing and repugnant spectacle that we can't stand without feeling betrayed and offended; someone who represents the rest of us is unpardonable. It just so happens that, for special circumstances, in two weeks that man had become a tough hero; he was representing himself. Guilt could no longer reach him.

"Crime"? No. "The great leap"—those really did seem like his own words, dark like the knot of a dream. His crime had been an involuntary vital movement like the reflex of knee to a tap: the whole organism had gathered so that the leg, suddenly incoercible, could give the kick. And he hadn't felt horror after the crime. So what had he felt? The astonished victory.

That's what it had been: he'd felt victory. With bedazzlement, he'd seen that the thing unexpectedly was working: that an act still had the value of an act. And even more: with a single act he had made the enemies he'd always wanted to have—other people. And still more: that he himself had finally become incapacitated to be the former man since, if he went back to being that, he'd have to become his own enemy—since in the language from which up till then he had lived he simply couldn't be the friend of a criminal. So, with a single gesture, he was no longer a collaborator of other people, and with a single gesture had ceased to collaborate with himself. For the first time Martim found himself unable to imitate.

Yes. In that instant of astonished victory the man had suddenly discovered the power of a gesture. The goodness of an act is that it goes beyond us. In a minute Martim had been transfigured by his own act. Because after two weeks of silence, now he'd very naturally started calling his crime an "act."

The truth is that the feeling of victory had only lasted for a fraction of a second. Immediately thereafter he hadn't had any more time: in an extraordinarily perfect and lubricated rhythm, the deep numbness he'd needed in order for this current intelligence of his to be born had followed. Which was as rude and sneaky as a rat. Nothing more than that. But for the first time as a tool. For the first time his intelligence had immediate consequences. And it had become such a complete possession of his that he could skillfully specialize it into securing him, and securing his life. So much that he had instantly started to learn how to escape as if everything he'd done up till now in his daily life had been nothing more than a vague rehearsal for the action. And then that man had become finally real, a true rat, and any thought inside that new intelligence was an act, though hoarse as a still-unused voice. What he was now wasn't much: a rat. But as a rat, nothing in him was useless. The thing was excellent and deep. Inside the dimension of a rat, that man was fitting entirely.

Yes; all this had followed the crime to such a perfect extent that Martim hadn't even had time to think about what he'd done. But before—during a fraction of a second—before the victory. Because a man one day had to have the great rage.

He'd had it. And for the first time, with candor, he'd admired himself like a boy who discovers himself naked in a mirror. Apparently, with the accumulation of thoughts of goodness without the action of goodness, with the thought of love without the act of love, with heroism without heroism, not to mention a certain growing imprecision in existing that had ended up becoming the impossible dream of existing—apparently that man had ended up forgetting up that a person can act. And having discovered that in truth he'd already involuntarily acted, had suddenly given him a world so free that he'd grown dizzy in victory.

That man hadn't even wondered if there was anyone who could act except through the intermediary of a crime. What he stubbornly knew, simply, is that a man would have to have the great rage one day.

—I was like any one of you, he then said very suddenly to the rocks since they looked like seated men.

Having said this, Martim once again plunged into a silence as total as meditation. He was surrounded by rocks. The wind that was hotly blowing was piercing him as it had on the plain. Hollow and calm, he looked at the hollow and calm light. The world was so big that he was seated. Inside he had the resounding void of a cathedral.

—Just imagine—he then started up again unexpectedly when he was sure that he had nothing more to say to them—just imagine a person who'd needed an act of rage, he said to a small rock that was looking at him with the calm face of a child. That person went on living, living; and the others were also imitating with studiousness. Until the thing started getting very confused, without the independence with which each rock is in its own place. And there wasn't even any way to flee from yourself because the others were solidifying, with impassible insistence, the very image of that person: each face that that person would look at would repeat in a calm nightmare the same deflection. How can I explain to you—who all have the calm of having no future—that every face has failed, and that this failure had inside it a perversion as if a man slept with another man and thus no children were born. "Society was such a bore," as my wife said—the man remembered smiling with lots of curiosity. There'd been a mistake and he didn't know where it was. Once I was eating in a restaurant, the man recounted suddenly getting excited. No, no, I'm changing the subject! he discovered surprised, since his father was the one who'd always had a certain tendency to change the subject and even in the hour of his death had turned his face to one side.

—Just imagine a person—he then went on—who didn't have

the courage to reject himself: and so he needed an act that made others reject him, and that person then could no longer live with himself.

The man laughed with his dry lips as he used the trick of hiding behind the title of another person, which at the moment seemed to him a very clever little move; then he was satisfied as ever when he managed to fool someone. Maybe he was vaguely aware that he was playacting and boasting, but faking was a new door that, in the first squandering of himself, he could allow himself the luxury of opening and closing.

—Just imagine a person who was small and had no strength. He was surely well aware that all of his strength gathered together, penny by penny, would only be enough to buy a single act of rage. And he was also surely aware that this act would have to be quick, before his courage ran out, and it would even have to be hysterical. That person, then, when he least expected it, carried out this act; and in it he invested his entire small fortune.

Quite astonished by what he'd just thought, the man interrupted himself with curiosity: "so that's what happened?" It was the first time this was occurring to him.

It's true that up till now he hadn't even had time to think about his crime. But, approaching it at last at this moment, he'd approached it in such a way that no court would recognize it. Could he be describing his crime the way a man paints a table on a canvas—and nobody would recognize it because the painter had painted it from the viewpoint of someone who was underneath the table?

What had that man, in just two weeks, ended up doing with his own crime?

He still wondered with a few remains of scruples: "was that really what happened to me?" But a second more and it was too late: if that wasn't the truth, it would become it. The man felt with a certain gravity that this instant was very serious: from now on he would only be dealing with this truth.

What had escaped him was whether he'd explained his crime this way because that's how it had really happened—or if it was because all of him was ready for this type of reality. Or, even, if he was giving fake reasons with the mere slyness of a fugitive defending himself. But a long past of tendentious bluntness wasn't yet allowing him to know where inside himself his fingers would feel the vein respond the way it responds when you touch on the truth of the dream. And for the time being he was someone still very recent, so that everything that he said not only seemed excellent to him, but also that he'd be stunned merely by the fact of having managed to walk by himself.

In fact, at that instant, his only direct connection to the concrete crime was a thought of extreme curiosity: "how could this happen to me?" He was feeling inferior to the events that he'd created with the crime. For with his habit of life he'd burst out, an unhappiness that usually only happens to others. And suddenly it was no longer just words that had happened to him. Martim was sincerely frightened by the fact that the disgrace had reached him too and—more than that—that he had been in a manner of speaking up to it. He had a certain pride that at last the crime that had up till that point only been other people's had finally happened to him.

The man kept looking at the table from underneath—and what mattered was that he was recognizing it. It's true that hunger was also making a punishing effort; the rocks, though, were waiting intransigently for him to go on. Then, in order to let him rest, his head wisely fogged over a bit.

After which, Martim started again more slowly and tried to think with great care since the truth would be different if you spoke it with the wrong words. But if you spoke it with the right words, any person will know that that's the table we eat on. Anyway, now that Martim had lost the language, as if he'd lost some money, he'd have to manufacture whatever he wanted to possess. He remembered his son who had said to him: I know why God made rhinoceroses, it's because He couldn't see what they looked like, so he made a rhinoceros in order to see it. Martim was making the truth in order to see it.

Oh, it's quite possible that he was lying to the rocks. His only innocence, besides the tendentious habit of lying, was that he wasn't sure exactly where the lie was. So, in the face of this ambiguity, his head defensively fogged over even more. And, with a little trick that brought him back to before his great leap, he became a simpleton.

Remade, then, he started his sermon to the rocks again:

—With an act of violence the person of whom I speak killed an abstract world and gave it blood.

And he said this with the stoic resignation of someone who had already figured out how to avoid placing the emphasis on lying or telling the truth. That man had just unbound himself once and for all. After which, he was very satisfied looking. The thing was getting better and better. From underneath looking up, he was recognizing the table more and more.

And now, sitting on the rock with a little bird in his hand, with his mouth dry from thirst, with his eyes burning—after his crime, that man would never again need another revolt. From now on he would have the chance to live without doing evil because he'd already done it: he was now an innocent.

Maybe with his unpremeditated crime he hadn't even meant to go that far. But that had come to him too: he'd become an innocent. And, by God, he'd never meant to do that much: but he'd also shaken off a certain suffocating piety since he now was no longer guilty—"if you see what I mean," he thought with deeply rooted fatuity, since he'd shaken off the great guilt by materializing it. And now, when he'd finally been banished, he was free. He was at last one of the pursued. Which was giving him all the possibilities of those who despair. "I killed several rabbits with one stone," he said.

The big and little rocks were waiting. Martim was quite confident because, since his audience wasn't any smarter than he was, he felt comfortable. Anyway that man had never had an audience, strange as that may seem. That's because he'd never remembered to organize his soul into language, he didn't believe in speaking— maybe because he was afraid that, by speaking, he himself would end up not recognizing the table he was eating on. If he was speaking now that's because he didn't know where he was going, nor knew what would happen to him, and that was placing him in the very heart of freedom. Not to mention the fact that thirst was turning him on like an ideal.

Moreover, the improvised audience wasn't cultured, and he then abused it the way he'd grown healthily accustomed to abusing an inferior and to being abused by superiors. His own lack of culture had always embarrassed him, he'd been in the habit of making interminably an always updated list of the books he'd meant to read but some new work would always turn up and that set him back, he who didn't even keep up with the newspapers; he'd even planned to read up on "group psychology" since he'd always dealt with numbers and since he'd always been a man who could easily imitate intelligence: but he'd never had the time, his wife would drag him off to the movies, where he would go with relief.

The rocks were waiting. Some were round and dead like moonstones; they were somehow cross-eyed, patient, those children. But the others were gemstones of the sun and were looking straight ahead. "Like jewels," he thought, since he'd always had a general tendency to compare things to jewels. The rocks were waiting for the continuation of whatever he had started to think.

Occasionally they had a glance of extreme life that would transmit to the man a painful urge of empty happiness. "I think," he thought suddenly, "that until I die I shall always be very happy."

The sun was hurting into the depths of his head, and the man forced himself to speak once again because he'd felt inside him a hard facility—as when you have something to say even though you don't know how, but when this minimum of inspiration gives us strength for the difficult search. He even wanted to speak because there is no law that prevents a man from speaking. And for the time being what was fascinating Martim was any absence of obstacles. Besides, he was well aware that the world was so big that soon he'd even have to hold himself back. The rocks were waiting, having come from all sides for the cabal—to which he was bringing, like a voyager, the latest news. Some rocks were little and childish, others big and pointy, all seated in the court of innocence. It was an unequal audience in which childhood and maturity were mixed.

—Childhood and maturity, he then said to them all of a sudden. Yet there was a time in which the world was as smooth as the skin of a smooth fruit. We, the neighbors, wouldn't bite it because it would be easy to bite, and there was time. Life in those days still wasn't short. And meanwhile—the trees were growing. The trees were growing as if there was nothing in the world besides trees growing. Until the sun darkened, people came nearer, puddles multiplied and mosquitoes emerged from the heart of the flowers: things were growing. Things were mature. It was richer and more frightening, somehow it was becoming much more "worth the trouble." The nights became longer, father and mother were foresworn, there was a nasty thirst for love. The kingdom was that of fear. And it was no longer enough to have been born: it was heroism being born. But eloquence was sounding bad. People were bumping into each other in the dark, all light was disorienting people and blinding, and the truth was only valid for a day.

All our difficulties were immediately stumbling into a solution. We were lost with the solutions that came before us, to tell the truth the world was coming before us with each step. In a few seconds an idea would become original: when we would see a photograph with shadow and light and paving stones wet by the rain, we would exclaim unanimous and tired: that's very original. Everything was deep and rotten, ready to be birthed, but the child wasn't being born. I'm not saying it wasn't nice — it was great! but it was as if the person could do nothing more than look, and Saturday night would be that hell of the general will if it weren't for poker. Yet nothing would ever stop, people even worked at night. Power had become great; the hands intelligent. Everyone was powerful, everyone was a tyrant and I never let anyone step on my foot, my cleverness became great with the help of a bit of practice. Though there were those who, despite being mature, had — "had like leprosy their childhood devouring their breast."

That last phrase the man said with conceit because it seemed to him that he'd organized the words with some perfection. Certainly what made Martim experience this perfection was the fact that his words had somehow surpassed whatever he'd meant to say. And, though feeling duped by them, he preferred what he'd said to whatever he'd really meant to say, because of the much more certain way that things surpass us. Which also gave him, in the same instant, an impression of failure; and of resignation to the way he'd just sold himself to a phrase that had more beauty than truth. The first thing he was wastefully buying with his new money was an audience — but this audience had already forced him into an organized truth. Which let him down with a bit of curiosity. Because just once, previously, had he spoken: he'd been drinking and gave a speech in a joyous house where the women also looked like seated jewels because it was already dawn and work was over, and they were childish and mature.

—Yes, though there were those who had childhood in their breast, as if only our future were in memory—he reported to the rocks. But it's also true that the moments of sweetness were very intense. And it's also true that a song heard long ago could make the whole machine stop and knock out the world for an instant. "A minute of silence," my wife's radio would say, "for the general's death." There was a furious unease in that instant, nobody looked at each other even though we didn't know the general. People were unhappy with all the strength of virility. There wasn't moreover any other way to be an adult, and we savored and took advantage of it, nobody was a fool. It's true that every once in a while someone would speak in an exceptionally low voice. Because everyone would come running from every direction in order to hear the low voice. But it's true that everyone would suffer from not being able to testify and from not being able to sign too.

—But—the man said a bit offended by the impassible naturalness with which the rocks would accept whatever it was he was telling them, he was used to foreigners who "have nothing to do with any of this" and just take pictures—but the world wasn't just that either! he said to them patriotically. There were also other very nice things! and that was why, much more than just putting up with each other, we loved each other so much, oh how we loved each other! And there were even flaking walls, the man said a bit distracted losing his footing. There were houses that still hadn't been sold, and lots of people still weren't studying foreign languages, he said envying those who were studying foreign languages. And even—when you reached a certain very intense degree of fatigue, as if taking off our shoes, suddenly the entire world would be unveiled before us. And even every once in a while—maybe because you'd opened the wrong door—people understood each other! Which would mean that sometimes once again there was nothing but growing trees, tall and calm. And, above all, above all there were the children arising from our battlefields, pure and fatal fruits of nasty love.

After Martim said what he had to say, despite being satisfied, he felt tired, as if there were a mistake in something he'd said—and he had to do the infinite sum of figures all over again. At some not-identifiable point, that man had ended up stuck in a circle of words. "Had he forgotten to inform them of something?" The rocks would surely get the wrong idea. For someone who's never seen a head of hair, a single hair is nothing, and taken out of its water, a fish was just a shape.

Out of honesty he wanted to make it clear that he was aware that it was the sun that was filling up his words, and turning them so blistering and big; and that it was the insistent sun, with its insistent silence, that was making him want to speak. But he was also aware that if he mentioned his own fatigue, the rocks would immediately stop hearing him, because after all it was only people in full command of their faculties who had the right, which is the way it should be. But since whatever he was saying to them was important to him, and since he couldn't explain to them that fatigue was only serving him as an instrument, Martim preferred not to bring it up.

Meanwhile, he kept feeling with discomfort that he'd forgotten to say some essential thing, without which the rocks wouldn't understand at all. What? Ah. "That time kept, meanwhile, passing." Meanwhile all of that, time kept fortunately passing.

Had he also forgotten something else? He'd forgotten to tell them that he might have invalidated his right to speak: that not having had a vocation, and being therefore free of urgings, he had never really specialized in a desire, and therefore had never had a starting point—which was certainly invalidating the way he was describing other people to the rocks.

Anyway, he'd also forgotten to tell them—but he wouldn't tell them this because it would be immediately misinterpreted and frowned upon—that he'd always taken advantage of whatever he could take advantage of, since he'd never been a fool. That he'd said to a friend that it was a bad idea, he'd done the thing himself and earned a pretty penny and felt that nice triumph in his chest, impossible to substitute by any other pleasure, and that makes a man love his fellow creatures through the fact of having defeated them. He'd forgotten to say that, promising once to get married, he hadn't even left his new address. But, that bit of mischief, only those who live can understand. And the person feels immediately misunderstood when he tries to explain. And that's how time fortunately kept passing, with the dogs sniffing the corners.

The fact is that, after the man remembered all that, he started to think his past life was quite nice, and a kind of nostalgia filled his breast. But, that too, only those who live can understand. What could he actually say, and that a rock would understand? "That time fortunately kept passing," since time was the hard material of the rock.

Time fortunately kept passing. Until it happened the way that food that you ate during the day got eaten and then you go to sleep and in the middle of the night the person wakes up vomiting. Time fortunately kept passing.

But, with time passing, despite what you'd expect, he'd started becoming an abstract man. The way the fingernail never really manages to get dirty: it's only around the nail that gets dirty; and you cut the nail and it doesn't even hurt, it grows back like a cactus. He had started becoming an enormous man. Like an abstract nail. Which would grow solid when occasionally he'd do something base.

Yes, that had been what slowly had started happening—the man astonished himself. The opposite of a natural rotting— which would be obscurely acceptable by a perishable organic being—his soul had become abstract, and his thinking was abstract: he could think whatever he wanted, and nothing would happen. This was immaculateness. There was a certain perversion in becoming eternal. His body itself was abstract. And other people were abstract: they all sat in the chairs of the dark cinema, watching the film. As they were leaving the cinema—not even forgetting the sweet wind that was awaiting us, and that you can't even imagine since it has nothing to do with the stupid sun to which a rock falls victim and of which it ends up being made—as they were leaving the cinema, in the sweet wind, there was a man there begging for change, so they gave some abstract change without looking at the man who has the perpetual name of beggar. Afterward they'd go to sleep in abstract beds that kept themselves in the air atop four feet, they'd love each other with a bit of concentration; and fall asleep like a fingernail that had grown too long. We were eternal and gigantic. I, for example, had an enormous neighbor.

Everything going so well! More and more purified.

But in the middle of the night suddenly they'd awaken vomiting, wondering between one nausea and the next—in the middle of the phantasmagoric revolution that is a light turned on in the night—what it was that they ate during the day that could have done so much damage. The nail bigger and bigger, at this point they could hardly fold their hands properly.

—Until one day, then, a man was made concrete in the great rage, Martim told them as if incarnating his own logic.

Until one day a man would go out into the world "to see if it's true." Before he died, a man needs to know if it's true. One day at last a man has to go in search of a man's common place. So one day a man loads his ship. And, at dawn, departs.

—Who has never longed to travel? Martim said trying painstakingly to transform whatever he'd thought into something he himself could understand: a table you put plates on top of.

—Picture a man ..., he then said turning with much sensuality to the third person.

That was when, absorbed by the game, he suddenly realized what it was with a shock of recognition. Because seated on the rock, what he was doing was nothing else but: thinking. He had become once more a triangle in the sun, maybe an disincarnated emblem for the disincarnated rocks, but not for the living rat that he wanted to be.

With a shock the man looked at the rocks that were now nothing more than rocks, and he once again was no more than a thought. For a helpless instant, caught in flagrante by his own self, the man looked around. But he'd already gone so far that he wouldn't know how to free himself from the useless vice except with the vicious assistance of another thought. For an instant he still sought that thought—which showed just how much he was still relying on the fact of being the nail that scratches the tablecloth and with the same nail erases whatever was written.

But in the next instant he noticed the process. And because that man didn't seem to want to use thought ever again even to combat another thought—it was physically that suddenly he rebelled in rage, now that he had finally learned the path of rage. His muscles tensed savagely against the filthy awareness that had opened around the nail. Illogically, he was struggling primitively with his body, twisting himself in a grimace of pain and hunger, and with voracity all of him tried to become merely organic.

When the hysteria of his thirst calmed, sweat was streaming down his face. His forehead was freezing, the physical effort of the struggle had left him weak and dizzy. The sun was exploding sparks on the rocks. Weak, his stomach dry, Martim had never seen anything as shining as the sun when it shines. The plain white with light was surrounding him. The silence had a bang inside it. That light he vaguely recognized: it was the excessive light from which you live as long as you've been a man.

Tired, he took a deep breath. One last belated spasm ran through him in a colic. And finally the last frenetic movement halted like the convulsion of a horse. When he opened the hand that had stiffly contorted—he saw then that the little bird was dead.

The man peered at it. Even its legs already looked old and were shivering lightly in the breeze. The beak was hard. Without anxiety, the bird.

Once again the man's rage had ended up becoming a crime. He looked at the bird with care. He was amazed by himself. Because he'd become a dangerous man. According to the rules of hunting, a wounded animal becomes a dangerous animal. He looked at the little bird he had loved. I killed it, he thought curious.

Then, as if he'd done some definitive thing, the sober and tranquil man got up from the rock. Whatever there was of uncontrollable rapture in an act is that every act went beyond it. With a bit of reluctance he forced himself to get up, and whether he wanted to or not he was forced to go now to meet the reward for whatever he himself had created. He stood slowly, avoiding thinking that he had killed exactly the thing he loved the most.

And as if he'd survived the death of the bird, he compelled himself to look at the world in the thing that he himself had just reduced it to:

The world was big.

In this world greenery was growing without meaning and starving birds were flying as if it were Sunday. The tree that he saw was standing. In the beauty of silence, the tree. That's how the man deeply saw. He looked straight at the carefulness with which the beauty of the tree was useless. Three hundred thousand leaves were shaking on the tranquil tree. The air had so much excessive charm that the man averted his eyes. On the hard ground the bushes were prancing. And the rocks.

That was what he'd had left.

That man standing there didn't realize what law was commanding the harsh wind and the silent shimmering of the rocks. But having laid down the weapons of a man he was surrendering without defense to the immense harmony of the plain. He too pure, harmonious, and he too without meaning.

What was surprising him was the extraordinary peace of hell. He'd never imagined it with this silence that was listening to each one of his gestures. Nor with the ingenious perseverance of a tree. Nor with this enormous sun within arm's reach. Not that thing that didn't need him and to which he had just attached himself like one more star.

After that, having seen what a person can see, Martim deposited with a certain courtesy the little bird beneath the big tree. The final thing to forget had been killed.

Then he started walking once more as if he knew whither. His steps were keeping him busy.

3

BY LATE AFTERNOON MARTIM STARTED TO IMAGINE—
because of the finer type of soil and by the occasional encounter
with fruit trees—that he might be getting close to some kind of
settlement. He tried to eat one of the unknown fruits that, green
and juiceless, did no more than scratch his greedy mouth. But a
fresher air was blowing, and bringing the smell of running water.
The earth there was blacker. And finding a grove of ferns gave
him a feeling of moisture that made his dry back shiver with lust.

The silence itself had turned into something different. Though
the man didn't hear a single sound, the little birds were flying more
excitedly as if hearing something he wasn't hearing. The man
stopped watchfully. There was a shift of the air as if a dinosaur
were going slowly along in some part of the globe.

And, walking along, sometimes the wind would bring him a
vague appeal, a more intense demand. It was an alarm from life
that delicately alerted the man. But one he didn't know what to do
with as if he were seeing a flower open and were simply looking.

Martim could barely make out his own feeling, taking care not
to notice too much and to stop perceiving. The disrupted clamor
was reaching him as if from very far away someone were whispering near his ear: that was the obscure notion of distance that

he had, and he stopped to sniff around. Awkwardly left to his own devices, he seemed to be trying to use his own helplessness as a compass. He tried to calculate whether he was close or infinitely far from whatever was going on in some place. As soon as he stopped, and once again the silence of the sun would remake itself and disorient him.

Probably that thing toward which, uncertainly, the man was walking was created by nothing more than his keenness. And that intense way of wanting to get closer—since at liberty in the field of light what that man was seeming to want was obscurely to get closer—in fact his stumbling way of wanting to get closer was no more than a substitute for his absence of language. Maybe "wanting" would be henceforward his only way of thinking. Martim kept moving ahead, without realizing that he was hurrying toward nothing more than an allusion of the wind.

Until unexpectedly the wind brought him once again, in a conquest of his own extreme attention, the same kind of uninhabited stridence as if the brightness were so insistent that it had become audible. The man then halted, nullifying himself cautiously. And his whole face sought to capture the direction of that other quality of silence. But then only the empty air hit his hair. His auditive acuity was seeming to have reached a blessing of invention—but right when his receptivity became the most acute, he had nothing to hear.

Since the breeze was blowing from the left, he concentratedly turned from the path he was following—and very studiously, with the meticulousness of an artisan, tried to walk in such a way that it would always be in his face. That's how his groping face tried to follow the path open in the air and that was promising—what? The wind, the wind perhaps. The man had no plan formed and, as a weapon, seemed to have only the fact of being alive. In the calmest afternoon, he had now fallen into an empty and humbly intense clairvoyance that was leaving him body to body with the most intimate pulse of the unknown. His will kept going forward.

Now, gradually more systematically, every time that the wind started to hit only one of his cheeks or even his neck, the man, patient as a donkey, would correct the direction of his steps until he felt once again his mouth being hit by moisture. And it was only this way that sometimes once again the calm resonance would reach him as if he had created it. His hard and subtle struggle was threatening to stretch on indefinitely.

But when that man reached the crest of the slope—as if he'd finally grasped an illusion he'd chased his entire life and touched in its own intoxication, suddenly captured by a whirlwind of the tiniest joy—the air was opening into a free and swirling wind. And he found himself in a full clamor that was as inapprehensible as if it were the sound of the sunset.

He hadn't been wrong, then! What was it? it was just the wind. What was it? but it was the top of a mountain. His heart beat as if he had swallowed it. He, the man, had disembarked.

It was a mood of celebration. Of empty and dizzying celebration, as inexplicably happens to a man on the summit of a mountain. He had never been so close to the promise that seems to have been made to a person when that person is born. Stupidified, he opened his mouth several times like a fish. He was seeming to have reached some thing that a person doesn't know how to ask for. That thing to which darkly he could only say: I got it. As if he'd provoked the deepest part of an imagined reality. Sometimes the person was so greedy for a thing, that it would happen, and that's how the destiny of the instants was shaped, and the reality which we await: his heart, anxious because it was beating so amply, was beating amply. And as for a pioneer stepping for the first time on strange ground, the wind was singing high and magnificent.

With which sense the tired man perceived it, is hard to say, maybe with the acute thirst and with his final renunciation and with the nudity of his incomprehension: but there was celebration in the air. Which in truth was as unassimilable to him as that almost invented blue of the sky and which, like all very soft blue, ended up making him dizzy in glory foolish and in noble glory. The interior armor of the man flashed. Unattainable, yes, but there was celebration in the air the way he'd been promised sometime in processions or in some calm face of a woman or in the idea of one day achieving that ends up hastening the achievement. And to that man, who was the overwrought type, it seemed that in a manner of speaking he had worked hard in order to reach this valuable and useless thing. It would be an imbecilic smile on his face, if a mirror reflected it.

It was only then that Martim noticed that he'd been walking on the immense crest of a ridge, whose first slopes he had certainly climbed in the night, figuring it was a difficulty of his own something that had been the difficulty of a climb in the darkness; and, later, thinking that it was his own fatigue when it really had been a gradual nearing of the sun. But what mattered was that he'd made it. The vehement happiness of the sky was increasing in weight the strange heart. There was a gravity in being there that he himself wasn't understanding. But to whose hidden meaning he was responding with the face a man has when the wind and the silence slap his face. Somehow, then, it wasn't a lie! Because, wavering from fatigue, there he was standing as if a man had a prophecy inside him. Standing, with his legs rooted in fatigue, with a trembling craving inside him like a man who is going to learn how to read. And at the edge of his muteness, was the world. That imminent and unreachable thing. His starving heart dominated awkwardly the void.

It was a surprising time. The man fortunately didn't even try to understand it. Maybe whatever was inside him was just echoes of what he'd heard someone say: "that on a mountaintop you unveil."

Except he hadn't unveiled anything. And if, in his numbness, he rudely recognized that instant on the mountain, it was only because a person recognizes the thing he desires. In language there was not so much as a word that could name the fact of, in the swelling of himself, his having reached the top of the mountain. Then Martim said out loud:

—Here I am, he said, and in the heart of some thing.

At least physically he tried with some dignity to remain on the level of what he'd found: he straightened up to his full fitting height. Which he couldn't stand for long. And he sat on the ground.

Sitting on the ground, the land was very lovely. A beginning of sunset was hovering in a grin of immobilized brightness. Harmony—an immense and meaningless harmony—was spinning in his empty head. The sun was shuddering fixedly with the discipline of stained glass. Now that Martim had strangely provoked his own arrival, he didn't know what to do. Thus, then, the man was seated, submissive, breathing. It was true, then. Much earlier than he could understand, but it was obstinately true.

Until everything went green. A transparence had pacified itself in the plain without leaving a brighter patch. Then his head hollowed by thirst suddenly calmed down.

—What's that light, father. What's that light? he asked with a hoarse voice.

—It's the light of the end of the day, my son.

And that's how it was. The light had transcended itself in a great mystery.

4

WITH THE NEW LIMPIDITY OF VISIBILITY, THE MAN'S lethargy disappeared. And as if now his energy were within his own reach and measure, he arises without any effort. An impersonal alertness had overtaken him like that of a tiger with soft paws. Now he was real and silent.

When he reached the point of the ridge from which you could only go down, he made out the house surrounded by green lands down below, as if at his feet, but in a tiny size that gave him an idea of the true distance. He then started to climb down the slope, softly encouraged at his back by the slope itself. Led by thirst as his only thought, the man didn't feel his progressive steps and found himself finally at the same level as this: the distant house, another man who far away was sitting under a tree, some dogs scattered across the ground.

Now Martim saw the house as an equal: it was bigger than he thought and there was a dense cluster of dark trees, he couldn't be sure how far from the house but certainly only behind it. The dark end of these woods was lost in the distance itself, and moved ahead and behind as he was looking at it, as if for a man who steps onto solid ground after the high seas.

With the lightness of fatigue, as if wearing tennis shoes, he was moving forward. A sly elegance had already overtaken him: he was getting ready to face people. And the closer he was getting, the more he was recognizing that quiet tumult of life that hours before he had sniffed out and to which he seemed to have given the intimate name of "ideal"—and which now, even not yet divided into sounds, was familiar to him. Without the fake joy of the ridge, which had become just a death from the past, and without the least promise; but reassuring like a place where there is water. His radiant dizziness from the ridge had already been transformed into mere thirst, and into indistinct cunning. It's true that the very high purple sky was still inebriating him a bit.

He kept going flexibly. By now his empty head no longer was any use to him. In fact his advance was seeming to be guided only by the fact of that man's being between earth and sky. And what was keeping him going was the extraordinary impersonality that he'd reached, like a rat whose only individuality is whatever he inherited from other rats. That impersonality, the man kept it up by a slight repression of himself as if he knew that, as soon as he became himself, he would collapse capsized onto the ground. The extreme individuality itself that he had reached on the mountain mustn't have been anything more than a spasm of the blind totality with which he was moving forward: levitated by fatigue, he was transporting himself without feeling his feet touch the ground, having as his only fixed point awaiting him the distinct house getting bigger and bigger, bigger and bigger. Very erect inside that that thinness of air that was surrounding him and that would be, no matter how untouchable it was, the thing that most would fasten that man to that place.

Though he knew that the fretful dogs had already sensed him, he hid behind a tree in order to observe. By pushing aside branches he could examine the layout of the house, now fully visible. What was confusing him was that, quite a bit bigger than the house, there was an ant on the leaf closest to the eye that he was peeking out with, framing—equestrian, red, the monument of an instant—his vision. Martim shook his head several times until freeing himself from the dimensions that the monstrous ant had taken.

The highest floor of the house didn't follow the greater expanse of the ground floor, and was arising in an obdurate tower. Martim, in his previous life, had learned to crave towers; he felt, therefore, a great satisfaction. Around the house, tufts of daisies formed in his tired eyes yellow and wobbling clouds.

But if the house had become clearer as he came nearer, it had lost the previous synthesis of distance. And from behind the tree the man's gaze couldn't reunite into a single vision the lack of logic that he was seeing: a porch covered with roof tiles, windows that simple calculation couldn't help him discover where they led to, doors that were halfway open so that he could see nothing but the shadow created by distance; railings delimiting areas that wouldn't be areas if not for the arbitrary railings. You could tell that all of that had been done little by little, added onto according to need or whim. It was a poor and pretentious place. He immediately liked it.

Realizing that it could look suspicious to be hiding behind the tree, the man finally revealed himself. Without feeling, he'd opened his arms a bit showing that he was unarmed. And as he moved forward—met by the dogs who were now barking furiously—he saw from afar the indistinct figure moving on the porch.

Already close to him, however, was the man sitting on the ground underneath the tree. The man was eating, and the smell of cold food made Martim wretch with desire. His expression became urgent shy and mean as when a face is begging. The smell came raw to his nose, he almost vomited out of nausea, so intense was the smell. But his body had gained a new urge, the difficult steps overtook him—and soon he was standing before the man, looking at him with meticulous eagerness.

Without breaking off his chewing, the worker was looking fixedly at his own bare feet as if he deliberately hadn't seen the stranger. With the keenness that hunger had given his perception, Martim didn't let himself be fooled: a mute communication had established itself between the two of them as between two men in an arena, and the one that wasn't looking at him was waiting for his chance to leap. A light pleasure of rage then overtook Martim, in a vague promise of struggle that he only managed to keep going for an instant. Having had a sensation of power covered his forehead with cold sweat. An extremely light joy put a bit of cynicism into his face.

—Whose farm is this? he asked finally giving in to the other man's more powerful silence.

The barefoot man didn't even tremble. He slowly pushed away the plate, wiped his full mouth:

—This is all hers, he said slowly making a gesture with his head, and Martim, following with furrowed eyes the direction being indicated, saw now from closer by the figure on the porch. I'm from here too, the man added accompanying the information with a fake yawn.

Whoever made the first unconvincing move would have given the other his rights. The evening was lovely, bright.

—I got lost, said Martim softly.

—On the way out of Vila lots of people get lost around here, the other said softer still.

—Vila?

—Vila Baixa, the man said pointing his head vaguely to the left, and for the first time raising his eyes with a declared distrust.

Martim looked, and to the left was nothing more than the infinite extension of the earth, the sky lower and dirtier. Feeling that he was being examined, he became even smoother.

—That's what happened to me, he said. I'm going to go back to Vila Baixa. But before I'd like a bit of water. I want water! he then said to him putting everything on the line.

The man looked at him fixedly. In a truce from the struggle, he took the measure of the other man's thirst. In his gaze was no mercy but human recognition—and, as if the two loyalties were meeting, they looked at each other clean in the eyes. Which were slowly filling with some more personal thing. It wasn't hate—it was a love in reverse, and irony, as if both despised the same thing.

—Only inside, the worker finally said.

He got up with a faked difficulty and a deliberate slowness. Standing, for an instant the strangers took one another's measure with their gazes. The mutual rage made them look at each other and have nothing to say to each other. Though each allowed the rage in the other the way enemies respect each other before killing each other. Weaker than the calm power of the other man, Martim was the first to look away. The other accepted without pressing his advantage. Martim, once more experiencing the warm contact of an aversion, started to walk toward the house, followed at a certain distance by the victor and feeling on his neck his calm threat.

The dogs were growling indecisively, holding back their impatience and the joy of a fight. The whole evening, moreover, was of a great tranquil joy. A hobbling hound painfully joined the others, with the distressed expectancy of a cripple. Everything was soft and stimulatingly dangerous, deep down nobody seemed to care what was happening, and everyone was simply enjoying the same opportunity. Things were spinning around a bit, happy at the wrong time. By God, I never saw anything so nicely done, the dizzy man thought. A blacker dog suddenly deepened the evening as if Martim had fallen into an unsuspected hole. It was this dog that vaguely alerted him and seemed to recall to him other realities. He was feeling so light that he was really needing to tie a stone around his neck. Then he forced himself with difficulty to remember himself. But, to his own disadvantage, the place was too lovely, and to his own disadvantage he was feeling fine—which removed from his perception the main use of his struggle.

The farm or plantation wasn't very big, if you considered only the part of it covered with work: a few broken cottages, the stable, the plowed fields. But it would be huge if you also counted the neglected lands that, here and there, just as a mark of ownership, the rough fence marked off. The green of the trees was swaying dirtily, new leaves were peeking out from among the dusty ones.

The roots were thick and fragrant in that late afternoon—and set off in Martim an inexplicable bodily fury like an indistinct love. As starving as he was, the smells were turning him on like a hopeful dog. The earth, in a promise of sweetness and submission, seemed sandy—and Martim, apparently without any intention besides seeking contact, crouched down and almost without breaking off his steps touched it for an instant with his fingers. His head went dizzy from the delicious contact with the moisture, he rushed ahead with an open mouth. Closer to the house, he saw that the porch was now empty. The roof of the stable was falling to pieces, here and there it looked as if it were only held up by the height of the invisible cattle, whose movements were slowly raking through the empty light.

The water from the rusty can ran from his mouth onto his chest, soaking his clothes that were hard with dust. From the stable came once again a tranquil stirring of hooves. The sun had disappeared, and an infinitely delicate brightness was giving each thing its calm final shape. A cottage off to the side had had a door, whose memory no longer existed except in the empty hinges. Martim wet his face and his hair—and up ahead was the irregular roof of a garage ...

Having reached the tense threshold of the impossible, Martim greeted the miracle as the only natural step coming toward him. There was no way not to accept whatever was happening because for everything that could happen a man had been born. He didn't wonder if the miracle was the water that was drenching him to the point of saturation, or the truck beneath the canvas garage, or the light that was evaporating from the earth and from the illuminated mouths of the dogs. Like a man who attains a goal, there he was exhausted, without interest or joy. He was aged as if everything that could be given him were already arriving too late.

Beneath the covering, the old but perfectly clean and cared-for truck. And the tires? crossed his mind. His myopic eyes couldn't make out the details of the tires. The difficulty, filling him with the doubtfulness of hope, rejuvenated him. He placed, fascinated and slow, the can on the earth and, with his dripping eyelashes, examined the truck, bending down to look at the tires calculating their possibilities in terms of kilometers.

—How can I help you, sir? a low and serene voice asked.

Without taking fright or rushing, Martim turned around his whole body. And his face encountered a woman's inquisitive face. Behind him, he felt the halted man on the lookout. He came over to the porch, his hips slowly swaying. Hunger was lighting up his eyes with great guile, his dark lips cracking as he smiled. Beneath the porch, the ground was covered with purple poppies, wilted and heaped together. That vision seemed to the man to be one of plenty and abundance. He looked at the living flowers, some of them stripped of petals, others yet to open, in tranquil waste: his eyes blinked from covetousness. He was perceiving everything at the same time, swaying, savoring the brightness of his eyes that had the brightness of light itself.

But, without knowing from where, from some direction a mulatta girl had appeared with her hair rolled up in curls, and who had taken up position with quick eyes, laughing. Not only did

Martim not know where she'd come from, he didn't know when she'd turned up—which made him cautiously aware of the possibility that other things were escaping him too. The dogs had come up panting, without daring to attack. The wind and the silence were surrounding them. The man hitched up his belt.

—So, how can I help you.

—I was looking, he answered shamelessly.

And he straightened up his torso in an effort at urbanity.

—That I know, said the woman on the porch.

—He was thirsty, that's what he said, the man behind Martim said, and the woman heard him without however taking her eyes off the foreigner.

—I've already had something to drink, he said with a certain candor, pointing at the empty can. The sun was hot, he added moving the position of his legs.

Martim had a quality whose benefits he didn't enjoy because that quality was he himself—a quality which, in certain favorable circumstances, few women could resist: that of innocence. Which would provoke a certain corrupt covetousness in a woman who is always so maternal and likes pure things. Protecting innocence, women were ogres. The woman on the porch looked at him then with great chilliness:

—That you had something to drink, I also know.

In some way everything that was ever going to happen to that woman was already happening in that instant. He realized it in the following indirect way: he ran his hand across his forehead.

The excess of the water he'd drunk was bubbling inside him, and gave him a nausea that could be taken for a desire to sleep or to vomit, and gave his face a goodness of suffering, like a halo:

—Well, Martim then said turning around unhurriedly, farewell.

Vitória seemed to awaken:

—What is it that you wanted?

Their eyes met and pierced one another without the one's meeting anything in the other, as if they'd both already seen many other faces. Both seemed to know from experience that this was one of many scenes to be forgotten. And as if both of them knew what this capacity for exemption meant, without realizing for what reason, each tried to guess the other's age. The woman was long past fifty. The man was around forty. The mulatta was waiting with a laugh. Part of the man's head kept stubbornly trying to find the thread that had escaped him: at what point had the mulatta turned up?

Which made him lose once again another important thread: tiny steps had drawn nearer and Martim hardly had time to make out the figure of a black girl before she hid like a bird inside a shrub.

The dogs were barking with their hot tongues hanging out.

—I was looking for work, Martim answered getting ready to leave. Is there any work here?

—No.

They looked each other in the eye without fear.

—The garden needs help, he said as he was moving away, and with his back already turned toward the woman.

—Are you a gardener, sir?

—No, he said turning around in vague expectation.

They looked at each other once more. For an instant it seemed to them that they'd be facing off like that forever, so definitive was the position of each of them; the dogs there. Martim heard a little laugh from a child or a woman. He looked at the mulatta but she was serious, with hot eyes. The hedgerow had moved with the child inside it.

—Who sent you? Vitória asked.

—Nobody, the man said, and if he was still standing it was

because he was propped up by the crimson tranquility of the poppies.

—What do you know how to do?

—Pretty much everything.

—I'm asking what your profession is, she said a bit roughly.

—Ah.

Another little laugh resounded close by him. Then, quite excited by the applause, he hitched up his belt getting ready to give a funny answer or to move. But he didn't say anything and stood there. It had seemed to him, with great intelligence, that the only way not to fall to the ground would be to stand there unmoving, and that it would be strategic to let events happen to him.

—Well? the woman repeated more impatiently.

He looked at her without expression, until bit by bit his eyes started squinting in a comic way:

—I'm an engineer, madam.

She looked slightly scandalized. She examined him with curiosity. He bore up under her gaze without effort. Maybe he'd realized that he'd impressed her, because a look of insolence made his face smile a bit bestial and happy as if he'd wrapped up a difficult task.

—You're an engineer.

—That's what I said, the man answered without arrogance.

Vitória looked at him as if professionally sizing up a horse. The man immodestly let himself be examined. Which suddenly shocked the woman. She blushed. Standing there, he looked indecently masculine to her as if this were his only specialization. Why hadn't he shaved? dirty, bearded, standing. She finally sighed, tired and uninterested:

—I don't have any work for an engineer.

The man turned to leave and, without interrupting his steps, repeated without insisting:

—I can do anything.

—I have a well that needs to be finished, she said suddenly full of mistrust and curiosity.

He once again stopped walking and turned around. The fact that, at a simple word of hers, she could make him walk or halt, had started to annoy the woman. Somehow the man's docility seemed like an affront to her.

—I can fix wells, he shook his head.

—The stable is collapsing! she said even more distrustfully.

—I saw.

—Sometimes I wish someone would hunt a few seriemas, she challenged him watchfully.

—I can shoot.

—I also need a few stones placed nicely in the stream to give the water some more power, she then said with chilliness.

—That can be done.

—But you're an engineer, that's no use to me! she said in a light rage.

The poppies were vibrating in red like good blood, and awakening in the man a brute life: he was struggling between hunger and numbness and happiness. Only the rich poppies kept him from capsizing. So it was, then, with some reluctance that, running his tongue through a mouth full of desire, he finally turned his back to the poppies.

—Wait, said the woman.

He stopped. They looked at each other.

—I don't pay much.

—But you provide room and board, he said between asking and affirming.

The woman looked quickly at him as if the room and board might have some other meaning. She then took her hands from the pockets of her riding pants. There were men with whom a woman could feel denigrated for being a woman; there were men with whom a woman straightened her body in quiet pride;

Vitória was insulted by the way he'd made her straighten up her head.

—I do, she finally said very slowly.

—It's a deal, the man said grabbing with an effort of his fingernails a final lucidity.

—I'm the one who will say if it's a deal. Where are you from?

—Rio.

—With that accent?

He didn't answer. With their eyes both agreed that it was a lie. But Vitória seemed stubbornly not to take notice of her own shrewdness. And trying to calm herself down, she asked another question:

—Besides being an engineer, what other work have you done?

The man's eyes blinked bright and almost childish:

—I can do anything, he said.

The answer clearly displeased the woman, and she made a gesture of uncontained irritation because he didn't know how to win her trust. She was getting annoyed by that man's clumsiness. She stuck her hands in the arms of her trousers, getting a grip on herself. Yet it would be enough for him simply to promise that he had experience with building wells.

—But have you already built wells! she asked pointing out to him imperiously what his answer ought to be.

—Yes, the man then said lying the way she wanted him to.

Once again she blushed at his submission. And then she looked at Francisco, trying to exchange with him a glance of union against Martim. But Francisco looked away and stared at his own feet. The woman blushed still deeper, roughly swallowing the rejection.

It was the first time she'd sought his support, and it had to be precisely now that Francisco had felt forced to withhold it: because he didn't agree with the way that woman was abusing the stranger. Oh, he didn't agree with lots of things. Which nonetheless he'd keep accepting—as long as she was still stronger than he was. The foundation of the farm was that woman, whose self-control Francisco despised the way you despise things that don't flow. But, from her, all he expected was strength, otherwise he wouldn't have any reason to obey her. So he averted his eyes in order not to see her weakness.

Martim didn't understand anything that was going on but he instinctively joined Francisco and tried to exchange with him a sarcastic glance.

This glance too Francisco rejected, looking ostensibly at a tree. That stranger hadn't noticed Francisco's fidelity to the woman, hadn't understood that he'd grown used to hating Vitória calmly, and that he couldn't be ordered around by a woman unless he safeguarded his own dignity with hate. And as if the woman had understood this, she'd never tried to establish the slightest tie of friendship between them: for Francisco this had become proof that she respected him. As soon as she started being nice, his own downfall would begin. What he respected in that woman was the power with which she didn't let him be anything more or less than what he was.

Feigning, then, interest in the tree, he also refused any connivance with the stranger. It was enough for him for today the insecurity that Vitória had given him while seeking a support that he didn't want to give: not only because he didn't agree with her way of destroying the stranger, as much as because he himself would disdain her, and start to disdain himself, if she needed a mere farmhand.

The new arrival felt rejected without knowing why. He didn't understand the rage he'd provoked. What he was vaguely noticing was a certain disdain in Francisco: a disdain that concerned him, Martim, as much as the woman, and as much as Francisco himself. And he had the odd impression that he'd fallen into a trap. In a dream of fatigue, he remembered stories of travelers who had spent the night in crazed houses. But that immediately passed, because if there was anyone dangerous there—it was obviously he himself. The impression of a trap nonetheless remained.

Rejected by Francisco, the woman then turned back with great determination to the stranger, whose stupid docility was now desirable. But suddenly she asked insulted:

—What are you laughing at, sir!

—I'm not, he said.

Then, without realizing that she was leering at him coarsely, the woman discovered fascinatedly that he wasn't laughing. It was the face that had a merely physical expression of mischief, independent of whatever he was thinking—the way a cat sometimes seems to be laughing. Despite being tranquil and empty, his features made him look like a jester, like someone cross-eyed who, happy or sad, would always be seen as cross-eyed. As if she'd fallen into a darkness, slowly she was looking at him. He's bad, she saw with her snout awakened. That man possessed a face. But that man wasn't his face. That bothered her and awakened her curiosity. That man wasn't himself, she thought without trying to understand what she was thinking; that man shamelessly was dragging himself along. And there he was standing in a complete exposure of himself, in a silence of a standing horse.

Which suddenly intimidated the woman as if she'd gone too far.

But now she couldn't help seeing what she was seeing. How dare he! she thought frightened and seduced as if he'd said something you mustn't ever say. In a perversion of some sacredly permitted law, that man wasn't making himself obvious. And his face had a horribly secret physical wisdom like that of a quiet puma. Like a man who only didn't violate inside himself the final secret: the body. There he was, totally on the surface and totally exposed. Whatever was uniquely whole in him, remotely recognizable by the woman in that instant of befuddlement, was the final barrier that the body has.

She stiffened severely. Because there was a great error in him. As big as if the human race had erred. "How dare he!", she repeated darkly without understanding what she was thinking, "how dare he!", she was startled, suddenly offended within everything that life had that was most intelligible. The nerve he'd had to reach this point of ... of dishonor, of ... of joy ... of ... The nerve he'd had to go so far as to—as to have that way of standing there! she stammered inside with rage.

She looked at him once more. But the truth was that that man didn't seem to be thinking about anything—she then realized a bit more calmly. In his face had remained the shivering sensibility that thought gives to a face: but he wasn't thinking about anything. Maybe that's what was horrifying her. Or, maybe, she'd been set off by the fact that he'd once laughed.

—You're no use to me, she said with strength, making up her mind unexpectedly.

But when, without the slightest protest, he was already near the stable, she shouted with rage:

—Only if you sleep in the woodshed!

And with fright, she looked at him. But he, without surprise, as if she could keep indefinitely rejecting him and calling him back, came nearer. The child, which had already come out of the hedge, immediately took shelter in the hideout. When he was once again closer, the woman asked unexpectedly:

—And might I at least know what an engineer is doing around here?

—Looking for work, he repeated, not even trying to make her believe it.

She opened her mouth to reply to this insolence. But she held back. And finally said serenely:

—Wipe your feet before coming inside.

5

VITÓRIA WAS A WOMAN AS POWERFUL AS IF SHE'D ONE day found a key. Whose door, it's true, had been lost years before. But, when she needed to, she could place herself instantly in touch with her former power. Without even naming it, she inside herself would call everything she knew a key. She no longer wondered about the things she'd once known so well; but she lived off of it.

It was, then, by beseeching the help of everything she knew that she later looked absorbedly at the plate of food that the man had emptied in the kitchen. She also tried to imagine him installing the woodshed door. She'd given him the door of the shed, a big and strange object to give someone. Since the totally unexpected arrival of the man had already broken a certain circle of order in which she was moving as if inside of a law, with reluctance she had to at least recognize that some thing had happened, though she couldn't say what. Then she thought, a bit embarrassed by her own free act, and somehow curious: "that's the first time I've ever given someone a door." Which rooted her in a dead-end sensation. It was the second time that the man had bothered her.

Without knowing what to do with the thought about the

door, she emerged from it trying to imagine that the man must now be fitting it with difficulty onto the rusty hinges. Probably still with that same face of fatigue and an almost-smile, and that immodest childishness that giants have. Or, maybe, he might be working to install the door with that same remote concentration with which he'd swallowed, with a thoroughness about every crumb, the food. It had been a long time since the woman had seen hunger, and, looking now at the empty plate, she furrowed her eyebrows. She couldn't figure out exactly when she'd felt the cruelty of that man. Looking at the empty plate, she then thought the way you think about a dog: he's cruel because he eats meat. But maybe the impression of cruelty came from the fact that, when he was standing in front of the porch, he was hungry and yet smiling: you could see the hunger on his face but he, in a capacity for happy cruelty, was smiling. Not cherishing oneself was the beginning of a cruelty toward everything. She knew this inside herself. But she, she at least had everything that she knew.

For the first time then, with a disagreeable brightness that she could no longer hide from herself, the woman realized that the man hadn't tried to give her the slightest reassurance nor had promised her anything. She herself had accepted all the risks on her own. The way one day, when she was caring with her skillful hands for a wounded dog—it had fainted. And she, feeling in her lap the unexpected total weight of the dog, had lifted her eyes solitary and responsible beside that soulless body that was now entirely hers, like a son. That man who had fallen there with all his weight.

—Rash old crone, she said suddenly very fatigued pushing away the dirty plate; the lack of love for herself swathed her in haughtiness.

And how could she introduce the new man to Ermelinda, without making her happy? But that was a problem for later.

Now, what mattered with an inexplicable urgency, was to try to guess what face the man was making while installing the door. Without connecting one fact to another, she went to examine the derringer. It was needing to be cleaned and oiled. The lady concentrated on the old weapon for a while which her stubborn and severe face, sitting in the kitchen. It was a face of someone who made her own giving up a weapon and an insult to others.

The worst thing was, however, telling Ermelinda. "Another worker didn't make a difference, even though he'd be living there," Vitória thought arguing reluctantly and slowly convincing herself—since so often one or two men had worked for a month and then left; just three days ago two men had quit. So why was she hesitating? Maybe because she'd have to confess to Ermelinda that the man was, or said he was, an engineer. And if that hardly mattered to her—she thought morosely, and accusing him of being an engineer—as long as he worked, since Francisco would keep an eye on him, to Ermelinda the fact would …

"I hired a man, he says he's an engineer but he'll do anything!", she imagined herself saying with asperity in order to cut off any comments her cousin might make. What comments was she afraid of? She stopped cleaning the derringer, and looked dreamy and hard at the air. Or just say to her: "Ermelinda, there's another worker who's going to sleep in the woodshed, so from now on you can't go in there, it's his room."

None of those phrases felt definitive enough to cut short Ermelinda's exclamation of rapture. And, when she imagined her cousin's enthralled face, the lady suddenly turned her own from the image she foresaw as if she couldn't stand it; without being able to stop, almost enraged, her heart inside her from starting to beat with fright. But having transferred to Ermelinda the disgust she was feeling at her own stupidity, she felt herself entirely guiltless; and, free to feel rage, she could no longer tolerate the curiosity with which her cousin would hear the news. It wasn't what Ermelinda would say that was filling her with the anticipation of resentment; since the fact was she'd never even been able to reproduce a single one of the girl's concrete phrases. It was her disguised expression of extreme joy, as soon as anything happened. And it was feeling herself forced, because she had to explain the man's presence to her, to reenter an intimacy with that face that would reveal slyness and gentle insidiousness — as if in her cousin's nebulous system a person's means of contact could never be direct, because danger and hope too were indirect. Ermelinda seemed to be always hiding that she understood. And her face would remain almost deliberately shapeless and suspended — waiting for a confirmation?

Oh no, it wasn't that. So what was it? Had it been a childhood of sickness that had made that girl develop in the shadows? that childhood of weakness that Ermelinda cherished as if it were her treasure.

But none of that explained her. And when she thought about Ermelinda without at least seeing her, her cousin seemed to slip away from other people's thoughts. And as soon as Vitória was accusing her, though just mentally, Ermelinda would seem suddenly to turn up innocent and frightened. How could she ever get to know her? Any direct contact was impossible. It was surprising how, if Ermelinda were thinking about the inexplicable hatred that she felt for birds and someone asked her what she was thinking about, she would only answer that she was thinking about "birds." It was surprising how the only solution would be never to ask her. Ermelinda acted as if a tree were blue — but if Vitória asked her what color a tree was, she'd immediately answer, blinking her eyes out of slyness, that the tree was green. What Vitória wondered about was whether Ermelinda really knew that the tree was green — or if she just knew that Vitória thought the tree was green. The trick would be never asking her anything. How could she ever get to know her? "How can it be that I, though I never do anything wicked, am wicked? and Ermelinda, who never does anything good, is good?" The mystery of things being the way we know they are, left the lady quite engrossed.

All throughout Ermelinda's stay on the farm, Vitória hadn't managed to interest her in its daily workings nor shake the calculated sweetness with which the other woman disguisedly waited. And that without Ermelinda's having said a single "no." The fact that she'd spent "her childhood bedridden" seemed to give her forever the right to an indolence that wasn't carried out without a certain ritual-like fussiness, and only addicts ignore the secret delights of addiction—Vitória, fascinated, was seeing the other woman care for her idleness with precision and the ease of affection.

At the beginning, paralyzed by the other woman's way of being, Vitória had let herself be dragged along by what the visitor had brought to the ranch almost transforming it. The fear of the dark—that tranquil darkness that after the cousin's arrival had gained a shapeless power. And the disguised allusion to death as if this were a secret never to be confessed. And hope. Fear, death, hope. A hope that was becoming concrete by waiting for events, as if the unexpected were within arm's reach. "From one second to the next some thing could happen"—that might have been what had been insinuated on the farm, and that was what for a while had infected Vitória. Until she, in sudden rage, had finally awoken, and started her own life back up again.

Though it was impossible to escape entirely whatever sneakiness there was in the other woman, and to stop hearing those dark and radiant phrases of hers that meant nothing but kept bouncing around in the air. "The horse feels when the rider is afraid," Ermelinda would say. "A halo around the moon is a sign of rain," she'd say—and the night would become bigger and deeper. "Be suspicious if a dog doesn't like you," she'd smile as if this were just a sign of whatever there was that was inexplicably promising. Ermelinda was a bit clairvoyant.

With the impossibility of making her work, Vitória at least had learned to fend her off. And, as soon as the first disturbance that the other woman had brought to the farm had passed, Vitória had hastened to teach her the basics of self-respect: the first thing she'd had to cut off severely in her cousin was her tendency to seek physical support and contact, to put her hand on her shoulder, to reach for her arm when they were walking together, as if both shared in the same delicious wretchedness. Once that first physical distance had been established, a kind of absence of relations had taken shape. And since Ermelinda, when she'd been widowed, had come to the ranch, Vitória and she had never gone into a clearer explanation. Until, as dust falls and heaps up, time had passed; and whatever had happened, irremediably had already happened. Ermelinda had ended up stowing her suitcases definitively and the useless objects she had brought—and, unable to drag Vitória along into her fears and hopes, had taken refuge in the laughter of the mulatta cook. From her previous life all that remained was waiting for the mail from Rio that would periodically bring her, sent by a pastry shop, a small package of almonds covered with perfumed sugar that she would carry around with her for days, economizing dreamily every single sweet.

Only once, in an afternoon of excessive heat and threatening storms, the tension had finally exploded inside Vitória, once and for all. And subsided when the rain had fallen breaking branches and swamping the fields. And when the light rain ended up calming down the farm, Vitória had wondered astounded why she had so unexpectedly made up her mind to reveal to her that, years before, when they were still in Rio, she'd seen through a

71

cracked-open door how Ermelinda threw herself into the arms of the man she'd later married.

And now, cleaning the weapon with a mechanical concentration, Vitória once again wondered what devil had brought her to the point of interrogating her cousin. Maybe it had been the rain that was looming but not falling? Or maybe the insistence of that face, which had specialized in waiting, had finally exasperated her: Ermelinda sitting there fanning herself, waiting, sweating and eating the almonds that smelled like an old handkerchief— and the rain threatening, and the smell of the almonds softening intolerably the air, filling the living room with that treacly smell of a letter stashed in a brassiere, and the hope … And then, as if the surface of things had to be slashed—but why?—Vitória had said to her that she "knew very well how it was that she, Ermelinda, had treated her marriage": that she'd seen the man run after her around the table in a ridiculous chase, she'd seen desperate Ermelinda laughing and running,—and seen suddenly how Ermelinda broke off the chase and threw herself into the arms of the surprised man who hadn't dared hope …

—And now that you finally know I saw it, don't you ever lie to me again! she'd said to her, and she herself didn't quite know what she was accusing her of, and had looked at her shocked.

—But that's because I was running away from him! …, the other woman had tried to defend herself: "that she'd thrown herself into his arms, yes, that she couldn't deny, but not because she loved him …"

And why had Ermelinda thought she needed to fight off the accusation that she'd loved him?

—And threw yourself into his arms because you didn't love him? Vitória had inquired, and at that point it no longer occurred to her that she'd accused her cousin of having loved him, so much that the other woman had had to defend herself and confess that she hadn't loved him—and it didn't occur to either that neither had the right to demand any excuses from the other. It was getting hotter and hotter and, about to cry, Ermelinda kept wiping off the sweat, trying to unburden herself of the uncomfortable almond in her mouth. She'd ended up spitting it onto her handkerchief with the judiciousness of someone who wanted to save it, tying the cloth into a knot and placing it carefully into her pocket—after which, about to cry, she'd tried to explain that she'd "been so alone with him, so helpless with a man running after her, that she'd ended up throwing herself into his arms." It was then that, perhaps inspired by the violence of the wind that was already starting to knock down fruits and kick up leaves and dust, Ermelinda had discovered with enchantment the word "torturer" which, over the course of the next few days, just out of pure pleasure and vanity, she'd started to use with frequency, with different meanings, some of which were forced. Clasping the box of almonds, she'd tried to explain that she'd been so alone with that man "that her torturer would have to be her support", and her misfortune would have to be her shelter, she'd said with relish. And, faced with Vitória who was then already drunk on her own unleashed rage, Ermelinda had stammered that "if a person comes up to me with a scythe, I'd stick out my neck just so that whoever killed me would at least not be my enemy"—she'd had the courage to say all this, and it took courage to say something that simply made no sense to either of them.

It's possible that if Ermelinda had managed to explain the absurdity of what she was trying to say and if the other had managed to understand—then there would have been peace between them, or at least fatigue. But Vitória had answered that "the bedridden childhood" didn't keep Ermelinda from being in fact as strong as a horse; to which the other woman, unexpectedly, had lowered modest eyes—which had intrigued Vitória who, after a moment of surprise, returned to more serious accusations. Ermelinda, dazed by the mooing of the cows frightened by the wind, had then started to talk about torturers—which led Vitória to say with much irony that, "as far as she knew," her husband hadn't been a torturer, "that he'd given her everything, that Ermelinda had wanted for nothing as long as the man had lived"; which had led Ermelinda to say that he'd been the best of husbands and that she wouldn't allow anyone to speak ill of the dead; to which Vitória had added that it had never crossed her mind to speak ill of a man who for all those years had put up with a wife who called him "my flower"; which led Ermelinda to cry from longing—both of them made desperate by the insufferable wind, by the dust that was coming into the room, the clouds closing up low and making sudden darkness.

And when the water had finally crashed down, it made so much noise that they couldn't have kept talking without shouting. With the wind settled down and fresher, the sweat had started to dry pleasantly—and a sudden peace had been established between them as if they had reached a conclusion. Haughty, covered in shame, Vitória had left the room. And started to avoid her cousin. A few people managed to do that to her: make her hate them and hate herself. Vitória never forgave them. Those people were in her way. Afterward, as if the most had happened that could happen between them, they hadn't needed each other again.

But that only sole contact had taken place long ago. And her incomprehensible memory didn't help Vitória, sitting in the kitchen, find a way to announce to Ermelinda the arrival of another worker. With a stoic gaze, she was grasping the derringer; enduring everything she knew. "With the frozen key close by my heart, I shout from my castle", she thought beautifully, because if she didn't give magnificence to the world she'd be lost. She was making whatever she knew magnificent—but whatever she knew had already become so vast that it more closely resembled an ignorance. To this, for an instant, she succumbed:

—If only I could fire a shot and make the rain crash down, she thought for an instant in which her head gave out in fatigue.

Because from the memory of the scene with Ermelinda all that remained to her was the vision of the blessed rain crashing down. And she was so badly in need now of another great rainfall, she thought with her strength once again taken up as if she had given an order or as if she had once again touched the key within her. The cornfield might dry up before the harvest ... And the grass for grazing. Maybe not, she wondered with her eyes looking skyward.

But the high sky and the daily reluctance of the sunset to turn into night—were promising nothing except the probability of yet another drought. It's true that the earth was still moist. And the green was luxuriant. But for how much longer? For days Vitória had been pretending not to notice that there were fewer frogs about: they were already deserting ... And that bit by bit the locusts were persistently filling the dusk. But the woman looked at the air with mourning: because the birds hadn't migrated yet! Which broadened her gaze into the hardness of hope, as if the authority of her faith were preventing the desertion of the birds. As long as they were still around, she'd keep on being a silent warrior.

Anyway—she sighed suddenly broken—the sooner she talked to Ermelinda the better, to avoid her finding out on her own and coming in all pale to announce: "there's a man in the woodshed!" She wouldn't be able to bear such a stupid phrase. And at the very thought of hearing it, her urge now would be to fire her cousin the way you'd fire a maid.

On her way through the parlor in order to go up to Ermelinda's room, she saw her, however, through the window, kneeling beside the new rosebush. She stopped for an instant to look at her before heading out to the yard—with that useless habit she had of looking people over when they didn't know they were being looked over. She peered out for an instant, sighed once again heroically, and, as if forced to reach a conclusion, since she'd already looked at her, thought: "she's just a girl, that's why she's still afraid; she's just a girl, that's why she's afraid of death." But I too have the right to be afraid! she told herself darkly, staking a claim. It was as if the other woman could still be offended. And she, she'd never be again.

She halted next to Ermelinda. She knew that she'd already seen her coming, though she hadn't even looked up; as if that's how you were supposed to behave when you're afraid of the dark or initiated into spiritism and into the secret of a way of living.

The girl, pretending she'd only just heard the steps, finally lifted a face that was sly with surprise. And it was as if the sweetness of this lie had made her face reach an expression at the same time of helplessness and blessing—and it was all, all fake. Vitória squeezed her hands inside the pockets of her trousers:

—What are you doing, she asked her calmly:

—Pruning the valiant rosebush.

—The rosebush doesn't scare you? she asked softly; she felt the need to wound that kneeling girl as if it was her fault that she herself had hired the man.

—Not this one: this one has thorns.

Vitória knitted her brow:

—And what difference does it make if it has thorns?

—Because I'm only scared, said Ermelinda with a certain voluptuousness, when a flower is too pretty: no thorns, too delicate, and too pretty.

—Don't be a fool, said Vitória with brutality, in any case it's in the body where things happen! And if you helped out with the work you wouldn't have time to be horrified by pretty roses or to hate the farm!

—And do you like the farm a lot? the other woman asked smoothly.

—There's a man in the woodshed! Vitória cut her off.

And as if she'd said something that up till this moment she herself hadn't realized, she sat there looking at her astonished, wounded. She immediately pulled herself together:

—He says he's an engineer, the reason he's here is that he really must be out of work. I'm going to give him lots of jobs. Francisco's going to keep an eye on him.

She'd said it. She closed her eyes for an instant with fatigue and relief. When she opened them, she saw that Ermelinda had come to a stop with her scissors in the air, and her face—her face once again had reached an extreme acute and tender note as if it was in order to reach that expression one day that a face had been made. "And I," Vitória thought, "who know about everything, and everything I know grew old inside my hand and became an object." She muffled her voice as best she could:

—What? What did I say that was so extraordinary that you're looking like that?

Ermelinda trembled:

—You didn't say anything, you said there's a man in the woodshed! she quickly obeyed.

—Well then, if you're pruning the roses, which is useless work when the drought is on its way, keep on pruning! she exclaimed without holding back. And don't sit there beaming!—no longer able to interrupt herself, she went on: beaming, yes! she said with pain, once again you're thinking that today is a great day! all it takes is for a hand to clap and you get happy, and scare me! it's a man who came to work, if he's no good he'll leave, and if he thinks that just because he's an engineer he's going to boss everyone around, he's quite mistaken! and that's it, and nothing more!

Ermelinda pretended to be so surprised that she looked at her with her mouth agape. Or she really was surprised, you'd never know for sure. "I was really abrupt," Vitória thought. Ermelinda examined her with the corner of her eye, fleeting—and started once more her vague work on the roses, and it was as if she'd wanted to be so discreet that she wouldn't let her notice that she'd understood; Vitória blushed, stricken.

Some time passed. They were silent, feeling the soft wind blow around them. The darkness was settling in bit by bit. For an instant the perfume of the roses gave sweetness and meditation to the two women.

—The flowers, said Ermelinda enveloped by the fainting avidity of the dusk, the flowers, she said.

—"The flowers are haunting the garden"? Vitória inquired attentively.

—Right? exclaimed Ermelinda surprised and grateful, you always put it so well! she said flatteringly.

Vitória was calm. She looked at her profoundly, once again immune to everything that girl was:

—I myself never said that. But since we live together I had to learn your language.

—Why does he say he's an engineer? the other woman asked quite carefully.

—Oh, I knew it. The question had to come.

—But what did I say wrong now?—and an almost real innocence infantilized an imploring face; but they both knew it was all a lie.

—Ermelinda, said Vitória closing her eyes gallantly, for three years you've been saying: "I'm afraid of little birds." For three years you've said: "what a funny thing it is when a tree moves." For three years I've been hearing even your silences. And I can no longer stand your bedridden childhood, that doesn't give you any rights over me. Ah, don't interrupt me: I'm well aware that from your bed you had plenty of time to see the birds through the window and to be scared of them! We live together, fine, you had to live somewhere; I'm also aware that you once took care of my father, but I also know that it was just the three days I needed you! I know everything. But I said clearly to you that—I wanted calm, I wanted—I wanted calm. Otherwise why didn't I sell the farm when auntie died? answer me! why didn't I sell it and why did I come here, since I didn't even know much about all this? And if I'd sold it, I'd have plenty of money and could have kept living in the city. That's right—she added amazed—and I could have stayed where I always lived … —Vitória awoke with sudden violence: What I forgot to ask was if you too were looking for calm when you came here. This, Ermelinda, is a place for a serene person like myself. No, don't answer me. It doesn't matter. For three years you've been bothering me, I have to tell you that. And today I'll tell you something else: enough already. You're altering my life with your—with your waiting. It's insufferable. This goes way beyond calm. It's as if I were breeding rats in the house, they run around without my seeing them, but I feel it, you hear? I feel their feet—their feet, Ermelinda—making the whole house shake.

—Why do you want calm? dodged Ermelinda cattily, trying to flatter her with a charming expression.

—I want silence, I want order, I want firmness—and while she was speaking it was seeming more and more absurd to her to have allowed a complete stranger to work there. —For the love of God, don't say that you have a premonition today just because the man was hired on a Thursday! You have premonitions every single day. It used to be your parrot with those dry screams that seemed to scratch my throat, but luckily he died. Your parrot, your premonitions, your kindness, your fear of dying, that's right! your fear of dying.

The other woman trembled a worried face:

—You think a drought's on the way? she broke in quickly, pale.

Vitória stopped short, thrown off balance by the interruption. Drought?

The bad woman looked at the sweetness with which the night was coming, moist and full, the way the world at certain moments loves us. It was March and a dizzy paleness was widening the vastness. Disturbed she smelt the rotten odor that was coming from the ditches. In the growing darkness the ditches seemed like cliffs that dragged her gaze invincibly toward an empty and involuntarily soft meditation. The extent of the lands was limitless, reposed ... And in the woodshed she saw with a start the lantern turn on.

The light now was waxing, now almost going out. With an intensity in which there was anxiety and aspiration, the woman surrendered to the struggle of the lantern as if it were some dark struggle of her own. The light at last, almost going out, survived. At first trembling, fogbound. Around it the total darkness had made itself.

—Drought? the woman repeated looking at the shed as if not seeing it. Maybe not, she said absorbed. Whatever has to happen, has great power.

6

MEANWHILE, LIFTING THE LAMP ABOVE HIS HEAD, MAR-
tim looked almost as big as the shed. Moist firewood was piled
near the pallet that he looked at with sensuality as if he hadn't
slept in years.

The lucidity to which he'd forced himself in order to reply to
Vitória's questions had already disappeared, and from his hands
had vanished the skill he'd needed in order to install the door.
With a brutality that the flickering of the beams on the walls
was making stammer and stagger, he breathed in deep the shed's
smell of wet leather, shook his head powerfully struggling not to
drown. Though he didn't need himself for anything, an elementary struggle was taking place within him in order not to capsize.
Because the threatening impression of losing important threads
was making him force himself to take notice of everything: when
the smoky light of the lamp would run atop the pallet, he noted
with a useless clarity a motionless belt on the big rusty nail and
the picture made of hard unframed cardboard.

To this the man drew with obedience the lamp nearer and his
own anesthetized face that was trying to awaken: on the engraving, in elegant and femininely drawn letters as on a patient embroidery, was written "St. Crispin and St. Crispinian." The man's

reddish eyes saw the two saints carrying out their shoemakers' work. He really liked the engraving. The hands of the saints were paralyzed for a moment on their sandals, in a perfect silence that the artist had happened upon by chance. Above the saints' halos—inside a smokey circle in order to render the future distance of the event—the same St. Crispin and St. Crispinian now boiling inside a cauldron. "Damn," the man grunted, "what was their crime?" But beneath the cauldron, before the future had come to pass, the green, blue, and yellow saints—colors that instead of violence were lending the engraving the great space that fits inside a church—before the future had come to pass, the saints had the tranquil concentration that fixing sandals demands, as if our task were the sandals.

In his weighty stupidity, which manifested itself in a smile of submission, the man made a point of bringing the lamp closer once again. Because, still deformed by the need for attentiveness that his flight brought, it seemed to him that there too was some important thread that was escaping him, and he then touched with timid fingers the cardboard face of the martyrs the way you creep up furtively to something that might grow enraged. Then, with the leisure of fussiness, he put on his glasses. But the truth is that the thread kept escaping him, and his eyes augmented by the glasses only stubbornly managed to repeat the vision without understanding it: in the smokey circle the cauldron boiling, beneath it calm instant by calm instant the shoes getting fixed. The man couldn't manage to take a step ahead. Though the mute scene of the picture gave the shed a perspective. The very woodshed smelled of shoemakers.

If that man still remembered what the world was like—in that picture there was some thing that he would certainly respond to if he were still a person. Whatever the man had learned and not forgotten at all, was still bothering him; it was hard to forget. Symbolic things had always bothered him a lot. But he was as coarse as the food that was weighing down his stomach. When he blew out the lamp, the darkness came full of wind through the window. And as if shadows were finding other shadows, fatigue knocked him over with a certain mercy into sleep.

Until a pale dawn began to stir. And the breeze blew the first weak life into that shed warmed by breath, leather, and intestines. Still not knowing what he was doing, the man sat on the pallet. Afterward, person of strong habits that he was, he got up.

It was a very lovely morning. When there's no light yet, and the light is just the air, and the person doesn't know if he's breathing or seeing. Besides, from afar the smell of the cows reached him, which always feeds a person with rapture: the smell of dawning cows came mixed with the great distance that he made out. Martim's eyes, rendered ignorant by the long night, looked then with astonishment at the fallow plot that the half-brightness of dreaming revealed through the window at the back of the woodshed. Apparently he'd forgotten that he'd slept in the countryside. On the plot, through the slight mist, he saw with childish curiosity a dirty and dry soil, hardened by the dawn. The man didn't anticipate anything: he saw what he saw. As if eyes were not made to conclude but merely to look.

Until, after another second of this absence from himself, and his head too was struck with grace by the incomprehension of what he was seeing. And in a mistake that he certainly needed, a mistake as correct as the correct fall of an apple, he had a feeling of finding something: it seemed to him that in the great silence he was being greeted by a plot from the tertiary era, when the world with its dawns had nothing to do with a person; and when, what a person could do, was look. Which he did.

It's true that his eyes took a while to understand that thing that did nothing more than: happening. That was hardly happening. Just happening. The man was "unveiling."

The plot had probably been an attempt, finally abandoned, at a flower or vegetable garden. You could see the remains of some work and some will. Certainly someone had once tried to establish an intelligible order there. Until nature, previously expelled by the plan for order, had sneakily returned and settled in there. But on its own terms.

Because, no matter what its period of glory and lushness had been, now the plot had the silence of something given over to itself. There were a few gray and hard rocks there. A bit of a fallen tree trunk. Exposed roots of a tree that had been cut long ago, since no more moisture was coming through the sideways cut. Weeds were growing vertically. A few had reached a height that was already making them sensitive to the bracing dawn breeze. Others were crawling and stuck to the ground, from which they couldn't be pulled without death. Rough earth was crumbling alongside an anthill; it was a tranquil disorder.

The man sat looking until the life that had set up in the plot started to awaken. Shining mosquitoes, as if they were bringing there the first shipment of light. The cautious little bird amidst the dry leaves. From one rock to the next, male and female rats were passing each other by. But in the brotherhood of silence, like a spindle whirring, you couldn't tell one movement from another. That was the restful confusion into which Martim had fallen.

During the incomprehensible days that followed—all the threads escaping him, receiving flummoxed Vitória's first orders, examined from afar by Ermelinda and hearing the mulatta's bottled-up laughter—it was with a clumsy effort that the man put up with the intense light of the countryside, as if he weren't up to understanding brightness.

But, day after day—once the punishing work was done that he wouldn't have been able to do if Vitória hadn't ordered him to—he climbed down from the open and superior light of the countryside, from which he arrived blind with incomprehension.

And led on by a sleepwalker's stubbornness, as if the uncertain shiver of a compass's needle were summoning him—he finally went to the tertiary plot of merely fundamental life, on the same level as his own. And with a sigh of someone returning to himself, he'd find the faltering shadow, the movement of the rats, the thick plants. In that vegetal cellar, which the light hardly dusted, the man would take refuge silently and coarsely as if only in the roughest beginning of the world could that thing he was enter: in the crawling plot the harmony made of few elements didn't go beyond him or his silence. The silence of the plants was at his own pitch: he was grunting in approval. He who didn't have a word to say. And who never wanted to speak again. He who on strike had stopped being a person. On his plot, sitting there, he'd just enjoy the vast emptiness of himself. That way of not understanding was the first mystery of which he was an inextricable part.

Because the tertiary plot was of a great perfection. Not even when the light was coming closer, would it manage to transform the feeling of silence: the brightness, arriving in stages and stages of silence, was reduced there to mere visibility, which is as much as eyes require. Because, to that man, much more had always been given than he'd needed; at least that's what it seemed to him now, sitting in his territory that so sufficed to him. And if visibility would reach the plot, it would reveal dead leaves decomposing, sparrows that got mixed up with the ground as if they were made of earth, the black and tiny rats that had made their nests in that rudimentary world.

Since it so happened that Martim had never understood anything about plants or animals, he found there plants and animals of new and rare species. The wharf rat was a large being of a rare and hairy species with a long tail. The plant was sticking its mouth to the ground. The bird, rising into a low flight, was a warning that the man was following with his mouth agape. And nobody was leading anybody: the plant dirty with dust was understanding itself in the same way it was coiling up. There was the dark air from which a thing lives. And Martim was nicely surrounded by the things that he understood: the flies were spawning. And the meaning of all that was the most primary meaning of that man: he was there as if there were a plan of which he was unaware but that a plant was joining with its mouth and to which he himself was responding sitting very obviously on the rock—sitting on a rock was becoming his most intelligible and most active pose.

And the thing was somehow so perfect that even the view of the distance was joining that world without God. Because when the man would lift his eyes—the distant trees were so high, so high like a beauty: the man would grunt approving. The stupider he got, the more he was in the presence of the things.

That's how, slowly, Martim's strength was reconstituting itself.

Despite only wanting from the farm board, food, and the use of the truck at the most favorable moment—the days started to fill up in ways he hadn't expected. And following one another in definite and rhythmic hammer blows, even though the days were the very threads that were escaping him. The mornings were fresh, the trees leafy, the tasks followed one upon the next. The mulatta would check him out and laugh, the black child was always hiding and keeping an eye on him. But he'd grown used to it. And was moving slowly like a man sowing seed. His great silence wasn't apathy. It was a deep sleepiness on the lookout, and an almost metaphysical meditation on the body itself, in which he seemed to be watchfully imitating the plants of his plot.

Slowly his strength was pulling itself back together, and that's how he spent the first week, the biggest of all those he spent on the ranch. At the end of the first week, Vitória had been ordering him around rudely for months, for months the man had been sweating in a punishing discipline. And to such a degree had whatever happened that week happened, and to such a degree had the invisible threads been connected that, at the end of seven days, that thing had happened that you unexpectedly take note of: a past. And at the end of a week there was worry and indistinct mumbling on the ranch the way it happens when, after a long time when everything has stayed without evolving, everything wants to transform.

Martim had also grown used without resistance to being constantly ordered around by Vitória who seemed to have discovered an incessant and impatient game: spying on him and inventing work for him:

—There's an Anglo-Arabian who needs to be brushed!

—Yes.

—In fact, she then said paying close attention, I think I need less of an engineer.

But the woman started to doubt that he'd heard her or understood.

—I said, she repeated while examining him surprised, that in fact I needed much less of an engineer!

—If you needed more of one, that's what would be tough, the man finally replied without seeming vexed in the least.

His tranquil face kept giving, however, the impatient woman the idea that he was permanently amused or occupied with something that escaped other people:

—That, she finalized, that's nonsense.

The air of the countryside had left him crude and wrinkled, with brighter eyes. He would move slowly across the great expanse, unencumbered at last by the absence of thoughts. But if his compact absence of thought was a dullness—it was the dullness of a plant. Since like a plant, he was alert to himself and to the world, with that same delicate tension with which the thick plant is a plant all the way to its furthest extremities, with that delicate tension with which the blind plant feels the air in which its hard leaves are inlaid. The whole man had reduced himself to that kind of watchfulness. What was happening to him was one of those periods about which, after they're over, people say: nothing happened.

7

IT WAS THE HOT AND INEXPRESSIVE FACE OF A MAN—
and one afternoon Ermelinda looked at Martim astonished to
see him so concrete in the midst of the vagueness of the fields.

Materializing the vast astonishment that she never quite knew
where to apply—she then was astonished by the coincidence of
that man's being exactly at the ranch, and she was astonished
by the extremely curious coincidence that she herself was at the
ranch. But—she thought forcing herself to some modesty—
there is no one fact that isn't connected to another, there's always
a great coincidence in things.

Right during the first week Ermelinda fell in love with Martim. First because he was a man and she so to speak had never
fallen in love, except for other times that didn't count. And then
because Martim, without knowing it, was a man in whose presence a woman didn't feel humiliated: he was shameless.

She was sitting in the afternoon shucking corn. The fact that
she'd accepted this chore might have already been the beginning
of a need to be by herself and let herself daydream. Daydreaming
was the usual way Ermelinda called "to be thinking."

On that afternoon, from where Ermelinda was seeing him,
distance was making the man a black point that the girl was
fixedly following as the only point of reference in the field. Until

her vision was muddied by the brightness, and thousands of black and luminous points made her close her eyes as if the man had shattered.

When she opened her now shadowy eyes, the field was once again empty: Martim had disappeared. What was left for her to see were the hated little birds flying calmly. And the high and haunted weeds trembling at the slightest hesitation from the breeze. Everything had once again become an antenna sensitive to whatever had never quite been said. As in a visitation, with the fretting of waiting Ermelinda looked. She was very thoughtful.

It was at that point that Martim reappeared in her field of vision. He, the concrete man who seemed to keep things from flying away. Since Ermelinda's way of seeing would usually make everything as unstable and light as she was herself. He, the man, turned up again. Vouching for reality. And that coarse body was counterbalancing the softness of the cornfield, the softness of the women and the flowers. With the naïve firmness that a man has, and that is his power, he was counterbalancing the nauseating delicacy of death. That innocent firmness that even Ermelinda's husband had had, even Francisco, even all the other men who had temporarily worked on the ranch. With a solidity that had no idea of its own worth, Martim's stupid body seemed to guarantee that never would death, most delicate death, win out. And the power of the man could justify her, Ermelinda, being so soft—that softness that without a man was as gratuitous as a flower and, like a flower, seemed to give itself to the nothing, and the nothing was death scattered with such subtlety that it even looked like life.

Ermelinda wasn't thinking about anything: she was daydreaming.

With her face bent over, she was husking the corn automatically. And differently from the hammer blows of Martim—which she was hearing one by one, waiting in sweet torture for the next—she told herself with the greatest care, at the beginning of a sensation of exasperating pleasure that she feared destroying if she gave it any more strength: "but who said anything about death, woman? I'm so alive," she said as if savoring a fainting and a heart in the field. Her face bent toward the corn wasn't seeing Martim. But with every blow of the hammer he was at last making material the unfurled field, and giving to that girl, so vague, a body. Ermelinda felt a shameful sloth against which, without any reason, she struggled by raising her head with a certain flair. It's true that her defiance didn't manage to keep going for long, and that bit by bit her once more heavy head bent over in meditation. The mechanical fingers kept working.

But sometimes she'd make a slight movement of her head, very quiet and lovely, as if chasing off a fly. Meditating was looking at the void. The girl was meditating.

It was then that she raised her head and stared at the air with some intensity. Because some gentle and insidious thing had mixed with her blood, and she remembered how people spoke of love as of a poison, and agreed submissively. It was some treacly thing full of unease. That she, conniving, recognized with tortured softness the way a woman who grinding her teeth recognizes with haughtiness that the child is about to be born. She recognized, at that, with joy and stolid resignation, the ritual that was taking place within her. Then she signed: it was the solemnity for which she'd waited all her life.

Afterward, like a woman who becomes messily active at critical moments, she pressed more powerfully on the raw cob, several kernels clattered, a neighing of a horse crossed the field and Francisco ordered it to stop, several kernels clattered in the bucket. It was some thing that might be love or might not be. It would be up to her, among thousands of seconds, to lend the slight emphasis that was all love was missing in order to be.

Ermelinda stopped with the ear of corn in her hand, her head was spinning a bit, satisfied, embarrassed. Because, in a second lost amidst thousands of others in the vastness of the field, subject to the law of the single cell that is fertilized among those that wither, she had just found out, as if she had chosen, that she loved him. Not directly, since she wasn't a girl with habits of courage. But this is how she'd chosen to find out that she loved him: "I'm alive," she'd thought. And as she thought "I'm alive" she'd for the first time realized that before she'd also thought about death, and that she'd also thought about the man. The ignorance of her own process gave her the surprise of innocence. And only then did she notice that now it was too late, that she had to love him. Painfully, haughtily, she'd lost forever the possibility of making up her mind. With relief, as when it's too late. A second before she could have still not loved him. But now, softly, presumptuously: never more. In the same instant she had a feeling of tragedy.

And now it was too late — whatever the generating sentiment had been, it had forever vanished into the air. It was too late: pain had stayed in her flesh as when the bee is already far away. The pain, so recognizable, had remained. But in order to stand it we had been made.

A bit astonished, the heat of the afternoon then enveloped her, nervous, heavy. Nothing had transformed in the field that was still full of motionless sun. Yet for an instant the girl didn't recognize it and didn't recognize herself, and if she looked at herself in the mirror she'd see big eyes looking at her but she wouldn't see herself. With the sharpness of surprise, she noticed a vein on her own hand that she hadn't noticed in years, and saw that she had thin and short fingers, and she saw a skirt covering her knees. And underneath everything she was, she felt a certain thing: her own watchfulness. A bit afflicted, she looked around. Out of an obscure need for preservation, she was trying to recover in the field that minute in which she had daringly accepted loving the man: she was trying to recover the minute in order to destroy it. But, stunned, she might have known that the need to destroy love was also love itself because love is also a struggle against love, and if she realized it that's because a person knows. She sought, desperate and offended, that minute that now she'd never again know if it had been fatal to the point of submitting her—or if in that minute she herself had been so extremely free that, in a gratuitousness that was already a sin and that you'd have to pay for in the end, she had aimed at.

She tried to recover the instant in order to destroy it, but that was painful and useless. Since everything had happened too fast. And the girl sat there with nothing more than this: with a pail filled with corn kernels, without even having something to fight against.

And so abandoned, and so solitary, as if everything that might come to pass in the future had nothing more to do with the solitary minute of glory that had long since vanished forever amidst the hammer blows. Those hammer blows that the girl, now emerged and astonished, heard louder and closer, fatal, fatal, fatal. Her strange liberty: she had chosen to head toward something fatal. It was the gravity for which she'd waited all her life. Once again a sense of tragedy enveloped her. And, strangely, inside it she was merely anonymous.

She then looked at the flies upon the rosebush. The grace of what she was living filled her with Christian modesty, and she humbly sought moral support in the flies that were blue inside. But what she saw were just bluish flies and the rose trembling because of the fly that had just made it tremble. After the whole world had become her accomplice for an instant, the girl had been dumped on her own.

Then she lowered her head and went back to work: the kernels of corn tumbled into the can rhythmically, hard drop by hard drop. The sun had suddenly widened into a great light, the hot wind blew. But some thing had certainly happened. Because the cry of the mulatta from the back of the house wrinkled the girl's face as if it had wounded her.

Uncomfortable inside the unexpected grandeur that her life had taken on, the girl pretended not to notice anything. After, revolted and taking refuge in consoling pettiness, where at least she was herself, she said to herself in defiance: "if I don't take care of myself, nobody will! what I'm going to do is drink more milk to get stronger because I'm not a fool!", she said with brutality. But as she said it, she herself lowered a head that was entirely distracted, breathing, breathing. Then she wiped off the sweat.

—The fence still hasn't been fixed! said Vitória at that moment to Martim.

Ermelinda shivered frightened by the fact that someone had spoken to the man: she hadn't imagined him, then! She took offense at the intrusion of the stranger as if he'd meddled with the love that had just been born.

—The fence is a wreck, added Vitória demandingly.

Martim never seemed to mind breaking off the job he'd just started in order to start on another: he'd start the new task with the same concentrated indifference with which he'd been perfect in the previous job.

—Wouldn't you rather finish up with what you're doing now? Vitória finally suggested, she herself having to supply the argument that he hadn't made.

But he didn't seem to be surprised by anything at all that Vitória might say to him. At first the obedience with which he'd listen to her gave Vitória an obscure rage in her bosom. In her fantasies, Vitória had the idea that, if she said to the man: "at night I sleep under my bed," he would answer: "of course, ma'am." The fact that he'd allow her to do anything whatsoever and give the most contradictory orders, offended her; and, even worse, that was surreptitiously removing an undergirding of vague heroism from which she lived and whose point was already long lost. But, bit by bit, she was being wrapped up by the way he'd permit anything in her or in himself. It was as if he were saying: "I don't see anything bad or good in sleeping under the bed." Ill at ease, she couldn't figure out what was so bad about sleeping underneath a bed: the woman blinked her eyes, disturbed. The solidity and calm of the man weren't transmitting either solidity or calm to her—they were just irritating her.

As for the man, his muscles were working with exactitude, slowness and certainty. And nothing would alter him as if he were dragging along with him, like a defense that others could not pierce, the great silence of the plants from his tertiary plot. To which he returned every afternoon as a man returns home. And where he'd sit on a rock.

And it was nice there. There no plant knew who he was; and he didn't know who he was; and he didn't know what the plants were; and the plants didn't know what they were. And all of them were nonetheless as alive as you could be alive: that was probably the great meditation of that man. The way the sun shines and the way the rat is just a step beyond the thick extended leaf of that plant—that was his meditation.

Martim had blue eyes and low eyebrows; his hands and feet were big. He was a heavy man, with an idea in his head. He had a mobile presence, watchful, as if he would only reply after having heard everything. That was his real side, and also his outer side, visible to others. Inside—requiring much more effort to reach the exterior form that had preceded it—inside he was a man of slow understanding, which at heart was a patience, a man with a stumbling way of thinking that sometimes, with the awkward smile of a child, could feel intimidated by his own stupidity, as if he didn't deserve so much: it's true that inside he was also shrewd, with an always ready possibility of availing himself and taking advantage. Which in the past had led him to ignore certain scruples and to commit certain acts that would be sinful if he were an important person. But he was one of those people who die without anyone's knowing what really happened to them.

In truth, seated on the rock of his kingdom, his so-called meditation was being boiled down to being a man with big feet sitting on a rock. What he didn't notice is that he was already starting to take some care to be exactly just whatever it was he was being. In his alert falling asleep sometimes a thought was already sparkling inside him as in a splinter of rock:

—The region is arid, he'd meditate with a great deal of profundity. Nonetheless there is coal, he seemed to be thinking, sitting straight up on the rock. Taking note was of a deaf virility. And it was as if a man, knowing how to wait sitting on a stone, well then! if a man knew how to wait sitting on a stone, then the moisture would favor the rotting of roots, nuts, fruits and seeds. That obscure logic seemed to him perfect and sufficient.

Sitting on the rock, he was also feeling satisfied by now knowing how to work so well in the field. His knowledge was slight, but his hands had earned a wisdom. "A man is slow and takes a long time to understand his hands," he thought looking at them. His thoughts were almost voluntarily enigmatic. And on his plot he'd feel that pleasure that in certain void moments you feel, as if everything really were essentially made of pleasure. The plant, for example, was just pleasure.

It's true that sometimes the intense quietude of the plants would already seem to deafly disturb him, and give him a first worry. Then he'd move the position of his legs, patient, without understanding. He didn't realize that he was there slowly manufacturing his first arrow and polishing his first dart.

He didn't even realize that he was already totally different from that man who had looked at the plot at dawn. He didn't realized that, shifting the position of his legs so often, he was having his first impatience, as he looked at this world ready to be hunted. Obscurely he was worried about starting to feel superior to the plants, and about feeling somehow man in relation to them. Because only man was impatient: he then shifted the position of his legs again. And more: only man was proud of his own impatience. The way he, shifting once again the position of his legs, unsettlingly was proud. It was a generalized vanity that would sometimes overtake him, and which still didn't feel embarrassed for existing at the same time as the prudence in not venturing beyond the reassuring somnolence of the plot around the woodshed. Reassuring but no longer sufficient. The man was uncomfortably growing.

But that almost merely physical restlessness would only overtake him at the odd moment. And it would still happen so far away from himself that it still hadn't altered the intactness of the world system in which he was in motion. And, soon, with the great pleasure that exists in holding back one's own energy, once again he was getting into the state of "knowing little." Since that was the essential condition of the plot. By not knowing, there was in the man a joy without a smile just as the plant fulfills itself, thick.

At times that man, who had always missed important threads, would grab at the earth like a person who possesses a parcel of earth. And he would sit there with a fistful of earth in his hand. Rude, with the earth in his hand; as the best way of being. What were that man's thoughts? They were merely profound thoughts, satisfactory and substantial. One afternoon he reached the point of thinking this:

—Extinct fauna is legion.

This was the kind of thought without possible retort. Still that same day he thought this:

—More than a billion years ago, one time … —Martim wasn't aware of exactly how much time was behind him, but since there was nobody around who could keep him from making a mistake, he sat up impassive, large. And kept making retorts of the finest quality. For example, another time he thought this: "under two meters of spoils, there might be a mastodon skull here." Thinking had transformed now into a way of rubbing up against the ground. It was, then, with the most legitimate pleasure of the meditation that he one afternoon remembered, just like that, that "buffalos exist." Which gave a great space to the plot, since buffalos move slowly and afar.

And whoever looked at him—so satisfied and dominant—would shake a head envying the luck that that man had had to be born when the masses of ice on the globe had already melted; he was savoring a favorable earth. What came to him, for example, was the desire to eat—and he noted it with approval. He now had all the senses that a rat has, and one more with which he was realizing what was happening: thought. It was the least perverted way to use it. He was letting himself be cleansed by the complete thing that there was in plants: with relief, he was leaning his wilted bits against the freshness of whatever exists. It was so damn good not to lie. So, sitting on the rock, he wasn't doing anything more than that: not lying.

For example, Martim wasn't sad. What he was was finally free of a whole moral duty of tenderness. That man had come from a city where the air was filled with the sacrifices of people who, being unhappy, were approaching an ideal.

—I'll bust the face of anyone who messes with me! he then said out loud practicing his soul and perhaps trying to unleash in himself a rage that somehow would bring him into harmony with that calm energy around him.

After which, he got up and peed serenely looking at the sky. The clouds were going by high up. He stood there, stupid, modest, haloed. His unity was surrendering as a unity.

—The region is arid, he then thought. Which gave him a very satisfactory taste. He looked at the arid sky. The sky was there, high up. And he down below. Greater perfection could not be imagined.

When he'd sleep, he'd sleep. When he'd work, he'd work. Vitória ordered him around, he ordered around his own body. And something was growing with a shapeless murmur.

8

RIGHT IN THOSE FIRST DAYS YOU COULD FEEL THAT there was a man on the ranch. And you could also guess that the person in charge was a woman: since despite the threat of drought and the fundamental needs of that poor attempt at a farm, what suddenly worried Vitória the most was the appearance of the place. As if until the man's arrival she hadn't noticed the slovenliness of the fields, she was now greedy to transform them. She seemed to be looking forward to the date of a party before which time everything had to be ready. A fever for precision had overtaken her. And the details to which she descended were like a fly taking off. By midmorning, there she was pointing out the crooked fence. And the calm strength of the man would uncrook it. From far off Francisco, brooding and skeptical, saw the woman pointing out the disorder of the odd flower beds—and smiling saw that in silence Martim was digging, cleaning, pruning. Between Martim and Vitória there had been established a mute already mechanized relationship that was fully functioning: constituted by the coincidence of the woman's wanting to give orders and of his acquiescence in obeying them. With avidity, the woman was the boss. And some thing in her had intensified: the happy severity with which she was now stepping atop something that was hers, disguising the glory of possession with a defiant glance at the passing clouds.

—And what about the stables? she interrogated him one day attentive, you never cleaned out the stables! she said to him impatiently, with that blinking of the eyes of someone who no longer knew what she wanted; but time was pressing.

That's then how Martim—as if he were copying in his work of making concrete an inevitable evolution whose trace he was fumbling about for—that's how the new and confused step of the man left one morning his kingdom on the plot to the half-light of the stables where the cows were more difficult than the plants.

His contact with the cows was a painstaking effort. The light in the stable was different from the light outside to the point that a vague threshold was established in the doorway. Where the man stopped. Used to numbers, he cringed at disorder. That's because inside was an atmosphere of intestines and a difficult dream full of flies. And only God feels no disgust. At the threshold, then, he stopped unwilling.

The mist was rising from the animals and slowly wrapping them up. He looked farther on. In the shadowy filth there was something of a workshop and of concentration as if from that shapeless tangle yet another shape were bit by bit taking concrete form. The crude smell was that of wasted raw materials. That's where cows were made. Out of disgust, the man who suddenly had become once again abstract as a fingernail, wanted to draw back; he wiped with the back of his hand his dry mouth like a doctor confronted with his first wound. At the threshold of the stable however he seemed to recognize the pale light that was being exhaled from the snouts of the animals. That man had already seen that vapor of light floating up from sewers on certain cold mornings. And he'd seen that light coming off hot garbage. He'd also seen it like a halo around the love of two dogs;

and his own breath was that same light. That's where profound cows were made. A person with little courage might vomit at the nasty fragrance, and upon seeing the attraction that flies had for that open sore, a clean person could feel sick in the face of the tranquility with which the standing cows were heavily wetting the ground. Martim was that person with little courage who had never placed his hands into the intimate part of a stable. However, though averting his eyes, he grudgingly seemed to understand that things had been set up in such a way that in a stable one day a child had been born. For it was correct that great smell of matter. Except that Martim was not yet prepared for such a spiritual advance. More than dread, it was a modesty. And he hesitated at the door, pale and offended like a child when all of a sudden the root of life is revealed to him.

Then he disguised his cowardice with a sudden revolt: he was offended that Vitória had pushed him from the silence of the plants into that place. Where, with repugnance and curiosity, he unexpectedly remembered that there was a dead age in which enormous reptiles had wings. Because in that place a person couldn't escape certain thoughts. There he couldn't escape the feeling that, with horror and impersonal joy, things were being fulfilled.

Might that have been what turned his stomach, or just the lukewarm smell? Hard to know. Yet it would have been enough for him to take a step back, and he'd find himself in the full fragrance of the morning which is already a thing perfected in the slightest flowers and in the slightest stones, and it's a complete work and without fissures—and that a person can look at without any danger because there's nowhere to come in and get lost. All he had to do was take a step back.

He then took a step forward. And, obfuscated, halted. At the beginning he saw nothing, as when you enter a cave. But the cows used to the darkness had noticed the stranger. And he felt in his whole body that his body was being tested by the cows: they started to moo slowly and were moving their feet without at least looking at him—with that lack of the need to see in order to know that animals have, as if they'd already crossed the infinite extension of their own subjectivity to the point of reaching the other side: the perfect objectivity that no longer needs to be demonstrated. Whereas he, in the stables, had reduced himself to the weak man: that dubious thing that never went from one side to the other.

In a resigned sigh, it seemed to the slow man that "not looking" would also be his only way to enter into contact with the animals. Imitating the cows, in an almost calculated mimicry, he standing there didn't look at anything at all, trying he too to dispense with direct vision. And in an intelligence forced by the very inferiority of his situation, he let himself grow submissive and watchful. Then, out of an altruism of identification, he almost took the shape of one of the animals. And it was in so doing that, with a certain surprise, he unexpectedly seemed to understand what a cow is like.

Having somehow understood, a heavy guile made him, now quite motionless, let himself be known by them. Without exchanging so much as a glance, he endured with grinding teeth the cows' getting to know him with intolerable slowness as if hands were running over his secret. It was with unease that he felt the cows choosing in him only the part of themselves that there was in him; as a thief would see in him the part that he, Martim, had of eagerness to steal, and as a woman would want of him something a child wouldn't understand. Except the cows were choosing in him something that he himself wasn't aware of—and that was bit by bit being created.

It was a great effort, the man's. Never, until then, had he become so much of a presence. Being materialized for the cows was a great intimate work of concretization. The fingernail was finally aching.

During a moment of lack of faith, the man felt certain that he was going to lose and that he would never manage the ascension into the stables. Since the odd wide glance was running unhurriedly over him, followed by a long moo of a heavy uplifted head: repudiating him. Amidst the intense heat of the stables, they were noticing his acid smell of people.

But it's also true that, by now, the joy of living had already overtaken him, that delicate joy that sometimes overtakes us in the middle of life itself as if the same note of music were intensified: that joy had overtaken him and was leading him instinctively in the fight. Martim already wasn't sure if he was just obeying the unformulated order by which cows end up forcing a cowboy to a peculiar way of looking and standing. Or if, in truth, he himself were the one who was seeking, in a painful spiritual effort, to free himself at last from the kingdom of rats and of plants—and to reach the mysterious breathing of the greater animals.

What he merely know—since he had already reached the same simply essential intelligence of a cow—what he merely knew was a simple law. That he oughtn't brutalize their own rhythm, and that he ought to give them time, their time. Which was an entirely dark time, and they were ruminating hay with drool. Bit by bit this too became the time of the man. Round, slow, uncountable by a calendar, since that is the way that a cow crosses a field.

Then—since things tend to reach a conclusion and to rest at a stage—the stables finally started to settle down. The heat of the body of the man and of the animals mingled in the same ammoniac warmth of the air. The silence of the man was automatically transformed. He finally had gained a dimension that a plant doesn't have. And the cows, pacified by the justification that Martim had given them, stopped paying attention to him.

In shaking jubilation, the man felt that some thing had finally happened. It then gave him an intense affliction as when you're happy and have nothing to apply the happiness to, and you look around and there's no way to give that instant of happiness—which up till now had happened with more frequency to that man on Saturday nights.

Some thing had happened. And though the threads were still escaping him, he finally had some thing in his hand and his chest puffed with subtle victory. Martim breathed deeply. He now belonged to the stables.

And finally he could look at it as a cow would see it:

The stable was a hot and nice place that was pulsing like a thick vein. It was from that wide vein that men and beasts had young. Martim sighed tired with the great effort: he'd just "unveiled." It was from that wide vein that a big animal would cross a stream scattering water that shimmers—which the man had already seen, having however had just that minimum warning of beauty that now was settling on a deep base. It was because of that pulsation that the mountains were far and high. It was because of this that the cows were wetting the ground with a strong noise. It was from a stable that time is indefinitely substituted by time. It was because of that throb that migratory groups left cold zones for temperate ones. That—that was a hot place that was throbbing.

All this the man might have felt because he felt so satisfied that he spat on the ground. After which, with his heart filled with heavy vigor, hiding his emotion, he held out his hand and gave a few slaps to the parched body of a cow. A great tranquil transfusion had begun between him and the animals.

You need to give soil to the corn! Vitória said to him irritated.

So he gave soil to the corn. But the cows were waiting for him, and he knew it.

9

BESIDES ORDERS AND CARRYING OUT ORDERS, THERE wasn't much to say. And whatever wasn't being said was starting to be missed. Ermelinda encircled him without coming nearer; he, barely looking, was guessing at her. And Vitória was trotting across the field.

For her, Martim still looked like someone who might burst out in laughter, like the inexpressive face of a clown beneath mischievous makeup: Vitória was worried. And getting exasperated by Martim's silence. The man's stupidity was suffocating her, but she didn't have anything to accuse him of because his work, though slow, was perfect. Vitória was worried. Her own strength was in a certain way growing, the woman seemed to be developing more and more and asserting herself.

And in the afternoon, when the heat would finally relent, she would stand on the porch looking at the things that slowly were being transformed by her will. Then her ambition would grow without an aim like a heat. And the desire to invent new orders just to see what would happen was born: she was the disturbed owner of all that, and was disturbed. She'd be outraged that there were nights that got in the way, during which no work would advance; and, as for the man sleeping in the shed, that seemed to her so cheeky that, if she put up with it, it was only because there was nothing she could do. Also by day, at a certain time, she'd get annoyed to know that the man was in the stables taking undefined care of the cows, carrying out with an excess of docility an order that she'd only given him once. And once again the night would come with its exasperating interruption. She could hardly wait for the next day, and her feeling of power was already so great that it had become uncomfortable and useless.

It was in this heavy fashion that the work was slowly moving ahead. At the sound of the plough, Vitória would close her eyes, her bosom agitated. In the ever-stronger heat, the work moving ahead. Which however seemed too slow to her: the woman standing on the porch unbuttoned her shirt collar unable to breathe. Because, coming from nowhere in particular, the threat of drought was getting closer surrounding them with shimmering heat. Each day it took the sun longer to die. It was an agony that the woman was putting up with while standing there, alone. Even after the sun disappeared, the farm would still reverberate for an indeterminable and worrying amount of time. By day it was that shining, those hammer blows, the sweat. But at night—she was well aware—there wouldn't be a truce. Drought nights keep in their bellies a radiant profundity like a light locked into a hard nut.

The woman on the porch bit distractedly her hand until, with suddenly severe eyes, she looked at her own wounded hand. That night she stayed out on the porch till late, examining apprehensively the thousands of stars that the strange clearness of the darkness was revealing. She worriedly sharpened her ears, and it was true: you heard fewer and fewer frogs, they were deserting…

At least as long as she was on the porch, dealing with stars and scrutinizing the vibrant dryness of the night, she was still powerful because she was working, coldly working and calculating. But when it came time to sleep, misery enveloped her. A haughty misery that was asking nothing. And, no matter how strong she'd been during the day, she then became small, silent, unfathomable. Poverty invaded her like a meditation. The little lady was lying in bed, calm, looking at the ceiling. And since nobody could understand her, she in revenge, with her eyes open, wounded, was calculating—calculating wounded like a prisoner in his cell. And every night she ventured further, every night her obscure threat was going to keep watch over the indecent sleep of the happy man.

With the vigor of the morning, the feeling of discomfort with regard to the man would dissolve, as soon as she discovered another field of activity: an anthill that needed to be destroyed, the open well that didn't seem deep enough to her and at whose side she would stomp an impatient foot. Afterward, she no longer seemed quite to know what order she wanted to give, she was feeling at her disposition that silent man who was shimmering in the sun, silent and with open eyes. Then her own power weighed her down, she galloped from one end of the field to another, giving more orders, staring authoritarian and interrogative at the mysterious parched horizon, she who couldn't allow herself the luxury of not being powerful, distributing her harsh efficiency among gallops—and there was no solution, the shirt was stuck to the sweaty body, she was afraid that the more powerful she was, the more she'd have to manage to get free of her own power. But there was no way to get out of the situation in which things had placed themselves and how to escape before she'd ordered around excessively the passive man and the malleable farm—before the man suddenly laughed? or before the lands of the ranch would open into arid cracks. Then the rage overtook her: one day she'd find out what the man had come to do on the ranch.

In this interim the farm was being beautified.

The farm was being beautified, and, with the heat, the tension was growing like an excessive happiness, the days going by bright, wide. As a sign of danger, there was only the agreement in which everyone was seeming to live. And the happiness. Vitória had never been so happy, and the one who was suffering for it was the whipped horse whose mouth was opening in fright. It was when it was spurred that the horse kicked and darted off—the woman, taken by surprise, lost her balance, grabbed on ferociously to the horse's neck. Chills ran down the woman's back, she was breathing terrified, without the courage to release that heavy neck, her legs were trembling: she remained motionless and with her eyes closed, letting the unbridled bay bring her to the pasture, letting it lower its indominable head in order to eat. The woman's whole body accompanied humbly the horse's head toward the hay, with closed eyes she was feeling it eat, it was a strange peace to be guided by the horse's disorientation, the farm being beautified, the wind blowing, tears of rage ran down Vitória's face.

—How long are you planning to stay here? she then asked the man, ready to fire him without wondering why.

—I don't know, he said as he kept digging.

—How can you not know! she inquired rigidly.

Forgetting that she'd been ready to send him away, she looked at him affronted. It seemed to her a disgrace for that man to be playing with time and bringing doubt into the mechanical running of the days, bringing these a frightening liberty as if any day now he could suddenly say yes, or no. Bringing indecision to her who, if anyone asked her how long she'd stay there, would answer "I don't know," meaning unlimited time outside her control—and not, as for him, a short time.

Yes, a short time. Without connecting one idea to the other, Vitória now seemed to want the man to work fast and twice as hard, and for the well, whose digging she'd forced him to interrupt in order to start working on the outer fences, to be begun immediately once again.

—But why doesn't he know if he's staying? Ermelinda was startled.

Ermelinda had been nervous lately, with headaches and palpitations. "Why doesn't he know if he's staying?" And as if they'd cut off the possibility of waiting for a more favorable time and for a natural ripeness, the girl felt intimidated, forced to define herself before the man left, and to have the green fruit itself, even if still incomprehensible. No matter what the obscure stages of love had been, these now would have to move more quickly. In order not to get bogged down in modesties, Ermelinda had already forgotten what she wanted from the man. She was just trying to get back that moment in which love, next to the bucket of corn, had been inevitable and great—there had just been that instant, on an afternoon now lost forever. But in that instant death too had seemed to her a ritual of life—there was that instant in which she'd faced down death with the same magnitude, like someone looking at the distance.

But it was no use: with the instant lost, she'd lost contact with fate. And once again she was seeing in death no more than mocking and pettiness. And she too had become once again petty to the point of being afraid to die, and was greedy and sly, and mocking because she was feeling mocked.

Yet something was telling her that nobody could die without first figuring out their own death. She looked around tormented. The bee, somehow, had figured out: she saw the bee flying. And Francisco in the same way. Who, mute, concentrated, was giving water to the donkey. As if giving water to the donkey, in that silent way, were a sign of being prepared. Ermelinda looked at him with envy. But she, she was petty: she wouldn't forgive death. What she wanted from Martim, she'd never be able to say: she wanted obscurely for through him her life to take on the dimensions of a destiny. She was confused, she only knew that she had to hurry because time had run short.

And, fake, scheming, she was trying to put herself in some way in a trance of love. Until finally, from looking at the man so much and pushing herself so much and demanding of herself, once again she started to feel that unease. Then, radiant, weakened by the effort, she'd love him. The field looked empty to her, gray, she was seeing the sick grass next to the chicken coop, seeing the dirty clouds, the weak hens cackling darting quickly around, the dissonance of the wheels of the plow was annoying her: it was love, yes. So much so that if the man turned up far off with the hoe—then—then this is what would happen: there he was!

There he was. Swathed in the power that he had over her and that she herself had granted him.

Until finally Ermelinda reached the point of no longer wondering whether she loved him. She was no longer ashamed to observe him while hidden behind the fence, and every feature of the man's face she'd rediscover with an exclamation of recognition and surprise. And when she'd discover, indefatigably for the thousandth time, that the man's eyes were light, she'd be surprised that so much had been given to her, a woman. His was a fine mouth, and that extraordinary beauty that only a man has and that was turning her mute, with a longing to flee—which made her peer at him bloodthirsty. She was trembling with the fear of no longer loving him. She'd never come close to him, and between them was always distance. But slowly the girl had spiritualized the distance and ended up making it a perfect means of communication. So much that, now, the distance alone was constituting enough space for her to unfold her love and reach the man: near him she would feel discomfited by him himself, and didn't know how to give him all the love.

Which didn't keep the girl from having become very active: she'd carefully calculate the steps she needed to take, nurturing her feelings with the foresight of an assassin. She'd bathe with fragrant herbs, take greater care with her undergarments, eat a lot to fatten up, try to be moved by the sunset, stroke with intensity the farm's dogs, bleach her teeth with coal, protect herself against the heat in order to stay untanned, grow apprehensive when she saw how much she sweated. One day she tried to tell herself a thing just to see if it would work: "I want to be the shoe he wears, I want to be the axe he grabs with his hand"—and afterward waited on high alert; and it worked so well that, from emotion, she lowered her modest eyes, confused, hiding a smile as best she could.

But Ermelinda didn't always need to work herself up. Sometimes love would attack her unexpectedly. That was when, rummaging through Vitória's desk in search of scissors, she found the list of instruments that Martim had made at the command of the owner of the ranch. Before even thinking, she was sure that it was his handwriting. Because her heart beat as if she were reading the very secret of the man: "a bigger shovel, two scythes," she kept reading. And what he'd written gave her such an impression of maturity that it hurt her. The words seemed full and painful to her, heavy with themselves. It was mordant to feel the power of the man in the words, a motionless and contained power— and yet all that right in front of her like a fruit that from then on can only rot. Since Ermelinda was quick, the vague idea of fruit brought her to the idea of "the harvest of death," since she'd read something about that, and she'd even seen engravings about it. Oh my love, she then thought, but her heavy heart didn't know how to express itself. His hands, which had written "those simple words," were big and ugly, making her sad. Ah my beloved, she said in an ending that was resignation. And while she was wondering if in love she'd give and receive life, she stole the list the man had made and kept it in her room. "My way of loving is so pretty!" she thought. She'd never been so happy. In fact she'd never even reached the point of needing him to love her. In the selfishness of her happiness, she was thinking this: too bad he doesn't feel what I feel, he doesn't know what he's missing.

On Friday, since he was close by, she finally said this to him:

—The heat is killing me.

And her eyes filled with tears: because she hadn't said anything, in a manner of speaking. Then later on she said humbly to Vitória:

—The heat is severe.

But Vitória answered her:

—You say cold is severe, not heat.

10

AS FOR MARTIM, HE HAD TIME. ACTUALLY HE SEEMED TO have discovered time.

At the end of the day he'd abandon his work in the field and go to the stable. With the same serene greed with which previously he'd gone to the plot by the woodshed. And free at last of the arrival of Vitória's orders, free of the ever more besieging presence of Ermelinda—the man every day would pick back up in the stable the instant interrupted the day before, uniting into a single theme the scattered instants that he spent with the cows, and making of them the single sequence. "As I was feeling ...", he seemed to think when he went into the stable—and kept doing what he'd interrupted.

The dark heat of the cows would fill the air of the stable. And as if some thing that no person and no awareness could give him, there in the stable was given him—he was receiving it. The suffocating smell was that of the sluggish blood in the bodies of the animals. No longer the intense sleep of the plants, no longer the petty prudence in surviving that there was in the skittish rats.

But the cows were already starting to bother him a bit. One day, for example, he awoke and opened the door of the shed to the first light. And since the day seemed to be given to him, that's how he received it. But—but he already wanted, for the first time, to do something with it. Because at the door of the shed, he for the first time was needing a deeper experience—even if he could never share it with the cows. Worried, he was detaching himself from them. It was a risk, and a first temerity. Then, looking how the field was big and full of light, he—he ventured and had the deeper experience. He blinked several times, hushed.

That's how that man was growing like a thing that while rolling along gets bigger. He was growing calm, hollow, indirect, advancing patiently.

He hadn't looked a single time directly at the mulatta woman. But she kept laughing. And a pacific power had awakened within him. It was a power—he still recalled it well. Alert, without any plan, he waited day after day for the moment when he'd make the mulatta stop laughing. Both the mulatta and the child were observing him disguisedly from afar without coming nearer. As for the child, Martim was avoiding it, confused, evasive.

But the woman would laugh a lot. In fact you could say that she was laughing too much. Without a thought, he knew what that laugh meant. And sometimes it was as if the laugh were a moo: he would then lift his head, groggy, summoned, powerful. But he was waiting. As if patience were part of desire, he was waiting without rushing.

The mulatta was a wide nature, as wide as her laugh—she'd laugh before knowing what she was laughing about. Life had settled into her in a dark and sweet way, and she was laughing at some thing; maybe she took pleasure in that thing. Though that same thing sometimes wound up inside her in rage the way a dog snarls. She was a person who erred without sinning. The slaps she gave her daughter were almost out of joy, and reinvigorated her all over. The man observed, without drawing a conclusion, that it was very common for her to start singing after beating the girl. The girl would dodge the blows, learning without resentment that that's the way it was, and that mother was that power that laughed out loud and that without vengeance beat her, and being a daughter meant belonging to that mother where vigor would laugh. The man would pretend to be interested in his work, just to dissemble. Because a person could understand himself entirely in the mulatta. The man found in her a past that, if it wasn't his, he could use. What she was arousing in a man was he himself. Martim would hardly look at her, and knew that she was there. With her you could speak man to man, except in order to get to that she was a woman.

Two days later, instead of going to the stables, he finally went over to the woman who was washing clothes. And stood without looking at her.

And without looking at him, she laughed. He meticulously broke a stick in his hand, and without looking at her knew she was young. Her hair had hard, long curls. Since Martim was a person who immediately liked whatever he needed, he immediately thought she was pretty. Finally he tossed the stick into the distance and looked straight at her: he'd have to leave her or grab her. He grabbed her unhurriedly the way one day he'd grabbed a little bird.

— You're strong as a bull, the woman laughed. He was concentrated. Clasping her shoulder, the man could feel her small bones and, a bit further up, the tendons and the fibers beneath the thin flesh: she was a young animal, he calculated her age by groping her. He was feeling the heat that came off her, and that's how it ought to be: body to body with the most intimate pulse of the unknown.

It was already dark when his gestures awoke the young girl. The man lit the lamp in the woodshed and she gave a little cry of anger. Something had twisted in rage. He looked at her curiously. She was vibrating with anger, God knows why.

And he stood alone, at the woodshed door.

Martim was very surprised because he used to know everything. And now—as a nonetheless much more concrete fact—he didn't know anything. He who had grown up a bright man, and around him everything used to be visible. He'd been a person who knew answers, he used to be without pain. The brightness from which he'd lived had made him able to carry out work with numbers with a patience that never altered; and, naked inside, clothes fit him well. Clever and elegant. But now, having removed the layer of words from things, now that he'd lost the language, he was finally standing in the calm profundity of the mystery. At the woodshed door, then, revitalized by the great ignorance, he remained standing in the dark. It was already almost night. Because he'd just learned this with that woman: to stand while having a body.

Then the days started to go by.

But if his tongue once had swollen too much in his mouth in order to express, and if in his head no air was circulating so that thought could be anything more than anxiety—now behind all brightness was the darkness. And it was from there that the dark flame of his life would come. If a man were to touch the darkness a single time, offering it in exchange darkness itself—and he had touched it—then the acts would lose the error, and he might be able one day to return to the city and sit down in a restaurant with great harmony. Or brush his teeth without endangering himself. A man had to surrender once. And only then could he live, the way he was living now, in the latency of things.

And then, maybe because one day followed the next, something started to happen slowly, engagingly, big, though the threads escaped him. It was that living there was as if that man no longer measured life in days nor in years. But in such wide spirals that he could no longer see them in the same way he couldn't see the wide line of the curvature of the earth. There was something that was a gradual essence and not to be eaten all at once.

That's how Martim's life started to overtake him: the days were big, pretty, and his life was much greater than he was. And he himself, slowly, became more than a man by himself. His previous knowledge had frayed, and, as for words, he merely was getting to know them like a person who had once fallen sick from them. And been cured. "After all his crime only had the size of a fact"—and whatever he meant by that, he didn't know.

He also started to understand women once again. He didn't understand them in a personal way, as if he were the owner of his own name. But he seemed to understand why women are born when a person is a man. And that was a tranquil strong blood that would enter and leave his chest rhythmically. While dealing with the cows, the desire to have women was reborn with calm. He recognized it immediately: it was a kind of solitude. As if his body in itself weren't enough. It was desire, yes, he did remember that. He remembered that woman is more than the friend of a man, woman is the very body of the man. With a slightly pained smile, he then caressed the feminine hide of the cow and looked around: the world was masculine and feminine. This way of seeing gave him a deep physical contentment, the still and contained physical excitement that he had every time he "unveiled." A person has highly spiritual pleasures that nobody suspects, other people's lives always seem empty, but a person has his pleasures.

It's true that he didn't yet understand individual lives: the two cousins seemed at the same time annoying and abstract, nor could he figure out what meaning there was in the life of those two women, and it hadn't occurred to him that understanding them would be a means of contact.

He didn't understand individual lives. But now that he looked at them as a whole—the mulatta who had been heavily his and who was now filling the pail with singing water, Francisco sawing wood, Vitória courageous, Ermelinda spying, and the smoke emerging high from the kitchen—that, that he already seemed to understand as a whole. And it was as if a warmth were evaporating from the efforts of them all, and it was as if that man were finally learning that night falls and that the day is reborn and that afterward night comes. And that's how it was. His body, in this understanding, felt nice, without the need for error that evil would be. And just as the cows calmly counted on the existence of other cows—the man was wrapped in the indirect heat of the others. And more: sometimes it was even as if, looking, he were the owner of a great factory, and the noise and the smoke were the sign of a progressive motion. Toward what? The man didn't ask himself. Though he felt—with the same vague worry with which the drought was gradually nearing—that he wasn't far from the question, unripe for now.

Meanwhile, the drought was approaching in the ears of corn.

—These are lovely days, said Vitória apprehensive, protecting her eyes with her hand.

They were great, bright and, as long as they lasted, threateningly infinite days.

—They're pretty! Ermelinda exclaimed, I even already took my tranquilizer!

The lizards, attracted by the promise of lightning and glory, were turning up in ever greater numbers, nobody knew from where. They'd pop up on the dry earth and roar. Vitória looked at the arid bodies that were multiplying, examined closely a few leaves that were already curling along the edges, raised her inquisitive face to a pure and deserted sky. In the field, the sun full of dusty butterflies:

—Lovely days like this come before droughts.

—Ah, Ermelinda said with her hand on her heart, they're so lovely that you don't know what to do with them.

And Martim? the scent of the earth was breaking out beneath

Martim's hoe. The grains were crumbling, the scent of grass in the light, the scent of certain secret herbs that the heat was making exhale, the confused herbs that were providing in their entanglement shadow for some kingdom darker than the visible one: Martim was working, the hoe was rising and falling, rising and falling. A branch in the shadow suddenly unfastened itself from another branch, startled the bee, making it fly until getting lost in the distance of the brightness … its flight hinted at a world made of expanses and echoes, that profound world that seemed to be enough for the light and shade of a cow and that is enough for a man who raises and lowers a hoe. Sweat was one of the best things that had happened to him: Martim was lifting and lowering the hoe. That thing without a name that is the scent of the earth disquieting him hotly and recalling with insistence, who knows why, that we are born to love, and then you don't understand yourself. That's when the bee returned illuminated. Which made the man stop working and sluggishly wipe off sweat, with his eyes wrinkled by the brightness—by that brightness that bit by bit was already starting to be Martim's too. His effort to understand was rough, sheepish:

—The field looks like a jewel, he then said blushing violently.

He afterward looked worriedly around as if someone had seen him do something ugly. He looked like a man who awkwardly wanted to give a flower, and ended up with the flower in his hand.

—The field doesn't look anything like a jewel! he said furious. The bee then got tangled in grasses as in hair, the ants in a long wavy line—and all this was starting to be Martim's. This was the bottomless abyss in which he'd thrown himself in his passage from the plants to the broader future of that big black horse that, at that very instant, walked by in the distance pulling the plow. And atop the plow Francisco sitting straight up, in the silent effort of watchfulness. All this was starting to be Martim's, because a person looks and sees. The cows were drooling, the bee ever more precisely annoying the air getting closer and closer to an imaginary center. And Francisco's cry suddenly gave dimension to the distance.

—I needed to speak to you, Ermelinda said to him at that same moment.

The man didn't interrupt the movement of the hoe in the earth.

—You could ask Vitória to plant sunflowers, she went on with a graceful smile.

—Ask Miss Vitória, the man replied without looking at her.

—That's just the thing, I'm afraid of her. Anyway—she said suddenly intimate—you need to be careful too. Don't get me wrong: she's very good, but she's so severe. She's very nervous.

As the man's face was still bent toward the furrow, the girl bent over too and from upside-down tried to guess at his expression:

—Just think, she said still bent over and speaking louder because she wasn't sure if he'd realized she was there, just think, she said almost yelling, that she once stepped on me, you hear?

Without interrupting his work, he looked at her quickly.

—Then she said it was an accident, Ermelinda added in a lower voice, now that she was sure the man had noticed her. Maybe it really was an accident, she added now hesitating to keep on lying because he'd finally looked at her.

—I said that she said it was an accident! she repeated when she saw him once more not paying attention, but I don't think it's true! that she stepped on me is something I'm absolutely sure of! she shouted at him watchfully, peeping to see the echo of her words in the man's face.

But her failed attempts didn't discourage Ermelinda: "that's just how it is," she was thinking, since "the time still wasn't right." What the right time would be, she didn't know. Maybe when she was little she might have heard of periods when the moon reaches fullness. She might have also learned about how animals need a minimum of security when they're together so that they can at least have the basic guarantee of not being interrupted. Maybe she'd heard more stories than she could understand—and what she'd had left, worryingly incomplete, was the notion of a right time. Oh, her plans were vague, very vague. She didn't even have a plan: her plans were so vague that she half-closed her eyes sheepish, and smiled. If by chance her plans might for a moment become more clear, sincerely astonished, she'd be offended. Because she'd been very sensitive lately.

When did Martim finally start to individualize her? She was almost ugly, though charming. Short and very black eyelashes outlined eyes that were noticed even at a distance, amidst the brightness of a skin in which not even the mouth had colored. The eyes were always blinking, cunning or perhaps anxious, as if the girl were always calculating the distance between herself and things. Only the eyes were positive. The other features were so much more indecisive that you could imagine that they might fall apart in order to form a new combination, as careful not to define itself as the first. She was an aged adolescent and, if there'd been any sorrows, they wouldn't have been of the sort that would give her wrinkles or hardnesses, but would have refined and erased her. The quick sparse instants in which the man had looked her straight on had been no use, since he hadn't found any support at any memorable place, be it uglier or prettier. Though, at certain moments when she ended up unprotected, in her face would appear a certain expectant frankness which if it lent her beauty it was that of a patient dog's face. Her face was then seen in all its nudeness like that of a blind man.

It was that weak face, auditive and trusting—without the lies of expression with which the girl so liked to adorn herself—that the man ended up recording. And he started to "not think about her," as a form of thinking.

—When I was married, I had everything, I didn't lack for a thing! she retorted the next day, perseveringly hovering around him and opening the basket of hard-boiled eggs in order to have a picnic while he was working.

Talking without pause, the girl saw once again that face with hard wrinkles, and once again was touched by the firmness of the man while the wind kept seeming to try in vain to wear him down. And, maybe, if she grabbed onto him, the wind wouldn't shake her either. Then the girl filled with a hope so strong and devilish that without a pause in her talking she took her tranquilizer from the basket and swallowed with difficulty the dry pill:

—How long did you say you were going to stay here? she asked him.

And when he said that he didn't know, once again the empty and painful rush spun her around, time was short, time was short, she didn't know for what, she only knew she had to hurry. So she started to speak with such volubility that the man felt his work become soft as if the blows of his hammer now had a counterpoint, and the girl were the echo of a man filling up the distance. Martim then looked at the sun and spat far off with pride. Ermelinda lowered her eyes with modesty.

11

BUT ON THE AFTERNOON WHEN MARTIM AND VITÓRIA went on horseback so that the owner of the plantation could show him where the maintenance ditches would be dug for water, on that afternoon in which they went up the same slope down which the man had once come alone—that was when he emerged mature from the darkness of the cows.

Because from the top of the slope, the woman was investigating the soil, he innocent and unsuspecting suddenly recognized the field the way he'd made it out when he'd arrived at the plantation for the first time. That time when, drunk from escape, he'd leaned exhausted on that vague thing that is the promise that is made to a child when it is born.

Sitting on the horse, in a flash of genial incomprehension, he saw the field. Stunned, watchful, atop the slope was that same freedom as if something were unfurled in the wind. And like the first time, the glory of the open air brought him closer to something that beat hard in his chest and that hurt in the extreme disturbance of the happiness that one sometimes feels.

But one he wanted this time, in a first unexpected hunger, to give a name.

Desiring something more than just feeling seemed to afflict

Martim, that confused sign of transition to the unknown worried him, his worry was transmitted to the horse that kicked obscurely touched, with the dazzled gaze that a horse has.

Because faced with that expanse of enormous and empty earth, in a suffocated effort Martim painfully was approaching—with the difficulty of someone who will never get there—was approaching some thing that a standing man would humbly call a man's desire but which a man on horseback couldn't avoid the temptation of calling a man's mission. And the birth of that strange anxiety was provoked, now like the first time he'd set foot on the slope, by the vision of an enormous world that seems to be asking a question. And that was seeming to demand a new god that, understanding, would conclude in this way the work of the other God. There, confused atop a frightened horse, he himself frightened, in only a second of looking Martim emerged totally and as a man.

In the same instant he also felt entirely uncompensated.

With his face beaten by the wind that immediately started to symbolize some thing, Martim saw down below the animals at liberty in the pasture. Ever since he'd understood the cows, for the first time he found himself above them on the slope. And this too beat in his chest. With his heart beating Martim then remembered unexpectedly how a man usually is: it was the way he was being now! In an agonizing feeling, he felt himself to be a person.

Martim was in some way humble, if humble meant the involuntarily triumphant way he was mounted on a horse—which was giving him height and fright and determination and a broader vision. In that unexpected humility he seemed to recognize yet another sign that he was emerging because only animals were proud, and only a man was humble too. He also wanted to give to that defenseless and yet daring thing a name, but it didn't exist.

It was somehow good that it didn't exist: not finding a name increased imperceptibly the worry that he was now savoring. For the truth is that, though intimidated, he was enjoying his own worry. As if the tension in which he found himself were the measure of his own resistance, and he were enjoying the novelties of a difficulty the way a man's muscles are intensified when lifting a weight. And he, he was his own weight. Which means that that man had made himself.

In that interim the barely contained impatience of the horses had increased Martim's instability and was pushing him toward a decision that he nevertheless was not aware of. The wind was joining Vitória's sharp figure to his, the pure air had made the horses blacker and bigger. The air was so light that the man couldn't breathe it all in, since you breathe bit by bit, since a person lives bit by bit—and he suffocated from not having room for more air, and yet "not being able" intensified his happiness, the enormous vastness surrounded him without his being able to dominate it, his heart was beating big, generous, uneasy, the horses were moving their feet with gallantry and skill. The constant wind had ended up giving the woman's face a soft physical rapture that didn't match her words about digging ditches, and the solitary bodies of both were having a tacit mutual understanding in the way that bodies agree that have the same final destiny: the heart of that man beat big and confused, recognizing. Being a person was being all that.

It was then that it seemed to him that the promise that had been made to him was his own mission. Though he didn't understand why it's up to us to keep a promise that nevertheless was made to us.

In that moment it was particularly nice to exist because there was also the very limpid afternoon air. And in that moment the mounted woman suddenly laughed out of annoyance because the horse had stepped back and frighted. With certain surprise the man heard the laughter in that woman who never laughed. Because everything was probably being displayed for Martim, the way flowers open at a certain moment and we're never around to see it. But he was. For the first time he was present in the moment in which whatever is happening is happening. And he! he was that man who for the first time was realizing, not only from hearsay, but worryingly firsthand. He was exactly that man. He was then surprised by this entranced way of recognizing himself. He'd just decided to be, not someone else, but that man.

And more than that: he himself had suddenly become the meaning of the lands and of the woman, he himself was the goad of everything he was seeing. That's what he felt, though he received from his thought no more than the throb. And held back, bristling, he remembered that this is the common ground where a man can finally step: wanting to give a destiny to the enormous void that apparently only a destiny can fill.

Then, in an urge of the same kind as the urge to want to give a name, he tried to remember what gesture was used to express that instant of wind and of allusion to the unknown. He tried to remember what he'd done when he'd been up on the Corcovado one day with a girlfriend. But, even if he remembered, there was no way to express it. In that first impotence, for an instant Martim felt woefully stuck.

But also feeling woefully stuck was being a person, he still remembered that! oh he remembered it so well: with distress he remembered that that distress was being a person—and up on the Corcovado he'd kissed the girlfriend with a ferocity of love. He remembered in time that there was no way to express joy and so you'd build a house or take a journey or love. He too, mounted on the horse, with the apprehensive look of someone who could make a mistake, was watchfully attempting to copy into reality the being that he was, and in that birth his life was making itself. And

127

the thing made itself in such an impossible way—that in the impossibility was the hard claw of beauty. There are moments that can't be narrated, they happen between trains that pass or in the air that awakens our face and gives us our final shape, and then for an instant we are the fourth dimension of whatever exists, they are moments that don't count. But maybe that's the anxiety of an open-mouthed fish that the drowned man has before dying, and then it's said that before plunging under forever a man sees his whole life pass before his eyes; if in an instant we are born, and we die in an instant, an instant is enough for a whole life.

The man, then, had finally remembered what he'd done with the girlfriend in the wind of the Corcovado. In order to express himself he might have been able to take Vitória, since now that he was a man, she had become a woman. But not only was she not docile, but that would be a gratuitous act without the perfect fatal weight that the desire of the body lends. So he sat hushed, awkward, not knowing what to do with everything in which he had so suddenly been transformed. It was then that, out of nowhere, out of pure clumsiness, he wanted to be "good" as a solution. He wanted to be good so much that once again he felt a kind of impotence.

It's true that the fleeting thought he'd had about the woman hadn't been entirely lost in the air. Some remains of it the woman felt, obscurely offended the way cats get offended on rooftops. Vitória turned toward him and while she was speaking about the ditches looked right at him, and he was indubitably that man: in him, she saw him. Which was unexpected. With the curiosity of someone seeing an artery burst and an unsuspected blood gush out, with repugnance and great haughtiness, she looked at him—and he was that man, not any other ever, but he himself, which made her avert her eyes severe. She remembered that one night she'd walked by the woodshed and heard the man snore. The recollection of this not only rendered him unmatched, as the reasonable probability that he didn't know he was snoring handed him back over to her in all his weight of unconsciousness, the way the fainted dog had once been hers.

Until—until another wave of breeze erased everything. Leaving as reality only the man and the woman atop the horses.

And of everything all that was left to the man was the slightly useless feeling of having finally emerged. And the heart of a living person. Which, if it wasn't much, gave him a very great power; as a person he was capable of anything. Maybe that had been what he felt. And in order to show him up to what point everything was converging toward an awareness—as when grace exists— Vitória at that same moment stretched out her arm pointing out in the distance a mountain with slopes softened by the impossibility of being touched ... Martim had then a kind of certainty that this was the gesture that he'd been seeking: so much do distances seem to need someone to determine them with a gesture. That's how the man chose to conclude that this is the human gesture with which one alludes: pointing out.

And it didn't even matter to him that the woman hadn't done it on purpose. Nor even that it was she, and not he, who had carried it out. In the mute potency in which he was, any thing that spoke would be considered by him as his voice, and any thing that moved would be a movement of his; and he could possibly say "the best moment of my life was when Napoleon's troops entered Paris," and he could say "the best moment of my life was when a man said give ye bread to those who hunger," and becoming his own hardest and most bedazzling work the growth of the trees— the wideness of the world had broadened painfully his breast. And if that's how it was that's because, having made himself, he started to require much, and much more than he was. So that, the woman having pointed out with her extended hand the mountain in the distance, it now no longer mattered to the man if it was she or a stone or a bird who carried it out, what mattered is that the gesture be carried out. That, without reluctance, he allowed. Except, as a counterclaim, he wanted to take up the task right where the woman had left it, and demanded that from now on he himself would determine that. And in that instant it was as if a whole future were being outlined right there, and he would only understand the details as he was creating them. Martim had started to belong to his own steps. He belonged only to himself.

In this interim, what happened was just that the woman was looking around seeking good earth where the ditches could be dug without obstacles. And in order to reduce the truth to pure reality, what was happening with Martim?

In truth Martim had only had a very sharp physical awareness of both of them raised by the horses, and, in perception sharper yet, was feeling the horses at liberty in the air. Which had given him a vague sensation of beauty, the way you have a worrying sensation of beauty: when some thing seems to say some thing and there is that obscure encounter with a feeling. Really noticing, you could honestly say that Martim hadn't noticed anything. So that, with the neighing of the horses, they simply turned to one another and, without there having been so much as an instant of interruption in the conversation about the ditches, the woman spoke about the drought, and he heard her, and agreed. And just as, if there were reincarnation of the spirit after death, the law would ordain that we not be aware of having lived, the moment of Martim's contact with whatever one is had gone unnoticed by him. All that was clear was just the thought that the farm was a place where he might just be able to stay a bit longer. Martim was very pleased with himself.

What made satisfaction no longer enough for him was the kind of tough tenacity that, as a first general step, was changing his posture as they slowly went down the slope. They sitting straight up, the horses wobbling their flanks.

Second Part

BIRTH OF THE HERO

1

BUT ON THAT SAME NIGHT, PACING EXCITEDLY FROM
one side of the other inside the smallness of the woodshed, Martim could hardly contain himself with what he'd gained. It was
joy. He didn't know what to do with himself as if he'd had some
news and nobody to give it to. He was very content to be a person, this was one of the great pleasures of life. Yet, inconsolable,
it seemed to him that he would never be compensated.

And for the first time since he'd fled he felt the need to communicate. He sat on the edge of his bed, his head happy between
his hands. He didn't know where to start thinking. Then he remembered his son who'd one day said at dinnertime: I don't want
this food! The mother had answered: what food do you want?
The boy had ended up saying with the painful fright of discovery:

—None!

He, Martim, had then said to him:

—It's very simple: if you're not hungry, you don't have to eat.

But the child had started to cry:

—I'm not hungry, I'm not hungry …

And since the radio was also on, the man had shouted:

—I already said that if you're not hungry you don't have to eat!
so why are you crying?

The boy had replied:

—I'm crying because I'm not hungry.

—I promise you'll be hungry tomorrow, I promise! Martim had said to him disturbed, entering out of love into the truth of a child.

Seated on the bed, with his head between his hands, Martim closed his eyes laughing very moved. It was joy. His joy came from being hungry, and when a man is hungry he rejoices. After all a person is measured by his hunger—there is no other way to calculate oneself. And the truth is that on the slope the great neediness had been reborn in him. It was strange that he didn't have any food but was rejoicing at hunger. With his heart beating out of great hunger, Martim lay down. He was hearing his heart demanding, and laughed out loud, bestial, helpless.

The next day Ermelinda more and more systematic returned:

—Sir, you might think I'm crazy, she said to him with the persistent look of the blind, but there's a place inside me where I go when I want to sleep! ah, I know that's funny, but that's how it goes ... If that place were closer, I could even say that it's on the left side of my head—because I sleep on my left side, she explained to him in passing, licking her lips—but that place is so much farther, it's as if were far beyond the place where I end ... but it's still inside me, it's still me, you understand?

Since it was the particular details of her life that made her, in her own eyes, unsubstitutable by some other person, when she was describing her specialties she was trying with effort to prove to the man that she was she herself. Since Martim hadn't looked at her, she then ventured a bit further:

—It's a place that's located beyond my death, she said at last, and suddenly became so pale that, moved to glance at her because of the girl's unexpected silence, he stopped smiling without knowing why.

But Ermelinda was well aware that it was still too soon to stop lying and stop charming him. She knew that it was too soon to show herself to him, and that she could scare him off if she were truthful, people are so afraid of other people's truth. Only through indirect means would she manage it. The idea that, if she didn't entertain him, she'd scare him off, was frightening her: now of all times that she'd gained so much ground that she'd managed to get him to hear her, even if he didn't look at her! Then, worried that she'd gone too far and scared him off, she laughed a lot and said jokingly:

—I know that in order to go to this place where I go when I'm tired, you take a left, that's how I manage to fall asleep, just think! Sometimes, in order not to get nervous, I want to bring a thing into my sleep with me, a thing from the day, you understand? a handkerchief to twist in my hand, a missal, just to give me some security and not have to go alone, just imagine how silly I am! she said with tenderness, looking at him straight on to see if she'd managed to infect him with tenderness for herself. But you can't bring anything or anyone, otherwise you don't go. There seems like there's just one place to go sleep or think. I, of course, don't want nor like to go back there at all! But—she said helpless—but after you go there once, you're immediately hooked. Can you believe—she added greedily—can you believe that I can't stop thinking about whatever I'm thinking about?—but she didn't tell him what she was thinking about, and felt the pleasure of someone who confesses in the absence of someone to hear it, as if she were robbing him while he was asleep.—Can you, sir, by any chance not think about whatever you're thinking about? It is, as they say, an obsession! a true obsession!—she was saying all playfully, without forgetting for an instant that, in a patient and perfect work, she should always flatter the man.

But also without forgetting that she was in a hurry. It occurred to her that, as she was speaking to him, she could accidentally reveal what she was, and the man would then notice how much she needed him, and for that reason no longer want her, the way it happens with people. At the simple possibility that he'd never end up liking her, Ermelinda shivered solitary, looked at the birds that were flying. Her work with the man was always so delicate, and demanded so much precision, that she wouldn't be able to do it if she just decided to carry it out or if she were sent to do it. It was a labor of infinite caution, in which a step too far and the man would never love her, where a step too far and she herself might stop loving him: she was protecting both of them against the error. And sometimes she seemed more as if she were protecting both of them from the truth.

—It's like an obsession! Do you think I'm crazy? she asked him, since she was aware that she lived from an idea and that this wasn't "normal."

—No.

—But other people don't seem to think that death … —Ermelinda quickly hid the revealing word with a flirty smile. I'm really not? she inquired coquettishly, I'm not crazy, am I? I'm so silly that you, sir, can't even imagine! she said to him as if promising him a whole future of attractive nonsense that he was only missing if he wanted to.

—You're crazy because you talk, he finally said, heavy.

—Ah, she then said with the sly look of someone who won't let herself be tricked, then I'm already seeing it all: you think I'm crazy! I already saw, you don't fool me! she said all laughing, speaking to him with deliberate intimacy—but her open eyes were thinking of something else.

Martim remembered a man he'd known and who'd traveled alone for a long time through the backlands and who, when he returned, would always talk about trees and snakes and little birds, to the fatigue and incomprehension of all; until the man had realized that a person doesn't talk about trees and little birds and snakes, and stopped speaking:

—No, he then repeated looking at her, and with a first kindness of curiosity in his voice, you're not crazy. It's just that you lead a very isolated life and no longer know what you say to other people and what you don't—the man stopped and looked at her, intrigued at having said so much.

He'd never said so much, and the girl's heart started to beat:

—That's right, she said gallantly.

With an instinctive wisdom, Ermelinda didn't show that she'd noticed his first step toward her, in the way you don't give a shout of joy when a child starts to walk so that it won't stop frightened for months.

As for him, he hadn't noticed anything. As for him, he was waiting with patient anxiety for the moment his work would be done.

In order to go—not to the plot with the plants, not to the cows in the stables—but, with the uncertain demonstration of a live jelly, to go once again to the slope in order to take up every day once more the instant of his education the day before. Where he'd stand, it was enough for him to stand, without knowing what to do. That need a person has to climb a mountain—and look. That was the first symbol he'd touched since leaving home: "climb a mountain." And in that obscure act he was fertilizing himself. That place was an old never formulated thought. As if his father's father had aspired to it. And as if from the invention of an ancient legend that reality had been born. That place had already happened to him before, it didn't matter when, maybe only in promise and in invention.

And only God knows that Martim didn't know what he'd come to do on the slope. But it was as true that some objective thing must be happening to him there that—since he'd grown used to authorizing his own nature with the final argument of the nature of animals—that it was enough for him to remember how a bull stands on top of the hill. Looking. That objective thing like an act: looking. Sometimes too a dog looks, though quickly and immediately thereafter worried, since a dog doesn't have time, he needs a lot of affection and is nervous, and has an afflicted feeling of passing time, and has in his eyes the weight of an untransmissible soul, only love can cure a dog. But it so happens that that man, for fortuitous reasons, was closer to the nature of the bull, and was looking. If it's true that if you asked him why, he wouldn't know how to reply, it's also true that if a person only did what he understands, he'd never take a single step.

Oh, you could say that nothing was happening while he was on the slope. And he wasn't asking for anything to happen either. The dusk of ragged light, the naked air and the empty space seemed to be enough for him. Even a thought word would sink the air. He was holding back. There, existing was already an emphasis. As if it weren't a daring and an advance for a person to be standing in the brightness. And it was as if there Martim were becoming the symbol of himself. He who, at last, had been incarnated as himself. The little birds, slipping away from the light, held themselves inside the darkness of the full branches. The brightness stayed there solitary, blue, sheer. It was dusk. And Martim was looking as if looking were being a man. He was savoring his state. It was a generosity of the world toward him. He was receiving it without embarrassment. Since, who knows why, he was no longer ashamed.

Until one day, in the face of the inhospitable and meaningless brightness, he'd finally thought, a bit worried and moving ahead: "by God, if we didn't create a world, this merely divine world wouldn't accept us." That was when it started to get dark. Dogs turned up watchful in the distance. The little birds came out of the foliage, and each ventured a bit further. Slowly the air grew denser, feelings started at last to show their less than divine nature, a deeply confused desire to be loved mixed with the human scent of the night, and a vague sweat started to seep out, spreading its nice and bad scent of earth and cows and rat and armpits and darkness—that furtive way in which we bit by bit take stock of the earth: we had at least created a world and given it our will.

The maximum of brightness had ceded to our peopled darkness: could that be what Martim was waiting for every day standing there? As if in this bending of brightness they had taught him how the harmonious union is done—not intelligible but harmonious, not with a goal but harmonious—as if in this bending of brightness toward darkness were made at last the union of plants, cows, and of the man that he had started to be. Every time, then, that the day became night, the man's domain was renewed, and a step forward taken, blindly, finally blindly the way a person moves forward into wanting.

Martim didn't wonder why on the slope he was completing himself so well, turning harmonious himself—unintelligible but harmonious—while he was looking at the immortality of the field. For now that was enough for him. A man who has walked a great deal has the right to have an inexplicable pleasure, just harmony, even without understanding—for the time being without understanding. Since, with calm presumption, he was saying to himself: "it's still early." It wasn't, however, just presumption. Because now he'd learned to count on the ripening of time, the way cows live off this tacitly. He now was seeming to understand that you couldn't brutalize time, and that its wide movement was unsubstitutable by a voluntary movement.

That's how, every day, when he was free of Vitória's orders, he'd go wait on the slope for the return of that instant when, stultified, he had neared the ranch for the first time and for the first time had been warned. And again and again he'd return. Repeating seemed essential to him. Every time he repeated himself, something was added.

So much so that Martim was already starting to get worried—he was a man, but there was still something that was unsettled: what is a man supposed to do?

2

UNTIL THAT EVENING ON THE SLOPE MARTIM STARTED to justify himself. The hard time of explanation had arrived.

There, before going ahead, he'd have to be innocent or guilty. There he had to know if his mother, who never would understand him if she were alive, would love him without understanding him. There he had to find out if his father's ghost would hold out his hand without fright. There he would judge himself— and this time with the language of others. Now he'd have to call what he'd done a crime. The man shivered with fear of touching something inside him the wrong way, he who was still wounded all over.

But because he profoundly knew he'd use even farce as long as he managed to emerge intact from his own judgment—in that way, if he didn't absolve himself, he'd be dumbfounded with a crime on his hands—because he knew you weren't allowed to emerge in any way but intact from the dangerous confrontation he had the courage to face himself and, if necessary, horrify himself.

And more: since you're only allowed to win, since at the point where you were you ferociously needed yourself, because beforehand you'd told yourself this: after the necessary judgment is when he'd have his great task before him. For there he would have to remember what a man wants.

Though it had occurred to him that he was inverting whatever had happened. That he hadn't committed a crime in order to give himself the opportunity of finding out what a man wants—that opportunity had been born incidentally with the crime. But he sought to ignore the uncomfortable feeling of mystification: he was needing this error in order to move ahead, and used it as an instrument. And, voluntarily leaving aside his confusion, the man at last tried to approach himself. With a sigh, he approached himself in clear terms and this is what he thought:

That he had not committed just any crime.

He thought that with this crime he had carried out his first manly act. Yes. Courageously he had done what every man had to do once in his life: destroy it.

In order to rebuild it on his own terms.

"So had that been what he'd wanted to do with the crime?" His heart beat heavy, irreducible, illuminated with peace. Yes, in order to rebuild it on his own terms.

And if he didn't manage to rebuild it? For in his rage he had broken something that existed into pieces that were too small. What if he didn't manage to rebuild it? So he looked at the perfect emptiness of the brightness, and the strange possibility occurred to him of never managing to rebuild it. But if he didn't manage, that didn't even matter. He'd had the courage to bet profoundly. A man one day had to risk everything. Yes, he'd done that.

And proud of his crime, he looked at the demolished world.

Demolished by himself, at his feet. The world undone by a crime. And one that only he, because he had made himself into the great guilty party, could re-erect, give a meaning and set up once again.

But on his own terms.

That was it, then. Then Martim wondered with intensity and pain: was that really it? Because his truths didn't seem to hold up for long under scrutiny without becoming deformed. And, for an instant, the truth could be this as much as any other: immutable was the field alone. It was then with the difficulty of a control art that Martim clung to just one truth and with difficulty pushed away the others. (Without realizing it, his reconstruction had already started off wheezing.)

It didn't matter to him that the origin of his present strength had been a criminal act. What mattered was that from it he had taken the urge of the great assertion.

That's how, then, Martim emerged intact from the judgment. A bit tired by the effort.

Well, and now the thing would be to remember what a man wants. That was the true judgment—and Martim lowered his head, confused, in penitence.

Oh God, it wasn't easy at all for that man to express what he wanted. He wanted this: to rebuild. But it was like an order you get and don't know how to carry out. No matter how free he is, a person was used to being ordered around, even if only by other people's way of being. And now Martim was on his own.

You needed to be very patient with him, he was slow. What did he want? Whatever it was he wanted had been born far inside him, and it wasn't easy to draw out the stammering rustle. After it so happened that what he wanted was also being strangely mixed up with whatever he already was—and that he nevertheless had never attained.

His obscure task would be made easier if he allowed himself the use of already created words. But his reconstruction had to start with the words themselves, since words were the voice of a man. That without mentioning that in Martim was a caution of a merely practical order: as soon as he allowed other people's words, he'd automatically be allowing the word "crime"—and he'd become just a common criminal on the lam. And it was still very early for him to give himself a name, and to give a name to what it was he wanted. Another step, and he'd know. But it was still too soon.

Then Martim went down the slope in order to tell Vitória that the next morning he'd start to dig the ditches. He went to the porch and waited for Vitória to finish speaking to Francisco.

The fact that he'd finally managed to think hadn't given him any directive. But, in his own way, he had owned up to his crime—and was feeling like a complete, tall, serene man. Standing on the porch, unhurried, he was hearing Vitória's hard voice and the assent of Francisco in rhythm with the woman's voice. Afterward, almost without realizing it, he started to hear the words as well.

— ... you need to get the tomatoes together too. And this time pack them better, Francisco. Better and quicker: this time the German's getting to Vila earlier.

Martim was listening, and waiting patiently. And that's when he understood what he'd heard.

So, then, she was going to meet a German. The German. So she'd be seeing the German. Stunned, alert, Martim turned over the phrase in his own head in order to see if he could make it lose its meaning. But however he repeated it, it was always the same: "the woman would see the German." She'd probably sell him some products from the farm! he thought, suddenly recovering the former voracious intelligence of his escape, and from one moment to the next dominating through a skill of reasoning that went beyond his normal capacity, as if now he could lose the weight of his body, crawl along and get mixed up with the shadows on the wall. In a feline sharpening of his memory, he instantly remembered that he'd seen Francisco cleaning the truck ...

"In order to go to Vila-Baixa or just to clean it?" He remembered that he'd already heard Vitória speak of the German—but

when? when! Or had he never heard it? No, he'd never heard it ...
And Francisco had already cleaned the truck! But the trip wasn't
happening today—could it be the next day? So she'd see the
German, he thought with the care of someone handling something treacherous that could unexpectedly rebel beneath his fingers and take on a life of its own. So she'd see the German, he
thought with care. But the thought, though very clear, didn't take
him anywhere nor lead him to any other thought. Captured, he
ferociously moved his head from one side to the other calculating
the distance of a jump off the porch. She'd see the German, he
repeated quickly and as stingy as a rat, and even his head looked
hairier to Vitória—who looked at him for an instant without
breaking off her orders to Francisco. "He looks like a dirty animal," the woman noticed while still talking to Francisco.

But soon the intimate darkness started fraying that had enveloped Martim and in which he was already starting to move with
skill. His head was slowly falling back into place. And when Francisco left and Vitória started to talk to him and give him orders,
Martim, forgetting what he'd come to tell her about the ditches,
looked her intensely in the eyes. And tried to guess, with the help
of that spare element that were two black eyes, if Vitória was the
kind of woman who would rattle on about what was happening in her own house: about a new worker, someone who wasn't
from around here ... But even if she didn't tell on him directly,
she might happen to refer to him ... and the German would guess
that it was the same one who'd fled the hotel in the night ...

"How close is she to the German?", Martim tried to guess,
looking her over avidly with his eyes. But he didn't find any reply in that face that, out of fatigue, had one day closed off forever. "Maybe she's not the chatty type ... but the German himself
might mention that night in which the guest ran off—and then
she'd find out!" Martim grew enraged against himself for never

having paid attention to that woman that he didn't know and whose acts, for that reason, he couldn't predict. Out of practical necessity, he then examined her for the first time. It was a thin and hard face, where the bones seemed to speak more than the flesh. It was a raised head. More than that, he couldn't find out.

And the journey would be when? how much time did he have to escape? "The journey can't be very soon!", he suddenly thought more lucidly, "because Francisco wouldn't have time to pluck and pack the tomatoes! the tomatoes still haven't even been harvested, since Vitória just told Francisco to do it now!", he remembered in a fury of joy. "Or have they?", he suddenly got confused.

—When are you going to Vila, ma'am? he asked no longer able to stand the doubt, and the question he hadn't planned but wanted to sound off-hand sounded brusque and imperative, suspicious even to his own ears.

Vitória stopped short, her mouth opened in surprise. It was the first time the man had spoken to her without being provoked.

—I don't know, she finally said, with knitted brows.

Then Martim, with the same sudden acumen that went beyond him and went beyond logic—saw that Vitória would turn him in. Then he lowered his shoulder and undid the tension. As if the first instant of certainty only gave him the relief of not doubting, peacefulness overtook him. He looked crudely at the woman.

Her face, beneath this undisguised tranquil gaze, blushed at being discovered. Stared at so nakedly, the face shrank in a rapid search for a posture, finally deciding on an expression of impassibility to which her blushing gave more determination.

Then the man understood even a bit later: that from the moment he'd stepped onto the farm, she'd decided to send him away. The only new element that had now been added was that she'd finally chosen the method.

Why hadn't he noticed, before, something that now was so

clear? he thought surprised. How had he not noticed that, day after day, that woman had struggled to decide, and that cumulatively she'd decided? How had he not noticed that each carefree step he'd taken—had made the woman, in an echo, move one step closer to the decision? Because the man speedily remembered certain glances from the woman while he was working, and which he'd barely noticed; he remembered the tone of voice with which she'd asked him so many times how long he'd stay at the farm. But why had she asked him that question? As if every time she were suggesting the idea of leaving voluntarily … In order to give him the chance to flee, and thereby free her from the difficult decision? He realized that from the moment he'd set foot on the farm, she'd guessed. Guessed as much as you can guess without knowing. Only one thing he still wasn't understanding, and he looked at her with curiosity: why she still hadn't turned him in. Vitória couldn't take the man's simple gaze, and averted her eyes.

"So that was her final answer," he thought. "And so there wasn't much time left," was Martim's next realization.

3

BUT IT WAS ONLY AT NIGHT, SITTING STRAIGHT UP IN bed and without turning on the lamp, that Martim fully understood what he'd meant when he'd thought that there wasn't much time left.

With a start he realized that in fact he didn't mean the time he had left to plan his escape. Although, from the moment in which he'd spoken to Vitória on the porch, he'd acted as if it were obvious that his escape needed to be that same night, before the truck was used by Vitória, and if he wanted to be far away by the time she met with the German. But as if the darkness of the woodshed were bringing him to his own darkness, he understood himself at last: it wasn't for the escape that there wasn't much time left. He'd been so busy planning the flight that he hadn't realized that he had no intention of escaping.

"He had to have everything before the end and had to live a whole life before the end." That was why time had run short. With a dazzled awe—because the truth is until that instant he hadn't really taken himself seriously, nor even realized to what extent he'd accepted the gravity, and, astonished, now was seeing that he hadn't been joking—with dazzled awe, it wasn't for the escape that he didn't have much time left. His own courage then left him wary. He was suspicious of himself.

And that wasn't all the man realized with surprise. In the violence of the ultimatum of now Martim recognized that the idea that there was no time to lose had been constantly with him, even before the ultimatum, disguised beneath the daily work, patient beneath the sleep in which a person moves slowly. Then, suddenly quite excited and pacing from one side to the other in the dark meagerness of the shed, Martim realized that now was only the guardian of a small time that didn't belong to him. And that his task was greater than time.

Now that he'd emerged to reach the point of a man on the slope, now that he'd emerged to the point of understanding his crime and knowing what he desired—or to the point of inventing whatever had happened to him and inventing whatever he desired? it didn't matter if the truth already existed or if it was created, since being created is what gave it worth as the act of a man—now that he'd managed to justify himself, he had to go on. And manage before the nearing end to—to reconstruct the world.

Yes. The reconstruction of the world. Because the man had just completely lost his shame. He wasn't even embarrassed to go back to use words from adolescence; he had to use them since the last time he'd had his own language had been in adolescence; adolescence was risking everything—and he was now risking everything.

He didn't have much time and had to start right away, in a manner of speaking. "From the reconstruction of the world inside himself, he would go on to reconstruct the City, which was a form of living and that he had repudiated with a murder; that was why time was short." "I don't think I'm such a fool at all!", he thought fascinated.

Understanding himself, finally, an enormous calm dominated the man. He wasn't even frightened by the senseless enormity of his aims. Once he'd destroyed the order, he had nothing left to lose, and no commitment could buy him. He could go out to greet a new order. Then, frightened, he wondered if any man had ever been as free as he was now. After which, he grew calm. Not because he was calm: in fact his body was trembling. But because, from now on, and starting at this very instant, he'd have to be calm and incredibly shrewd in order to manage to follow along with himself and follow the speed with which he'd have to act. He'd have to be calm. Now that he'd reached on the mountain his own greatness—the greatness with which we are born.

That greatness—oh, just the size of a man—that had been buried as a shameful and useless weapon. Being a man had been something without a point. But greatness which he was now at last needing as an instrument. For the first time Martim was profoundly needing himself. As if at last—at last—he'd been summoned ... Which left him bashful in the dark. And since in the dark not even the walls could see his face, Martim made with great relief a face of pain, and then of embarrassment because of the joy he'd had, and then of pain.

He sat at last on the bed. And in a cold and calculated plan decided that his first struggle would have to be with himself.

Since, if he wanted to reconstruct the world, he himself was no use ... If he wanted, as a final term of his work, to reach other men—he'd first have to destroy totally his former way of being. In order for the beggar at the door of the cinema not to be an abstract and perpetual person, he'd have to start way off, and from the first beginning. It's true that there wasn't much left to destroy, since, with the crime, he'd already destroyed a lot. But not altogether. There was still ... there was still he himself, which was a constant temptation. And his thought, the way it was, could only give a certain and inevitable result, the way a sickle can only give a certain kind of cut. If he'd obtained the first and coarse destruction with the act of rage, the more delicate work still remained to be done. And the delicate work was this: being objective.

But how? in what way be objective? Because if a person never wanted to err—and he never wanted to err again—he'd end up prudently remaining in this stance: "there's nothing as white as white," "there's nothing as full of water as a thing full of water," "the yellow thing is yellow." Which wouldn't be mere prudence, it would be exactitude of calculation and sober rigor. But where would it take him? because at the end of the day we're not scientists.

The work was this: being objective. Which would be the strangest experience for a man. As far as Martim could remember, he'd never heard anyone mention an objective man. No, no—he got confused a bit tiredly.—there had been men like that, there had been, yes, men whose soul had come to exist in acts, and for whom other men hadn't been great fingernails; there had been men like that, he no longer remembered who, and he was a bit fatigued, a bit solitary. Because his plan was so easily escapable to his own perception, so refined amidst his merely uncouth strength, that he was afraid that instinct wouldn't rescue him and that, as a desperate measure, he might become intelligent. And he for the time being was still nothing more than a vague thing that wanted to ask, ask and ask—until bit by bit the world started taking shape in reply.

Martim hesitated tired, looked around, pulled himself together a bit. He was moving forward by jumping back, with apparent freedom. What sometimes gave him support, and a generalized morale to continue, was the recollection of the successful pleasure he'd had with women. But, right after, the fact of never having managed to get a bicycle paralyzed him: he could, then, fail. All through his life, like a dripping faucet, he'd wanted the bicycle. Once again his plan seemed too fragile to him, and that breathing thing that he was in the dark seemed to him very little, as the beginning of a conversation. Martim got all entangled as if he had more fingers than he needed and as if he himself were botching his own path forward. The desire then came to him for a child to start to cry so that he could be kind to it. Because he was helpless and felt the need to give, which was the form in which an awkward person knew how to ask. His ambition was big and helpless, he would have liked to hold a child's hand; he was a little tired.

"Why do I want so much?", the habit that had ended up once again by making other people's hunger an abstraction hinted to him then, the same habit that is the fear a man has. "And if I didn't take myself seriously?" he thought shrewdly, since that had been the old solution, and that of many people. "Because if we suddenly gave importance to whatever really is important to us — we'd lose our lives." But it's also said that he who loses his life, gains his life.

Having spent his rest time in discouragement, Martim stirred worriedly: he'd have to violate himself every time the habit returned. Since from now on he wasn't even allowed to interrupt himself with a question — "why do I want so much" — any interruption could be fatal, and he would not only risk losing speed but balance. Growth is full of tricks and self-ensnarement and fraud; few are they who have the dishonesty necessary in order not to nauseate themselves. With ferocious self-preservation, Martim could no longer allow himself the luxury of decency nor of interrupting himself with a sincerity.

4

IN THIS INTERVAL DAWN ARRIVED.

And digging the first ditch in the morning light, at the same time that his thick hands were obeying him, Martim had already started to dedicate himself to a work of infinite exactitude and alertness. Which was to appropriate oneself and, with oneself, the world? Was that really what he was doing? But was it really important to know what he was doing? He was doing a dream— which was the only way that the truth could come to him and that he could live it. Could it then be indispensable to understand perfectly what was happening to him? If we understand it profoundly, do we also need to understand it superficially? If we recognize in its slow moving our own shaping—the way you recognize a place where you've been at least once—do you have to translate it into words that compromise us?

Blindly, then, and having as a compass nothing more than intention, Martim was seeming to want to begin from the exact beginning. And to reconstruct in his way from the first stone, until reaching the instant in which there came the great bypass—what had been his impalpable error as a man? Until he reached once again the instant in which the great mistake had once appeared unleashing the useless vastness of the world. And when, once the path he'd already traveled was remade bit by bit, he reached the point where the error had happened, then he'd go in the opposite direction from the bypass. In the morning light it seemed that simple to him, and he was as fresh and clean as a boy going to school early in the morning. In the morning light it seemed that simple to him: when the world was remade inside him, he then would know how to act. And his action wouldn't be the abstract action of thought, but the real thing.

Which? "Anything," he said with tranquil insolence. And if time were short, if Vitória turned him in before he was ready, and he didn't have any freedom left over for action—he would at least have managed to know what is the action of a man. And that too was a maximum. (Oh, he'd been warned that if you explained yourself nobody would understand, since when you explain how one foot follows the other nobody recognizes the stride.) Oh there wasn't much time, yes, he knew. He could almost hear the enormous silence with which the hands of a clock were moving forward. But he didn't feel revolted by being the guardian of such a short amount of time: the time of a whole life would be short too. That man had already accepted the great contingency.

On the first day, then, he asked of himself no more than objectivity. Which became a source of cares and deceptions. For example, a little bird was singing. But as soon as Martim tried to make it concrete, the little bird stopped being a symbol and suddenly was no longer whatever it was you could call a little bird. In order to make up for it, the roosters and hens became in his rigorous eyes the day itself: they were rushing around, white among the smoke, the morning sun, if Martim wasn't quick he'd miss it, the roosters were running, sometimes opening their wings, the hens without having to take care of the eggs were free, all this was the morning itself and if you weren't quick you'd miss it—objectivity was a dizzying glance. Martim immediately learned the question of rhythm: when his eyes would try to do more than describe things, all that remained of his effort was an empty rooster shape.

Moreover, in his work of constructing reality, there was as a point against Martim the novelty of things no longer being obvious; he kept bumping up against it. Against him, too, was the awareness of the precise time. Though Martim had a great advantage: if life was short, the days were long. In his favor he also had the fact of knowing that he ought to walk in a straight line, since it wouldn't be very practical to lose the train of thought. Against him there was a lurking danger: because there was a savor and a beauty in a person's getting lost. Against him was also the fact of understanding little. But above all in his favor there was the fact that not understanding was his clean point of departure.

Fine: that was a first attempt at reconstruction and with a clean point of departure.

But—but could he have started too much from the start?

For he looked toward the empty field and it seemed to him that it went back to the creation of the world. In his leap backward, because of a calculation error he'd gone too far back—and because of a calculation error it seemed to him that he'd placed himself uncomfortably in front of the first perplexity of a monkey. As a monkey, at least he'd be replaced by the knowledge that would make him scratch himself and that would make the field gradually reachable by jumps. But he didn't have a monkey's resources.

Could he have started excessively from the start? And afterward it so happened that, despite his heroism, there was a practical question: he didn't have material time in order to start from so far off. He already didn't have much time left to go back over what had taken him almost forty years to travel; and not only to travel in a new way the road he'd already taken, but in order to do what he hadn't been able to do up till then: reaching understanding, going beyond it by applying it. Just for that there wasn't much time. Much less to begin, in a manner of speaking, from nothing! And yet, if he wanted to be loyal to his own necessity, he couldn't trick it: he had to start from the first start.

Which, digging and digging, suddenly seemed to him easy once again. Since each minute could be the whole time—if a person were free enough to oblige that minute. Martim was aware of that because once, in an already lost minute, he had accepted rage, and a path had opened like a destiny in a minute. And later, in a minute, he hadn't been afraid to be great; and without modesty, in a minute, he'd accepted, as if it were his own, the role of a man.

That's how, then, that having already lost on the mountain his original modesty, Martim was losing without noticing his final chains, until it already was no longer monstrous for a person to give himself the function of a person and to "reconstruct." Which seemed quite easy to him. To this day everything he'd seen had been in order not to see, everything he'd done had been in order not to do, everything he'd felt had been in order not to feel. Today, though his eyes may burst, but they'd see. He who had never faced anything straight on. Few people would have had the opportunity to reconstruct existence on their own terms. À nous deux, he suddenly said interrupting his work and looking. Because all he had to do was start.

But as if he'd had a childish dream he looked back at the little bird who was singing and said to himself: what do I do with him?

Since already in his first vision a little bird didn't fit. Everything had been given to him, yes. But broken apart and in pieces. And he, with too many parts left in his hand, didn't seem to know how to put the thing back together. Everything was his to do whatever he wanted with it. Yet his own freedom was rendering him helpless. As if God had granted his request excessively and given him everything. But had at the same time withdrawn. The prairie was all Martim's, and along with it a little bird who was singing. And his too, in this short time, was all of life. And nobody and nothing could help him: it had been exactly this that he himself had prepared with care, and even with a crime had prepared it. But if he'd slyly started by the easiest part—what was simpler than a little bird?—then he wondered embarrassed: what do I do with a little bird singing?

He then looked at the little bird with severity. But he—he didn't know how to deduce. It's true that, concentrating and full of lots of goodwill, by staring at the little bird, he managed a maximum tension that resembled a sensation of beauty. But that's it. Nothing more. Would seeing the little bird singing be the limit of his intuition? is two-plus-two-is-four the great leap that a man can take?

As you can see, this first day of objectivity was sleepwalking. If he tried to go from the spirit of geometry to that of *finesse*, things stubbornly didn't have a *finesse* reachable by his big mouth and by his inexpert hands. His was, then, a great spiritual effort. And a little dull. What helped him out is that he had the persistence of people who, not having enough foresight to make out the difficulty, see no obstacles. What also helped him out was that, having grown used to the fact of not being brilliant, he thought that once again the difficulty was his alone; so he forced himself. Until he reached a point of worried responsibility in which it seemed to him that if he wasn't aware that the flowers were growing, the flowers wouldn't grow.

Yet—yet, on that same day there were moments in which, because he was applying himself to trying to understand, it was as if, rapping the dry earth with a rod, he felt that there was water there. It's true, as well, that that was where his cleverness stopped.

It was at night that Martim had a thought more or less like this: whether the story of a person were always the story of his failure. Through which…what? Through which, period. Then, reluctant to use this thought, he took refuge in the thought about his son. Since the love for his son was one of the truths he liked best.

5

AS THE DAYS PASSED, NOTICING THAT HE WAS MORE present, the women took for stability the morose appearance that Martim had taken on and that came from the fact that he was training instant by instant, with the stupid face of a thinking man, with the patience of the shoemakers on the engraving, a way to open a path forward. Sure then that she'd finally receive the reassuring reply, Ermelinda asked him with the security with which a woman establishes dominions in order to settle in with children:

—How long are you staying?

—I don't know, he answered.

Once again Ermelinda was astounded. And as if her shiver were communicated impalpably to Vitória, both women more active started to act as if time were running out, Vitória growing impatient with the ditches that were hardly progressing, would spy on him from her horse. And a new rhythm was felt on the ranch.

And Martim? Martim was working—looking and working, ironing out the world. His rough thinking kept nonetheless stubbornly anchoring in what he kept considering to be more primary—from which he would gradually start to understand everything, from a woman who had asked him for years "what time is it" to the sun that rose every day and the people would then get out of bed, to understand the patience of others, to understand why a child was our investment and the arrow that we shoot. Could that be what he wanted? that's not quite known. He for now was shaping himself, and that is always slow; he was giving a form to whatever he was, life making itself was hard like art making itself.

All that was becoming barely demonstrable. The truth most recognizable to all is that that man was confused. As was said, only persistent ambition made him not see obstacles along a path that, thanks to the grace of stupidity, was easy for him. His grandiloquence, however, had a bit of humility: since he'd come to accept that every moment has no power in itself, he'd started to rely on the cumulative power of time—"the passing of many moments would bring him where he wanted to go." And that's how his humility turned into an instrument of patience: he was working without stopping, the ditches were opening deep.

The small population of the ranch was looking at the sky, scrutinizing it and working. Everything was shivering in a heat that was growing by degrees without making its transitions felt. The twigs were trembling, the heat doubling every object into a flaring refraction. From the depth of his own mystery, Martim was looking at the plants that in their innocent lushness still didn't seem to feel the threat that the crimson sun was sparkling: the drought. He was looking. Now that he had courage—everything was his, which wasn't easy at all. He was looking, for example, at the prairie that had become his battleground, and there wasn't a breach through which you could enter into what belonged to him. What was he merely seeing? that everything was a soft prolongation of everything, whatever existed was joining whatever existed, curves were creating themselves, crowded, harmonious, the wind was eating the sands, beating useless against the stones. It is true that, in some strange way, when you didn't understand yourself, everything would become obvious and harmonious, the thing was quite explicit. Yet, while looking, he had a hard time understanding that obviousness of meaning, as if he had to make out a light inside a light.

And that's how Martim sometimes would lose his objectives. Was there really even a planned goal, or was he just following an uncertain necessity? to what extent was he determined? Martim might well quickly reach a conclusion. But if you purified yourself, the road becomes long. And if the road is long, the person can forget where he's going and end up in the middle of the road looking dazzled at a little stone or licking with pity his feet wounded by the pain of walking or sitting for an instant just in order to wait a bit. The road was hard and lovely; the temptation was beauty.

And all this is to say that in that interim some thing had happened.

An insidious thing had started to gnaw at the crossbeam. And that was something Martim hadn't counted on. It was that he was starting to love what he was seeing.

Free, for the first time free, what did Martim do? He did what trapped people do: he was loving the harsh wind, loving his work in the ditches. Like a man who had set up the great meeting of his life and never arrived because he'd got distracted offended examining little green leaves. It was in such a way that he was loving and getting lost. And the worst part of it is that he was loving without having a concrete reason. Just because a person who was born, would love? and without knowing why. Now that he'd created with his own hands the opportunity of being neither victim nor hangman, of being outside the world and no longer having to bother with pity or with love, of no longer having to punish nor punish himself—unexpectedly love for the world was being born. And the danger there is that, if he wasn't careful, he'd give up on moving forward.

Because another thing had happened too, as important and serious and real as sadness or pain or rage: he was contented.

Martim was contented. He hadn't foreseen this added obstacle: the struggle against pleasure. He was overly savoring the details of the stable. With surprise, he was satisfied with so little: in carrying out tasks … It was quite enough for him to be a person who gets up in the morning. The almost-dark sky was enough for him. And the foggy earth and the cool trees, and he had learned how to squeeze milk from the cows who in the dawn would moo lukewarmly. Like this: I am a man who squeezes milk from cows. The current of grace was strong in the morning, and having a body that lived was enough. If he wasn't careful, he'd feel he owned it. If he wasn't careful, a taller tree would make him feel complete, and a plate of food would buy him in the moment of his hunger, and he would join his enemies who were bought by food and by beauty. Worried, he was feeling guilty about not transforming, at least in thought, the world in which he was living. Martim was getting lost. "Was there really a goal?" Now it was already happening to him to have an admiring and benevolent vanity in relation to his "escapes," and visualizing himself as a big horse that we have at home and that sometimes does its fantastic runs around, free with impunity, led by the beauty of the contentment of the spirit that is equal to the way our body doesn't come apart. Exercises in living. Martim was taking pleasure in himself. Miserably, just that. As you can see, he couldn't have been happier.

It was with a superhuman effort that Martim tried to conquer every day the vanity of belonging to a field so great that it was growing without meaning; it was with austerity that he conquered the taste he had for hollow harmony. With effort he was surpassing himself, forcing himself—against the current that was dragging him along in its grace—not to betray his crime. As if, with his contentment, he were stabbing his own rebellion. So he'd force himself harshly not to forget his commitment. And again he would place himself inside in a spiritual state of work: a kind of trance in which he'd learned to fall when he needed to.

His state of work consisted in adopting a doltish pose of purity and vulnerability. He'd learned the technique of staying vulnerable and alert, with an idiotic face. It wasn't easy at all, it was even very hard. Until—until he reached a certain imbecility he'd been needing. As a point of departure, he was creating for himself an attitude of amazement, becoming defenseless, without any weapon to hand; he who didn't want to even use instruments; he wanted to be his own instrument, and with naked hands. Because, after all, he'd committed a crime in order to be exposed.

But if that attempt at innocence was bringing him to an objectivity, it was to the objectivity of a cow: without words. And he was a man who needed words. So, with patience, he was correcting the exaggeration of his imbecility: "I also need not to force myself to be dumber than I am," since there also weren't all that many advantages to being an imbecile, you couldn't forget that the world isn't made up of imbeciles alone. He adopted, then, as a new working method, the opposite path and struck a resolute pose that recalled a defiance. It wasn't hard to keep that pose. Yet more than that, he couldn't manage—and he was all eager like a man who winds himself up for a kilometer race and then bumps up against the fact that he only has two meters to run—he deflated disappointed. It was revealed that the pose of no longer being an imbecile had been a task beyond his real capacity to stop being that way.

It's true that when it was occurring to him that the end wasn't far off, he already no longer needed to spur himself on or create techniques in order to continue his monstrous task. When it was occurring to him that he had to have violently everything, and "revelation" too—once again his hurry was becoming perfect, tranquil and concentrated like that of the shoemakers beneath the cauldron. And his own contentment seemed to be a necessary part of the slow work of the artisan.

Oh he was very helpless. He simply didn't know how to approach whatever it was he wanted. He'd lost the stage in which he had the dimension of an animal, and in which understanding was silent the way a hand grasps a thing. And he'd also already lost that moment when, on the top of the slope, all he'd really been missing was the word—everything had been so perfect and so almost human that he'd said to himself: speak! and all that was missing was the word. What point was he at now? At the point where he'd been before the crime: as before, he was now something that might have had a meaning if it were viewed from a distance that stuck him into the proportion of a leaf of a tree. Seen from close up, he was too big or could no longer make himself out. Basically, he was nothing. And it was with effort that he gave himself some importance. Because, in fact, he had a great deal of importance: he was only living once.

And the fact is that now it was too late: despite his contentment, he'd have to go on. Not only because he had to save his crime. But because, even heading backwards, he felt he was advancing.

He felt that—that's right—that he was almost understanding. It's true that, due to a calculating error, he'd started too much from the start; it's true that the green of the weeds was so violent that his eyes couldn't translate it; it's true that it was already occurring to the man to have destroyed the world in order never to receive it whole again, not even a single time the way you receive the extreme unction. All this was true, yes. But that's because sometimes resistance seems ready to crumble ...

There was a tranquil resistance in everything. An immaterial resistance like trying to remember and not being able to. But just as memory was on the tip of the tongue, that's how resistance was seeming ready to crumble. That's how, the next morning, when he opened the door of the woodshed to the freshness of the morning, he felt the resistance crumbling. The clean morning air was shivering in the bushes, the cracked coffee cup connected to the fogless morning, the leaves of the palm trees were shimmering darkly; the faces of the people were red from the wind like that of a new race walking through the field; everyone working without haste and without stopping; the yellow smoke coming out from the back of the fence. And, by God, that has to be more than great beauty, it had to be. Then, with scruples, resistance crumbling, he almost understood. With scruples as if he had no right to use certain procedures. As if he were understanding something entirely incomprehensible like the Holy Trinity, and were hesitating. Hesitating because he'd learned that after understanding, it would be somehow irremediable. Understanding could become a pact with solitude.

But how to escape the temptation of understanding? without managing to vanquish a certain sensuality, he understood. In order not to jeopardize himself at all, he became enigmatic, in order to be able to draw back as soon as he became more dangerous. Then, careful and cunning, he understood this way: "How to keep from understanding, if a person knows so well when a thing is there!", and the thing was there, he was aware, the thing was there. "Yes, that's how it was, and there was the future." The wide future that had begun from the beginning of the centuries and from which it is useless to flee, for we are part of it, and "it's useless to flee because some thing will be", the man thought quite confused. And when it was—oh how could he explain himself in the face of such an innocent morning?—"and when it is, then it will be", he said humiliated by the little he was saying. And when it would be, the man who is born will be astonished that before ... "But maybe it already is?", it occurred to Martim with great astuteness. "I even think it already is" he concluded with dignity of thought. Then, somehow satisfied, he adopted an official pose of meditation. He meditated, while he was looking at the morning in the field. And who could ever say why butterflies in a field broaden in obscure comprehension the vision of a man?

That's how by scurrilous means Martim finally reached a state, jumping like a hero over himself. And that's how, by means impossible to recapitulate, he ended up finally freeing himself from the beginning of beginnings—to which out of ineptitude he had clung for so long. A phase had closed, the most difficult one.

6

THERE WAS SILENCE AND INTENSITY UNDER THE SUN OF the farm.

Nobody could tell how Martim's mute vigilance had been communicated to the others, since he kept working calmly with the same face that said nothing, and his eyes had the expression that eyes have when the mouth is gagged. Yet there seemed to have been established a deadline after which everything would be impossible. The communication of his intensity might have been done by the deeper blow of his hammer or maybe by his walking in hard boots or by his sudden disappearances—they'd look for him and not find him but, before their concern about his absence grew, he'd turn up as calm as if he'd arrived from nowhere in particular:

—And where have you been? asked Vitória dismissively.

The man's answer didn't reassure her. The stability of the man didn't fool her; all that was going to end, she was well aware. Vitória gave him new tasks, invented little jobs, and no longer let him out of her sight. With limited time, the woman had acquired an instinctive knowledge and was carrying out so many acts that in the middle of them the essential one might involuntarily escape.

But if Vitória didn't seem to know what she wanted, Ermelinda knew. And she hovered around the man closer and closer:

—Just look at this fern! she said to him in the afternoon, just look how much it's grown lately! it's so pretty that it's gone floppy.

But the man didn't understand what she was hinting at in too-veiled terms. And nothing was happening. If the emotion of his feelings was giving him a very lovely ignorance, it wasn't very efficient. And if Ermelinda were bathing in the back and forth of her efforts and busying herself with the beauty of her plans—nobody was understanding. At the same time, why not? When she was a girl, out of a pure tendency for subtlety and weakness, she'd said to a boy she'd liked: "I'm going to give you a rock I found in the garden"—and he'd understood that she liked him, so much that he'd given her in return a matchbox with a cookie inside. And then, continuing in her vocation for adroitness and in that tortuous path of graciousness of hers that spared her from being offended by truth—truth might seem to Ermelinda to be an inferior form, primary and in a manner of speaking "without style"—after she'd thank her husband for giving her a new dress by saying to him: "it's a lovely day today, isn't it?" For some mystery in her process of becoming, she'd always avoided being totally understood.

And yet, it was with no exclamation of horror that, inside herself, she was facing the simple crudity with which she wanted to have that man for herself. Maybe her delicateness, incomprehensible to other people, came from the very delicateness of her reasons for wanting him. Her reasons for wanting him were those of a woman who wants love—which seemed terribly subtle to her. And as if that strange reason wasn't enough, she'd braided it with an even more subtle reason: that of saving herself—which is a certain point that love sometimes attains. All that, then, was making her ununderstood. Which didn't make her suffer exactly, because it was part of the order of things: since she didn't understand others, it also didn't occur to her to be understood.

There was however a very intense practical problem: her process of living simply wasn't giving her what she wanted. And the result is that she involuntarily looked like pure without, however, even wanting to be. Just to avoid the rudeness of becoming bright. She, for example, had never confessed to a priest that she was afraid to die; instead she'd told him full of intentions and with a great refinement of allusion: "I think a rock is so much prettier than a little bird"—with that she might have meant, who knows, that a stone seemed to her closer to life than the little bird who in its flight reminded her of death, which, naturally, would mean that she was afraid to die. The priest hadn't understood, and she'd left without confessing, frightened not to have had an answer. It had been years since that girl had had the satisfaction of a success.

—Look at this fern! she said to the man because a person can't say "I love you."

The man's face was hot and ruddy, dirty with grime. She looked at a man's hot face, and the strength in that girl was as little fragile as the strength of a woman, but she'd mentioned ferns and the man hadn't understood, and his face remained simple and unreachable. And the girl started to grow desperate because now she'd already started to convince herself that it wasn't by speaking of ferns that you summoned a man. She didn't know how to summon him and was flailing in the empty urgency that the man, as he was hammering, was communicating to her.

So, the next morning—as soon as Vitória had mounted a horse and the dust of its hooves was still yet to settle once more on the ground—Martim noticed Ermelinda next to him in the stable where he was bathing the cows. Standing like a student.

She was standing and not saying anything. In despair the girl was trying for the first time this crude approach: not saying anything. Martim made a curious grimace that he himself wouldn't have known how to interpret: because, without knowing exactly how, he'd just understood. Maybe because Ermelinda's mute face had the intensity of everything she wasn't saying. When Martim understood, he then felt very contented. She was charming, with that fresh look in her daring not to speak, in her trembling courage of just standing there: so that he'd know.

—When is Miss Vitória coming back? he finally asked.

The girl tried to answer but her voice gave out. Her emotion at being understood was powerful, as if someone had finally crowned the only way she had of expressing herself: in that moment she was finally receiving recognition for her art of living. The instants passed without her heart, calming down, giving her back her voice. But with the experience she had of failing, she knew that you can't throw yourself with closed eyes, everything would be lost again, and she'd have to go back exhaustively to speaking of ferns. Then, violating with effort something she'd wanted to be so much darker and prettier, so much less brutal, she answered out loud and with closed eyes, throwing herself off a bridge:

—Vitória's going to be gone for a while because not till noon is Francisco going to meet her in the cornfield, she'll only come back at two for lunch, I heard her say that myself!

She stopped astounded. For the first time in her life she was saying something directly. Her heart recoiled inside her chest as if in order not to touch a disaster.

The man looked at her curious, watchful, patient. It was true that "not thinking about her" had been a way of really thinking. But until this instant he'd managed to keep her inside himself surrounded by a neutral and bright element, while he himself was dealing with other things. And if he wasn't quite surprised when the girl, like now, was imposing herself, he looked at her with a certain coldness. He seemed to accuse her of not having known how to wait for him to call her himself into the focus of his attention. Once again he was being pushed along before he was ready, just as he'd been tossed by Vitória into the stables.

He put down the pail of water in order to say some thing. And the way Martim let her know he'd understood managed not to endanger him at all:

—I'm going back to the slope at noon.

But by eleven Ermelinda was already standing in the sun, serious, her heart beating, the birds flying and the great tree waving.

A certain point had been attained, at last. What seemed to alarm her is that there was no longer any question of going back—at last too late, which left her heroic. And beside there was that excited and joyous unease, of a pernicious joy, that secret of hers against the world: nobody knew what was going on with her, what a secret.

Yet, more than anything else, she, with her heart all dry and aching—she, she was playing for keeps.

If she failed, she'd come back ragged, shoes in hand: that was the idea that Ermelinda had of a person failing. Though she also didn't know what it might mean to fail, since she was dealing with immaterial things—she'd grown used to considering immaterial "the things of the spirit" and didn't have a very clear idea of the spirit, and it seemed to her that now some thing was happening to her more or less of spirit—and in those things you're never quite sure if you'd failed or not, it was a question of thinking in one way or another. But, at the same time that she saw herself with shoes in hand, she had that intimate warning that she wouldn't fail: that she'd touch one of the vulnerable points of life with a sure hand, despite its trembling. That trembling that came from the importance of that moment that was at last—at last—insubstitutable by any other. Rarely in life had she had the chance to face some thing that is not substitutable. "At last I'm going to live," she said to herself. But the truth is that this seemed more like a threat.

Which didn't mean that she'd lost her grip. For, as if she impartially ignored the importance of the event, she had time to strike various poses that seemed to remove that importance: she messed with her hair, as if a certain hairstyle were indispensable, pursed her lips and widened her eyes as if in a drawing of an innocent and beloved woman, recreating with much emotion the famous love affairs. While inside she was wilting confused. Because she knew she was risking much more than it superficially seemed: she was playing with something that would later be a forever inscrutable past.

In order to distract herself, she quickly remembered what she was going to say to him. How was it again that she was going to say it to him? Like this: "destiny is such an odd thing." She'd say that to him. Not because she was an artificial creature but because, thanks to an experience that was no longer differentiated into facts, she'd ended up learning that "at least with her" acting natural didn't work. When she relied on naturalness, it wasn't truth that would emerge. Naturalness was for someone who had limitless time that would give the chance for eventually certain words to end up being said. But someone who had the time of just a single life, would have to condense herself with art and maneuvers. That girl was deathly afraid to spend her whole life without having the chance to say certain things that already no longer seemed important, but she was stuck with the stubbornness of saying them one day.

After remembering what she was going to say to him about destiny, she inescapably returned to the idea that she was playing with something that would later be a past closed to her understanding. A bit world-wise, she knew that in the moment things seem right and afterward no longer do. And she was vaguely wondering—while her worried heart was beating across the whole prairie and her gaze seemed to follow it with apprehension—vaguely she wondered if later, when she was returned to the average days that judge us, she'd be up to understanding herself, and to perhaps having to forgive herself. Even now she was already wondering what her future inscrutable memories would be like. For she was aware that she was stingy: she wasn't a person who forgave herself easily.

Yes, all that would come. But she had to risk everything. Because time was short, that headstrong girl had to know if love had saved, as if in order to tell someone later. Martim—as Vitória had said in a moment of rage—looked like he had nothing to lose. But—Ermelinda guessed suddenly learning inside herself—there was no such thing as having nothing to lose. What there was was someone who risks everything; since underneath the nothing and the nothing and the nothing, there we are who, for some reason, can't lose. That she found out right there, standing. Somehow that man had come to bring to herself the problem of playing for keeps and risking whatever we are—that Ermelinda was fated to know forevermore. Maybe the mere sight of him, since eyes see much more than we do. What Ermelinda only knew was that she had, as a final bet, to take the risk. That was when it seemed to her, in a sudden sensation of great unease, that the world is malignant. Which gave, yes, but which said at the same time: "don't come to me afterward and tell me I didn't give you anything." The thing wasn't given out of friendship but out of hostility.

Standing there, at eleven o'clock on the 17th of April, frightened, she was greeting this way in which the offer was laid down for her without goodness. She who had worked so hard to get what she herself didn't seem to be up to understanding. But now nothing more depended on her. In that rare instant—in which "it hadn't happened yet," "it's still going to happen," "it almost already happened"—she called, in an effort of understanding, "the instant before the man turned up." Giving a title, she was trying to appease the world.

171

The girl ran her hand across her forehead, her whole soul congested. According to what she was feeling, she figured that her face must be ugly and reddish, profoundly regretted not having a beauty that might correspond to the instant in which she was going to be a man's. That's not my face! she rebelled, that face isn't me. In the despair of maybe not being accepted by a man who was so much more elegant than she and so much more man than she, once again she tried to make her eyes bigger and her mouth heart-shaped. In her opinion they didn't make an "attractive couple," and that idea not only wouldn't get out of her head but it made her uncomfortable to the point that she had to hold back tears: it seemed to her that nature wasn't giving its blessing. The day was so pretty that it added to her disgrace.

Oh, if she'd had more time, and nothing had to be rushed! she thought desolately shaking her head. She could have even sent for some fabric from Vila in order to make a new dress. But how long would this man stay on the ranch? And what about death? no, she didn't have time, time was short, the birds flying in the distance seemed to wait unhurriedly for her to come back and join them. They, they who weren't in a hurry, they who were sure. And who were flying waiting. Waiting for her to come join that serene and disturbing freedom ...

The girl, with her tight shoes, shivered with fear of herself. She was afraid to purify herself so much that she wouldn't need anything more. How could you imagine a being who doesn't need anything? it was monstrous. "I don't want to progress," she said doggedly, recalling the line from a clairvoyant who really wanted progress. But what would be left of her, if progress were stripped away? what would be left would be a whole body, what would be left were desires, and so much dust. What would her freed soul do, without a body in which to exist? It would hurt in the windows until the living people said: what a windy day. And in the summer she'd be the unease of nights stuck inside the gardens.

That was when standing there, amidst the thousands of unnoticed beatings of a heart that was so well connected to its own purpose, that knocking sounded more deeply than she knew the way you know someone: a deep and hollow knocking as if the heart could roll toward an abyss. And as always she wondered: but could that be sickness or life? Amid a thousand butterfly palpitations, that tragic knocking … I'll go to the doctor, she decided with the greed of a glutton, I'll go to the doctor. The cold inside the sun made her shiver.

Oh, but even then, up till now life wasn't serious—for she had a body where she could moan, she went to a heart, she had monthly cramps, she had a body where she was happening. But then? then? The clairvoyant girl suspected that it might not be just a thought that someone might guess in the air and that they'd call, according to her, inspiration. It wouldn't be enough, in the liberation, to peek impatiently at the dawn in order to take shrewd and canny advantage of that concretization of light—and be. Nor would it be enough for her to look at the dry sky for days on end in the hope of joining the rain in order to be able to cry. She'd grown too used to life, she was accustomed to certain minimal comforts, she needed somewhere to hurt, somewhere to bleed if she cut a finger. Oh God, why didst thou choose me to be clairvoyant and to understand and know?, she thought beneath the weight of her vocation, I'm only human, givest me not a task that is beyond my powers. And death was clearly beyond her capacity.

Oh, and if she was to be haunted—if that's what they expected her to be, and she wasn't sure what they expected of her—then she'd need at least an entire house, and an extra floor, she calculated fussily. And for the doors to open by the absence of her hand, for her steps to ring out beneath her lack of feet—but … but all that set into motion just by memory? How difficult her memory would be. "How was it that I could play piano while I was alive? but how did it go again?", she'd wonder. So much money spent on teachers in order to end up playing with the anguish of a single finger. Having as an audience a possible living woman frightened by her own imaginings?

No, no, she didn't plan to scare off a woman with her difficult memories. Deep down—she reflected with the fixation of worrying about details beforehand—deep down she might be happy to find the body of someone where she could sleep. And a flesh where she could explain herself. Since the thing that would hurt, more than anything, would be her own absence. For example, there it would be, like now, the water of the river. Except she simply would no longer need to drink! the way an amputated leg bothered someone who no longer needs to walk: would she stay behind with the function of the leg but without the leg? Then— then all that would be left to her would be to contemplate the water. But would she be her eyes or the landscape itself? And— and how to hear? wouldn't she herself be the sound? And, bit by bit, ever more free, could it be that she'd at least think? Since every thought was the child of things, and she would have no more things. She would at last be free.

As horribly free as the detested field. As free as perhaps could no longer be free, even, that thing nonetheless already so free that was a bird. Since even a bird was still full of hot feathers, and so dirty with intimate blood.

Above all—just as one day as a girl she'd become a young woman—above all one day her first repugnancies would begin, in a sign of the terrible refinement. In a sign of progress. First of all, she'd probably start avoiding warm things, in order not to be sullied. She'd avoid anything that had needed, in order to exist, to be in the world though only for a second. Until she'd end up being something that, when someone felt it, would say: I am an empty man, I am an empty man.

"Nonsense," she said suddenly freezing, "when the time comes,

I'll make up my mind; maybe that isn't even the way it happens." But this thought didn't calm her. What I'm missing is self-confidence, that's my problem; she was aware that right now she wasn't going to make up her mind in the least.

Oh, what am I thinking? she then startled herself. How could she have gone so far in her freedom of thought? And—it occurred to her—couldn't that freedom be the start of another freedom...? Since thinking was always such an adventure without guaranteeing... Ermelinda then started to sweat, now fully awakened from her reverie, feeling herself standing in the field. The birds were just what was left over, as the only real proof of her dream. The birds, which she looked at intrigued. As if all she had left, from an entire dream, was a pen in her hand and didn't know why or where the pen had come from. She looked at the simple birds, and didn't understand what was happening to her, like someone who awakens from a fright and doesn't know what nightmare set it off.

Suddenly she didn't know anything. And she wondered with a start if the man had really said "noon." And if he really was referring to today. And if Martim had really understood her. Or maybe she was the one who hadn't understood? But, feeling her feet squeezed by her shoes, she remembered with relief that, while she was putting them on, she'd been sure of the reality of what was happening to her. And then she made up her mind courageously to trust more in her previous certainty than in her doubt now. "Everything is true," she told herself with violence, "all this is true," she said, now anchoring herself in the sensation of sin she'd seemed to have run after all her life: "the evil is being done," she thought with strength, and her vision darkened with savor and revenge, the sun was burning her—evil, which was the symbol of being alive. The birds were flying, gliding in the burning light. She looked at them as if raising a fist against them. They who were the opposite of evil: they were death and beauty and progress.

The sun was making her head hellish, the flowers were crackling with light and heat. And in her tall shoes, which she'd taken from her suitcase at the wrong time, her feet were sweating fatigued. All decked out and unhappy, she waited. Truth be told, that girl no longer quite knew what she was waiting for. If a certain point had been reached, she no longer quite knew which. "But if I left now, tomorrow suddenly I'd understand all this, and could no longer return." Then, resigned, she put up with it, a bit astonished. After all she was a small person stuck in a bigger situation. She'd wanted the bigger situation, so she needed to put up with it. Which gave her an impression of a punishment. And of irrecuperable advance. And, as could happen at moments of great importance, the moment itself seemed not to have any importance. She was so in touch with the moment that she didn't see it. It was for that reason that dreaming was superior to reality: when she was dreaming she was well aware of what was happening. Whereas, in such a real moment, the truest sensation was her shoes. And, in a reasoning error that happened a lot with her, she wondered if it had been worth so much work and so much dreaming labor to end up with this: taking her shoes out of the suitcase. She felt like unlacing them to rest her feet. But she knew, as if this were the fruit of a great experience, that if she unlaced them, her feet relieved for an instant would never again fit into the shoes. And, by analogy, if for an instant she got out of the situation in which "she'd been put," she'd never fit back into it. The bones of her toes were crackling with sensitive bones.

At that moment it was noon. The flowers were lit up from the inside and the red roses were a clang: from very far off Martim noticed the girl like a dark stain in the air.

The garden was extended by two or three sharp shadows that the ditch was stretching into the ground. The immobile sun was making the plants heavy, in a wakeful silence in which everything could happen: Martim came closer and closer with the hatchet in his hand. Things were waiting deserted. But the honeysuckle was trembling like a lizard before dying.

Then—looking at the violent motionless roses and walking toward them, as if looking and walking were the same perfect act, looking at them who were restraining themselves in red—a billow of power and of calm and of listening passed through the man's muscles, and a man wandering in the sun is a man with a power that only whatever is alive knows.

From less far off he saw her standing in the sun; a woman's face hardened by shadows and brightnesses, with stains of light across her dress. With perplexed eyes, he wondered how a person could invest so much in another person. And if he thought this it was because, while he'd been working, he seemed to have slowly transformed the simple girl into some vague and enormous thing. Only when he got closer did he discover with surprise that the girl's face in fact was fresh and without color. The discovery somehow reconciled him to the fact that she was simply herself, and not the guardian of a great hope. And it seemed to him that the murmur of cold water among the stones was also flowing inside her. Not that he loved her. But as if it were because of love. Watchful, he came closer while looking at her. So extinguished among the demonic flowers. Without disillusion, then, he saw her exactly as she was.

And she, she looked at the stranger. Before there was in the girl a silent heat of communication from her to him, made of begging, sweetness and a kind of trust. But standing before him, to her surprise, love really did seem to have ceased. And tossed into the situation that she'd created, feeling alone and intense, the only reason she was still standing there was because of determination. The way when she'd once prepared a whole week excitedly for a dance and, right then, disappointed, had taken the taxi to go to the dance; exactly what she'd wanted. Ermelinda was sad, surprised. And at the moment in which he finally was right there in front of her, she looked at him with resentment as if he wasn't the one she'd been waiting for, and they'd sent her nothing more than an emissary with a message: "the other one couldn't come."

Martim hadn't reckoned on his own shyness, and was embarrassed. So that there was nothing Olympian between them. It was very hard to create a solemn situation the way Ermelinda had wanted it all her life, and to which the man, without realizing it, had adhered with hope. The girl lowered her eyes with a sigh: she wasn't up to the great love stories. At the moment in which she most wanted to be herself—with that idealized individuality that the years had created for herself—at that moment her whole personality groaned as if it wasn't real, and yet it was, since that invented personality would be the maximum of herself. And what she felt now was only a paltry anxiety that was concretized in the unreachable ideal of finally taking off her shoes. And in a despondency that she hid with a smile in which there was no glory, but a certain disconsolate sweetness. She'd wanted so much to have a lover! But now it seems she no longer did. Even, truth be told, the question of dying or not had lost its importance, and seemed to her suddenly something distant and slightly uncomfortable.

Why then didn't she tell the man the truth and immediately go away? But she was feeling the truth in the form of a weight in her heart, and didn't know what it was. Though it was weighing her down more and more as if all of her were her own numb heart. Why then, if she opened her mouth, wouldn't that solitary truth come out in words? Ermelinda didn't even open her lips. In the desire not to lie she'd tell him: I don't love you. But she seemed to know something more: that she loved him, that she loved him. It was just that the things of the world weren't made for us, just that we'd had to come to terms with everything for which we'd nonetheless been born, just that suddenly it was as if love were the desperate clumsy shape that living and dying take, just that it was as if even in that moment the absolute had rendered us helpless; and the forever untransmissible truth that there was in her heart was the weight with which we love and love not. And yet, for all that, the solution was exactly love. "Don't offend me," she thought looking at him, less to protect herself than to save what they had both created almost outside themselves and that they were then offering to both of them.

Thus, then, Ermelinda only found out that she loved him when the man took a step and she thought he was leaving. In a fright, she extended her hand to hold him back. And understood that if he left, she wouldn't be able to stand it. She then saw that the truth was that she wanted him. As for the rest—as for so clearly not wanting him—she resigned herself to not understanding. Then she smiled at him, fawning, without hope.

Intimidated, the man felt the need to do something. So he took her hand. The woman's hand was freezing.

—Are you scared of me? he was sincerely astonished because after all the girl was the one who'd offered herself to him.

—I am, she said with a broken voice, dropping any pretenses. But don't worry about my fear, she said tired pacifying him. I, for example, am not worried about it, she said as if she were the mother of both of them or the nature that forgives us.

—Scared of what? he said very curious, bracing himself for a vanity.

—I don't know, she said confused. I don't know, scared be-cause—because you're made in a different way than I am, I don't know …

—What!

—Oh, she said desperate, but that's how it has to be! it's right! how else could it be!

—But be what? the man asked stupefied.

—Oh God! she said crying, I mean that you're a man and I'm not a man, but that's just how it is! she exclaimed attempting the great effort at conciliation.

—Ah, he said intrigued.

Martim's curiosity, with ignorance now added to it, grew blind, instinctive. He'd dropped her hand when he felt how cold it was—but this time it was without effort that he took it back again. And the small hand was light between his hands hardened by those calluses of which he was proud and which were there like a stigma. This pride in himself then moved him a great deal. And with pride he could clasp that hand with security.

When a man and a woman are close by and the woman feels that she is a woman and the man feels that he is a man—is that love? The sun a hundred and fifty million kilometers away was burning both their heads. "Oh, deliver me from my mystery!", she begged him inside her. And as if everything entered the same serene and violent harmony, life became so beautiful that they looked at each other in the eyes with the tension of a question, incomprehensible eyes of man and of woman. Sometimes people feel alone and with the question, but it doesn't hurt—or if it hurts, that's the way in which things are alive. "If you only knew how much I love you," the girl looked at him, "and it's forever." She, who at least once in her life wanted to be able to say "forever."

And Martim? When they went into the woodshed, after passing through hedges and hedges as through doors and doors, what he loved in her had already ended up mixed with the alit flowers, mixed with the smell of rotten wood, the good smell of the moist earth that stuck to the axes—as if he'd been thrown into his first human love. In the shed the incandescent flowers were losing their grip. There it was like a stable and people grew slower and bigger like animals that neither accuse nor forgive themselves.

He looked at her, and she seemed to have kept her body in a cool dark place like a fruit that must get through an adverse season unscathed. Her arms had golden hairs, which gave her the value that golden things have.

But it's true that in the disorder of a first encounter there was a moment in which both, finally forgetting whatever they had painstakingly wanted to copy into reality, there was a moment unprepared by either, a gift of nature, in which both needed to know why the other was the other, and forgot to say "please"; a moment in which, without the one's offending the other, both took what was owed without stealing anything from the other, and that was more than they would have dared to imagine: that was love, with its selfishness and without which there would also not have been an offering. One gave the other the greed of being loved, and if there was a certain sadness in submitting to the law of the world, that obedience was also their dignity. It was the selfishness that gave itself whole. And as if in the girl the desire to offer a gift were bigger than anything she had to offer him, she didn't know what to give him, she remembered mothers who give to children, and she wasn't feeling maternal with that man, but with the great power of the unreasonable she also wanted to give him, just to finally go beyond whatever you could and finally break the great mystery of being just one. She gave him her entirely empty thought inside of which was all of her. In wanting to give, more than in wanting to give oneself, something had been made: she'd gained the minimal destiny that the brief insect too requires.

It was with an obedient and grateful look, like a woman's, that she warned Martim that she was going to mend his clothes. Especially, stubborn, what she wanted was to linger in the safe environment that the man, living in the shed, had ended up creating there: spurs on the ground, the sickle, muddy boots, palpable world. Taking, calm, the clothes that needed mending, she felt a much smaller happiness than she was capable of feeling, but it was a question of that thing that you want to be: concrete. Then she looked at him: thank you for being real, her open eyes said.

The man didn't understand, but puffed up his chest a bit. As for her, now she could without lying use the word love, and with so much artless hope as if she didn't know it. Because, in a perfect movement, the world had become once more whole and even had its old mystery—except this time, before the enigma closed, Ermelinda had placed herself inside it, as enigmatic as the enigma. Then the girl got up, as if giving the man an order to go away and leave her alone.

—You are my master, the haughty and mute way she was standing there was saying, serene and without humility.

He seemed to understand, and he didn't want to be anybody's master, and he whistled as a disguise, then looked at his own shoes: women were always more wanton than men, he was embarrassed. She was noble. "She got what she wanted," Martim thought offended in his own chastity and disguising it with a new awkward whistle. "You are my master," the way she was standing there was saying with tyranny; he grunted in agreement, uncomfortable, wanting to get rid of her. Her shoulders were narrow and breakable, her skin that of a child, and, as if he had broken the girl's present time, there was something ancient within her. She had a lithe waist. My God, the man said to himself, she's a ghost. He was comically abashed by her fragility. "Little and weak, but a virago like all the rest," he thought with malice but didn't think what he'd thought was witty at all, and it didn't even give him any pleasure; what he felt, in fact, was a certain pride in her, he was admiring her. Women always stretch things out more than needed and immediately created families. And he was proud to be her victim: that was the awkward homage that the man managed to pay to her.

—Thanks for my liking you, the girl's gaze was also saying, but this the man didn't understand, and only blinked his eyes. After, as if he'd had time to feel better, he nodded his head in assent, since she'd taken up for an instant the destiny of them both.

And maybe because his submission to that woman was the way that he himself was making her submit, as he left the shed Martim became powerful and brisk, and a bit cheeky.

7

MARTIM BREATHED DEEPLY AS IF UP TILL NOW HE'D been gagged. Because it was sweet and powerful for a man to go and a woman to stay. That's probably how things ought to be. Heading toward the water of the river in order to moisten his face he was feeling proud and calm. Now that he'd had a woman it seemed natural to him that everything would become understandable and within arm's reach. Large was the prairie: a multitude of shining spots against an obscure and uncertain background, within reach was the water that the sun had made into a hard mirror, and that's how it ought to be, he approved of the earth's way of being. Without modesty, like a man who is nude, he knew that he was an initiate. Faced with the water that was killing him with its sickle-like shine, everything was his, a dizzy happiness filled his head, he was still feeling in his arms the weight that a submissive woman has. Initiated like a man who lives. Even if he didn't have time to be more than a man who lives. It was a rare instant, and without vanity that's how he took it, and before he wrapped up he touched it with his whole soul so that his soul could at least have touched the enormous reality.

"What would the woman do by herself in the shed?", he thought, and what would she want from him? The lucidity turned excessive by happiness made him understand that she was expecting a word from him, and that she was stuck to him by the final hope. And who was she? that had suddenly become important, who was she? for if he got stuck in a cell with only a leaf of grass in his hand, in that leaf of grass was everything an entire field could tell him. And if he nabbed an ugly and disregarded woman, a woman among thousands of women, in her was the whole world expecting from him hope. But what could he give her, except mercy? It was in that instant that, uncertain and badly orchestrated, for the first time the ancient word mercy slipped inside him. But he didn't quite hear it.

For when he thought of Ermelinda he'd started to think of his own wife listening to the radio while time dripped by, and receiving presents with a sigh: "don't look a gift horse in the mouth," she'd said with a sigh. And while thinking of her, he thought of his son, about whom he'd never wanted to think directly. He thought of his son with the first and happy pain as if having had Ermelinda in his arms had finally given him his son. That son he'd made with so much care and who had come out so lovely, and who was quite tall for his age. And he thought of seeking out the mulatta's daughter from the first time he'd surprised her looking him over, he really was needing a child.

And with his son, the love for the world had overtaken him. He was now feeling very moved by the richness of whatever exists, moved by his tenderness toward himself, so lively and powerful he was! so kindly he was! strong and muscular! "I'm one of those people who understand and forgive!", that really was what he was, yes, touched, missing his son. The halted sun kept digging deeper inside him, love for himself gave him a grandeur that he could no longer hold back and that stripped away the rest of his modesty. Next to the shimmering water nothing felt impossible for him. Now that, as a first step, he'd reached through his son that point in which pain mingled with ferocious joy, and joy was painful, since that quick point must be the big needle of life and the encounter of him with himself—then, just as the soul of a dog barks, he incoercible said: ah!, to the water.

Ah! he said in love and anguish and ferocity and pity and admiration and sadness, and all that was his joy.

But why then wasn't that enough? Why wouldn't it be enough for him just to cry out? Because it so happens that he wanted the word. As long as he was being who he was he'd be stuck to his own breath waiting for it to join itself, living with that word at the tip of his tongue, with the understanding almost about to reveal itself, in that tension that ends up getting confused with life, and that is itself, it so happens that he wanted the word.

And now that he was getting to know the wavering of a human love, he'd never been so close to it. The weeds were trembling it ... The water was shining it. The black sun was expressing it in its own way. And the prairie was becoming tenser beneath the man's gaze.

Why then wasn't he saying the word? The sun was stopped. The water muddled. Martim before it. Why wasn't he saying it? Because everything was so perfect that he was beside the point. The hard glass of the water was looking at him and he was looking. And everything so reverberated and motionless, so complete in itself, that the man didn't wet his face, didn't dare touch the water and interrupt with a gesture the great static. Everything was bursting with silence. With the scent of hot grass that the wind brought from afar he inhaled the revelation trying uselessly to think it. But the word, the word he still didn't have. The foot, the foot with which a man steps, he didn't have it. He knew that he'd made himself. But he still didn't know what a man does. Otherwise what would the freedom he'd gained been worth?

The writhing sun was burning his head leaving him calm and mad. It was then that under the truth of the sun he finally wasn't ashamed to desire the maximum. And through the love for his son he chose that the maximum could be attained through mercy.

Was that the word? If it was, he wasn't understanding it. Was that the word? His heart beat furiously, crestfallen.

Not out of mercy transformed into kindness. But the profound mercy transformed into action. Because, just as God writes straight with crooked lines, even through the errors of action ran great mercy and love. Since a person had that strange capacity: that of feeling mercy for another man, as if he himself were a separate species. For by now he didn't seem to want to reconstruct just for himself. He wanted to reconstruct for others.

Martim had just "unveiled."

Had he just discovered gunpowder? No matter, each man is his own chance.

But through which action would love run? From monstrous thought to monstrous thought, he calculated with lucidity that if he got a new way of loving the world, he'd transform it in some way. The most important thing that could happen in the land of men—wasn't that the birth of a new way of loving? the birth of an understanding? It was. Everything for Martim was unexpectedly harmonizing ...

Then, drunk on himself, dragged along by the foolishness to which logical thought can lead, he thought with tranquility the following: if he grasped this way of understanding, he would change men. Yes, he wasn't ashamed of this thought because he'd already risked everything. "I'd change men, even if it took a few centuries," he thought without understanding himself. "Could it be that I'm a preacher?", he thought half delighted. It so happened however that at least for now he didn't quite have anything to preach—which abashed him for an instant. But only for an instant: because in the next moment he was once again so full of himself that it gave him pleasure.

The rest of his prudence then fell, and without any shame he thought more or less this: even if he spoke of his "unveiling" to just one person, that person would tell another, as in a "goodwill chain." Or else—he thought sprightly—that person transformed by the knowledge would be perceived by another, and that other by another, and so on and so forth. And in the air there would gradually be the stealthy news in the same way that fashion spreads without anyone's being forced to follow it. Because what were people besides the consequence of a way of understanding and of loving of someone who is already lost in time? "That's how he lived," one person would say to another like the awaited password. "That's how he lived," the rumor would spread.

Martim had finally enunciated. The only thing that held him back a bit was the sudden facility in which he'd fallen. But maybe that's really how it was: that after being enunciated, the truth was easy? The obscure plan then seemed as perfect to him as a perfect crime.

And full of himself, bursting with sun like a frog, the task seemed big and simple to him—while he now was mixing the powdered cement with water, preparing mortar for the water-tank. The cauldron of the saints might be burning above his head but he was concentrating on the sandals. His urgency was tranquil. Not an urgency that made him want to skip any steps, but an urgency like that of nature: without an instant lost, when the pause itself was a move forward. He mixed the cement with exactness, with uninterrupted urgency as the thousand shivers make the vastness of the silence and the silence moves on. "The thing is progressing," he thought.

He found this thought of his excellent and his feeling excellent too. He grew emotional and serious, stopped working for an instant. "I offer this that I felt in homage to my mother," he thought vaguely, already a bit distracted. Afterward, having happened to come into closer contact with whatever it was that he'd thought, he found it "nonsense." But afterward he really regretted thinking it was nonsense and said to himself offended: "let's also not be so dumb as to think it's all poppycock." Since poppycock was a very long word, which quickly lost its meaning, he finally ended up with nothing at all, and a taste of nothing in his mouth. That alerted him to the need to take care not to become vague, which was a legitimate temptation—but if a person didn't specialize, he could easily get lost, as they say about doctors. It was very hard to be global and nonetheless maintain a form. He couldn't lose himself from view.

So he tried to gather himself, a certain plan started to be outlined, the cement was thickening, he applied himself with perfection to his work, tranquil hours passed.

And the first fresher breeze blew.

That's how, when Ermelinda pushed the door of the shed, evening had been made. Like a continuation of the shadow of the room, the whole evening had been ruined and smelled in the shaky shadow of roots with ants. The girl's eyes were wide, tranquil, avenged. She'd managed to absorb the security of the man against the countryside, and armed with her talisman she looked in serene defiance: the countryside was nothing more than a bigger shed where a thousand trees had room to lose themselves in the distance, the world was a place. Just that. And the countryside had lost its limitlessness. She crossed without effort the crowd of lawn, the flowers now tamed. There wasn't a wrinkle on her face. She looked like an Indian carrying a pitcher on her head and balancing herself in order to balance the pitcher. Nothing was contradicting her. Such moments happen too.

8

AT NIGHT MARTIM HAD AN EXCELLENT IDEA THAT
would turn out to be the opposite of excellent. The truth is that
later the man compared the excellence of the idea and the sub-
sequent disappointment with a round fruit he had once eaten —
a pomegranate — and that under his teeth had proven hollow.
Which had given him, as its only prize, an instant of absorbed
meditation and a contact with experience.

That night, then, he turned on the lamp, put on his glasses,
took a sheet of paper, a pencil; and like a schoolboy sat on the
bed. He'd had the sensible idea of ordering his thoughts and summing up the results he'd reached that afternoon — since that afternoon he'd finally understood what he wanted. And now, just
as he had learned to calculate with numbers, he got ready to calculate with words. The exaltation that had come to him from
the sun that afternoon had already abandoned him. He was now
a slow and studious man, with the face that a woman has as she
threads a needle. His face was concentrated on the chore.

It was with slight surprise that his thought proved as rough
as the swollen fingers that were clasping the pencil. To start off,
the pencil seemed too delicate for him to carry out his resolu-
tion, which had also been too determined. He didn't know that

in order to write you had to start by abstaining from power and turning up for the task just because. From the lamp the blackened smoke was rising and enveloping the engraving of St. Crispin and St. Crispinian. Occasionally the sound of the piano distanced by the silence would reach the shed. Ermelinda was playing. Time was passing.

But in the half-darkness of the shed, and without the advantage of the drunkenness of the afternoon, the man seemed to have disappointedly lost the meaning of whatever it was that he wanted to jot down. And he was hesitating, biting the tip of the pencil like a laborer wrongfooted by having to transform the growth of the wheat into numerals. Once again he twirled the pencil, doubting and doubting again, with an unexpected respect for the written word. It seemed to him that whatever he threw onto the paper would be definitive, he didn't have the nerve to scratch out the first word. He had the defensive impression that, as soon as he wrote the first, it would be too late. So disloyal was the power of the simplest word upon the most vast of thoughts. In reality the thought of that man was merely vast, which didn't make it very useable. Yet it seems that he was feeling a curious repulsion toward turning it concrete, and even a bit offended as if they were making him a sketchy proposition.

Once again he got bravely ready to start and moistened with his tongue the tip of the pencil.

And deflated, wearing glasses, everything that had seemed to him ready to be said had evaporated, now that he wanted to say it. Whatever had filled his days with reality was reduced to nothing in the face of the ultimatum to say. As you could see, that man wasn't an achiever, and like so many others, he only felt the intention, with which Hell is filled. But in order to write he was naked as if he hadn't been allowed to bring anything with him. Not even his own experience. And that man in glasses suddenly felt plainly diminished in the face of the white page as if his task weren't just to note down something that already existed but to create something that would exist.

Could there have been a mistake in the way he'd sat on the bed or maybe in the way he was holding the pencil, a mistake that had placed him before a bigger difficulty than he deserved or hoped for? He looked more as if he were waiting for some thing to be given to him than that some thing was supposed to come out of him, and so he waited piteously. He lightly transformed his position at the edge of the bed and reduced himself austerely to be just a seated man who was going to note down something that had already been thought. And once again he was surprised: it was incontestable that he didn't know how to write. He smiled awkwardly. The way a docile illiterate might ask someone: write a letter to my mother saying what I think. "What's happening to me anyway?", he worried suddenly. He'd grabbed the pencil with the modest intention of noting down his thoughts so that they'd become clearer, that was all he'd wanted to do! he insisted irritated, and didn't deserve so much difficulty.

But as in stories in which the distracted prince touches by fatal happenstance the only prohibited rose in the garden and terrified breaks the spell in the entire garden — Martim had carelessly executed among a thousand innocuous gestures some unfamiliar act that involuntarily had transported him into the face of something bigger. The lantern was smoking a black thread. He looked at the shed that was trembling in the dark light. The walls were hesitating. The wind was knocking at the door. And around him the void was blowing in which a man finds himself when he's going to create. Woebegone, he had provoked the great solitude.

And like an old man who never learned how to read he measured the distance that separated him from the word. And the distance that suddenly separated himself from himself. Between the man and his own nudity could there be some step that could possibly be taken? But if it were possible—there was still the strange resistance that he was putting up. For in him had just awakened that inner fright of which a person is made.

Not believing in what he couldn't explain, he knitted his eyebrows as if that would help thread the needle. What was he waiting for with his ready hand? for he had an experience, he had a pencil and a piece of paper, he had the intention and the desire— nobody had ever had more than that. Yet it was the most helpless act he had ever done. And he wasn't able to such an extent, that not being able had taken on the grandeur of a Prohibition.

And at the very thought of breaking the Prohibition, he recoiled, once again opposing the immaterial resistance of a hard instinct, once again cautions as if there were a word which if a man said it … That absent word that nevertheless sustained him. That nevertheless was he. That nevertheless was that thing that only died because the man died. That nevertheless was his own energy and the way in which he breathed. That word that was the action and the intention of a man. And that not only did he not even know how to mumble, as he seemed profoundly not to want to … In vital prudence, he was defending it inside himself. And just by imagining that he could say it he closed up austere, insurmountable, as if he'd already ventured too far. Suddenly susceptible, he'd fallen into a sacred zone which man doesn't let woman touch but two men sometimes sit in silence at the door of a house at nightfall. Inside that solitary zone the choice would be to let yourself touch with humility and debasement—or shelter the integrity of the man who neither speaks nor acts. He'd fallen into the avarice that had always made his life something personal. And that had become "doing," which would be surrendering, the impossible action. A coward in the face of his own greatness, he was abstaining.

Without a word to write, Martim nevertheless didn't resist the temptation to imagine what would happen to him if his power were stronger than his prudence. "And what if I suddenly could?", he wondered. And then he couldn't fool himself: whatever he managed to write would only be because he couldn't manage to write "the other thing." Even within the power, whatever he said would only be because of the impossibility to transmit another thing. The Prohibition was much deeper ..., Martim surprised himself.

As you can see, that man had ended up falling into the profundity that he'd always sensibly avoided.

And the choice became even deeper: either leave the sacred zone intact and live from it—or betray it through what he'd certainly end up grasping and which would be just this: the reachable. Like someone who couldn't drink the water from the river except by filling up the bowl of his own hands—but then it wouldn't be the silent water of the river, it wouldn't be its frigid movement, nor the delicate avidity with which the water tortures stones, it wouldn't be whatever a man is in the evening next to the river after having had a woman. It would be the bowl of his own hands. So he preferred the intact silence. For what you drink is little; and from what you abandon, you live.

Thus, from punishing approach to punishing approach— Martim's having had along this path a feeling of suffering and of conquest—he ended up wondering if everything he'd finally managed to think, when he'd thought it, might not have been just because of his incapacity to think another thing, we who allude so much as the maximum of objectivity. And if his whole life hadn't been just allusion. Could that be our maximal concretization: trying to allude to what in silence we know? All this Martim thought, and he thought a lot.

And there he was. Who had just wanted to jot down, no more than that. And whose unexpected difficulty was as if he'd had the presumption to want to transpose into words the glance in which two insects fertilize each other in the air. But maybe—he then wondered in the perfect darkness of the absurd—maybe it's in the final expression that's our way of transposing the insects glorifying each other in the air. Maybe the maximum of that transposition is exactly and only in wanting . . . (And that's how he was saving the value of his intention, of that intension that he hadn't learned how to transform into action.) Maybe our objective was in our being the process. The absurdity of that truth then enveloped him. And if that's how it is, oh God—the great resignation that you need to accept that our greater beauty escapes us, if we're only the process.

Thus, then, seated, quiet, Martim had failed. The paper was blank. His eyebrows knitted, watchful.

But what do we know about what goes on inside a person? Because he, who was failing, couldn't call his failure suffering, even if the disillusionment and the offense received had emerged onto his face, so few are the feelings that the flesh allows. But how to call suffering the fact that he was going through the truth of the Prohibition as through the eye of a needle. How could he even rebel against the truth. He was his own impossibility. He was he. He'd reached this point of the great tranquil anguish: that man was his own Prohibition.

Suffering? He thought with his face irreparably offended as he looked at the blank paper. But how could he not love even the Prohibition? if it had pushed him as far as he could go? if it had pushed him up to that final resistance where . . . Where the only unreasonable solution was great love. When a man is intimidated only great love occurs to him. Suffering? Only not being able to is how a man would know. A man anyway was measured by his neediness. And touching upon the great lack might be a person's aspiration. Would touching the lack be art? That man was savoring his impotence the way a man recognizes himself. He was frighteningly enjoying what he was. Since for the first time in life he was learning how much he was. Which was aching like the root of a tooth.

A great sweetness enveloped him, as when you suffer. He couldn't face without pain the empty paper. Where his action had failed.

But had it? Because the compensation was fatal too. He couldn't help admiring the perfection of the Prohibition. Since, in a perfect balance, it so happened that if he didn't have the words, he had the silence. And if he didn't have the action, he had the great love. A man could know nothing; but he knew how to turn, for example, toward the setting sun: a man had the great resource of altitude. If he wasn't afraid to be mute.

Oh, not suffering. Because in his impossibility to create he hadn't had the worst thing: he hadn't been dispossessed. In everything else that man had deceived or been swindled, they'd robbed him or he had cleverly robbed. But in his passage through the great void, for the first time in his life, he neither deceived nor was deceived. The thing was clean: since we were dealing with a person, the clean result had then been to carry out the experience of not being able. It even seemed to him that few people had had the honor of not being able. Because, in a genial sensation, born perhaps of his pain, he found out that the most accurate result was to fail. Suffering? he thought with an offended face. But how not to love the Prohibition, if carrying it out is our task? the involuntary writer reflected in pain.

Martim had now started to get entangled in a curious sensation of having grasped some extraordinary thing. He'd gone through the mystery of wanting. As if he'd touched on the pulse of life. He who had always been dazzled by the spontaneous mystery of his body's being body enough in order to want a woman, and his body's being body enough to want food—he now had touched on the source of all that, and of living: he'd wanted … In a general and profound way, he'd wanted.

To his disadvantage, in a way that was a bit too profound. Since there he was confused, without understanding why he had the feeling that he'd fulfilled himself, despite not having taken a step beyond the personal realm. He looked at the empty paper. Goodness then enveloped Martim, as it does when you suffer. In his helplessness he had the temptation of calling on God. But, not having the custom nor the belief, he felt afraid of provoking such a great presence, now more careful about not touching the garden's forbidden rose.

—I don't know how to write, he then said.

He'd given up. His impression was that he'd saved himself by a hair. Great was his relief for having escaped unscathed from the hollow darkness. Though he also felt that none of his future thoughts would arrive exempt from his true cowardliness that had only now been revealed. No heroic act of his would be totally free of that experience that immediately became as old as wisdom.

He took off his glasses, rubbed his tired eyes, put the glasses back on. And relieved, abandoning at last that thing that the spirit hadn't wanted to give him, he felt ready for a more humble task. Modest, studious, nearsighted, he simply noted: "Things I need to do."

Writing that phrase he wasn't the same person who had faced possibility and its frightening promise. He was someone who had given up on the truth—which one? now never again! oh he'd never know again!—and dedicated himself to a truth that was so much smaller that it already had its borders in talent; but the only truth within his reach, the only action within his reach. Humble, knowing with a remote start that he'd been "close" but had managed to escape, the man became more humble still. Even a phrase as modest as "things I need to do" seemed to him too ambitious. And in an act of contrition he tore it up. He wrote still less: "Things I'll try to find out: number 1."

Then it so happened that Martim knew what the first thing was that he needed to try to find out but he couldn't manage to give it a name. It even seemed to him that he'd only know the name in the instant that he got it, as if a person only figured out what he wanted when he found it.

Well, the much simpler reality is that it was with effort that that man was trying to stay on the level he'd been at that afternoon beside the river. He was now reduced to his own proportions and without the lesser grandeur of the sun. He'd lost his faith and his purpose. And was looking at the poor woodshed with astonishment. Even so he insisted on going on and, next to "thing number 1" to try to find out, he wrote "That," since what he was managing to do was allude. And he reread the phrase.

And that was when—that was when he had his first great thrilled pleasure with which you inevitably love whatever you've made. The still-wet phrase had the grace of a truth. And he liked it with a shiver of creation. Because he recognized in it everything he'd wanted to say! Moreover he thought the phrase was perfect because of the resistance it was offering him: "beyond that, I cannot go!", so that it seemed to him that the phrase had touched the very depths, he was groping its resistance with ecstasy. It's true that a second later, at a glance, Martim noticed with distaste the writer's great mistake: it had been his own limitation that had reduced the phrase to what it was, and the resistance that it offered might have been the resistance of his own incapacity. But, since he was a person who was hard to overthrow, he thought the following: "it doesn't matter since, if with that phrase I at least managed to suggest that the thing is much more than I could say, then in fact I did a lot: I alluded!" And then Martim grew contented as an artist: the word "that" contained within it everything he hadn't managed to say!

He then wrote: "Number 2: how to connect 'that' which I find out with the social situation."

Because that's what he wrote. He'd lost the habit of thinking, and once the vocabulary was lost, he couldn't manage any other expression to mean what he wanted to say except this: "social situation," which seemed very nice and clear to him, and which had a little touch of erudition that had always been an ambition of Martim's: erudition, being external, was confused with the primary idea that he had of objectivity, and always gave him the satisfactory feeling of being right.

When the man reread his body of work, already with his eyes blinking from fatigue, reality spun around, and he faced the paper with the physical and humble concretization of a thought, and he had an empty and wide laugh—where for the first time the sense of ridiculousness appeared, undermining for the first time his greatness. That man who was trying to construct his greatness and the greatness of others. Then, in a painful defense, he started to laugh, a little bit against his will and a little bit in order to show off to himself, and a little bit out of masochism, and a little bit to show how much he was a martyr who was pretending not to be suffering but was waiting for God to divine with repentance and pity that his son was suffering and that he was only laughing out of heroism, a little bit so that God would repent, offering him his disguised suffering like a sock in the face, like someone saying he's not suffering but who is suffering, and is sanctified inside his pain. Then Martim bumped up against a less flattering reality and one less possible to dramatize: he bumped up against the fact that he was just a confused person who'd forgotten the books he'd read but who still retained from them many dubious images that he was chasing after, his terminology was out of style, he'd never gone beyond his first readings—the reality that he was a man of slow comprehension, and, why not say so?, not too intelligent, a man with a clumsy way of thinking, a badly informed person and who moreover didn't know what to do with the little information he had—and who, helpless then, had to count on himself, which made him constantly rediscover gunpowder, as if a person only had one resource: himself, "at least that's how it is these days," and then he was laughing, which was foolishness because God didn't even take offense at the error of having created whatever he, Martim, was, because God made up for it with more efficient achievements.

Out of pure self-martyrdom he laughed once again. And since he hadn't laughed for so long, he started to cough, choked. He then stopped laughing because the feeling of saliva having entered his nose gave him the unpleasant suggestion of a physical error: it was as if his body too were failing. He blew out the lamp and lay down.

But with the laughter his tiredness disappeared. And in the dark he was worried. The rose he'd accidentally touched in the garden had left him kicking like a horse holding back a gallop. By this point things had somehow lost their material size. Nobody would ever face for a second the void from which things emerge without ending up forever with the indocility of desire. Stung by a will to get closer, he was untamable and anxious. What's wrong with me? he surprised himself. Alert, sniffing around. A minute later he recognized that he was in the state of soul for acting or for loving. It so happened that he couldn't do one thing or the other: having no experience in dealing, without hurting himself, with the creative act, he avoided it; and the night was empty, without the love of a woman. "I've got insomnia," he then said to his wife in a tone of complaint and accusation.

Martim didn't know what to do with his desire and how to apply it. From one thought to the next—most of them escaping him—he reflected that if he'd failed in the creation of the future, he still had the already created past. In an intense desire, he wanted to have at last some thing in his hand. Which seemed to him easier and less susceptible to disappointment: the clay from which he'd already happened was at least a material from which to depart. Then, with the same attitude of severe goodwill with which he'd tried to create his plan of action for the future, he turned back to his memory. "Oh remember that trees exist and children exist and bodies and tables exist," the man said to himself trying to awaken himself to a maximum objectivity.

And really he became objective and clear. But what had he managed to get? Little rocks; he was looking curiously at the little rocks of facts, ancient hard little rocks, unswallowable, irreducible, imperishable. Drowned in a sea of pebbles. Not only reality, but memory too belongs to God. The man turned around in the dark. He had got stuck inside the construction of his own past. Nothing had ever left the world, nothing had ever entered the world; they were always the same little rocks, the die had always been cast, and improvisation was impossible! because those were the elements—the ones that were already there—and suddenly they'd closed the door, and nothing more had been allowed to come in or out. And if, for the future, he wanted to make a new construction—he'd have to destroy the first one in order to have little rocks to use, since nothing more could enter the game and nothing more could leave: the material of his life was this right here. But, he thought, what infinite variation! with the same little rocks. You'd go to a clairvoyant, she'd give the rocks a shake, one would jump out, and she would say mysteriously wearing glasses and fake hair, before dying of cancer: I'm seeing a little rock.

But it so happens, he reflected with an intense desire to give up on the future, it so happens that with these little rocks something is at least definitively organized. And we fit inside it. It's true that sometimes we fit in with an arm paralyzed by the construction, or with one eye closed by the mortar that has been hardened by a construction that dried too quickly—but something is at least definitively organized, and if we hardly fit, the truth is we do fit. What will we do? we'll construct with the same little rocks another definitive organization, knocking down the first one beforehand? Or will we make up our mind sensibly to fit into the first one? It's true that in order to fit into the first one, we can't eat much. Since if we get fat, we won't fit, and if we grow we won't fit, and we'll end up with trousers that are too short, looking meditatively at our exposed feet. But let's be careful, it's all about being careful. Oh although we are very careful. Until we forget how much we've grown and fattened up recently—and yawn distractedly, and the construction ends up too short. That's what's called unease.

That's what that man was calling unease. Had that man committed a crime because he'd gotten too fat? Martim turned over, sick, with a stomachache: he wasn't fitting. By now, his thinking had started to echo inside a church, which was giving him a respect that was made of fear and of respect properly speaking. And just as, for some unknown reason, every time our steps get loud, we instinctively try to walk without making noise, the man now tried to go forward on his tiptoes. His thought had taken on the echoing grandeur of a nightmare. And the man suddenly thrashed with the old nausea of thinking, oh would he never be more than a creator of truths?

Until, fortunately, he realized that the creation of the world was making him colicky. Then, happy to be able at last to submit to a pain, he lay on his tummy and, at the heat of the contact, started to fall asleep.

But that was a night of many lessons. You have to be patient, sometimes a night is long.

Because in the shadows the birds had perceived the acidity of the dawn and, long before this shined onto a person, they were breathing it and starting to awaken. There was a bird, especially, that all but drove Martim crazy. It was one that was calling its mate in the dark; with patience and calm, it was calling, calling. Until the thing started growing to the point that Martim leaped up and flung open the window. At the open window, he was greeted by the bird's sudden silence. More with his nostrils than with his eyes, the man noticed that the darkness wasn't stable and that the bird was already living a dawn that, for him, Martim, was still the future. Which, vaguely, seemed to him a bit symbolic and satisfactory. He turned around and lay back down. And once again the patient little bird started up. The calm chant calling brought the man to the breaking point: he covered his ears.

But, by covering his ears, he didn't hear the little bird.

It was only then that the man realized that in fact he was longing to hear it. It seems that often we love a thing so much that in a manner of speaking we try to ignore it, and so often it is the beloved face that embarrasses us the most. And for Martim who had so sought explanations for his crime—it occurred to him then that he might have fled the world because of a love he couldn't stand.

Vanquished, he took his hands off his ears, and docile now, suddenly accepting the beauty of the little rocks, accepting the maddening song of the bird, accepting the fact the dawn precedes the perception of the dawn—the man started to listen with sentimentality to the little bird that was pleading. And more than that: a bit shy, Martim wanted it too. In the dark he smiled amused and stinging, because Ermelinda wasn't the kind of name you shout out, and his virility wouldn't have let him perch in a tree. And even because, if he called her, that woman might very well come. And he didn't want her so much that he desired her to come. Martim smiled again, quite sad. Because the colic had returned, he flipped onto his back, and this time fell asleep.

That night had been a great experience. Of the kind that you can't claim before a court without missing the words and without embarrassment overtaking a man because he, after all, has to be responsible for what he says, to know what he's talking about, and to understand what's going on with him.

It's true that he hadn't totally given up. In his agitated sleep, that stubborn man tried to construct in a dream another house with the same rocks, since there aren't any others to use. In every construction he attempted, he forgot something outside, or he put too much stuff inside, and the construction crashed down. And that was when, for the first time, the man seemed to see some advantage in the fact that rocks are harder than our imagination, and immutable and intransigent, that human nature of the rocks or that thing of rock that is our nature. For the first time, he was relieved that the creation of the world wasn't his task: for in his construction he found himself suddenly like a man who had constructed a room without a door and been stuck inside it.

In his agitated sleep, he sat once or twice on the bed. But his hurry was the useless hurry of a man who is sitting on a train that he's not driving; sitting on the bed, devoured by a thought that didn't occur to him so sharply during the day: that the day was near in which Vitória would go to Vila and meet the German. Time was passing, time was passing, time was passing, and the indefinable future was dawning.

9

ONLY WHEN VITÓRIA WENT BACK TO THE CORNFIELD with Francisco did Ermelinda have the chance to turn up with a basket of food:

—For a picnic in the woodshed, she said hoping he'd be over-joyed by the surprise.

But, annoyed, he murmured something about how women were crazy about picnics, and for an instant she wilted in disap-pointment. Only for an instant did she have to make the vague effort to pretend that "everything was all right." Because, even though she ate the sandwiches by herself, she pulled herself back together quickly, and now was talking with volubility, inebriated by the joy that, "like it or not," existed in a picnic. Without blink-ing, Martim received cynically several drips of saliva in his face. For some reason, he tried to be ironic and rise above the situa-tion.

But the truth is that for him it was relaxing to have that woman who gave herself so easily, as if having her at his disposal were already an achieved goal: to that point he'd already dominated her. The sillier she was, the more she was his: she was making up for the difficulty that Martim was having with himself. And, in a relief that seemed to him must have been that felt by the man when woman had been finally created—taking away at last his

freedom and at last making it impossible for him to be formidable—he was already smiling, hardly hearing her. The girl was the
type who allows, without getting offended, a man to wander off,
which he did naturally as if they were married. And soon, absent,
already smiling, he was flattered by the nonsense that flowed out
of her with sweetness and that let him drift off to sleep in peace.
The girl had a smell of a box of face powder that was making
him a bit nauseated.

—Don't you want to take a bath? he'd said to her one day
with great delicacy, because I can't stand that smell, he said uncomfortable.

—But it's powder! she said surprised.

—I know, but I can't stand it.

—Fine, she said thoughtfully. And she never again smelled of
powder.

She was now caressing his hair with attention, ingratiating,
distracted, small:

—Do you believe in the other life? she then asked him, immediately smoothing his hair with more intensity as if blowing on
a sting so that it wouldn't hurt so much. For an instant he was
surprised as if, looking like a little bird who was nibbling lightly
with its beak, she might just lunge forward. But it was only an
instant of mistrust, his, and he smiled, seizing her, whole and soft
as she was, and as curious as a woman is curious, which reminded
him of his wife.

—No, I don't, he said.

—Silly! she said laughing. Since in intimacy people were used
to insulting each other, insulting each other would be an intimacy, and that way they felt quite nice together. Too cowardly to
be able to stand love alone, they had already with a certain haste
moved beyond it, entering into familiarity and losing with relief
the greater size of things.

There, familiar at last, she entirely revealed to him, the man examined her. She wouldn't be pretty, if a person didn't love her. But she had the beauty that you see when you love the thing you see. Every mother of an ugly daughter should promise her that she'd be pretty when the wisdom of love illuminated a man, he thought. Around Ermelinda's dark pupils, for example, Martim saw a lightly amber circle, which without love would have escaped him. He also saw that the birth of the hairs on her neck was softer, and those threads too short to be tied up in her braids were dangling in light in the air. On her arms the light hairs were gilding the girl as if she couldn't be touched. Once loved, she was of rare delicacy and beauty. He looked at her curious, sympathetic. She was capable of making a man happy; but strangely she'd had to trick him with little ruses until she made him happy, and only then had she shown him that she hadn't tricked him and that the happiness she was giving him was real.

All this the man was vaguely realizing, and was looking at her, feeling the fine energy that was emanating from her and that he himself had awakened within her. Which she herself had forced him to awaken within her—so that she, as she was doing now, could give him in exchange this fine energy. In the whole siege that Ermelinda had carried out until capturing him, she'd used dubious methods, lying, unpleasant; just as from a dirty art life is revealed. The love of both of them was something he owed her, and owed the wise unscrupulousness of that girl who, having gotten what she wanted, was there, rendered wholly innocent by her own prize. All this the man thought, with tranquility and wisdom, because they'd just embraced very concentrated, and that's how he was feeling now: meditative and tranquil.

Afterward she asked, having on her face the innocence of very curious people:

—Did you ever like another woman as much?

He then, in the haze that feminine repose was giving him, with half-closed eyes and almost without having heard her, continued his own thought about the other woman and said this:

—She sought me out, not because I was I or she was she, but she sought me out with the laziness she had. She was very lazy, he said with pleasure in recalling it. And she'd interrupt me to say she'd gone to the dentist. She was always asking me what time it was. Every once in a while she'd say to me: what time is it.

—Oh, I'm so lazy! Ermelinda said, I'm so lazy: all I want is to be happy but not to have to do all this work to make myself happy. I'm such a different kind of person! very lazy but wanting things. What are you thinking? she then asked with sudden worry—since he was lying there, suddenly inaccessible as if a circumference of one centimeter of isolation were surrounding him. What are you thinking? she implored accusingly.

—Nothing, he said simply.

She sighed lightly, pacified and immediately dreamy, immediately herself isolating herself safe within her own circumference.

—I always wanted a thing so to speak forever, she said.

Since in relation to others he was very sensible and used an offensive adult tone, he said:

—That's absurd.

—Right, she said agreeing just in order not to end up alone, because when she would tell the truth she would find the sudden wall of others defending themselves. It's absurd, she agreed lying out of good sense.

Neither questioned what they meant by the word absurd, nor realized that they'd left behind, untouched, the very thing they'd been asking about. That's how the conversation went about "forever"—which they'd think about later, when each once more had the guarantee of being alone.

—Was she pretty? Ermelinda asked suddenly greedy.

A bit startled, somewhat offended because a man's wife ought to be untouched by a man's lover, he awoke lightly and looked at her:

—I don't know, he said quite mistrustful, trying to figure out if Ermelinda was polluting some sacred thing. I don't know, he then said a bit more calmly, the lucidity of sleep returning. I don't know, we haven't seen each other for such a long time, we once spoke to each other directly, as if we only had souls. What time is it, she'd ask me. She'd say to me: what time is it? I went to the dentist today! that's what she'd say to me: today I went to the dentist.

—It's been a long time since I went to the dentist. Thank God I have good teeth, but it's actually quite nice when I go because I take advantage of it and spend a few days in Vila, I take advantage of it to go shopping, I go to the movies, I miss the movies so much.

—She had good teeth too, he said a bit annoyed.

—Why, I didn't mean she didn't, I'm talking exclusively about myself, because after all I don't even know who "she" is, she said trying to offend him by speaking to him with sudden ceremony.

Since the girl's monotonous and sweet tone was filling the woodshed, he, from the depths of the half-light in which he was lingering, said to her:

—Imagine a person who needed an act of violence, an act that made people reject him because he simply didn't have the courage to reject himself. A cowardly person, maybe?—he stopped distressed, and sat on the bed.

—Lie down, said Ermelinda with anxious authority because she'd never had him at her disposal for such a long time, and she still had so much to say.

He looked at her with suspicion for a moment, but then laughed mollified:

—There's no danger in my telling you, he said enjoying the fact that she didn't understand him, because I'm telling you what I am, and nobody can denounce what other people are, nobody can even make mental use of what other people are—Martim thought it was so funny to use the old word "mental" that he laughed; it was a strange and empty word, and he was getting annoyed.—After I'm done speaking, you'll know even less about me: that's always how it goes—when we reveal ourselves, other people start to unknow us.

—What? she asked intrigued, interrupting for an instant her own thoughts.

He then realized that he'd said too much, to the point of getting her interested, and glanced at her quickly. But either she hadn't heard him or wasn't interested. Then, stimulated by her presence without importance, he said:

—Imagine a person—and repeated the whole thing.

Then, like a cock proud he'd sung all by himself in the yard, he grunted with gusto and shook his head several times, agreeing.

—But when I manage to get to Vila, she said, I've got so much to buy that there's no time. My ideal would be to spend a whole week in Vila, but Vitória doesn't want to.

—You don't much like women, do you? he said with curiosity.

—Well, she said reluctant and concentrating, on a desert island I'd rather be with a man.

Only after she said it did she notice the implicit mischief, and she smiled excited and modest about her own capacity. He too laughed a little, examined her with an affection also made of cold curiosity. In that moment Ermelinda was quietly swallowing a pill taken from the picnic basket.

—Why do you take so many tranquilizers? he asked smiling.

—Ah, she said with simplicity, it's like this: imagine a person is screaming and then another person puts a pillow in the other person's mouth so as not to hear the scream. So when I take tranquilizers, I don't hear my scream, I know I'm screaming but I don't hear it, that's how it is, she said adjusting her skirt.

Embarrassed by the painful secret she'd confided without the slightest pain, he laughed. Ermelinda suddenly noticed his gaze, stopped short, grew aware of herself—"I'm someone who makes another person see me"—and made a falsely peppy face, playing the role that he was surely expecting of her. But unexpectedly, as if this time she'd heard her own scream, she said to him intense, hard, without any hope:

—I love you.

—Yes, he said after a pause.

Both sat quiet for an instant, waiting for the echo of what she said to die.

Then, since she'd bent over for a moment, some apple peelings fell from her blouse. Which, even before he understood it, confirmed somehow the sweetness of that girl. He smiled while catching the peelings, turned them over with his fingers, and then started not to understand: no doubt about it, they really were apple peels. Without interrupting her chattering, she saw him with the peelings in his hand and said:

—Because perfume is so expensive.

—But the peelings are already withered, he said scrutinizing her attentively.

—They are? she was startled examining the peelings with much curiosity. Just look at that. I'll put some new ones in today.

She was simple and a woman, and he could laugh at her—and as another form of laughing, he for the first time caressed her face, pushing away with great delicacy the braided sections of hair that were framing her narrow face. And the face that appeared, stripped and strong, made him suddenly retract his hands as if he'd accidentally stepped on an animal's tail.

How much of what she said was a lie?! how much was she pretending to be a woman? since that girl's jaws were wider than he'd supposed, and gave her a tough air of beauty that he didn't want in her. Had she pretended to be weak? since with her jaws showing, like those of a preying animal, she revealed herself to be bloodthirsty and supreme. He was astonished mainly the way a child is astonished when it touches something that moves, and looked at her accusing her.

Having, however, in his fright, retracted his hands—the hair immediately fell back into place, and a face once more indecisive refuted the vision he'd involuntarily had. And now, without the power of the chin, the eyes lost the horrible victorious expression that had come to confirm to Martim certain vague thoughts, immediately pushed aside, that that girl was using him for some purpose—which annoyed him. He'd created the freedom of being alone and of fleeing entanglements, but each time the invisible circle was closing in around him: the way we eat ourselves! Vitória more and more watchful, as a strange way of demanding something from him; Ermelinda with the jaws of ambition revealed for an instant. And he, in the face of those strong women, felt abjectly innocent, with astonishment he was seeming to be the purest one of all. And he was slinking away in order not to be contaminated; everyone else's life was starting to be darkly intermixed with his own. But what about he himself? he himself, disguising his anxiety, how often had he tried to make out the mulatta's daughter, without even knowing why he so badly wanted contact with a child, as if only she were as pure as he was. Had the former man returned? the former man who seemed to need a purity he wouldn't know how to use? Once again, somewhere along the way, had he taken the wrong path, and gone back to being the former man?

—What is it you liked about me? Martim asked high-handedly.

—Ah, Ermelinda said voluptuously as if he'd finally touched on the best part of the question, and her whole attitude was now like that of someone who was finally going to have a nice chat between women. I just don't know! she said intimately, and the man had the disagreeable feeling that she wasn't talking to him but talking about the two of them to some third person. It started, she said, with a kind of curiosity, and then it went on, and on, and when I saw it wasn't curiosity, it wasn't anything else: it was you and I!

—But, he said a little annoyed, what did you like about me?

Ermelinda looked at him a bit astonished, almost resentful. Immediately inside her something closed up with hardness; and she looked at him without the slightest love. A temptation occurred to her to try to offend him with the truth that he so dangerously was asking—as if the truth was that she didn't love him. But she was well aware that she loved him, and she had a laugh of relief as if changing the subject:

—I had a kind of awful fascination with what you are! she said as if making up a story, since she'd just chosen another truth that was equally true, except that this was one she could tell him without lying. I don't know exactly what you are, but I'm so fascinated because of that. It happened little by little, in a short amount of time. I can't tell you what I like about you, I can't separate you into parts. I think that I feel that you're a whole person, she said very nicely.

—But how did it happen that you liked me? he said hard as if the girl were turning him amorphous.

—I don't know, certain little things, I don't know, little things I don't even remember.

The man's demanding gaze made her retreat and, because she was wounded by the lack of care with which he'd asked her such a dangerous question, the girl suddenly became insolent and ironic:

—If I fall in love again, I'll take notes every day about what I felt so I can report back later! But I'm sure, she said with a generalized disdain for people, that when I look at my notes I'll have a handful of dust.

Since a handful of dust was what she was having now. And what the girl now had was a past full of so much disappointment that it had made her ironic.

But in the evening, her body being much cleverer than she was, she got a headache that expressed her perfectly. In the evening, lying in her room, dealing at last with a nice, solid, satisfactory headache, like someone who has a nice and nourishing meal.

Things didn't always happen the same way. Since the next time they were together, perfection enveloped her. There in the dirty woodshed, Ermelinda became irradiated. Vitória was far away, the field was entirely cut off by the closed door of the shed. And the girl was the way she wanted to be: forgetting her fear, in a crackling happiness, talking endlessly. Everything that evening seemed so safe to her that she could even enjoy herself in reveries: finally caught and concrete, she no longer feared going too far and not having anywhere to come back to. She was anchored, and was venturing into liberty at last, without fearing the possibility of going beyond the almost inexistent dividing line between her and the field. At last so safe that she could even lie. And she could, as she was doing now, if only she wanted, invent a character that, even if it didn't symbolize her, pleased her as a choice: that's how, talking to Martim, she was leaning her head back, which gave her a look somewhere between daring, ambitious, and cruel, not herself possessing any of those three attributes, nor wanting to.

Or else she'd pretend to be absentminded and thoughtful, though in truth she was as attentive to her work of pretending as a seamstress is to the details of her sewing. Living with Vitória, who knew her too well, was horribly restrictive: Vitória knew all too well how to deal with her. Whereas Martim didn't know her, and with him she could invent new life. And above all an engineer, "an educated man"—maybe before he left he'd tell her the word that would remove her fear forever? She'd put her hopes in him because she'd known several educated men who didn't believe in God and didn't believe that you lived after death.

Oh, he'd leave, yes. But she wouldn't worry about it. As long as he left the word with her, maybe of disbelief, that would give her forever the same security that his presence was giving her. That man would have to leave behind the living part of his life. That thing that makes a person exist in another person's eyes: Ermelinda looked at him avidly and someone might say she hated him, but it was just ambition, and just hunger. A bit paler, then, because time was short and now was the moment to ask him for the word—a bit paler, taking care not to be too bright and reveal herself, she said with a sharp and unpleasant laugh:

—For example, I don't understand what infinity is! just think!

Through the chuckling with which she was disguising herself, she looked at him intensely as if through a keyhole, and her heart was beating.

Martim was that evening nailing down a few loose boards in the walls of the woodshed, and looked at her aslant, amused.

—I'll bet, she said quite gracefully wagging a finger near to his face, I'll bet an engineer knows things like that!

Martim unhurriedly pushed the uncomfortable finger from his face, and kept working.

—How could it be, she continued struggling to keep the flirtation going, trying to remove from her face the expression of urgency, and from her eyes the pleading for help—how could it be that the world, for example, never ends? and never starts either, for example ... That's horrible! isn't it?

The girl's voice trembled a bit and he, who was smiling flattered by the fact that she was ignorant, looked at her quickly:

suddenly she was so imploring and moved that, illogically, it seemed to the man that she'd come with her annoying picnic basket in order to, through all those labyrinths, ask that question: how can it be that the world never ends nor begins. Martim was intrigued and laughed again:

—The idea really is monstrous, he conceded.

She was hanging on the man's lips with an attention so complete and, for the first time, was so heedless of herself, that her face ended up entirely exposed—and Martim saw a pale face, neither ugly nor pretty, with features that seemed to have been made for a sole expression: of expectation.

—What's monstrous? she asked frightened as if instead of having given her a hand to lift her up, he'd pushed her even further down.

—The idea of a world that never began nor ever ends, he said a bit annoyed by the fact that the girl had put him in a situation of saying something that neither she nor he understood.

—Well? she said, all of her waiting with her head askew, well?

He didn't understand what she was waiting for, and repeated:

—Well what?

—Well? she repeated as if keeping at him were clarifying in and of itself.

He shrugged, hammered another nail into the board, and said:

—So, then imagine the reverse: a world that one day began and that one day would end. That idea is just as monstrous.

Ermelinda kept waiting as a deaf person extends a deaf ear. But, realizing unexpectedly that she was very serious and that men don't like that, she gave a laugh—which nonetheless was too quickly exhausted. Her mouth then seemed to suffer, she twisted it several times involuntarily:

—I'm leaving, she said slowly, getting up and shaking the crumbs from her lap.

The next day, as soon as Vitória disappeared, Ermelinda, in her painstaking work, spoke with Martim about the death of a turkey, and about what would be happening now with the turkey that had been eaten. And she guided Martim so well that he ended up saying, maybe inspired by the proverb about the turkey who dies the day before:

—The thing is so well done, he said, that nobody dies the day before. You die exactly at the instant of death, not a minute before, the thing is perfect, he said.

But it was exactly that perfection she was afraid of! Ermelinda looked at him rigidly. Martim grew a little embarrassed. But guided by an intuition that was born of the very tender way he always treated her, he said illogically, fumbling and feeling generous without knowing in relation to what:

—We don't know where we come from and we don't know where we're going, but we experience, we experience! and that's what we've got, Ermelinda, that's what we've got!

Martim couldn't interpret the girl's blank gaze in which the pupils seemed suddenly to be yet another inexpressive feature of the face, and not something with which to see oneself. It was as if she'd just cut off in herself the possibility of thinking. Which made Martim stir uncomfortably: he didn't know how much what he'd just said was worth, neither for her nor for himself. "We've already started to say things to each other that end up swimming in the air," he thought as if this were the sign of an inescapable transition and the delicate way things get corrupted, without anything that could be done about it. Martim had noted that they were already "chatting."

But the next day, as soon as Vitória had gone off, Ermelinda came back and, with the haughtiness of someone who no longer has much to lose or to hang on to, asked the man: "what's destiny like."

This time, though, without understanding why the engineer was so angry all morning—maybe because he was already tired of her?—this time, instead of responding, he repeated dazed: destiny? what's destiny like?!, he repeated with a surprise that wounded Ermelinda. Afterward, the impossibility he had in expressing his own anger gave the man's face, for an instant, a horrified look that Ermelinda, exulting, interpreted as participation—until she discovered that the repetition of the question was just a violence and a fatigue: no matter what the next word was, it would come like a jab. She waited intimidated.

—What destiny, what the hell! he finally said, furious.

The girl didn't cry. She immediately changed the subject to things that could flatter him: saying that the farm had changed so much since he'd come, that everything looked fixed up and new, "that now it was all different." And if that didn't quite transform the man's gruff expression, at least it calmed him down and pleased him. And the girl calculated quickly, with blinking eyes, that she still had the right to come back to the woodshed a few more times. Not many, since time was passing ... her face wilted in anticipation. With a hope that tried to be stronger than her disbelief, she promised herself: maybe next time ... She didn't interrupt herself another second to ask herself honestly what she expected from Martim.

Third Part

THE APPLE IN THE DARK

1

AND THAT'S HOW THE DAY ARRIVED WHEN VITÓRIA LEFT
for Vila Baixa with the truck full of tomatoes and corn, and the
truck looked like a harvest festival. Everyone watched it leave
with a smile and a retch, since everything everyone had worked
for had finally reached its term. And if it had been exactly for that
that they'd worked hard—it was with a smile and a retch that
they were watching the truck garlanded with the yellow corn.
Vitória, disguising a seriousness, looked at them for an instant,
solitary with the product of her effort. Embarrassed, they bid
her farewell.

Martim stood watching her drive off. Until not even the slightest dust still rose from the earth. And until, after the sound of
the wheels had left even his memory, the field pulled itself back
together in silence and wind.

The time was up.

Without the presence of Vitória a sudden lull dominated the
plantation, in a state of emergency. And as when someone is going
to die or depart, and then the sun shines and then the plants rip-
ple their palms—that's how the little birds were flying watchfully.

And that's what the plantation was like where people seemed

to have worked in vain, and yet that wasn't true. No matter from which angle Martim looked at the farm, he seemed to see if from the distance of years and years gone by: the farm seemed depopulated, you could feel the breeze blowing. And because some important thing was going to happen in such a near future—Vitória's meeting with the German—the plantation was relegated to the past, the flowers standing in the wind, the dry rooftop shimmering in the sun.

There was a silence as when drums are struck.

As for Ermelinda, she was quite wounded because she no longer loved him. For she no longer loved him. The great attraction that justified an entire life had passed. She was wounded and melancholy. It was a dead pain. Here's the water—and I no longer need to drink it. Here's the sun—and I no longer need it. Here's the man—and I don't want him. Her body had lost its meaning. And she, who had concentrated herself wholly in the anticipation of the day in which Vitória would go to Vila and would leave her the man for herself, at last without sneaking around, at last without precautions—she only sought him out once when she said to him sad, honest, indirect:

—One day I loved a man. Then I stopped loving him. I don't know why I loved him, I don't know why I stopped loving him.

Martim, worried about the German, didn't know what to reply and then asked:

—And then you became his friend?

And if he asked in such a way it was because he was helpless and needed friendship.

—No, she said looking at him slowly. No. Friendship really is very lovely. But love is more. I couldn't have friendship for a man I'd loved.

—And then? he asked with an anguish whose roots he himself didn't understand.

—Then, she said, then I cried from sadness, even without pain. I was asking: make me suffer for love! But nothing happened, I was free once more.

—And wasn't it nice to be free?

—It was as if the years had gone by and I saw on a face that before had been everything to me, I saw in that face whatever love is made of: of ourselves. And it was as if even the most real love were made of a dream. If that's being free, then I was free.

Since Ermelinda had never said that she'd loved him to the point of having had a life, Martim didn't find out that he himself was the now-unloved man, nor understood that she'd stopped loving him. But as if imploring from her a truth that was more compassionate than reality, he pleaded in despair on behalf of someone else:

—But what was it that kept you from becoming his friend? he asked.

—I was alone, she said.

The man grew sad, dark, heavy. Nothing had been said that could be remembered later. But they looked at each other with a smile worse than death, silently submissive to nature. Scratching the earth with a foot, keeping his hands in his pockets, Martim said inside himself quietly, intensely: "please!" He didn't quite know what he was asking, and said "please." But it was as if a man who was dying of hunger said politely: please. The back that Ermelinda turned to him in order to leave didn't have a face, it was a narrow and fragile back. Yet with what bitter vigor did they say to the man: no.

And the drums kept beating.

The field now belonged entirely to Martim for whatever he wanted to do or think about it. But the wait for whatever was going to happen had cut off his communication with what had now become a desert. And the truth is that the man no longer wanted anything at all. He didn't even know what it was he'd wanted so much. In the same way that love had died in Ermelinda, the lack of desire was giving silence to the heart of the man. He sought out his own hunger: but the silence was what was answering him. He was experiencing the worst thing of all: no longer wanting. The first moment was very bad, he hardly calculated that not wanting was so often the most desperate way of wanting.

Although in certain instants, during an imponderable variation of time, the plantation would change and show a closer face, and impose its living field. And then for an instant the man and the plantation would vibrate once again at the same level of present time. And once again, as he looked at the world, once again the man felt that promising tension that seems to be the maximum that a person can attain, the way you take notice of a stone because it resists the fingers. More than tension? He tried within himself to go forward: but no, that seemed to be the limit. If he wanted to exceed the resistance of the stone, and suddenly nothing would happen. Momentarily challenged, Martim still tried to grab the interrupted thread of his slow construction, and at least suffer. But time was really up.

On Saturday Vitória returned dusty and aged, with the empty truck. She'd struggled so much—and bemusedly managed, agedly managed; Martim didn't understand her. While the woman was talking about the sale, he tried eagerly to read her eyes and, in these, to read whether she'd talked to the German. But what he managed to learn was just what she said without any enthusiasm as if fatigue had stripped away the interest of the major news: it was already raining six kilometers from Vila Baixa.

And it was from the woman's apathy that Martim learned a lot: some important thing must have happened, so important that it removed the power from the fact that it was already raining not too far away from the farm. So important, for example, as if she'd spoken to the German. Vitória said nothing more, and disappeared inside the house.

Would she have seen the German? With little excuses Martim hovered around the house, vainly looked for Vitória: that was the only element he had for his calculations.

Until, when with lowered head he'd stopped looking for her, he saw her again. But as if seeing a stranger. She was coming from the end of the hallway, against the light. He didn't exactly see her body but only her walk, as if seeing only the spirit of the body. Bit by bit, now closer to the brightness, she started taking shape until she became opaque—and the man blinked looking at her in fright. Because her hair was loose and wet from the shower and she was no longer wearing the long dusty pants that already belonged to what Martim thought about her. For the first time he saw her in a woman's dress and she was a stranger. No toughness could sustain itself with moist locks of hair on the shoulders. Looking at her for the first time from the viewpoint of the body, she earned in his eyes a body. Which was no longer feisty as he'd always seen it, and whose strength had given the man a reason to struggle obscurely against that strength. It was a body that was so much more docile than the face. Scandalized, rueful, Martim looked at her: it was indecent how feminine clothes stripped her nude as if an old woman revealed the anxieties of a little girl. With modesty, he averted his eyes. Just as Ermelinda had refused herself, Vitória—who before had given him a firm outline—was now refusing to give him a shape, and leaving him free. On the face with its loose hair was the same tired gaze with which the woman had returned from Vila Baixa, and which he in vain had sought to interpret. It was also the first time he'd seen her tired. The woman's eyes, as if they no longer wanted to contradict anything, were on the surface, black. Martim tried to prompt her so that she would be stronger than he was. But she answered:

227

—No, tomorrow we're not going to do the ditches. The teacher is coming with his son.

Their eyes met and nothing was transmitted or said. Or maybe a god would have been needed in order to understand what they said. They might have said: we are in the nothing and touching upon our silence. Since for a fraction of a second they had looked at each other in the whites of their eyes.

What was it that Martim had first heard of the teacher? It must have been during his first days on the ranch, when in his numb eyes he could hardly tell Vitória from Ermelinda. "As good as the teacher"—had he heard that phrase? And if he had, which of the women had uttered it? Martim unexpectedly remembered another phrase: "It's the last Sunday of the month but the teacher can't come, he's sick."

Who had said it? Martim cursed himself for not having paid attention to everything, now that he was needing every detail in order to understand. He'd only got the impression of threads escaping him—but which ones? Could the teacher be the same person as the German? And in this case the son ... could the son be the one he'd thought was the German's servant? No, since Vitória had referred to him calling him "the German" but was calling the visitor the next day "teacher" ...

And suddenly Martim could no longer see any danger in this arrival: the teacher, as far as he could tell, visited on the last Sunday of the month, though by coincidence he hadn't turned up until now. And the next day was exactly the last Sunday of the month! There was nothing suspicious, then. It was a simple visit ...

The only suspicious thing was the unexpected break in Vitória's behavior: she wasn't giving orders and the only time he'd spoken to her she'd wriggled away like a shy woman.

At the same time Martim couldn't be sure if the change in Vitória was real, or if she just seemed different to him because she was wearing feminine clothes and because she'd let down her graying hair. Yes, it must just be a superficial transformation in her appearance. But then it occurred to Martim with acumen: "and why had Vitória suddenly transformed the way she dresses? what's the reason?" Without managing to find any logical explanation, he was suspicious again.

That Saturday, having stopped work on the ranch—"why had Vitória wanted them to stop work? oh, maybe just because she wanted in her dry way to celebrate the sale of the produce?"— having stopped work, the ranch had become even more vast as if it were already a Sunday, a mild wind was coursing through the countryside without obstacles. Martim was on the loose, suddenly the sequence of the days was cut. It was raining near Vila, and the news that the drought was going to end was calming everyone down, at leisure. On the silent Saturday evening fell quick and gentle. Martim didn't even see Ermelinda. And that bothered him too. They'd given him a sudden liberty. He missed the circle of women that before had restricted him. The mulatta no longer seemed to come out of the kitchen. Nobody was looking for him. Martim wandered through the field without knowing where the danger would come from.

It was therefore with a racing heart that he saw the little girl playing near the corral. The drums had suddenly ceased.

His first keen movement was to rush over to grab her before she too could run off. But he slowed his steps in order not to scare her. He could hardly contain the fear that she too would balk. With a casual gait, his heart racing from thirst, he moved forward. And when he was beside her, out of fear and delicate feelings, he didn't look at her.

But the girl—the girl raised her eyes from the bricks she was playing with. She looked at him—and smiled. The man's heart clenched in the affliction of joy: she wasn't scared of him!

Maybe she never had been! he then thought. For an instant a suspicion ran through him: "had he been imagining the whole time a danger in Vitória's meeting with the German and had he invented that emptiness on the ranch—the way that now it was being clearly proven that he'd been just imagining that that child was afraid of him?" For the girl was smiling at him, and now pointing out with her finger the little instable construction she'd obtained with the bricks ...

There was however another possibility: that the child really had feared him and had only just grown used to his presence in the area now. If this last hypothesis were correct, and if he hadn't just imagined the girl's fear or rebuff—then the danger of the German might also still be a reality! Fearing to get proof that he'd been right, he looked at the girl without the courage to speak to her.

The girl was stacking the bricks, tranquil. And he, standing there, was slowly starting to be moved by the kind indifference with which she'd allowed him to be there, grateful that she was treating him like an equal, that same obvious way that children have of playing with each other.

—In this funny house, the girl said suddenly showing him the bricks, lives a funny man. His name is Funny because he's funny.

"Oh forgive me," the man said to himself obscurely, timid, happy. A child was the arrow we fire, a child was our investment—he was so keen on her that he took care not to look at her. He stayed quiet, his heart beating as he received human goodness. He was big and awkward, and feeling abandoned didn't improve his clumsy situation. He remained quiet, afraid of making a mistake. He so much wanted to get it right, and didn't want to pollute the first thing that was being given to him. Oh God, I've already ruined so much, understood so little, refused so much, I spoke when I shouldn't have spoken, already ruined so much.

He who for the first time was experiencing the worst solitude, the one that has no vanity; and so he wanted the girl. But he'd ruined everything that had been given to him! To him, who once had been given once again a man's first Sunday. And of all that, the thing that bit by bit was left, was a crime.

Martim didn't find out what word to say to the girl without his heavy hand's breaking. The child was silent. Maybe it was silence too that she was expecting from him. But what kind of silence did she want to share with him? Ready to give up on everything he himself wanted, he was desiring to be just whatever the girl wanted him to be. A child was a man's commonplace, he wanted to partake of her.

But the silence of the busy girl was different from the silence that he'd shared with the cows and it was different from the silence of the cold peak of a slope. He went quiet. As a first offering of himself, he then abstained from thinking. And that's how he neared the natural heart of a girl. Between the two of them, slowly, the silence became a silence that would fit into a matchbox, where children keep buttons and pinwheels. Both remained, then, in a secret calm. Except he was afraid because he'd already ruined so much.

Then she said:

—One day I went to Vila and walked into the pharmacy, said she who knew so well how to speak without breaking that silence in which they were understanding each other and which he, his heart soft now, was loving. When I went into the pharmacy I ran and didn't even fall. Then I weighed myself on the pharmacy scale with mama.

She adjusted the bricks and added politely:

—You know something? I don't weigh anything. Even mama said so. She said that I don't weigh anything at all. Then I ran and didn't fall, and I almost crossed the street by myself but I'm smarter than the cars. Mama doesn't want me to sleep in her bed and sits there reading magazines, reading magazines, reading magazines. At night then she went out with high heels but I didn't cry: I slept, slept, slept. Tomorrow morning when I got up I stubbed my toe here on the bed in my room. Do you think it hurt? she inquired and sat waiting with yellow and calm eyes.

When the man finally managed to speak, he said with effort:

—I don't know, little girl, I don't know.

—Well it didn't hurt, she informed him with impersonal goodness.

She was almost black and had tiny teeth. She started once more to place one brick atop another, and then looked up—at the tall man who was standing. They looked at one another. The man's heart gave in with difficulty, he couldn't swallow his saliva, an extremely painful sweetness softened him. Oh God, then it's not with thought that we love! it's not with thought that we construct other people! and a girl escapes from my strength, and what are you supposed to do with a little bird that sings?

The girl was looking at him attentively.

—Don't you want to give me a thing? give me a thing, she said attentive, expectant, and her little face was that of a prostitute.

So the man didn't want to look at the girl. He looked hard at a tree, stoic.

—Gimme, you hear? anything at all! she said very intimate.

—I will, he said hoarse.

Suddenly satisfied, pacified, her face became childlike once again and extremely polite:

—Did you know that José's grandmother died one day? she said to him by way of thanks.

—No, I didn't know.

—I swear by Our Lady, she said without insisting. I even went to her death.

She arranged her bricks a bit better, sociable, careful, maternal. But a slight worry passed over her face—she raised it with her eyes blinking and once more a fake flattery appeared in her features which were mature, sweet, corrupt:

—You really will give me a little thing? give me a little present? It doesn't have to be today, she allowed avidly, but tomorrow? yes? tomorrow?

—Tomorrow he said lost, tomorrow he said with horror.

—Tomorrow, yes! she repeated bossy, laughing. Tomorrow, silly, is what comes while we sleep!

The horrified man stepped back. He couldn't get away immediately. But when he managed to wrest himself from the child's grasping claws he almost ran—and since he looked back with incredulity he saw with still more horror that the girl was laughing, laughing, laughing. As if he were horrified by himself, he was almost running. The water—the water was infected, the girl hadn't wanted to give him the symbol of the child. For the first time then he thought that he was a criminal, and he got all confused because, being a criminal, he'd nonetheless felt horrified by impurity. And what confused him still more is that that child was pure too, with her sharp little teeth that bite and her yellowish eyes, expectant and foul and full of hope, eyes forgiven and delicate like an animal's—he was almost running. What was it he too needed so much, but froze up when someone asked him for it? He saw once more Vitória with her gray hair that now seemed to him luxuriant and lascivious, felt in his heart the hardness with which Ermelinda could stop loving—"are we bad?", he wondered perplexed as if he'd never lived. What dark thing is it that we need, what greedy thing is this existence that makes a hand grasp like a claw? and yet that greedy wanting is our strength and our clever and helpless children are born from our darkness and inherit it, and beauty is in this dirty wanting, wanting, wanting—oh body and soul, how to judge you if we love you? "Are we bad?"—this never had occurred to him except as an abstraction. Are we bad? he wondered, he who hadn't committed a crime out of wickedness. Not even his own crime had ever given him the idea of rottenness and retching and pardon and irreparability—like the innocence of the black girl.

Now it was night and everything was calm. He spent the night waiting. The drums beat the whole time. He couldn't stay lying down. So he sat on the bed and waited all night long.

2

ON THE LIMPID SUNDAY THAT SEEMED TO HAVE DAWNED in advance the man got the impression that he'd merely invented the danger. In the round sky the angels were clasping the tips of the clouds—that's how he got the idea of an inoffensive peace.

Seeing Ermelinda later with her wavy coiffure made it clear that she'd disappeared the day before in order to curl her hair: so that's all it had been! And—why not?—the calm might just mean the day before the last Sunday of the month because now Martim was understanding how much of a revolution it represented to be visited by the teacher and his son: in the joyous morning two screaming hens were grabbed and turned up dead in the kitchen. From the larder marmalade emerged to fill a cake.

And at eleven o'clock, behind the woodshed door, he finally saw an old car approach. The short fat man who was emerging from it didn't look like the German in the slightest! and the mistrustful youngster who was with him looked shyly at Ermelinda and Vitória who were waiting nicely dressed on the porch. Afterward the visitors disappeared into the house ...

So it had all just been his imagination! Almost laughing, running his shaking hand across the dryness of his mouth, with relief Martim listened for an undetermined time to sounds of conversation coming from inside the house, the noise of plates; the din was familiar, innocent and reassuring. Free at last of the tension, the man fell into bed and slept deeply.

When he awoke, the evening had composed itself tranquil and vast. And a short time later Vitória turned up. She looked even more tired and vanquished, standing erect in front of the wood-shed door:

—Since you're an engineer, she said, and he's a teacher, you two have things to discuss.

As Martim didn't reply, she added even more fatigued:

—The teacher is intelligent, he makes amazing puns.

She made an empty pause.

—We're waiting for you, sir, all right?

Martim ran his hand across the rough face that he hadn't shaved in days. She noticed the gesture and made another of inexplicable dismay:

—It doesn't matter, she said, the teacher is above things like that.

She was already leaving, broke off her steps. She seemed to make a decision and explained to him:

—He's not the principal but he's in charge of the whole school because he's got lots of personality. He makes great puns. He's very intelligent and superior.

Sleep had made Martim calm and nourished, and now that there was no more danger he looked at her waiting.

—The teacher's in charge but he's very paternal with the students, his theory is that a teacher can be very strict with the students.

He wasn't asking any questions and was looking at her serenely. She was pretty and tired. He'd never seen her so dressed up. She waited a bit longer, and both of them were for the first time talking about something besides work. That's when Martim, realizing that this was a novelty, looked her over distrustfully.

—He's strict with his students, very strict, she repeated monotonously and without seeming to pay much attention to what she was saying. One day a student was talking in class, and then at the end of the class, in front of them all, the teacher called the student up and made such a moving speech, calling him son and asking him to lift his feelings to God, that the repentant boy couldn't stop sobbing. Nobody laughs at the teacher, he doesn't allow it. The students laugh at the other teachers, but not at him.

—Yes, said Martim as a doctor would to a patient.

—The student cried so much, said the exhausted woman, that they had to give him a drink of water. He became a veritable slave of the teacher. The teacher is very well educated. The boy became a veritable slave, he's very well educated.

For the first time Vitória didn't seem to mind Martim's silence. And standing there, as if she had nothing else to do and no plans to leave, her features puckered up from fatigue, she kept reciting:

—To this day the teacher uses the boy as an example. The boy now looks like an angel, he grew paler, he looks like a saint. The teacher was so pleased with what he accomplished, it was such a great moral victory, that he even put on some weight, she said exhausted.

—He put on some weight, Martim repeated cautiously as if afraid to awaken her.

—He put on some weight, she said awaking a bit frightened. But he was suffering! she added quickly as if Martim had accused the teacher. He's good, he suffers like a person who's in charge! she said in rebellion, he has a heart of gold! she said looking at him with a certain rage. He suffers the suffering of others, the suffering that others have in their hearts! she added with sudden ardor.

And as if knowing that Martim hadn't understood a word, she looked at him with resentment.

The teacher was occupying the best chair in the parlor and in the arrangement of the scene, at a glance, Martim understood what the man represented in the little group. Ermelinda had just sat at the piano, with her very curled hair, looking distracted and tense. The mahogany of the furniture had been dusted. Martim stopped at the door and nobody seemed to have seen him. Maybe only the teacher who, with a sign of his finger to his mouth asking for silence, seemed to address specially the recent arrival. His son was chewing his nails with lowered eyes. Vitória kept her attention on an embroidery, in a hunchbacked and feminine position—Martim couldn't see her face and sought it, looking in it for the severity which was what he loved in her eyes. Martim sat near the door.

Ermelinda was playing without looking at the keyboard:

—I managed to memorize it, she said very softly. Feeling, she added as an order to herself.

The feeling came from her fingers with ease, which she seemed to be proud of, considering perhaps the fact as a sign of refinement:

—I can already play without even paying attention, she let them know once again leaning her head slightly back.

—Don't speak! the teacher suddenly said as if he were suffering, music oughtn't be interrupted with words! he said suffering from the fact that he himself had been forced to speak.

Martim was surprised by this rudeness.

—The teacher is a spiritualist, said Vitória suddenly to Martim as if that explained it.

Without looking at the keyboard and without needing to pay attention any longer, Ermelinda's music emerged mechanically and lightly in the Sunday truce. The piano was off-key enough to have a sound of crystal and clavichord, and the notes seemed to play themselves with the delicate impersonality of a pianola; the sound was somehow escaping pure as when you hear something and don't know who's playing. Ermelinda herself seemed to be stirred at last: the music had apparently started to say so many and such confused things to her—maybe about love, to go by the expression of anxiety and sad desire on her face—that she stopped playing and abruptly turned around on the swivel stool with a surprised look that communicated nothing to the others.

—Music is spirit itself, the teacher said with great assurance.

—I, said the son suddenly, what I like is opera, for me that's the best.

The teacher went red, looked at the floor.

—I've already explained to you, he said very low and soft, that you are mistaken.

—Opera's the thing, the boy repeated with courageous stubbornness; his face was pale and ugly.

—You are mistaken! the teacher shouted exploding. I've already told you, young man, that you are mistaken! the teacher shouted with eyes lost in suffering and rage. I've already explained to you that opera today is considered second-rate music! you're the only one who doesn't obey! I've already explained!

—Maybe, the boy said with painful haughtiness, but for me opera's the thing.

The teacher looked at him with bulging eyes. The vein in his neck was pulsing. The boy then lost his strength, lowered his head and started chewing his nails again.

—The teacher is a very emotional person, said Vitória simply to Martim.

At this phrase of Vitória's, the teacher seemed suddenly to calm down, the pale color returned to his fat face and as if he'd unexpectedly made up his mind to forget the problem with his son, he turned resolutely and tranquilly to Martim:

—So then, he said with extreme attention, what do you have to say about our Vitória?

Vitória lowered her head toward her embroidery and a blush came to her face.

—All that dryness—the teacher said—covers, if you'll excuse the beauty of the words, a heart that is breaking from love.

Vitória tried to protest slightly, choking:

—The teacher—she said with a confused and imploring voice, and Martim didn't know if what she said was praise or an excuse—the teacher ought to write a novel!

—I couldn't! the teacher leapt, that's the thing! I couldn't, he exclaimed painfully, I couldn't because I have all the solutions! I already know how to figure everything out! I don't know how to get out of this dead end! to everything, he said opening his arms in bewilderment, I know an answer to everything!

Nobody seemed to understand very well what he'd meant, nor why that would make him unable to write novels. As if he himself noticed that nobody had understood, once again he seemed to abandon the problem then, leaving it unfinished—and turned to Martim with greater calm, cooler now.

Feeling the teacher's watchful eyes upon him, Martim lowered his own and trying to control himself picked up the already half-tanned cowhide that was in the corner of the parlor. When he calmed down, he realized that he'd also picked up a hammer and that he was now hammering the leather, tanning it. Vitória looked at him astonished as if he'd gone too far, and worriedly scrutinized the teacher. He, swallowing such insolence with difficulty, closed his eyes for an instant and his face seemed to be asking God for humility. When he opened his eyes, he was really already smiling with understanding and irony, and could look impassively at that man who without warning was hammering a cowhide.

—Since this morning, said Ermelinda who could no longer stand the silence, this since morning I've been so thirsty! Thirsty, as they say, as a dog.

—I don't think that's what they say, if you'll allow me—the teacher said politely, but with the quickness of a stingray—they say hungry as a dog, if you'll allow me, he repeated with a bow, somewhere between ceremonious and disgusted.

—But what I am is thirsty …, she ventured very shy.

Vitória destroyed her with her eyes. The other woman averted her eyes and crossed her hands.

Vitória had gone back to her embroidery. Martim was hammering softly. The evening had spread smoothly, entering the parlor and making the silence. Nothing was making the evening more obvious than the blows of the hammer at intervals: at each blow, distance was becoming farther off, the branches leafier, more lost whatever was lost, a hen cackled in the shadows. And a vague desire seemed to be born as when you dream. The teacher's son, left to his own devices, was biting his nails with melancholic voracity. Vitória was keeping a darkened face above her embroidery. Ermelinda seated on the stool, her back to the open piano, was facing them all with an intense and motionless smile as if her face were shining in and of itself without the help of thought. Martim with his head lowered was cadentially assuaging the cowskin. The smell of leather and the blows of the hammer were stripping from the scene its total immobility and gave it a progressive motion: bit by bit the more intense smell and the hammer blows brought the situation to an end—Vitória lifted from the embroidery her widened eyes, the teacher's son coughed and frightened at himself looked at his father, Ermelinda blanched her smile a bit, her dry lip got lightly stuck on a tooth. Martim, unconscious author of the destiny of those moments, kept hammering. The teacher kept his eyes half-closed, somber, where a shrewd glint was thinking. Vitória noticed it with disquiet and jumped the gun:

—I dreamed, she said out loud, that I was surrounded by ships.

—Lit up or dark? Ermelinda immediately asked waking up.

—What difference does it make! exploded Vitória.

Ermelinda lowered her head.

—Lit up is prettier, said Martim looking with softness at Ermelinda.

Vitória turned quickly toward him, hurt. The teacher immediately examined him, closing his eyes still more: it was the first time that Martim had spoken.

After a second of fright, Ermelinda laughed a lot:

—Lit up is prettier, it is! lit up is happier, she repeated with zest.

—From the outside, my dear friend, said the teacher with great coldness, from the outside a ship is much more total than from the inside, he said with an experienced and bitter smile.

Once again nobody understood and nobody seemed disturbed not to have understood. Realizing this, the teacher blinked several times. Night had fallen. Vitória got up slowly and turned on the lights.

The teacher was now speaking calmly, lounging in the chair, which was letting his fat belly stick out. Martim didn't know whether they were expecting him to go or to stay.

—Let us divide the journey of humanity into stages, the teacher was saying.

The hammer blows had ceased, the frogs were croaking. The teacher was speaking and playing with the key ring, twirling it in the air and without letting it go snatching it with his hand. That was when the keys fell.

Martim automatically bent over to grab them. But the teacher, apparently without hurry, was quicker than Martim and grabbed them. And as if he'd tranquilly shown what he was made of, he smiled at the other man. Still with the gesture in his hands, Martim looked at him with surprise: he wouldn't have thought that the little fat man could make such a jovial movement. Then the teacher, understanding, laughed still more and started to twirl the keys once again.

The man was demonstrating some thing—Martim's mouth dried out a bit, he wasn't taking his eyes off the keys. Vitória too was following with fascinated eyes the rotative movement of the teacher's little hand.

—By dividing the journey of humanity into stages, we may reach the conclusion that we are today in the stage of bewilderment. We might say that modern man is a man who no longer finds a lesson in the perennial lesson of the ancients. Subsequently I would say ...

Vitória was listening to him sitting straight up, a sleepwalker, looking at the keys. At last the teacher broke off, looked at his watch. He held his breath for an instant and finally said:

—My game is the human charade, he said clearing his voice with a hack. You're not contradicting me, sir? he suddenly asked. You, sir, an engineer?

As if something had finally happened, Vitória stirred with a start on the chair. Stultified by long motionlessness, Martim moved the position of his legs:

—Yes, yes, he said.

—All that is human interests me, you're not contradicting me, sir?

—No ...

—I, said the teacher with pleasure, am a born mystifier.

Vitória grew anxious. Martim moved his gaze from the teacher to Vitória and from her to the teacher, trying remotely to grasp what was going on; an incomprehensible circle was closing around him, he was disturbed without knowing why.

—Exactly because the human charade—which is what with a touch of English humor I like to call the human mystery—exactly because the human charade, as I was saying, interests me is why I'm wondering this: what is an engineer, a man let's say of such high quality, doing here?

Well. So that's why they'd summoned him.

—Let's say, what did a man do in order to leave a place like São Paulo, since the accent makes clear the locality of your excellency's origin, and not Rio de Janeiro as your excellency claimed. As I was saying, what did a man do that made him leave an exalted field, like that of constructing a city, which is the function par excellence of an engineer, what did he do, as we were saying, in order to end up in the vicinity of Vila Baixa, where the only resources are those of the spirit? Moreover: your excellency didn't even know where he was, as noted by an ignorant and illiterate man like Francisco, who doesn't have the gifts of scheming that spiritual evolution lends a man, but *quand même* has the instinct of inquiry. As we were saying, what did a man do or think that made him come here? what did he do, I ask quite clearly, since your excellency just agreed that my game is the human charade?

—Guess, said Martim trying to smile with dry lips.

The teacher didn't hesitate: he opened his eyes and looked at him with crudity. Martim smiled, pale.

—I shall, the teacher said abruptly.

He got up looking at his watch at the same time.

Behind a hedge, while the others were taking leave on the porch, Martim sought in vain to make out the faces in the dark but all he got was just a general tone of leave-taking. He tried violently to analyze each dark face and make out another clue, though the very violence with which he was wanting it made his search more difficult. The yellowish light that was echoing weakly inside the house wasn't enough for him to make out more than shadows, and the buzzing of blood in his own ears didn't allow him to pick out words. Internal disorder had left him both acute and lost, as if extremely attuned to a void. Nothing seemed very real to him, and he was being tripped up by the extremely strange fact that the teacher, not being the German, nevertheless …

At last the car went off, the two women slowly went up to the porch and disappeared inside the house.

3

THE DOOR OF THE MAIN HOUSE, AS IT CLOSED, ISOLATED him outside. Soon a light was being lit on the upper floor. And Martim remained alone panting in the darkness.

"Very well," he said with fake ease and good humor into which he inserted a bit of irony, "and now," he added friendly and polite, "let's go to sleep." He felt that in some way he was being stronger than he was, and he was overtaken by self-pity. "Very well then," he repeated with sarcasm.

At the same time that he was deciding to lock himself in the woodshed and as a first step calm down his hot head, he took himself stunned and distracted in the opposite direction. At first the lack of understanding of what he himself was intend-ing to do made him stagger, and he moved forward almost in backward jerks. Afterward the direction of his flight became yet another obscure impulse—and when he suddenly understood himself, panic overtook him and he was almost running. "Very well," he yet said like a man who had time to straighten his shirt before dropping dead. That was when he started to run for real, to run unleashed toward the river, and his nebulous goal was the woods, the dark woods. Overtaken by the murmurings of his own panic he crossed the cold water bumping into the rocks, his legs were terrorized by the iciness of the black water, he ran very scared, and entered the woods—but the edge of the woods wasn't enough for him, with the covetousness of a scream what he wanted was the black heart of the woods, he couldn't run freely because of the branches but he was running getting cut up and breaking branches like a wild horse.

Until unexpectedly he felt that he'd made it to where he wanted to be and halted panting, with his whole chest beating, his eyes wide open in the shadows. And God can bear witness that he didn't know what he'd come looking for in the woods. But, without managing to get back his breath, there he was, and the mere possibility of not being there frightened him. The heavy air was close to his face as if the dark were full of the breathing of a dog.

There the man sat snorting out loud, his eyes open and nasty. He was feeling elementarily protected by the darkness, though it was the darkness itself that scared him the most. No thought occurred to him, his famished soul was feeding off the total blindness of the shadows, and he was breathing rough and shrewd, he heard with great greed his own breathing that had become his most primary guarantee: as long as he was breathing, he'd be very clever. He was moving his head from side to side, ready to leap, which, if he did it, he'd do while giving a ferocious cry. To feel that he'd have the means of giving that cry also calmed him down. Though none of those guarantees made him stop trembling and gnashing his teeth.

He ran his hand a few times across his mouth—and with astonishment realized he was grinning. Unable to wipe the idiotic grin from his mouth, he then looked in the dark at the hand that had touched the smile, as if it might come back wet with blood. His teeth were gritting light and precise, without Martim's having anything to do with them. And as if they'd just told him that he was afraid, he laughed.

Because it was a fear that had nothing to do with the equations he'd developed before the teacher's arrival—as if the fear were happening to someone else. Except that someone else was frighteningly—himself. Who was he? Martim had fallen so far into himself that he didn't recognize himself. As if up till that point he'd just been playing around. Who was he? He had the intuitive certainty that we're nothing like what we think we are and we are what he was being now, one day after we are born we invent ourselves—but we are what he was now. Martim had in truth fallen the way a person falls into madness, and so he was gnashing his teeth. It would be a chaotic truth only as long as he tried to understand it. But in itself it was entirely perfect. And he—he was the one who was gnashing his teeth. Gnashing his teeth in a fear that made him forget that he'd initiated a task of a super-man. He was afraid as if he'd finally fallen into the trap—in that trap that he'd ignore as long as he could, but as if frustrated if he didn't fall into it, Martim who had been made in order to fall. Yet he was still ignoring it and his fear was petty as if he'd stolen, not the grandly punishable fear of one who murders but the fear of one who steals.

Bit by bit the darkness calmed him down. But immediately thereafter it started to scare him, and his eyes shined a lot. Until the impassibility of the darkness that had just terrified him, once again calmed him down with the same quality of impassible permanence, and he stopped trembling, as suddenly as he'd started.

Immediately taking this as a sign that the crisis had passed and it hadn't been more than a crisis, Martim said mechanically to himself: "very well then!", and got ready to pull himself together as quickly as possible, hurrying to join himself to the past that the teacher's threat had interrupted. To his surprise, he couldn't. Then he ran his hand across the mouth that was still smiling. But he simply couldn't. An instant of real fear had made him come to his senses. And the man spun around without support from any of the thoughts that, just a few days before, had started to make him the man he'd invented being. Now of all times! now when he'd started to feel that the sandals were almost ready, already near the realm of the smoky circle where the cauldron was boiling—now of all times was the end of his journey! But what had he reached at the end of the journey? Fear …

Crying from rage and fear he gritted his teeth and punched the tree a few times, and the more his hands hurt the more he felt compensated and the more his rage grew, and the more his fear closed his so unfamiliar heart. At the point he'd reached, it was as if not a single step had ever been taken! As if all his steps had been useless. Oh fool, fool! he said to himself crying. He'd had everything within his reach but—"I don't know how to figure it out! I didn't learn how to figure it out!", he said punching the tree, "not even the little bird fit into the construction, much less me!"

After which, as if he'd said something so formidable that it managed to be incomprehensible even to him, he calmed down sniveling. "Nonsense," he then said running his hand across his bearded face and feeling by touch that the smile hadn't left his face. He blew his nose with fussiness.

As if not a step had been taken. For in the dark he was now just that shapeless thing with a single basic feeling. In a single leap backward, he once again had just distanced himself from the territory of the word—he who had started to be able to do more than stutter. And as if not a step had been taken, he was now indistinguishable from a frightened horse in the dark. But the truth is that Martim in that moment no longer even wanted one of the minimal things he'd proudly wanted, and was even surprised that he'd ever desired them, he found them strange the way a man in the hour of his death would be amazed that he'd once worried that the tailor was late. Now he miserably wanted just the immediate and urgent solution to fear, and greedily he'd make any bargain.

The worst thing is that there wasn't even any glory in that punishment, nor martyrdom: that thing with frightened eyes that one day had rashly risen to the crime and then to the mountain, that thing that he was could no longer be distinguished from a beast that had dared flee its pen: both would have the same indiscriminate punishment, the fear that was suddenly reducing them to the same serious destiny.

Suddenly it really did seem to Martim that until now he'd been traveling down superimposed paths. And that his true and invisible journey had really been made beneath the path he'd thought he was walking along. And that the true journey was now emerging suddenly into the light as from a tunnel. And the true journey had been this: that he'd emerged one day from his man's house and his man's city in a quest, through adventure, exactly for this thing that he was now experiencing in the dark, in a quest for the great humiliation, and with that he was ferociously humiliating with relish an entire human race. Fear humiliated him and he then violently blew his nose.

If he'd initiated a man's task, now it was seeming to him that he had played around with things you don't play around with: he'd touched the illusion too closely. And he'd sought to understand more than was allowed and to love more than was possible. In order to enter life, a monk would renounce — not act. Had his mistake been to act? He'd committed a total act but he wasn't total: he was scared in the same way you love a woman and not all women, he was scared in the same way you have your own hunger and not other people's; he was just himself, and his fear had his own size.

So in the dark, not knowing exactly what he was fearing, the man feared the great crime he had committed.

Face to face with the word crime, he started to tremble again and to feel cold, without managing to undo the grin that had turned up again. And the criminal felt so much fear that for the first time he understood in all its inexpressible meaning what was meant by salvation.

Salvation? His heart then beat powerfully as if the limits had collapsed. Since, maybe, that might be the great bargain he could strike—salvation. Everything then that in Martim was individual, ceased. He only now wanted to join the saved and to belong—fear had brought him to this. To salvation. And with his heart wounded by surprise and joy, it seemed to him for an instant that he'd just found the word. Could it be in order to seek this word that he'd left home? Or would it once again just be the remains of an old word? Salvation—what a strange and invented word, and the dark was surrounding him.

Salvation? He was startled. And if this were the word—so could this be how it was happening? So he'd had to live everything he'd lived in order to experience something that could have been said in a single word? if that word could be said, and he hadn't yet said it. He'd wandered across the whole world, just because it was harder to take one single step? if that step could ever be taken!

The absurdity enveloped the man, logical, magnificent, horrible, perfect—the dark enveloped him. However, from the little he understood, he seemed to feel the perfection that there had been in his obscure path that led to the woods: there was in his steps an impersonal perfection, and it was as if a lifetime had been the time rigorously calculated for the ripening of a fruit, not a minute more, not a minute less—if the fruit ever ripened! Because the fear seemed to him to establish a harmony, the terrifying harmony—I tell thee, God, I understand thee!—and he once more had just fallen into the trap of harmony as if blindly and down crooked paths he had carried out in pure obedience a perfect fatal circle—until finding himself once again, as he was finding himself now, at the same point of departure that was its own final point. And if that merely circular path had just rendered useless all the steps he'd taken, at the very bottom of his fear the man suddenly seemed to consent to this path, with pain and with fear he seemed to admit that his unknown nature was more powerful than his freedom. Since what did freedom ever get me, he cried to himself. I did nothing with it ...

What had the deep but powerless freedom ever got him. He'd tried to invent a new way of seeing or of understanding or of organizing, and he'd wanted that way to be as perfect as the way of reality. But what he'd experienced had been just the freedom of a toothless dog. The freedom to go in search of the promise that was surrounding him—the man thought trembling. And so vast was the promise that, if the person lost sight of it for a second, then he'd lose himself from himself in a world so empty and complete that it didn't seem to need yet another man. He'd get lost until exhaustively, and born out of nothing, hope would arise—and then once again, as for a toothless dog, the world would become something he could wander through, touchable. But only touchable. Then whoever screamed louder or yelped more melodiously would be the king of the dogs. Or whoever knelt deepest—since kneeling was still a way of instant by instant not losing the promise from view. Or whoever revolted. His strike!

His strike, which was the only thing of which until today he could be proud.

Until once again the desire of a toothless dog was born? Yes, that's how it was. And all of this until dying one day? Since we do die. In his fear the man saw that we do die. And if it wasn't for the pain—which was our answer—it would be only like this: would we have died one day?

But not so simply! shouted the panicked man. Since in the

dark he seemed to have the great intuition that we die with the same intense and impalpable energy with which we live, with the same kind of offering that we make of ourselves, and with that same mute ardor, and that we die strangely happy despite everything: in submission to the perfection that wears us out. To that perfection that made us, until the last instant of life, sniff with intensity the dry world, sniff with joy and accepting … Yes, because of the inevitability of love, accepting; out of a strange adjustment, accepting …

Was that it? Almost nothing! the man revolted yet again, but my God that's almost nothing.

No, that's a lot. Because, by God, there was much more than that. For each man there was probably a certain non-identifiable moment in which there was more than sniffing: in which the illusion had been so much greater that it would have reached the intimate veracity of the dream. In which stones would have opened their stone hearts and animals would have opened their secret of flesh and men wouldn't have been "others," they would have been "us," and the world would have been a flash that we recognize as if we'd dreamt of it; for each man there would have been that non-identifiable moment in which we would have accepted even the monstrous patience of God? That patience that allowed men for centuries to annihilate other men with the same stubborn error. The monstrous goodness of God is in no hurry. That certainty of His that made Him allow a man to murder— because He knew that one day that man would fear and in that instant of fear, captured at last, at last unable to avoid looking at his own face, that man would say "yes" to that harmony made of beauty and horror and perfection and beauty and perfection and horror; the perfection that wears us out.

And this man, with the great respect of fear, would say "yes," even knowing with shame that this would be his greatest crime perhaps: because a man essentially lacked the right to think all of this was beautiful and inevitable, a man essentially lacked the right to join the divinity—how much right did a man have to be divine and say yes? At least not before gathering his things!

But no. Even without knowing how to gather our things, the man would end up committing the crime of saying yes. Since once the incomprehensible knot of the dream was reached, you'd accept this great absurdity: that the mystery is salvation.

Oh God, Martim then said in calm despair. Oh God, he said. Because our parents are already dead and it's no use asking them "what is this light," no longer asking them, we have to ask ourselves. Our parents are dead—when will we finally face that? Oh God, he then said. Because he looked at the darkness around him and the way every other being was definitively in its own house and nobody in the world would lead him, then in his flesh in colic he was inventing God. And it was enough to invent Him so that from the depth of centuries of fear and helplessness a new power might grow gigantic in a place where nothing had existed before. A man in the dark was a creator. In the darkness the great bargains are struck. It was by saying "oh God" that Martim felt the first weight of relief in his chest. He breathed slowly and with care: growing hurts. He breathed very slowly and with care. Becoming hurts. The man had the painful impression that he'd gone too far.

Maybe. But at least for a moment of truce he was no longer afraid. Except that he felt that unexpected solitude. The solitude of a person who instead of being created creates. Standing there in the dark, giving in. The solitude of the complete man. The solitude of the great possibility of choosing. The solitude of having to manufacture one's own instruments. The solitude of already having chosen. And of having chosen of all things the irreparable one: God.

Until, alone with his own greatness, Martim could no longer

stand it. He found out that he'd have to shrink in the face of what he'd created until he fit into the world, and shrink until becoming a child of the God that he'd created because only thus would he receive tenderness. "I am nothing," and then you fit into the mystery.

And that man with a frightened gaze, with fear reborn, only wanted now one thing from this world: to fit inside it. But how? The wind filled his mouth with dust, the wind that he'd only now noticed and that frightened him too. He started to tremble once more, ran his hand across his dry and avid mouth. The fear of never reaching the goodness of God overtook him. He had called on the power of God but still didn't know how to provoke His goodness. That was when he suddenly said to himself: I killed, I killed, he finally confessed.

Since maybe that was what they were expecting of him in order to deliver him from fear? and he was offering his crime as a hostage.

But—he rebelled immediately thereafter justifying himself to God—someone had to sacrifice himself and bear suffering without consolation all the way to the end and then become the symbol of suffering! someone had to sacrifice himself, I wanted to symbolize my own suffering! I sacrificed myself! I wanted the symbol because the symbol is the true reality and our life is what's symbolic to the symbol, just as we ape our own nature and seek to copy ourselves! now I understand imitation: it's a sacrifice! I sacrificed myself! he said to God, reminding Him that He Himself had sacrificed a son and that we too have the right to imitate Him, we have to renovate the mystery because reality gets lost! Oh God, he said in self-defense, dost thou not respect even our indignation? my hatred always saved my life, I didn't want to be sad, if it weren't for my rage I'd be sweetness and sadness, but rage is the daughter of my purest joy, and of my hope. And dost thou wish for me to give up the best of my rage, thou who hadst Thy own, he accused, because that's what they told me, and if they said it they weren't lying because they must have felt in their flesh thy rage, he accused.

What happened, then, was that Martim feared his own rage as we fear our own strength. Darkness was all around him. And the silence that enveloped him answered that that wasn't the way he'd fit in the world and that that wasn't how he'd deliver himself from himself. And he—he wanted to fit. But how? It would nevertheless be so simple. If animals were their own nature, we were the beings to whom things surrendered: it would be so simple just to receive them. All he'd have to do was receive, that's it! So simple.

But a person doesn't know how.

How? how am I supposed to do it? he asked himself. The wind was leaving his mouth dry with dust. More than the fear of being turned into the police by the teacher, a total fear was making him want to give in at last. In fact he now no longer knew if he wanted to accept because there was no other way out, or if because accepting was taking up a great and obscure meaning that was coming toward the unknown creature that he was. He now no longer even cared if, in the act of accepting, he had been aware that he was betraying the most valuable part of himself: his rebellion. Not even just his own rebellion. But the rebellion of others too. He, who had made himself the depository of other people's rage. He, who had needed a great crime in order to prove some thing. Martim knew that he was betraying his own sacrifice. Nonetheless that's what he wanted. Although, being aware of his betrayal, he was now a very old man. He could no longer be understood by an adolescent. Never again, never again would he be understood. Not even by himself. More than that: he was aware, as if he'd taken a blood oath, that no thought of his in the future would ever deliver itself from the mark of his now-revealed cowardice, that cowardice that is the necessary submission of a man, and his experience. He was aware that he could never again start to be free without recalling the fear that he was feeling now.

He knew it. But in the darkness of the forest he only wanted to be delivered. How? Without any experience, he didn't know how a person accepts. As if there must be a ritual that not only symbolizes submission but completes it. Oh it didn't even matter to him that, as soon as he accepted, a new lack of meaning would be immediately organized within the kaleidoscope. A harmonious and intangible lack of meaning, in a system closed once more which once more he couldn't enter. What really mattered was belonging to a system—and delivering himself from that nature of his that suddenly made a man start once again to tremble from his head to his feet. Oh it didn't matter, since he'd already gone too far, and being afraid was too late, it already meant belonging to the salvation, whatever that meant. What did it matter if that was the word or not! we who allude, we who only allude.

In the night in the forest the enormous fatigue was making the man lose his lucidity, and instinctively his blind thought wanted to seek the remoter source. He was guessing that in that dark source everything would be possible because in it the law was so primary and vast that inside it the great confusion of a man would fit too. Except that, before being admitted into the first law, a man would have to lose humbly his own name. That was the condition. But someone shipwrecked had to choose between losing his heavy riches or sinking with them into the sea. In order to be admitted into the vast source, that man was aware that he'd have to believe only in brightness and in darkness. That was the condition—and after that step he would be a vanquished part of whatever he was discovering and loving.

The wind was blowing stronger in the trees, in the darkness the ripped-off leaves were hitting him in the face. With his chest wounded and sweet, he inhaled the moisture that was approaching. He wondered curiously if it might still rain that night. Since he didn't have the courage to leave the warm coat of the forest, he realized that the rain would come to meet him there defenseless. And at that idea, he once again started to tremble with fear of the dark and of the rain. He too, just like the others—since they'd told him that this happened even to the most vigorous, and sailors were aware of this.

Like the others, one day in rage he'd attained his strength. And in repentance, his sweetness to the point of honey. Until, transfigured by his own nature, now he was saying nothing and in the dark seeing nothing. But being blind means having continuous vision. Could that be the message?

But first your rage and your repentance. Until in extreme unction a man would come and, so that this very man could save himself, beg you with a threatening face, in that summing-up cry with which we try to understand whatever is ours: "say yes! once! now! right here! say yes once before dying! don't die damned, don't die enraged! the miracle of blindness is just this: saying yes!"

So that was what they wanted from him? For him to say yes. In exchange for everything he knew, what did they ask of a man? In exchange they were asking a man—to believe. He could eat dirt until he exploded but he's asked to believe. He himself may have stolen other people's bread—but he's asked horrified by himself to believe. That he's never done an act of kindness—but he's asked to believe. That he's forgotten to reply to the letter from a woman who was asking for money for her child's illness—but he's asked to believe.

And he believes. "I believe," said Martim frightened by himself, "I believe, I believe! I don't know what the truth is but I know that I could recognize it!" he insisted, "give me an opportunity to know what I believe in!"

But that wasn't given to him. And then, since he didn't know what the truth was, he said to himself in the forest: I believe in the truth, I believe in it just as I see this darkness, I believe just as I don't understand, I believe just as we murder, I believe just as I never gave bread to the hungry, I believe that we are what we are, I believe in the spirit, I believe in life, I believe in hunger, I believe in death!—he said using words that were not his own. And because they weren't his they had the value of the ritual that they were only awaiting in order to deliver him from fear, the only password: I believe.

The man sniveled ashamed. A new and painful dimension had opened inside him. Which "God" silently must have foreseen in His strange vision of us. In truth the man for an instant seemed to have lost his relativity, just as a horse sometimes gets helplessly absolute. Could that be what God had patiently hoped he'd understand? that was what he'd promised him. But even if God could speak, he wouldn't have said anything to him because if he'd said it he wouldn't be understood. And even now the man wouldn't understand.

Humiliated, the man sniveled wiping away his tears, a bit intimidated. The first lightning finally opened the sky—the main house lit up and went dark again. After an instant of silence the dry thunder rolled down the mountains in reply. Until collapsing into the rumbling murmur of quietude. Sniveling, the man thought that this was a harmony.

Then the wind started to blow harder, making the windows shake. And Vitória sat on her bed.

No thought had yet occurred to that lady but her heart heard the thunder clearly. It was the rain that was supposed to come. It was the rain that was supposed to come! She recognized it by the suffocation of the air and by the rage of the trapped wind, it was the rain that was supposed to come. Her heart was ferociously overjoyed: triumph, her triumph, she had known how to wait.

Only then did she understand with a bit of astonishment that she was awake. It was cold and yet she was asphyxiated, with her heart swollen in her chest, maybe because not a single drop had yet fallen.

Then, sitting in the darkness and as if there hadn't been any break, she took up the thought she'd had when she saw Martim for the first time in front of the porch: a man standing there whose face showed the rude beatitude of having satisfied his thirst—and already then she couldn't say if she thought that was pretty or ugly. And as if it were very natural to be thinking about the man in the middle of the night, the lady once more seemed intrigued by that indifferent face upon which nevertheless the physical traits were of pure malice. But it was like a tiger who seems to laugh and then you see with relief that it's just the shape of the mouth. Which, however, didn't quite calm her down since physical things also have their intention. What softened in the man his danger was the contradictory duality of the physical face with an expression that didn't confirm it. Out of a wicked curiosity the woman imagined that if besides the malicious features the expression too became malicious, then—then she would have seen the face of laughter and of evil. She then shivered with pleasure.

The pleasure surprised her, she turned over in shock. Her shock might have come from being awake in the middle of the night or from thinking about the man. She immediately adjusted her sheets, getting ready severely to go back to sleep.

She knew however that it was a lie and that she wasn't getting ready to sleep. So, then, she lay quiet in the darkness. The compact darkness would allow for anything because her face wouldn't even be seen by the walls. And as it always does, the night seemed to be whispering to her that she could have any thought. As if the animals had escaped into the black field before the storm broke and the lady could take advantage of the wind in order to mingle furtively among them. I love you, she ventured with care giving a first cautious sample of herself in the dark in order to see if it was true that nothing would happen to her. And nothing happened. The lady seemed disappointed as if she'd really hoped that after the daring phrase the darkness would turn into day or that at last it would start to rain or that suddenly she could be transformed into another person.

Though the phrase had echoes and echoes in the temporarily subsided wind.

Nothing had happened. A tranquil sadness filled the room. If love was what that lady was feeling with her body hot from sleep. If love was this beastly sadness mixed with rage and with shadows; shadows were her love. That thing that was as if she were the only living person in the darkness couldn't be love. She'd never heard of love like that. But the wind was blowing ... And uncertain she was seeking love the way darkness seeks darkness, as the flame of a candle seems to want to go out vanquished at last by something that is so much greater than the little flame of a candle. If it wasn't love, the man owed her this before going away: the lady had bit by bit grown as stubborn as you get in the middle of the night.

The window was opening onto the opaque night. That opacity that would transform into a shivering transparency when the darkness at last gets wet. And the lady, trying to calm down, told herself that she'd surely fall asleep as soon as it started to rain. "That was the only reason she wasn't sleeping." For now, no matter how much her eyes were piercing the darkness, they found nothing, and no obstacle that kept her from going ahead. Out of habit she was seeking some blockade, until now obstacles had always been a great support for her. But now surrounded by love, by wind in the trees, by permissiveness. It wouldn't even be the embrace that would symbolize the love of that woman. Sitting there, she'd already reached the point of using the soul that was the blackest part of her body, and the saddest part. I love you, she tried again with a hard and haughty voice. But love couldn't be that. Loving that way was melancholy. "The animals are on the loose," she then thought softly, softly, melancholy.

"What animals?", she jolted when she realized what she'd thought, and the little flame of the candle tried a final justification before surrendering. "What animals?", she wondered forcing herself austerely to a logic that "astonished" her, and being astonished would mean defending herself. But she herself answered with the obstinacy of pleasure: "the animals of which the darkness is made."

After which, the woman tried painfully to get herself together: she had to stay as lucid and clear as she was during the day. Hadn't she finally managed to live tranquilly on her plantation, taking care of her tasks? Hadn't she managed at last to get rid of that threat which was the anxiety of living? and get rid of that hard and empty ardor that would have taken her you'd never know where?

I did! she answered herself with pain, feeling her great loss. And hadn't she managed to get God with so much effort? I did, she responded astounded. What she meant by God, can't quite be known. But she'd done it. So what she logically ought to do was lie down and sleep.

She'd done it, yes. But as for someone cured of an addiction who can no longer fight the temptation—a man had turned up who by the transitory nature of his passing through seemed to demand as an ultimatum that she do it again. And renew her decision. Why would a person have to decide every day and every night? what freedom was the one that that woman hadn't even requested? And as if she hadn't already with so much effort chosen, again and again she'd have to choose; as if she hadn't already chosen. The speed of the man's time on the farm recalled in an obscure echo another transitoriness and another urgency—which ones?—and were giving her the final opportunity. Opportunity for what? And the heavy soul, which with such pride had given up, felt it had to choose between joining forces in the struggle or giving in. Giving in to what? She'd hardly looked at the man for the first time in front of the porch, and in rage had guessed that once again she'd have to decide.

"Which doesn't mean that I didn't struggle!", she shouted to herself in revindication, demanding enraged the right to receive mercy. She who, out of caution, had turned the man in to the teacher. And wasn't that a sign of struggle? It was. Then, since she'd done her duty, since she'd turned him in, she was going to sleep tranquilly.

But she kept sitting there. I love you, she ventured with care. As if loving were obscurely the way to reach her own limit, and the way of surrendering to the dark world that was summoning her. How unhappy I am, she thought with the tranquility of someone gazing into the very far distance. Unless what she was feeling was happiness. Since they looked so much alike. She grew still, sitting, listening to the frogs. Still, with her wound from love. And all by herself in order to figure out, without the resources of understanding, the fact that she'd turned the man in. The calm expectancy of the night was hounding her in the way that silence forces speech.

Suddenly Vitória came to her senses: "Anyway," she thought with authority, "anyway I have my rights and duties, and there's no reason to be awake in the dark, anyway I'm not lost in Africa!"

But she was. The frogs were croaking as if they were inside the room, the black wind was coming in through the window. The woman shivered. "That dark and good and muffled thing that was evil." The only word that remained from the unknown thought and that occurred to her in another shiver was: "evil." Evil? why use that dreadful word? Yet that was what she was feeling: in the dark, all surrounded and muffled and greeted. What steps had escaped her in order for her to reach the point in which darkness was greeting her? Would she only feel of love its cruelty? In love whatever there was of diluted feeling for life was gathering into a single instant of fright, and the rage from which she lived had transformed in the presence of the concrete man into the mortal hatred that was love, as if the scattered green of all the trees were gathered into a single black color. In love whatever there was of the vague foretaste of life was gathering into a single instant of fright.

And yet—yet you might say that she was loving that fright and that darkness, and that that's where the nasty joy in which the woman was in the dark was coming from. Her crude-fingered ambition had returned. Touched by whatever it is that you don't know how to call by any other name, except that of love—so different from what you expected that love and softness and goodness would mean—her ambition had returned, wiping out the bright and busy days on the ranch. In the dark of the bedroom, the obscure ambition, the obscure violence, the obscure fear that made her attack, she who out of fear had turned the man in.

The night was made for sleeping. So that a person never witnesses what happens in the darkness. Since with her eyes blinded by the shadows, seated and still, that lady seemed more to be peeping at the way the body works on the inside: she herself was the dark stomach with its nauseas, the lungs in tranquil bellows, the heat of the tongue, the heart that out of cruelty never had the shape of a heart, the intestines in an extremely delicate labyrinth—those things that while you sleep never stop, and that at night augment, and now were she. Sitting with her body, suddenly so much body. At midnight Cinderella would be the rags that she really was, the carriage would be transformed into a big pumpkin and the horses were rats—that's how it was invented and they didn't lie. At midnight you entered the realm of God. Which was a realm so dense that a person, unable to traverse it, would get lost in the means of God, without understanding his clear ends. For there was that lady confronted with her body that was a mean, and where suddenly she'd got entangled without being able to leave. And God's means were such a weighty power of enveloping darkness—that the animals were emerging one by one from their lairs, protected by the gentle animal possibility of the night. "It's dark," the lady said as an expected sigh to initiate herself into hell, since the means of God seemed like a hell. And the hell was the path of one who was worshipping the means of God. Absorbed, still, she was listening to the frogs. Being a frog was the humble and rude form of being an animal of God's. And as if purity and beauty were no longer a possible path of serving him, the lady also looked like a frog in her bed, with that basic demon joy that things in the dark have, curled up as they are, and they themselves so dark. Like a green animal, then, sitting on her bed ...

The night was made in order to sleep because otherwise in the dark you'd understand what was meant when they spoke of hell, and everything a woman doesn't believe in during the day, at night she will understand. For in the dark of the bedroom, with a weight of pleasure, she was seeming to understand why they said "hell" and why people wanted hell. She was seeming to understand what is meant by the figure of a black monk in childhood stories. And what's shadowy about the flight of a great butterfly. And if she looked now at a dark dog it would be no use to know that inside it lived no demonic soul: for now the lady might find out what was meant when they made up that a black dog is inhabited by evil. Because in a black dog some thing is being said. And motionless, without committing a single sin, she also knew what was evil and what sin. And if bats didn't exist, they'd end up coming through the window at nightfall: just to say with their winged form what we know. "Everything I know is hidden," she was feeling, and she was sitting on her bed, captured by what she knew. But it was also true that, as long as she wasn't obscure, her heart wouldn't recognize the truth.

Her eyes were supple, uneasy, intense. Maybe she was also understanding why God, in his infinite wisdom, gave and or-dained only a certain few words to be thought—and only those. It was so that we should live from them, and only them. Maybe she'd understood, since she remembered, out of nowhere, that the teacher had said that there had been a time when it was considered heresy to have in liturgical music more than one melodic line; yes, the teacher had said it was considered demonic. That's because, with more than one melodic line, you were delivered unto riches. The dizzy woman remembered stories she'd been told about tranquil men who'd gone to pieces for having experienced living at night a single time, and then they'd abandoned wives and children, and then started to drink in order to forget what they'd felt or to meet the expectations of the night.

Suddenly the lady, who'd been dragged along by the stream of her feelings, ran her hand over her face trying to wake up. It had been an involuntary mistake of hers to wake up in the night that is made for sleeping, as if she'd opened without meaning to the prohibited door of the secret and seen Bluebeard's livid wives. It had been an involuntary and forgivable mistake. But it was already more than a simple mistake not to have closed the door, and to have given in to the temptation to win power in that silence where, because she hadn't wanted to limit herself to using only His comprehensible words, God had left her all alone. Probably she'd been counting on a God stronger than her error and stronger than her desire to err. But the silence was surrounding her. And the lady, in the face of his cupidity, was sitting up. My God, I forgive Thee, she said closing her eyes before moving ahead irrepressible in her joy.

And all that was love. That's how, then, it happened. With that darkness and that silence and that wind and the shaken trees. But I forgive Thee for its being thus because I want it to be thus.

Nice and healthy, with the misery of her lust. Which wasn't

even the lust of love. It was more serious than that. It was the lust of being alive. The frogs were now enormous, with their mouths open near the window. The claws that were emerging from those neckless heads, those ragged mouths croaking an ancient noise, the little monsters of the earth. And for an instant, in a torture of joy, the woman too seemed to have claws in her bed, since something happens in the wetness of the night. Amidst her suffering, now entirely fulfilled, only a minimum of awareness was keeping her from joining the frogs beside the window. A minimum of awareness inside her waking nightmare was keeping whatever was darkness inside her from joining the orgy of the frogs. That effort that half-awake she made not to be an animal, since we already have their ears and the innocent face we have too. A minimum of awareness was preventing her, so favored at last by the waxing wetness, from following the scheme of whatever there was of lament and howling inside a person. And which the darkness of the prairie was promising, temptingly, to bless.

Feeling perhaps that she was no longer afraid, she dared wonder:

—Why did I turn him in?

But even in the muffled darkness remorse gave acidity to her blood. And the worst part of remorse was not understanding the use of her revenge: why did I turn him in? Then, in a balsam, she remembered a sentence from a children's book: "The lion is not a cruel animal. He doesn't kill more than he can eat." The lion is not a cruel animal, he doesn't kill more than he can eat, the lion is not a cruel animal—and was it her fault, if her hunger was so great? But could she ever eat as much as she'd killed? she who'd already killed so much, she who'd already killed so much. Sitting up in bed, she'd killed more than she could eat. That right there was her great fault. Her childish fright was that, having turned the man in to the teacher, the man would be turned in.

If the lady had thought that in the dark she'd have no remorse for what she'd done, she'd been mistaken. Even in the dark the inexplicable point was aching. And humiliated she could no longer stand the weight of her little crime. That desire to burn in the Hell to which everyone is summoned and so few are damned. She didn't have the strength of badness, the flesh is weak: she was good. And the demon was as difficult as sanctity.

She'd turned him in, and the man would certainly end up getting arrested. Oh God, she then said haughtily without begging, take pity on a weak heart. Because she, she couldn't. She was feeling nothing more than scorn in the face of the pettiness of her crime, and didn't even want solace. Solace seemed mean in the face of the depth of the dark light that is what suffering was, and where once again she seemed happy and frightened.

But a minimum of awareness was making her realize that in a moment she'd finally have the strength to free herself from her nightmare and to free herself from her evil joy in the darkness. In a moment the lady would finally have the strength to leave that joyous state into which she'd dangerously fallen like someone who falls into a hole while looking for a path. She'd already gone so far that she'd only manage to understand what was happening to her if she called it a nightmare. Because it had to be a nightmare to be alone with that hot feeling of living that nobody can use. God who out of pure goodness, considers this feeling a sin. So that nobody will dare and nobody suffer the truth. Alone with the hot feeling of living. Like a rose whose loveliness nobody can use. Like a river that only exists so that its murmur can be heard. A hot feeling that the woman couldn't translate into any movement or thought. Useless but alive. Imponderable but alive like a bloodstain on the bed. There she was like a dead man who had stood and started walking, the heat of her life suddenly was lifting her slowly, and would bring her serious and blind to seek in the night her fellows.

When it finally started to rain, the lady had reached a point of silence in which the rain looked to her like the word. Surprised by the sweet and unexpected encounter, she surrendered without resistance to the water, feeling in her body that the plants were drinking, that the frogs were drinking, that the animals on the farm were hearing the noise of water on the roof—the announcement had spread nebulously and was soaking the whole ranch: it was raining, raining, raining. Let it rain, she said. Because in this way too I love you, she thought before falling asleep, the darkness too was goodness, we too were goodness.

It was a bit later when Vitória awoke as if she'd slept for hours. And finally free of the nightmare, she was astonished to find the night in the same place she'd left it.

What had happened is that she'd slept so deeply for a few minutes that her body was heavy from hours of sleep. When she went to the bathroom, she saw in the mirror a calm and puffy face. Thirst was alerting her a bit, the sound of rain on the hollow leaves was making her thirstier yet. She went down to the kitchen where, from the fruits, she plucked a big mango. Watchful, she beat it against the wall, vaguely taking care not to wake Ermelinda with the soft noise of the mango against the tiles on the wall—until she felt engrossedly the fruit softening inside its peel, full of its own juice. Meditating, Vitória bit the peel, spit it out and through the hole sucked out all the nectar. She then tore off the peel with her teeth, ate the yellow flesh until she reached the pit.

Only when she was at the sink brushing her teeth did the sobs rise in her chest. Then, with her arm folded against the wall, hiding her face inside them, the woman waited patiently for the crying to pass. After which, she wiped away the tears and looked at her teeth in the mirror.

Then she went onto the porch. While she'd been in the bathroom the rain had stopped. The night was retired and serene; small indeterminate noises were nuzzling the darkness. Shivering from the pleasant cold she could make out from the porch the path that would bring her to the woodshed and, in the secret confusion of the bushes, almost make out the door. She went down the stairs.

She breathed slowly until she felt her lungs full of the black and wet air. Pushing aside branches she managed to reach the small clearing that preluded the door. She could almost hear the silence that was coming from the shed. She could hardly suppose that a living someone was existing inside that darkness, besides she herself who was breathing softly, with her head bent, listening, listening. Where could the man be? She recalled a time when she'd heard him snoring. If the idea hadn't been so absurd, it would have occurred to her that the shed was empty; she'd always been able to feel when a place was empty.

It started to rain again. The drops were running down the boughs, slapping with delicacy the leaves and spreading across the vastness of the field. Green lightning revealed in a flash the unsuspected height of the sky. Another bolt placed a previously invisible tree all of a sudden within her reach. And the thunder was rolling toward the abyss. "I"—said the old woman—"I am the Queen of Nature."

Clasping her robe to her breast, she then came closer until she could feel the door's smell of wet wood. And, a bit deeper into the smell, the rotten smell that was coming from the billets in the shed. Her hands ran slow and lively across the door. It gave way noiselessly. She slowly pushed it and, as she opened an unknown door, the woman seemed more concerned about her own cautious figure in the dark than about the fright the man would show when she awoke him. She remained motionless, neither inside nor outside the shed, with her watchful face wet.

But the kind of instinctive obstinacy of will that had led her that far seemed to have been extinguished. Before even ending the act the inspiration that had fed her had dried up. And as if in that night the woman had been enveloped in countless layers of nightmare and every time she freed herself from one of them she'd mistakenly thought that she'd finally reached the last one— only now was she entirely awakened from the dream. She ran her hand across the face down which the water was flowing freely. Even the trip to the kitchen and the mango she'd eaten belonged to the nebulous part of a dream and of a power. Why had she gone to the woodshed? she wondered curious.

She then remembered that at a certain already unidentifiable moment she'd meant to warn the man that she'd turned him in to the teacher. That, then, was what she'd come to do in the woodshed. But if until she'd arrived there she'd seemed so determined to the point of not even questioning herself—now suddenly she didn't know the next step to take. She was reduced to being a woman next to a door on a rainy night. Could it be that if someone saw her they'd say "look an old lady in the rain?", she wondered meditating. "I am the queen of the animals," the lady said.

Nobody in the world knew that she was there. And nobody ever would—since now she almost seemed sure that she wouldn't speak with Martim and that she'd go back to bed traveling back down the rainy path. "Nobody in the world would ever know"— which suddenly widened the great darkness of the countryside, and the woman got lost in it, in herself, the trembling queen of nature. That thought of a complete secret that only the rain could share gave her pleasure as if she'd finally done something beyond her human strengths. She shivered with joy. With the wet wind the night hit her hard in the face—the lady received with delight the unknown pact.

It was with the same previous care, but without the same emotion, that she turned around to leave. Soon she was arriving at

271

the porch, slipping on the wet steps and the moss; soon she was crossing the parlor and the hallway without making the slightest noise, leaving behind her the wet tracks of a biped. But when she reached the top of the staircase her caution became useless: her foot had stepped on something that rolled and rolled and rolled. With her back glued to the wall, holding her breath, she withstood with horror the object's rolling step by step unhurriedly like the minutes of a clock. Maybe it was the lost spool of thread. And had she heard, or just thought she'd heard, the creaking of a bed in Ermelinda's room? The silence remade itself bit by bit, the shadows returned to their places.

Only when she reached her room did her heart start to beat with violence. She stood in the dark and while she was trembling from the daring of what she'd done—now she wasn't sure if the daring was having gone to the woodshed or turning him in to the teacher—while she was trembling all over from what she'd done, she was already starting to smile in triumph. She didn't flick the light switch because she was afraid of the unpleasantness of the farmhouse's yellow and weak lights, to which she'd never grown accustomed: every time she'd turn on the light it seemed to her that it only gilded the darkness. Without turning on the light, without making any noise in order not to set off again the suspicious rumble in Ermelinda's room, Ermelinda who slept like a bird, Vitória took off her robe, slyly pulled back the sheets and slyly got into bed; she quickly covered herself up to her chin and lay with her eyes wide open in the dark, savoring the still shivering comfort of a dog who goes off by himself in order to lick his wounds, with the human gaze that animals have.

It was only then that it also occurred to her that there hadn't been any act … That she'd gone to the door of the woodshed and come back; just that. Just that? Her eyes opened wider in the dark. With surprise—not with pain, with relief—with surprise her life at the farm was totally intact. Everything then became clear; when she'd turned the stranger in, she'd just been defending that life. So much so that in the brightness of the next day a thousand little tasks awaited her. One thing she had at least managed: it had rained. It was raining. "And," she thought illogically, "since the man still hadn't gone, she still had time." A new indistinct noise from Ermelinda's room made the lady seek obscurely until no longer thinking: she froze up even more in search of the sleep that would refute it all.

As for Ermelinda, she too took a while to understand that she was awake. Lying down, her eyes looked tranquilly at the darkness of the ceiling. Then she started to make out the crickets separate from the silence. And then the noise of the calm frogs started to be born to her ears. Her attention then sought a certain rhythmic noise that she was no longer hearing: a noise inside the house itself or inside her dream, something that strangely was connected to the staircase. She remembered that she'd dreamed that it had gone down the staircase one step at a time. And she'd dreamed that a rat had rolled down the stairs. The house was tranquil beneath the rain.

But when she finally realized that she was awake she wondered in sudden fright how long she'd been awake. She stirred quickly, started really listening to the hoarse frogs next to the window and heard the noise of the wind in the leaves—everything that had been deafly in the background took the hard form of reality. "It's now," she thought with cold hands.

She didn't even need to think what the "now" meant since her heart had already beaten with the knowledge. She was aware that if she remained an instant longer alone in the dark she'd end up once again feeling the expanse of the field in the dark, the little flowers that even at night kept existing in a soft smile—through the same process that had made the frogs and the wind real.

As if she'd been bitten, in less than one second the girl was standing, in less than one second she was wrapping herself in the sheet and running down the hallways with her slippers in her hand. Without wondering why she'd found the door to the porch unexpectedly open, she crossed it in a wind of sheets and hair. And only when she reached the clearing near the woodshed—after conquering in a single instant of almost audible fear the distance that separated her from the man—did she with a muffled exclamation notice that she'd found the porch door inexplicably open … And that the woodshed door was open too …

That was the final sign that maybe that impossible thing might have already happened, that thing impossible to conceive except when it happens: there was no longer any barrier between life and death, the doors were all open.

The girl then froze in the clearing with her wet sheet, rigid, without taking another step. Her terror was tranquil in the rain that was falling. And standing there she seemed calm. She'd been captured without warning. Captured by her religion and by the chasm of her faith and by the awareness of a soul and by a respect for whatever can't be understood and which you end up worshipping, captured by whatever it is in Africa that makes the drums be struck, by whatever makes dancing a danger and whatever makes the forest be a person's fear. Unable to move, with respect and terror for her own thought that was floating away from her, and the rain seemed to be evolving from the earth the way smoke rises from ruins. But it wasn't the ruins the girl was afraid of, it was the smoke. And it wasn't death she was fearing. What she respected, with the veneration one has for a forest, was the other life. Standing there, looking at the empty fields where one day she would wander freed from her body. With that indirect way of wandering that her soul would have: at the same time backward and forward and to the side. So alone after her death. Entirely alone. Handed over at last to the dream that dragged her along in life, she who had so badly misunderstood the miracle of the spirit.

The girl therefore stayed quiet in her sheets like a great white butterfly. And she couldn't offer anything, as the sacrifice of an exchange, for death. She had nothing precious for a martyr's gift. There was no possible bargain. The thought of death was the most final point that her thought could reach. And from which as well her thought couldn't even step back. Since stepping back would mean meeting, as in a nightmare about being chased, the great fields of this earth, the inflated and empty clouds in the sky, the flowers—everything that on earth is already as soft as the other life. The small and perfect flowers swaying in masses in the field … didn't they have the serene madness and the delicateness of the "other life"? When she had to face her fear head-on, the extremely soft scent of the flowers would chase her like a little bird flying around her head. That delicate girl preferred the rat, the body of a bull, pain and that continuous work of living, she who had so little knack for living—but she preferred all of this to the horrible and tranquil cold little joy of the flowers, and to the little birds. Because they too were on the earth the nauseating mark of the latter life. Their presence, innocent reminder, was stripping away the security of her own earthly life. And it was then that, even the houses with their inside lives, seemed to her to be constructed too flimsily, unaware of the danger that there was in no longer being deeply rooted in the ground. Yet only the girl seemed to see what others didn't and something the solid houses didn't even suspect: that they had been built carelessly like someone who falls asleep in a cemetery without realizing it. The houses and the people had just alighted on the ground, and as little definitive as a circus tent. That succession of temporary constructions upon an earth that didn't even have borders to mark off where one person lives in life and where he lives in death—that earth that might be the very place where the soul one day would wander lost, sweet and free.

But if the girl managed to see, coming from the distance toward which she herself would head one day, if she managed to see the little birds ... which ones? which would be the other "signs"? how to discern them underneath their disguises? Sometimes suddenly she'd notice on the so-solid tree their suspicious softness. But how, how to discern the other signs? Though sometimes silence would blow.

All that girl's work, who had one day fallen into the mystery of thinking, was to seek uselessly proofs that death would be the serene total end. And that would be the salvation, and she would gain her life. But, with her tendency toward nitpicking, all she was managing to get was signs to the contrary. A hen who was flying higher than normal—had that naturalness of the supernatural. Hair that always grew so fast would make her so pensive. And a snake "but it was there just a minute ago, I swear! and now it's gone"!—the speed with which things vanished, the speed with which she lost handkerchiefs and didn't know where she'd left the scissors, the speed with which things were transformed into others, the automatic evolution of a bud mechanically opening into an open flower—or the head of a horse that she would suddenly discover in the horse, the head stuck on like a scared mask atop that solid body—all that was obscurely a sign that after death measureless life would begin. For this had been the way Ermelinda had taken note of beauty: through the side of it that was eternity. And if there are thousands of ways to see, the girl had forever snagged on to one of them.

Oh but not this time!

There in the clearing, suddenly and in an unexpected movement of liberation, she released her feet from the soaked earth—and in a flight crossed the threshold of the door throwing herself in search of the man with the despair of a bird in the cage. And when her body struck his, she didn't even wonder at finding Martim standing and fully clothed and soaked, as if he too had just come into the woodshed.

And the stupefied man, seeing her with her rumpled hair, wild as a chrysanthemum, only realized what was happening when he finally recognized the figure of the girl. And he couldn't say whether she'd run toward him or whether he himself had thrown himself onto her — to such a degree had they frightened each other, and to such a degree was each the other's solution to not being terrified by being so unexpectedly united. She clung to him in the dark, that big wet man who smelled of verdigris, and it was strange and voracious to be embraced without seeing him, just trusting in the avid feeling of a desperate touch, the rough concrete clothes, he seemed like a lion with wet hair — was he the hangman or the companion? but in the dark she'd have to trust, and she intensely closed her eyes, surrendering entirely to whatever was unknown in that stranger, alongside the knowable minimum that was his living body — she clung to that dirty man in terror of him, they grasped each other as if love were impossible. It didn't even matter if he was a murderer or a thief, it didn't matter why he'd turned up at the farm, there is at least an instant in which two strangers devour each other, and how could she not like him if she was once again loving him? — and when his voice resounded in a grunt in the dark, the girl felt saved, and they loved each other the way a married couple love when they've lost a child.

And now the two were embracing in the bed like two monkeys at the Zoological Gardens and not even death separates two monkeys who love one another. Now he was a stranger, yes. No longer because she didn't know him — but with her way of recognizing the particular and impassable existence of another person, she was accepting the stranger in him as the obeisance of love. In that moment she could say: I recognize you in you. And if grace also illuminated the man beyond the fear of finding something, she too would be at last for him the great stranger—and he would say to her: and I recognize in you, you. And that's how it would be, and it would be everything, since this probably was love.

The girl took his hand and feeling it hot and still wet, sighed deeply and gave a little laugh. Because she could hardly believe her own cleverness: that night she'd vanquished the fear. And even dazed by sleep she'd known to run to a man, since a man didn't have the softness of women, a man refuted for an instant the other life. Lying there and pensive, Ermelinda understood what one day a fearful girlfriend had said to her: "I want to get married because it's very sad for a person to be alone." Ermelinda gave the phrase an entirely special meaning of warning, because the friend was also someone who, for example, was afraid of the dark. And it was true, reflected Ermelinda quite sensibly. Since as long as she herself had been married, her husband had his schedule and his habits, which did so much to push away the wideness of the world. And even while she'd lived in the city it was different: in shops and markets life was smaller, you could fit into it without fear, and not like in the cursed countryside. She should have stayed in the city and remarried; that, yes, that's what she should have done. And tomorrow, tomorrow she would let Vitória know that she was leaving, since right now she was getting proof that that's what she should do, now that she was curled up next to Martim, and a man was taking away that freedom that a person alone feels as a forewarning of the greater freedom.

So it was with a smile of sleep on her face, well armed with whatever she might say to Vitória the next day, that the girl left the woodshed still dazed, stepping on the debris of woodchips and mud, walking with care in the dark in order not to fall.

And it was then that, as if her eyes were looking at her straight on, she had the idea of herself as if she were seeing herself: and what she saw was a girl all alone in that dripping world, with a shoulder uncovered by the sheet that was hardly enfolding her, her hair loose and that face in whose easy indecision had now appeared the joy of living.

And, seeing herself, she froze so suddenly that her feet drowned in the puddle of water and her unsupported hands clawed at the tree that in the dark had been tossed in front of her. And as if she herself were a distracted outlander who suddenly had seen that girl all by herself in the rain — she shivered all over. She was alive and shimmering in horror. Could she be living in this life or already in the next? she might have gone past the vague horizon like the little birds who go and come back ... She wondered if in fact she might have died without knowing it in the arms of the man since to him she'd given her body, and her soul was there white and faltering, with that sweet joy that the girl didn't realize could also come from the body.

Maybe because, having tripped, she was almost on her knees and didn't need to be daring in order to do what her heart was asking; maybe because being outside the house for the first time at night had broken some law of possibility — now she didn't need to be courageous in order to complete the semi-gesture of the fall, and then she knelt beside the trunk that had wounded her and without any shame asked God to let her be eternal. "Just me!", she begged, not as a privilege but in order to facilitate for Him the tremendous exception. Ah God, let me always have a body! The tears were running down her still happy face that, alarmed, hadn't had time to change its expression. My God, she confessed at last feeling that with this she was committing a great sin, I don't want to see Thee ever! She was horrified by God and His sweetness and His solitude and His perfume, she was horrified by the birds that He would send as messengers of peace. I don't want to die because I don't understand death! the girl said to God, don't judge me so superior that you'll give me death! I don't deserve it! despise me because I'm inferior, any life is enough for me! I'm not even intelligent, I was always slow in school, why then make me so important? all you have to do is ignore me and forget me, who am I to die! only the privileged should die! who's asking Thee for the truth! give it to whoever asks!

Her face had leaned against the trunk as against another gnarled face, and she was smelling that scent of dirty mud that is so reassuring and simple: the scent of her own life on earth, leaned then with love and greed against the dirty trunk, to which her mouth stuck imploring. And out of pity for herself, it was as if God were saying to her:

—It's the right way. We live and we die.

Hadn't that been what she'd felt on the afternoon when she'd threshed corn? Whosoever accepts the mystery of love, accepted that of death; whoever accepts that a body we pay no mind nevertheless carries out its destiny, then accepts that our destiny surpasses us, that's to say, we die. And that we die impersonally—and therewith surpass whatever we know of us. By carrying it out there was some impersonal thing to which a girl simply was saying amen—and the only one shouting was clawing at a pain or a scare and becoming personal. The girl was confused and tired, leaning against the trunk. Deep down she was understanding herself and understanding. Her form of understanding was what, because of the mystery of words, had made itself so difficult.

That was more or less what she felt in a state of sleep and love, embracing the good trunk of the tree for the love of which we were so well made, clinging to the tree, savoring so its good and hard knottinesses, hoping she'd have many and many and many years to smell the scent of things, happy birthday. The wrong posture was buckling her over. But she couldn't bid farewell to the warm perfume that was coming from her sleep and fatigue, perfume of a body living, and once again inhaled the freshness of the wet leaves, that scent of rain that is like a bitter taste of nuts—and in her blind hands she felt the rough tree that was made for our fingers, and at her knees the wet earth, everything that is our joy, everything that gives us such pleasure, and if that's why we were so well made, then—then Ermelinda, very tired now, felt like giving in at last and at last following her vocation which was one day to die.

4

WHEN MONDAY DAWNED, THE SUN WAS SO STRONG THAT the water in the puddles was panting hotly and the bees were already circling the wounded flowers, and it was as if there had been a party whose decorations hadn't yet been taken down. Soon a new heat had settled in there, made of leaves of green wool and of the moistness of bodies, a depetaled heat, and already by nine o'clock the soul was withering amidst the mosquitoes. A few unripe fruits had crashed on the ground for the curiosity of the ants; on the surface of the puddles of water were dustily stuck the fallen threads of spider webs. Though some diligent spiders had already made new sparkling links in the air. It was with a heed of unconscious hope that that the gaze would accompany the silken threads traveling from one tree to the next, remaking the space burst by the deluge. At nine o'clock only the spiders' threads were delicate in the light. Everything else had the brutality of a satisfaction, a sogginess of felt that takes a while to dry, and the weight of its own weight. It had rained everywhere.

With new strength the mulatta was singing in the hot kitchen. The night's rain seemed to have been something everyone just imagined, what happens at night doesn't apply to the day. Martim's eyes were reddened by insomnia. The fatigue had turned out to be worse than he'd expected and his mouth had the taste of unslept sleep. "I was in the woods last night," he thought stubbornly reducing what had happened to this: he'd been in the forest and when he came back Ermelinda had come into the shed. "A hussy," he thought fatigued and without malice, looking at the girl from afar and seeing her with her hair once again sensibly tied back as if nothing had happened. Sunday night seemed absurd to the man, and he really didn't quite remember the details; having been in the forest "after all didn't mean anything"—and that's how he spit on the plate from which he'd eaten. "Later, later I'll think", he said to himself, "there's still time." It would be very easy to take the truck at nightfall, and by the time they heard the sound of the motor he'd be far away. Relatively speaking he had time: "Later," he thought.

The mulatta was singing and Ermelinda drinking her coffee said to her:

—Sweetheart, last night I was so afraid to die that you can't even imagine! it really seemed that the world was going to come crashing down!

—Heaven forbid, Miss Ermelinda! said the other woman happily.

Both laughed. But they fell silent in mutual understanding when they heard Vitória's steps crossing the parlor. Once again with her old black pants and with her open shirt on her chest, with her hair rolled up, Vitória was coming from the field. Nobody knew when she'd had breakfast, she'd awoken so active as if, along with the rain, she'd lost some time that she needed to get back.

—Today's the day, the mulatta murmured indicating Vitória with her head, today's the day we're going to have trouble—and Ermelinda agreed in silence.

But on her way through the kitchen Vitória didn't even look

at them. She was worried about other problems—she'd made up her mind, for example, that it was finally time to cut down the old apple tree that only rarely produced fruit and even then it was acidic; and above all it took up so much good earth. But now the moment of decision had arrived, since lightning or wind had broken off a few branches that were dangling like old rags from the trunk.

Martim balked a bit: he thought it was too bad to destroy the beautiful tree. Vitória insisted and turned red from insisting so much. He was looking at her, listening to her arguments, and opposing a mute resistance. The woman wanted more and more for the tree to be taken down, as if the repugnance that the man was showing for that work were turning her on.

And so, after a few orders had been given to Francisco and other measures taken, Vitória followed Martim and his axe, and set herself up near the tree in order to watch—and was so resolute as if chopping it down would only take a few minutes. One of her feet had determinedly rested on a rock.

Martim started morosely to give the first circular cuts. She, as if prepared to watch a violent and rapid destruction, grew worried about the man's slowness, and could hardly control a face goaded on by the sun:

—Faster, she finally muttered quicker and in a low voice, no longer holding herself back.

He didn't turn around nor interrupt the slow rhythm of his blows.

—How long will it take for it to fall? the worried woman asked.

—Depends.

—Maybe you'd like me to get Francisco to help? maybe you can't do it all by yourself? she suggested already impatient for the answer.

—No need, he said at the same time that another total swing of the axe was vibrating. I do it slowly but surely.

"But I don't want slowly," she thought striking with her boot at the roots that were spread knottily and would pop out in excrescences even far from that old and black tree that, powerful, was hardly trembling beneath the blows of the axe. They fell silent, the sun was rising and gaining in power. It was a restless silence, full of flies. The axe blows took on a regulated rhythm— small chips were flying off moist and white showing how young the tree still was inside. The woman sat on one of the bumps of the roots, and the man without stopping his work looked at her quickly. The silence continued, the flies were shining filthily, bluish, the worried dogs were sniffing themselves. In the distance you could hear a whistle, in the distance a downswing; the flies were shining black.

The woman's heart started beating a lot when she finally asked with a calm face, but so unsettled that she didn't hear her own voice:

—Why did you come here, sir?

She heard nothing in reply. Only the blows of the axe were ringing out making the circle on the trunk deeper. And with great relief she came to believe that she hadn't spoken and that she'd only heard her own thought. Her ears, which had been prepared for an answer, only made out the murmur of the river. But he answered:

—I separated from my wife and left.

Still without realizing that only now was she finding out that he was married, she said:

—At first I thought you were on the run! she then said with much harshness.

—In a way, he said.

And having said it, he broke off his work without haste. He

tossed the axe into the distance. He turned around and looked at her straight on.

The woman went a bit pale. A slight tick made her mouth wrinkle at the same time as her left eye, which gave her the appearance of the guiltlessness of people caught in flagrante.

—You, ma'am, Martim noted without anger, wanted me to take down this tree just so you could keep me in one place and ask me questions.

—Me? of course not! she replied, and the truth had been so suddenly revealed to her that the woman felt innocent in the face of it.

—I already told you: I separated from my wife and left.

—But you looked like you were on the run … —she couldn't help herself saying full of curiosity.

—These are things a person runs from too, he answered with extreme watchfulness, without for a second taking his cold eyes from the woman's face.

They stood there looking at each other, both of their faces were raw in the open air, and reddened by the sun. There wasn't a wrinkle in the woman's face that wasn't exposed but since she didn't know it she suddenly lifted her head with great self-assurance.

Then, though the thick tree was only wounded, Martim turned to leave as if he'd finished the job.

—Stay, she said hastily. I want to talk!

—I've already told you, he repeated more roughly. I separated from my wife and left. Does the teacher need to know more than that? he added tranquil, cruel.

She didn't seem to have heard but blanched:

—That's not what I want to talk about! she cut him off quickly, surprised at herself.

Martim stood rigid waiting strictly as if planning to leave as soon as she said what she had to say.

—I want—I want to talk about Ermelinda, she suddenly made up.

He raised his eyebrows in sincere surprise, and his eyelids more open for an instant left his blue eyes quickly nude, in suspicion. The woman didn't immediately go on, as if she were sure that she'd keep him there longer with silence than with improbable words.

—What about her? he asked looking at her from the side in defense.

—Here's the thing, she said slowly as if there were no more rush since now inexplicably he seemed to be the one who had the haste of curiosity. Here's the thing, she repeated as if she still wasn't quite sure what to say.

Then squeezed by the man's now overbearing expectance, she repeated:

—Here's the thing: Ermelinda is a very impressionable person, really sensitive.

They stared at each other.

—The slightest thing has an impact on Ermelinda, any little thing makes her lose her composure. She—said Vitória licking her lips—she loses her balance over the silliest things. She's very impressionable, really very sensitive. When she came to live with me, just after losing her husband, I was well aware of the type of person I was going to have in the house, since, I don't know if you know this, sir, she spent her childhood bedridden. But she'd have to live somewhere and she didn't have any money, so she came here. Since Ermelinda is very sensitive, I feel a bit responsible for her, you understand? I always pay close attention to her life, you see? Oh, please, she's not unbalanced, oh not in the least: I've never seen anyone who loses herself less. But what happened is that she, being very kindhearted and charitable, didn't take the laws of spiritism as just symbols. She didn't quite understand what spiritism is and mixed it up a little with Catholicism, you understand, and then she ended up a bit different from us. Understand that I don't mean that her head isn't screwed on right. To the contrary. But she allowed herself the privileges of madness without being mad, said Vitória with the sudden avidity of admiration, and her face clenched up from envy and bitterness.

The intrigued man said yes with his head. And stood waiting for the sequel in vague suspicion, though his face in foreboding was already a bit malicious.

—So, said Vitória after a pause and once again running her tongue over her lips—so, since I'm responsible for Ermelinda …

She paused again, and this time looked at him indecisively no longer knowing what to say. But he, unappealable, was waiting.

—What I mean, the woman began again suddenly in a strong voice as if she were about to speak of an entirely different matter, what I mean is that it might have been good for you to be a bit careful. I mean: I know perfectly well that it's a bit much what I'm going to ask you, but I'd like you to keep her from one day becoming, let's say, interested in you, sir … Oh, no overly powerful feeling, she said subtly as if she understood the objection that would occur to him, no overly powerful feeling! she repeated with sudden assuredness for having had the chance to interrupt him with her penetration of spirit. Ermelinda isn't capable of that! But perhaps you might … Well, because I can't depend on her. She loses her cool at the slightest pretext, when she gets a little excited she immediately turns red, she gives little shouts … look, for example, she doesn't eat much, but if we encourage her by being a little friendly, she seems to think that she'll reciprocate our friendship by eating a lot, eating with the greed of a charwoman …

She suddenly stopped. Because, if before the man had waited with surprised eyes, now the capacity for laughter was clear on his face.

—I know, she continued stoically painfully wiping the sweat

from her forehead, I know that this isn't up to you, sir, oh I understand very well, you don't need to argue with me: I know very well that a person can, let's say, take an interest in someone without the other person, let's say, at least seeing it coming …

Could the horrible malice in the man be just that particular cast of his features, or was it also already his expression? Unease inhibited her, she waved the fly away from her chin.

—But the thing is, she then said nobly, since I can't count on the good sense of Ermelinda, who has, as I was saying a bit earlier, the possibility of one day becoming interested in you, sir, I therefore have to count on your own help! she concluded with relief as if she'd just laid out some very logical reasoning. A light triumph shivered in her voice: she'd never thought she finally manage to deliver herself of the nightmare of the phrases.

As for the man, he seemed quite content. And looked at her: she was so immaculate and satisfied!

—You, madam, fear that one day she'll go to bed with me, he said with enormous pleasure, is that what you're afraid of? But that would never happen, my lady! And now there's no longer even time for it: you, madam, are the one who knows this best, isn't that right? you and the teacher! But what sincerely shocks me is that a head as clean as your own could lower itself to imagine such a thing! by God you outrage me!

The woman went mute, her mouth agape … the man looked at her with meticulous attention, full of delight.

—What I mean—she suddenly responded, ignoring with difficulty his rudeness—what I mean is that, let's say, the world is too much for Ermelinda because she is very sensitive, the woman said forcing herself into a drawing-room tactfulness and, without realizing it, her hand had gone up to her neckline closing it a bit. The world, she concluded shocked without paying the slightest attention to what she was saying, is too much for Ermelinda, she can't stand it, she added all over.

—Yes she can, the man said unexpectedly in a morose tone, without looking at her but without running off.

The woman's heart gave a squeeze. Not because of what he'd said and what she'd hardly heard. But maybe because she hadn't expected any reply at all. Only now was she realizing that the two of them were standing there talking; only now was she seeing that she wasn't talking to herself. And, by God, neither had she made up that undeniable wound in the trunk of the tree, and she hadn't made up that feeling of soft offence that was coming from the man toward her, nor had she invented that sun that was blotching everything in her eyes: only now had she fully realized that she wasn't alone. And feeling that she'd communicated filled her with trembling excitement as if after having lifted a weight she saw with amazement that she'd already lifted it. She'd gone farther than she thought she ever could, and now it was too late to turn back. Even if nothing else happened, she could never deny what had already happened … She'd gone further ahead than she could turn back, and her skin shivered like the skin of a hen. Everything around her then seemed to her to be infected by the same possibility of ending up becoming real, a possibility suddenly sweetly revealed: the tree that was nearly intact was nonetheless ready to break, the sun of today that was nothing more than yesterday's rain, everything that was solid nonetheless always ready to break—and even in the eyes of the man the woman could almost make out the overwhelmed place that exists in the coldest eyes, the vulnerable place: possibility.

"And if I really spoke?", it occurred to her. Would the man understand her? Or not? And for an instant—in the face of multifarious unequal things that nonetheless were receiving in the field the same sun—for an instant there wasn't even a contradiction in his simultaneously understanding her and not understanding her as if that was the only way it could be. If she spoke? But how could she guess in that stubborn body of a man how much of her he'd understand. And deeper yet, more inexplicable yet—how could she herself know how much her own words would be the ones she spoke or the ones she left silent.

Just initiated into the sweetness of communication, any obstacle seemed to her impassable as if she'd been handed the miracle of the juice that feeds the plant and she then said: it's impossible. She didn't know that certain things either happen on their own or never happen at all. Accustomed to her own power of determination, she'd ended up thinking that she was walking because she wanted to and sleeping because that's what she'd made up her mind to do. And now she was thinking that before speaking it was essential to know how to speak. In a light despair of happiness she looked at the field and the weeds and the flies: and everything was making itself by itself, everything had the wisdom of living. But she—she didn't know how to make herself. How unhappy I am, she then said to herself tranquilly. But could unhappiness be that imminence toward which everything suddenly seemed to her to be leaning, and that great risk that a person runs? And if exactly that were our happiness. "I think this is what it means to be happy," she thought with curiosity. For if both of them were standing there talking ... for if the river was running fat and slow ... for when she raised her eyes the thick crown of the tree lit up ... for if the beetles were crackling in the air ... for if the instants never repeat and if knowing this is what gives us that delicate thirst ... what happiness could she desire besides this one? She wanted them to assure her that whatever she was feeling was so real that it was about to happen. She wanted—wanted for everything she knew no longer to be hidden.

—You didn't understand me, sir, she said swallowing her saliva in the severity of her joy, I don't mean that Ermelinda can't take it. Ermelinda could reciprocate, let's say, even love, but she wouldn't be able to resist. Ermelinda has the sickness of the soul, says … —she was going to add "says the teacher" but stopped herself in time.

The man didn't reply. Vitória felt that not only had she not convinced him but that he might think she'd said too much. And if that's what he thought that was because, unused to speaking, she herself had had the painful impression of having blathered with voluptuousness. She of all people, being accused of talking too much! pride stung her mixed up with pain:

—Everything in Ermelinda is hanging by a thread! she shouted at him as if that were a final order.

—And in you, ma'am? he inquired very calm.

Even before feeling the question with a little shock, because of what it was implying as a personal insult, Vitória unwrinkled all over: it was soft to hear him speak of her. "Ma'am, ma'am, ma'am." The respectful and sweet word was finally breaking something woven in her chest, she who had always been afraid of not being respected.

—Not in me, she replied without vanity. I am strong.

An instant later, and it occurred to her that in fact she'd just told the man that she was strong enough to stand love. Could she have simply offered herself to him? Her eyes blinked several times as if this thought had blinded them with surprise. Since she didn't speak much, she didn't quite know how much words usually reveal about thoughts, and her heart beat in horror: could the man have understood? And the worst thing, she thought in revolt, is that it was a lie: love wasn't what she wanted!

On Martim's silent face fortunately the expression was empty. She'd been afraid that he'd show he'd understood. And right afterward, for an instant, she wanted for exactly this to happen: for him to say he'd understood and for everything to collapse at last. In the next instant she'd kill him if he'd dared understand. She couldn't bear the idea that he would think it was obvious for her to love him, especially because it wasn't true, she revolted.

—All right, I'll be on my way, Martim said.

He went off and his boots were already starting to make a hollow noise on the wooden plank.

—Wait, she said with a rough voice, I'm not done speaking.

He turned around obedient, with the same rhythm of steps with which you walk away.

—I want to tell you, she said pale, that I wasn't asking you questions about your life, as you thought. Your life is of no interest to me. You work, you get paid, and that's all I need or want to know. Is that understood?

He laughed. For the first time he laughed:

—Understood.

He turned around once more in order to leave.

—Wait, she called. When I'm done speaking you can leave, sir, I'm not used to people turning their back on me.

Once again therefore he stopped. And once again headed back toward her. But this time he broke off his steps at a greater distance from the woman as if he knew that soon he'd be leaving and that soon she'd call him back: so he stopped halfway.

She was still standing straight up, hard. She was whiter.

—I also want to say that you, sir, shouldn't be so presumptuous as to judge by appearances. You don't want to say anything about your life, but I am well aware that you also don't want to be judged simply by what something might seem to be, since you are vain and disguised. So then don't judge, when you see an aging woman running a ranch, she said with great authority as if she'd said something intelligible.

When she'd said "aging" he hadn't protested but she thought she'd noticed a certain surprise in his eyes, and her heart tightened in joy.

—What I mean to say to you, she went on with pride, is that my life isn't just this—and she waved a trembling hand at the sunny lands of the farm.

—Those things aren't meant to be said, he murmured heavy, fleeing with his eyes.

—But I want to say them! she shouted quickly as if he might physically prevent her from going on. Listen, she said halfway between an order and a request, accustomed as she was to telling him what to do, listen.

—I'm not a priest, he said with brutality.

—But listen! she repeated with the same violence.

—I don't want to know your secrets, he then said very severe.

—You're scared, said Vitória illogically.

—Scared? ah not that either—since he'd noticed in time that she was trying to drag him into her life—ah that too is going too far. I'm not scared: it's that there's no point in speaking about such things.

—But listen! I mean to tell you that my life isn't just this.

—But why tell me? he exclaimed furious.

—Because I need a witness! she responded in a despair of rage. Don't think that my life is just this. What would you say, I wonder what you would say, sir, with that look of someone who looks down on other people's life, what would you say if I told you that I'm a kind of poetess! she cried.

Martim looked at her with such shock that she was paralyzed. A slightly yellowish color spread across the woman's surprised face.

—Then look, he suddenly said laughing and shrugging his shoulders, I wouldn't say a thing.

—I'm a kind of poetess, she repeated as if she hadn't heard his interruption, it's just that I don't write because I don't have time. But I collect sayings and thoughts, I have a huge collection, she said surprised and knowing she'd just ruined her collection forever in its secret and would never copy down another saying, because not being understood by the man was disorienting her. I collect thoughts, she said very uneasy. I have lots of inner life. I'm someone who's curious about life, she then exclaimed with sudden discomfiture, everything in this world interests me and I study in the open book of life. And my inner life is very rich, she said and shook her tied-up hair as if it were loose in curls.

Martim quickly looked at the tree as if he and the tree were exchanging a furtive glance.

—I even started a poem once, she said astonished, forcing herself to go on since she thought that speaking consists of saying everything, and at the same time she saw seeping toward nothing her uselessly sacrificed modesty. The poem started like this: "The queens who reigned in Europe in the year 1790 were four".—That man was going to know everything, and she'd be left with nothing … — But the poem wasn't going to be about queens, understand? she said almost crying with rage, it was just because of the beauty, understand?—but she knew that he didn't understand, she knew that success and failure were all there was, and between these two nothing existed, and that was why she'd never emerge from limbo in order to prove that through the phrase about the queens the poem would take its subtle momentum; and since she knew that she'd never prove to others the infinite grace that can lift off into flight from a simple phrase, then she, who only believed in success, didn't believe in the very veracity of whatever she was feeling; and there she was wound up in the inexplicable poetic phrase that once uttered had left her with four queens in her clumsy hand. —It was just because of the beauty! she said with violence.

They stood in silence. The woman was panting. But what she couldn't say to him, what she couldn't say is that she was a saint. That, opening her mouth several times in agony, she tried to do and couldn't. That, that you couldn't say to anyone.

—You needed to find a love, madam, he said with a serious

expression, and thought it was so funny that he grimaced in order to keep himself from laughing.

She looked at him incredulous, open-mouthed.

—What do you know about me or about anything! she finally said, and was so surprised with her audaciousness that she hardly knew what to reply.

—True, I don't know anything, he agreed softly. But I can try to find out. You, for example, just asked me why I came here. And you, ma'am, he asked somewhere between amused and cynical, why did you come here?

—How stupid, she said furious, that's such a stupid question, so stupid. It's as if I—as if I asked you this, as if I asked you: why are you alive!

—Because I have a certain instant in view, he said with smooth speed.

She looked at him perplexed, affronted. The man, satisfied with himself, looked at her smiling with impudence. But some thing in the woman's face made him blink his eyes in a feeling of discomfort. Like addicts who recognize one another, he'd just seen in her himself. Which was unpleasant. In her was that thing that also existed in him, and which he only didn't point out because it hurt inside him too and because, whoever had it, suffered from it. Martim averted his eyes.

—Anyway, she said pulling herself back together, if the question is "who" and "why" someone came here, that's for me to ask and not for you. You, sir, are positively not in a situation to ask, but to answer.

Martim made a tired gesture of agreement that revealed to what extent his patience was up. And since at the same time he'd opened his mouth, the woman thought with surprise that he'd finally answer her and say why he'd come to the farm … It was then that she made an energetic movement with her hand, preventing him from going on. Since Martim hadn't intended to answer her, he didn't understand what she meant by such a sudden movement, and looked at her intrigued.

She too had been astonished by the unexpected automatism of her own arm. The gesture had preceded her in her understanding of the gesture. She looked at Martim, surprised, attentive, as if in his face there might be the explanation for whatever it was that had only been revealed in his face that she didn't want to know the reason for his coming to the farm. It was as if, by knowing facts, she could lose the direct knowledge that only in that instant she noticed that she had of the man—for it was with surprise that she discovered that she knew him deeply. She only didn't know him superficially. But in her own skin she knew him, and from the moment she'd seen him for the first time: the way she'd known him had been the way she herself stood up straight when she saw him; one of the deepest ways of knowing someone was in the way you responded to what you were seeing. And now, looking at Martim, the woman was afraid to lose that unsubstitutible contact that was telling her about the most secret nature of that man standing there; and about whom, knowing nothing, she had the limitless knowledge that comes from looking at oneself and seeing. Facts so often disguised a person; if she knew facts she might lose the whole man.

Oh, hers was a blind knowledge. So blind that, knowing him, she nonetheless didn't understand him. It was a step before knowing. As if she'd gone through everything she didn't know about him and were heading straight to the patient beatings of that heart. "I know you in my skin," she thought in an unpleasant shiver, and the body cringed resentfully at that intimacy that had made of her he himself. And which was making her someone else. That someone else … Suddenly she was afraid of whatever it was she'd never know about herself. Since in her flesh she was understanding in silence that the rainy night had been more than a nightmare; that Sunday night had been the dark opening toward a world whose first joy we can hardly divine, and knowing that a person dies without knowing, and that there were hells to which she hadn't descended, and ways of grasping that the hand had not yet divined, and ways of being that out of great courage we ignore. And that she herself was the other never-worn person. In more than fifty years of life she'd learned nothing essential that could be added to what she already knew—and whatever in those years had remained intact had been exactly whatever she hadn't learned.

And one of the things that nobody had taught her was that strange way she had of knowing a man.

—And you, ma'am, why did you come here, Martim repeated resigned to wasting time since she wouldn't let him go. His gentle tone came from knowing that, if he repeated the question enough times, that woman, who was just waiting for a simulacrum of insistence, would end up talking.

Vitória made an impatient gesture, her face got ready to reply to the insolence. But unexpectedly she calmed down and said:

—I didn't have anything to do in Rio. I came to here to create a life, to make my life.

—And did you? he asked irritated.

—But I know one thing! she exploded. That only saintliness saves! that you have to be the saint of a passion or the saint of an action! or of a purity, that only saintliness saves!

Martim looked at her white with rage, trembling without knowing why.

—What? she asked vigorously. I'm just wearing out your freedom! what, sir, so you don't recognize it? she said with great austerity.

She wasn't exactly sure what she was referring to, and he understood without being exactly sure what she was referring to. But if it had been any other way, their mutual understanding would have been poor, our understanding that is made through lost words and through meaningless words, and it is as hard to explain why someone was overjoyed and why another was devastated—because we don't count on the miracle of lost words; and that's why it was always so worthwhile to live because many were the spoken words that we hardly heard but they were spoken.

For an instant neither hesitated to comprehend one another inside the incomprehension:

—I do recognize it, he then answered entering for a brief second into a more perfect world of understanding, we who have a fineness of comprehension that escapes us. From which Martim immediately exited in order to look with astonishment at that woman who had said nothing and with whom, nevertheless, he had just agreed. He looked at her, and as always it seemed to him that he wasn't getting the main thing about her or about anyone else—though it was this principle that he had to come to terms with blindly.

—Well then, said the woman, don't be surprised at what you yourself provoked: my freedom, she said, and then she was surprised because she realized that she didn't know what she was saying and that she'd gotten lost in a play of words.

Then they remained silent as if in order to give to that thing, which had the fragility of an indiscernible mistake, time to be reabsorbed by forgetfulness.

But upon seeing the man's somber face, the lady didn't know how to interpret it and feared that she'd frightened him. Though she was nasty, she'd always had the painstaking compassion not to scare other people with the truth:

—No, she then said quick and begging, you, sir, oughtn't think I meant I was pure or saintly, she explained to him like a mother who assures her son that she is none other than his mother so that her son won't become the son of a stranger and won't become a stranger himself. You didn't understand what I meant when I spoke of saintliness. Don't think that I meant by that that I'm good, she went on because, more than anything else, she didn't want him to think she was "superior" and then admire her with disdain. —I didn't mean that I'm good, she repeated, forcing herself to a frankness that hurt her but that gave her almost immediately a relief and a resignation—I never did a thing for the poor in Vila Baixa, all I do is suffer on their behalf. Don't let it cross your mind that I mean that I'm a saint … —Her chest ached with joy because, at least in a negative way, she was telling him the truth—and how else to tell the truth, except by denying it delicately? how else to tell the truth, without the danger of giving it the emphasis that destroys it and how to tell the truth, if we pity it? more than fear, pity.

The woman felt calm knowing that she hadn't confessed simply because the man hadn't received her for confession: nothing then had been said. She was needing to speak, yes; but she was tactfully avoiding being understood. As soon as she was understood, she'd no longer be that profoundly untransmissible thing that she was and that made every person be his own person—since Vitória thought that was what happened in communication. Could it be from that surrender of the self that she was protecting herself? or was it fear of the imperfection with which souls touch one another? But she wasn't just scared of that. It was that, lacking the apprenticeship in communication, she had the instinctive delicacy of abstaining.

—I didn't mean by that that I'm pure—she tried to calm the man down. My soul is dirty, my life is gruesome, I'm not good, I … —Saintliness was a violence for which she lacked the courage; somehow a rotten person was more charitable than a saint, saintliness was a scandal for which she lacked the courage. —I'm rotten, you understand? I'm rotten as … I'm rotten as a disappointed woman! she said unexpectedly with a certain coquettishness.

—Disappointed? he said leaning toward her chivalrously and attaching himself without realizing it to the dignity the woman was wanting to lend to her confessions.

—In myself, she concluded gloriously, shaking her tied-back hair.

Oh God, lady, how you bore me, Martim thought.

"He doesn't see you," Vitória then thought in an effort to transmit her gaze of which Martim only noticed the effort but not the meaning, "he doesn't see that if I wanted to I'd be up for anything, did my life have to be pure? And I wanted to be up for anything and got ready every single day. Not moral purity," she thought. And in that moment Vitória realized that, by mistake, she'd ended up falling into moral purity and that, as a life, she'd never reached purity … That was more or less what happened, and then she said to him a bit astonished:

—I am not pure …

Lady, how you bore me, Martim thought. "That entanglement of a woman who was afraid to die — is that what it is?", he wondered, since Ermelinda was as alive as a flower is alive, duality confounded him; "and the entanglement of a woman who was afraid to live — is that what this is?", he also wondered confused, since that woman had in her ashen wrinkles more death than life, and yet it was life she was afraid of; "and the entanglement of a man who … of a man who didn't want to be afraid?" Yes, and meanwhile the sacred cows. Was that it? But to have given those words to facts that weren't even facts, ended up being unsatisfactory for the man. So, failing to define what was happening to them, and because Martim wanted, even without her hearing it, for there not to be the slightest doubt about his feelings, he thought quite clearly: "You bore me. I know all this and I don't care. Maybe there's nothing else besides this anxiety, but I don't want any more of it. I simply want you to go to hell," he concluded somber, "I don't care about this any more." He looked at her. Probably an impoverished body that was trying to take shelter in thoughts? the body that, when exacerbated, could become spirit.

The confused woman was being so sincere, that the veins of her neck were popping out in the effort to speak the truth—or to lie, it didn't matter to Martim. He had nothing to do with any of this. And he was tempted to say to her absurdly: "I know you're telling the truth but, to be honest, I don't believe you." Oh, the boring female. Sometimes that man was so nauseated by women that it strengthened him all over in his own clean masculinity. And now, out of pure satiety, if that woman was at an extremity he wanted exactly the opposite extremity.

In sudden fatigue, cornered by the woman, all that Martim in that instant would ask of men and women is that they be unaware of themselves, with just the little light that is enough in order to get out of the dark, the light of the dog's eyes in the darkness of the dog: that was all that now, so tired, he was wanting; because it wasn't much, because it was more than enough. "You wear me out," he thought heavy, rude. Indifference was making him look at her with the crude precision with which he'd watch a writhing ant. "At the point where I am now, mute and tired, I'm sickened by the contortions of the soul and sickened by words", he thought. At the point where he was, he was big and his hands were covered with calluses, and the soul is big, the trees are big. The sun was big and the earth extensive. All it really lacked was another race of men and women—the race he'd create, if he could. With sudden brutality, the man thought that "living was the only thought that anyone can have," and that the rest was just the words of women like Vitória, and living was the maximum conquest and the only way to respond with dignity to a tall tree. For, recalling the noble decency that existed in his tertiary plot, at that moment that's how Martim wanted to be.

And the woman who was there ... —he looked at the stranger. Mouth, teeth, belly, woman, arms, all that had had the chance to be a clean plant. But all of it corroded and wrecked and lifted by the spirit. You bore me, you're a mistake, you're the mistake of a plant. "From now on," he discovered with a tiredness that right then removed from the discovery the dazzle that one day he'd feel when he understood what it meant and when he figured out how much love there was in this—"from now on I want whatever is the same as something else and not what's different from something else. You talk too much about things that shine; yet there's a pith that doesn't shine. And that's what I want. I want the extreme beauty of monotony. There's some thing that is dark and doesn't glow—and that's what matters. You annoy me with your fear, since even that shines. From now on I want whatever is the same as something else." And she still had the nerve to tell him she was someone who'd been disappointed.

—You're afraid, ma'am, he said using futilely any old seriousness and trying, out of a certain politeness, to match the tone of an abstract polemic that the woman, in the sun, was making a point of keeping elegant.

The lady could barely believe what she'd heard:

—Afraid?!

Afraid? her? Her impulse was to laugh, as if laughter could reply to such an absurdity. Afraid? She shook her head, incredulous. She who kept the ranch in line like a man. She who ordered around that man standing there, unafraid of herself or of him? She who deafly had fought the drought and had conquered it! she who had known to wait for it to rain. Afraid? She who walked with dirty boots and with her face bared without being afraid of ever being loved. She who was courageously depleting her father's inheritance in order to keep that ranch running, without even wanting to know why, courageously waiting for the uncertain day when that farm would be the biggest one in the area, and then she could finally open the gates. Afraid?

Her whole body revolted against everything there was of incomprehension in the man, and of injurious in the word, all of her got ready for a gesture that would make her own indignation burst out, but none of them seemed strong enough. Afraid! She looked at him, surprised, bitter; what did he know about her, that man. How could he ever understand her great courage, that man whom she was now looking straight in the face without the least fear—for the first time noticing in that face how stupid it was: on the closed forehead you could guess at his difficulty in thinking, there was a painful effort in the face of that man. And she shook her head, bitter, ironic. Because she knew he was an engineer, she'd never really thought about his intelligence. But looking at him stripped bare, how stubborn and slow he was. The man's face had the sleepwalking perseverance of the stupid.

—Afraid, yes, he said patiently as if speaking to a child.

The repeated injury made her shiver, and this time all of her got ready to retort with an insult. Her afraid … her mouth twisted in sarcasm.

But instead the features of her face suddenly surrendered. She couldn't take it any more. Afraid, yes. Afraid, yes. She remembered that being afraid had been the solution. She remembered how once she'd accepted humbly being afraid like someone who kneels and with a lowered head receives baptism. And how her courage, from that point on, had been that of living with fear. Her, afraid? And suddenly, as if vomiting out her soul, she cried with pride her fifty years of muteness:

—Afraid, yes! what do you know about any of that, sir, afraid, yes. So listen and try to take it if you can, take it if you're not afraid. I've been afraid before. I took care of my old father for years, and when he died I ended up alone—The woman interrupted herself: when her father had died, she in one stroke had ended up with all of herself for herself alone; and in the awkward urge of people who get a late start and already without any talent for it, she'd wanted for the first time to do what was called "living", and which in a first and hesitant step of glory would be to go by herself to a hotel and stay by herself and concentrate and have the highest part of herself like a monk in a cell, and it would be in that furtive way that she'd make her first bow to ... to what?— I'd gone to be by myself and concentrate, she said with vanity, and I cut myself off from everyone and took a boat with my suitcase—but already when I was on the boat, already on the boat that bad thing was happening that I recognized, that ordeal, that almost good but dangerous feeling—I'd hardly set foot on the boat which was wobbling all over, and everything was already touching me and leaving me aching, curious, alive, full of curiosity—but wasn't that what I'd wanted? wasn't that exactly what I'd gone off to find? it was, but why didn't I want to realize what was happening? why was I looking at everything with a head held high, faking it? I reached the island in the evening—my heart tightened when I saw the big old hotel with the high-ceilinged parlors and the flies in the dining room, and the people were resting on the terrace and looked at me walking through them, I was begging their pardon; that place was lacking the protection that exists in the smallness of a cell, I'd gotten it completely wrong. I didn't know anyone on the terrace and I didn't let anyone guess that that's what was making my heart thump. I put my suitcase in my room, but I felt an urge to take the boat and go back, but that would mean failure! somehow I'd gone to suffer whatever was happening to me, since wasn't that the life I'd wanted? and if

I wasn't up to accepting it, just because it was cruder than I'd expected—that would be failure and desertion. But much stronger than the shame of deserting was the anticipation of what a night alone in that room would mean, so I went down the stairs, and without the slightest shame I asked for the timetable for the return boats, and to my fright the horror was confirmed: they told me that only the next morning. So I went out of the hotel calmly, but outside was the open and bright air, it was evening, and there was the blue sea with the horizon with the finest line I ever saw to this day, and the beauty was such a pain, and I was so alive, and the only way that I'd learned to be alive was to feel helpless, I was alive, but it was as if there were no answer for being alive. So I went quickly back to the hotel, driven out by the light of the beach, and swallowed with so much courage my dinner amidst the strangers. After dinner I tried to take a little walk in the night outside the hotel, since wasn't that what I'd planned? wasn't it that encounter with my own day and the encounter with the night itself? but outside the hotel was the beach shimmering all over in the dark. Lovely, all white with lots of sand, with the dark sea, but the foam, I remember that the foam was white in the dark and I thought that the foam looked like lace, there was no moon but the foam was white like lace in the dark. Then I went quickly back to the room and quickly transformed into the daughter of an old father because only as a daughter had I known calm and composure, and only now was I realizing the security I'd lost with the death of my father, and I made up my mind that from now on I wanted to be nothing more than I'd always been before, nothing more. I put on a clean and ironed nightgown because that was a pleasure I used to have, and I combed my hair quite a bit because those were the habits by which I understood myself and recognized myself, and I smoothed out my hair so much with the brush until I managed to make myself a thing that was neither crude nor exposed. I was full of flattery for myself: I was treating myself with ceremony and trying to see if I could find a way to feel some camaraderie with the frightened coward I was being—and who so repulsed me—but I pretended that everything was perfect, I even sighed with comfort in bed with the book in my hand, the book I thought I'd never open on the island. I knew that my eyes weren't reading, but I'd never let myself be convinced that I was pretending, and that I hadn't come in search of reading on an island, I was trying to ignore that God was giving me exactly what I'd asked for and that I—I was saying "no." I was pretending that I didn't notice that I'd constructed a whole hope for whatever was finally happening to me, but that there I was wearing glasses with the open book, as if I loved so much that I could only shout "no". But I also knew that if in that exact moment I didn't take up the calm thread of my previous life, then my balance would never return, and never would my things be recognized by me. And that's why I was pretending to read—but I was hearing the waves of the sea, I was hearing, I was hearing! That was when all the lights in the hotel suddenly went out. Just like that, all at once, without a sound, without the slightest warning, nothing. Only the next day did I find out that at nine o'clock the lights went out to save electricity, all the lights went out, and I sat there with my book open in my hand, I ended up in the dark as I'd never been before, only last night did I end up in that dark for the second time in my life—just like that, with that simple way of being in the dark, I never had been, and I'd never been in the dark with the sea. It was as dark as if I were looking for the hotel and didn't know where it was, the only touchable thing was the book in my hand—the fear, the fear you accused me of, sir, didn't leave me a single movement, but after the surprise passed—then something burst through that I had really barely held back until that instant—the beauty of the beach burst through, the fine line of the horizon burst through, the solitude I had voluntarily arrived at burst through, the swaying of the boat that I'd thought was so nice burst through, and the fear burst through of the intensity of joy that I can reach— and no longer able to lie, I cried praying in the dark, praying something like "never again, oh God never again let me be so daring, never again let me be so happy, take away once and for all my courage to live; may I never again go so far ahead inside of myself, may I never again allow myself, so merciless, grace", because I don't want grace, because I'd rather die without ever having seen than to have seen a single time! because God in his goodness allows, you hear, allows and advises people to be cowardly and to protect themselves, His favorite sons are those who dare but He is severe toward those who dare, and benevolent toward those who don't have the courage to look straight on and He blesses those who abjectly take care not to go too far in rapture and in the search for joy, disappointed He embraces those who don't have the courage. He knows that there are people who can't live with the happiness that's inside them, and so He gives them a surface they can live off of, and gives them a sadness, He knows that there are people who need to fake it, because beauty is arid, why is beauty so arid? and so I said to myself "be afraid, Vitória, because being afraid is salvation." Because things mustn't be seen straight on, nobody's that strong, only those who are damned have strength. But for us joy has to be like a star smothered in the heart, joy has to be nothing more than a secret, our nature is our great secret, joy ought to be like a radiance that the person never, never ought to let escape. You feel a pang and you don't know where: that's how joy ought to be: you shouldn't know why, you should feel like: "but what's wrong with me?"—and not know. Though when you touch some thing, that thing shines because of the great secret that was smothered—I was afraid, because who am I without restraint? When the next day I was sitting on the boat I thought I'd died. But as if, before dying, I had taken communion.

Martim was pale. Oh what he would give to offend that naked and shameless face.

—I don't believe a word of it, he said.

But as if they had understood each other beyond the reach of words, the woman wasn't offended by what he'd said. Nor did he repeat it, as if he really hadn't opened his mouth. He just averted his eyes because he didn't want to see that face that was aching. And she, she just sighed. They were as tired as if they'd performed some violent exercise. Somehow the woman's stupid explosion had done them both good, since inexplicably, besides being tired, both of them had now calmed down.

Anyway nothing seemed to have happened. Nothing is as destructive of spoken words as the sun that keeps on burning. They stood in silence, giving themselves the time to forget. Through a tacit pact they'd forget that slightly ugly thing that had happened. Neither of them was young and they had some experience: some things a person has to have the manliness not to notice, and take mercy on ourselves and forget, and have the tact not to notice—if you wanted to keep a moment of comprehension from crystalizing us, and life from becoming something else. Neither of them was young, and they were prudent. So, then, after the explosion, they remained silent as if nothing had happened because nobody can live from fright, and nobody can live from having vomited or having seen someone vomit, those weren't things you should think about much: they were the facts of a life.

The lady wiped the sweat from her face and looked, at a glance, at that narrow forehead, at that frizzy hair. Once again calm human stupidity was restored on his face, that opaque obtuse solidity that is our great strength. They looked at each other in the void of the eyes. Without pain, one seemed to ask the other: who are you? The main thing about the other, as they looked at each other, they weren't getting, and yet it was once again the main thing they were dealing with. Until, because they were so empty, their eyes started to fill up and become individual, and each was no longer imprisoned by its absorption in the other. Then they looked at each other frankly, as if touched by the same sentiment: "let's be frank since life is short." But they looked at each other merely frankly, without having anything to say, except this: extreme frankness. Afterward they averted their eyes without grief, in mutual agreement, experienced; and once again waited an instant for frankness, which never has words, to have time to pass, and they could go on living.

Without pressing, she said calmly as if they'd just had a friendly chat:

—Naturally, if on that night on the island I'd known that it would all blow over, I would have taken the risk of being unhappier. But while it's happening you always think it's eternal. And it also just so happens that while it was happening I didn't understand that I was getting exactly what I'd gone there to look for, I didn't recognize it totally, and thought I was making a mistake. Naturally, after that, my approach started being much more careful. I already knew that you shouldn't go directly, the way I had. Never directly, she said as if in a recipe. I also want to tell you that I was afraid, yes, but not because I felt sorry for myself. I don't feel sorry for myself, she said without vanity.

And, by God, she didn't.

—It was just a question of learning that you don't go directly, she then said conciliatory. And I learned that by myself. Always by myself, she added with a certain simplicity.

—Why did you never think to ask for help from someone? he asked annoyed, not quite knowing what he was saying.

—Don't you understand, sir, she said irritated once again, that

I can't ask? because I need so much that nobody could ever give me? don't you see that I would ask for more than they could ever give me?—In her exacerbation the lady was forgetting that she had no right to be irritated, since, if the man were listening to her, it was just as a favor or because she'd forced him to listen; and forgetting that he, after all, had nothing to do with any of that.

—Nobody, said Martim unexpectedly emphatic, nobody can ask for more than they can receive from someone else! Human nature, he said very satisfied, is all the same: nobody can ask for more than someone else can give, because asking and giving is all the same act, and one wouldn't exist without the other—and besides, nobody makes up something that doesn't exist, ma'am: if asking was invented, that's because the answer exists of giving! he said very firm and contented.

—But ask whom? she bellowed.

—Well, said Martim stumbling and already losing interest, that's the question. But something else also exists—he added suddenly serious and voluptuous—something else also exists: you have to know the technique of asking! because, ma'am, things aren't that way at all, ma'am! it's not just saying "gimme!", and that's the end of it! You often have to trick the one you're asking, he said intimately, sensual. You have to, in a manner of speaking, ask in disguise. You, madam, who are an intelligent and well-read lady, must have learned this too. Let us, for example, imagine that you were married and needed a pair of shoes, he said suddenly extremely interested in the problem, while the woman was staring at him with eyes baffled by surprise. If you needed a pair of shoes, the most advisable thing to do would never be to say to your husband: gimme shoes! The advisable thing would be to say bit by bit every day: my shoes are old, my shoes are old, my shoes are old, said Martim unable to keep himself from laughing. You understand? he said, and your husband one fine day would wake up in the morning and, without in the least knowing why, would say something like this: Vitória, my love, I'm going to give you a pair of shoes! Because in order to ask for help you also need technique! Getting a request is very frightening to people who, nevertheless, madam, sometimes are desperate to give, do you see what I'm saying? you need technique! For everything, moreover, you need technique! For example, he went on enthusiastically, you can only manage to express what you mean, for example, when you express it well! You need technique. You need to know how to live in order to live, because the other side, madam, is lying in wait for us at every step: a blunder and all of a sudden a man who's walking along looks like a monkey! a single misstep, and instead of being aghast people laugh! A weakness, madam, and love is perdition. This requires art, madam, great art, since without it life makes mistakes. And great wisdom: since time is short, you have to choose in a fraction of a second between one word and another, between remembering and forgetting, you need technique!

—Technique? she repeated stupefied.

—That's right, he said bored with the knowledge to which she'd forced him.

The lady was looking at him, entirely imbecilic. The man smiled embarrassedly, without knowing how to get out of the jam he'd got himself into:

—I'm going to the stables, he then said in a low voice, with discreet modesty as if asking if he could go to the bathroom.

But she suddenly awoke:

—Listen.

The insistence on the same word was starting to wear the man down and make him give in. He stopped once more. He was feeling used by that woman as if she were slowly turning him effeminate: there were women like that, who broke whatever they touched. Like a suction cup, she was extorting something from him; something that wasn't precious, but at the end of the day was he. What she was doing with whatever she was extorting, he didn't know. He looked at her without pleasure, without curiosity. He no longer seemed to have any strength to resist the word "listen" which ended up breaking him, resigned. With slowness, without the least defense, he braced himself to listen to her.

—Listen, she then repeated, more gently like a mother who scared her child with an involuntary cry. Listen: before I came here, I was different, she then said as if going back to the beginning of time, which gave the man a prior fatigue, and his face a heroic expression of sacrifice. Not that I really was different, the lady added with certain kindness, but because I didn't always have this farm.

She paused. Because—working hard to show consideration for the man she was somehow nullifying—the meaning of what she had intended to say had escaped her. The heat had left them moist and salty.

—I was living in Rio, she went on, and her tone tried to be unpretentious as if having lived in the city would enlarge her too greatly in the man's eyes. But I myself was the one who wanted to come here. I know, I know it was a mistake, you don't have to tell me, the lady added with that vanity of hers that was so easily susceptible. But I was led astray, what can I do? to err is human, I was led astray like a woman led astray by the promises of a man—oh, no, there wasn't a man, if that's what you mean or at least are thinking, she interrupted herself flattered by the hypothesis that might have occurred to Martim. But how can I explain it to you? she asked, as if he were eager to understand, though there was no question in the man's resigned face. Because I thought I could find here …

What had she, actually, come to find? The passion for living? Yes, she'd come to find the passion for living, discovered the disappointed woman, and a bead of sweat dropped sadly from her nose.

—I'm going to tell you how it happened, she then said with effort, and probably that woman had already had her speech prepared for years. This is how it started: once some relatives came to visit us in Rio, and I left Ermelinda to take care of my father, and I went around showing them the city, I mean showing it to my relatives. We always went by car, my uncle rented a car. It was already getting cold … We went so far, but so far, driving around, driving around … I'd never seen such wide highways, it was cold, every day I wore a new blue dress I'd never had a good occasion to wear. And we ate in a lot of restaurants! to have fun and also to get to know the restaurants. It was the first time I'd ever done things like that … eating stewed meats with sauces … I have to tell you—she informed him—that I always had a certain disgust for fatty foods, I always preferred dry things, my food was always so simple! since I'd already ended up adopting even my father's diet …

—But in the meanwhile, continued the woman with a face suddenly brightened by pleasure and by the unexpected access to an unreachable ideal, in the meanwhile on enormous platters the fatty pork chops kept arriving, and when I was leaving the restaurant, you could see that the fruits at the grocery store were bursting and then … —She went quiet. Interrupting herself, however, only made her feel, as if brought by the breeze, the scent coming from inside the grocer's, the whiff of rotten pineapples and the hot feathers of hens—and she then smiled with her face bright, mysterious.

—When I was leaving the restaurant, I'd also put my new jacket on my shoulders, but not even because of the cold, only because it seemed to me that some thing was happening to me. I don't know, she said wiping away the sweat painfully, but it was as if I'd seen that things are much more than their dry shell, see what I mean? it was as if I'd seen that, if before I'd been nauseated, that was because already then I was aware that the danger was underneath the dryness—I don't know why, but during those days of travel it seemed to me that everything that existed was—was horribly ripe, you know what I mean? and I was feeling as tired as if I was about to fall sick. To tell you the truth, it didn't even feel like winter. It's incredible, but it didn't, and the cars honking, the groceries so full of fruit ... the fruit almost rotten, almost—almost I don't know what, said Vitória sweetly, loving, and, because of her pure intimacy with the man, didn't try to explain herself better.

Martim took his handkerchief from his pocket and wiped his face. The woman saw that he wasn't understanding. But now it was sweetly too late to stop, now it didn't even matter that he didn't understand. She stood for a moment with a ragged gaze, reduced to remembering by herself how at the restaurant her mouth shined with the dripping sauce, which slightly repulsed her; how in those days it had seemed to her that you had to be moved by ugly things; and then, with a nausea that she suddenly couldn't separate from love, she'd admitted that things are ugly. The smell of the grocery seemed like a hot smell of dirty people, and you had to be moved by those things that were so imperfect that they seemed to be begging for her understanding, her support, her forgiveness and her love; happiness was weighing down her stomach, in those days. Yes, and she'd felt that she could love all that. It was surprising, it was horrible; as if it were a wedding night.

In that instant the woman shivered, remembering that exactly those strange days of happiness had brought her later to go off to the island by herself—in search of more. And that, then, she'd failed.

She looked distrustfully at the man, without seeing him. It no longer even hurt her that Martim didn't understand her. Because a woman eventually has to speak.

—During the days of that trip, she informed him with humility, it was as if I were about to get sick …

—Maybe because the food was fatty? he suggested with his head boiling under the sun and his dry hair crackling.

"A man without a vocation should at least have the advantage of being free," Martim digressed absorbed. But everyone was summoning him to exercise an occupation. And the truth is that, under the sun, he was as definitively entangled as he'd been before; wherever a man might step, a city was installed, all that was missing were tramways and cinemas. Ermelinda wanted him to … what was it exactly that Ermelinda wanted? And Vitória was forcing him to receive her for confession. It was hard not to go along. Vaguely then a new explanation for his crime was born in Martim—that crime that kept getting more elastic and amorphous, and the man already had left it so far behind that he really seemed to have committed an abstract crime, and in fact his crime now seemed more like a sin of the spirit, merely. Thus, under the sun, persecuted by the presence of Vitória, he thought thus: "that the only way to be free, the way a man without a vocation has a right to be, had been to commit a crime, and make other people no longer recognize him as one of them and demand nothing of him; but if that was the right explanation, then his crime had been useless: as long as he himself survived, other people would call him." Burning under the sun, it seemed to that man tired from the unslept Sunday night, that this was the most reasonable explanation for his crime. Worried, he also knew that he was just digressing.

That's when it occurred to him that this was the right time to be arrested. So that they could tell him, at last, what his crime had been. It was time to be arrested and let other people judge him, since he—he'd already made a legend of himself.

—It's possible, said Vitória distressed, it's possible that the meat really was very fatty, and I'd been following my father's diet for so long! she added distracted.

They stood in silence, the man scratched himself.

—Did you consult a stomach specialist, ma'am? asked Martim, not exactly because he didn't understand her but because he was trying to see if, reducing honestly what she was saying to a question of something the doctor could take care of, everything would return to its real proportions.

—The fact is that it was slightly because of those days of travel that, years later, I thought I shouldn't sell the farm I inherited from my aunt, and decided to live here, she concluded unexpectedly, frightened as if she'd reached the goalpost long before she expected to, and without at least being ready to get there.

—Ah, he said as if he'd understood.

Once again they stood in silence. The woman had finally stopped wringing her hands.

—I think, she said in a final sigh, I think that I thought I could find at this farm whatever happened to me on the days of that trip. I mean, those things I was seeing when I'd come out of restaurants. Of course, not in the impossible way like I wanted to find on the island. To find here, yes, but within my reach, every day and bit by bit within my reach—she said, she herself feeling irremediably obscure, and capsizing in the inexplicable.

And suddenly everything seemed to her to be really inexplicable. It's true that living in the countryside had come to give a passion to her purity; it's true that during the first months she'd been touched by the plenitude of the laziness with which the plants would grow straight upwards, and that in the first months nature had come to lend an ardor to her confusion. Yes, that was true ... But it was also true that, down paths that were now impossible to retrace, she'd ended up falling into the cruel brutality of a moral purity; and her arteries had grown rigid like those of a judge.

Yet that wasn't the only truth! she claimed, since there she was, tough woman, blossoming so simply in front of a man who wasn't even hearing her, like a drop of water that no longer can bear its own weight and falls wherever it falls; the thing had enough power of self-direction in order to happen by itself. And it was also true that at the same time in which she'd stiffened into a morality that she herself didn't understand, she'd drawn nearer on the inside, without at least knowing it, from deprivation to deprivation, to some living thing.

—I suppose, she said to the man, that I thought I might find all that at the ranch. But afterward—she added surprised as if only now realizing it—afterward I got a bit mixed up …, she said and smiled awkwardly, forgivable, with the charm of helplessness on her face.

What Martim had least expected was a smile. And he awoke intrigued. Becoming retrospectively more alert, he managed to reproduce in his ears the end of the woman's phrase: "I got a bit mixed up." It was, however, that phrase that, less clarifying than any other, seemed to transmit to the man a kind of total comprehension, as if, out of tenderness, he was no longer unaware of anything about that woman. In the effort of looking at her and of understanding her, the material of the man's face had ripped open at last, and a kindly expression came to the surface, the shadow perhaps of a thought.

Vitória noted it, moved, sad, modest:

—As I was saying, that was why I came here. It was a mistake. But I do so many other things for the same reason that I can't explain it! she said simple, perplexed. It's as if there were some event awaiting me, and then I try to go toward it, and I keep trying, trying. It's an event that surrounds me—it's owed to me, it resembles me, it's almost me. But it never came closer. If you'd like, sir, you can call it destiny. For I've tried to go out to meet it. I feel this event the way you feel an affliction. And it's as if, after it happens, I'd become someone else, she added tranquil. Sometimes I get the impression that my destiny is just to have a thought I haven't yet had. I long for that event, yes, but at the same time I've done everything I could to put it off, I don't know how to explain it to you. I've even already longed for this time now, in which I'm living without it—since I got used to a way in which at least everything is, for better or worse, in a place. Often I felt that if I gave up, but really gave up, the event would come closer. But since I'm scared, I avoid it. Even before going to sleep I read in order not to allow it any room to happen... But once—she said serene—once, while I was waiting for a tram, I got so distracted that when I snapped out of it, when I snapped out of it there was wind in the street and the trees, and people were walking by, and I saw that the years were passing, and a guard signaled to a woman to cross the street. Then, you understand, sir? then I felt that I, I was there—and it was in a manner of speaking the same thing as if the event were there... I don't even know what event it was, because almost before feeling it, I already recognized it—and without even giving myself the time to learn its name, I in a manner of speaking had already fallen to my knees before it, like a slave. I swear I don't know what got into me, but my heart was beating, I was I, and whatever needed to happen was happening. Oh, I know that if I got so scared it was because being on the street had nothing to do with my father, nor with my life, nor with myself, it was something so isolated as if it were an event—and yet, despite all that, I was there surrounded by wind, the tram going by, with my heart beating as if I'd just had a thought. That was one of the times in which I had the greatest contact with what I like to call "my destiny." I felt it the way you feel a thing with your hand.

The man looked at her austere, serious, without understanding. Because beauty was upon the woman's face.

—What you needed, ma'am, was someone by your side who backed you up, he said like a priest. Everything we don't understand, is solved by love. You needed to find a love.

But instead of getting annoyed she replied with a hoarse voice:

—I've had so many, she said hoarsely. When I was young I had so many.

They looked at each other with interest, but a bit tired.

—Once, she said with sudden clumsiness, once I was spending the holidays with my aunt, how funny, right here! it was right here! she said faking astonishment just in order to lend some interest to the story—It was right here, when my aunt was still alive! what an odd coincidence, my God, life sure is like that.

Since the woman had stopped, he said without much patience:

—And then?

—It was the first time I'd ever set foot on this farm, and I never thought it would end up being mine, she went on striking again the note of coincidence. I was on holiday and I saw an older boy lighting a bonfire in the middle of the field. I stood there looking, there was a boy looking too! she exclaimed guaranteeing the veracity of the fact, that boy's actually already dead, she said hoarsely. I saw the older boy lighting the bonfire, the hot dust of the leaves was flying, warming up—warming a person up. The boy who already died said a thing, if I'm not mistaken I even think he said this: look at the bonfire. The older boy said nothing and kept feeding the bonfire, his face kept getting darker, darker and darker with the flames, also because it was almost nighttime. And I ... was there—I, very young, very pretty, I was crazy oh crazy and nobody knew, when I remember what went through my head, I was so idealistic! standing there, just like that, and I—I loved that boy, I loved that boy and loved the bonfire he was lighting. He didn't say a single word! a single word.

Since she'd spoken of love, almost grudgingly and conquering a sudden discretion, the man glanced at her body, looked at it roughly, without mercy, without malice. To tell the truth, she wasn't half bad. Martim suddenly looked at her watchful, mistrustful, as if they'd been tricking him all this time: since she was something that was "the same," she wasn't something "different." He then averted his gaze, with caution:

—And he surely loved you too, ma'am, he said hiding his discomfort.

—But he knew I was there, she retorted. I was young, I didn't have a drop of makeup on my face, I was pretty, idealistic, I was wearing my new red coat, he knew I was there.

—And so that was your love? Martim asked with a delicacy that she hadn't thought he was capable of.

—Yes, she said a bit disappointed, wiping away the sweat. That too was my love.

—It lasted as long as the bonfire, said Martim foolishly, maybe trying to copy situations in the past or things he'd read; but his tone sounded uncertain, he didn't know how to spare her from facing the poverty of her love story.

—It lasted as long as the bonfire, she repeated surprised looking at him. But if you'd seen—she said all of a sudden whisked away by sweetness—if you'd seen how there was—there was a little dawn—and a little horizon because of the bonfire. There was all that. The two of us—she suddenly added begging as if asking Martim to bear in mind as well such a soft detail—the two of us were standing, he almost the whole time with his back toward me—Oh, she then shouted misunderstood, you, sir, mustn't forget that I was different from the way I am now, I'd reply so quickly to everything, as soon as a leaf would fall, I'd see it immediately. It wasn't happiness in the way that people talk about happiness these days, times have changed so much, these days we demand more of ourselves.

She fell quiet, a bit dizzy. A covetous love for her own story had overtaken her. There she was in that moment standing there—rich, dizzy, heavy, gaining right there, while she'd spoken, a past she'd never suspected ... "But I still have a whole past behind me!", she cried to herself in a rapture of surprise. She'd even been pretty! she'd even been young—something she'd never be in the future. She shivered at the thought that if she hadn't told Martim about the boy at the bonfire, he might remain forever ignorant of events of hers, hers by right. Since it was only by telling him that she'd remembered ... As if only now she'd learned that a boy and a bonfire were feelings too, and that that too was her life, ah, maybe you should give vehemence to whatever you'd forgotten, maybe.

The woman then wondered absorbed if there might not be a thousand other things that had happened to her ... And which she simply didn't yet know. She wondered, with the seriousness of a discovery, if she in fact hadn't chosen to live off a few past facts, when she could have lived off of others that had happened just the same—and were hers by right—just as in that moment she was living off the boy at the bonfire. There she was, dizzy and heavy; her past revealing itself to be as full of possibilities as the future. Oh more than the future. Because the past has the richness of what's already happened.

—And, naturally, you'll never like anyone else again, ma'am, said Martim with irony.

—Why? she replied distracted. But that was a love.

—And where's the boy from the bonfire? he asked politely.

—But how am I supposed to know?, she said shocked because with that question the man was revealing that he hadn't understood a thing.

She was reduced, by Martim's incomprehension, to remembering by herself. Moreover, just then she wasn't asking for more than that: to think by herself, like someone who received a letter and is waiting impatiently for the undisturbed moment to read it. In her first cautious steps toward an unexplored past, Vitória was trying to recall the boy from the bonfire a bit better. In that inferno of fire, on that gentle evening, that boy who was moving with the somber delicacy that an animal has … That's how Vitória saw the boy in her own past. And to think that the boy had always been there! That young man, tall, dark, stirring the fire, stirring through his own autonomous existence and exuding his own heat. And life was great inside him, life had space inside him. He wasn't nervous, oh not a bit. There were people like that: life was great inside them but that didn't make them nervous. Oh how many memories she had, and she'd never touched them! avid as she was to live, when … when in fact she'd already lived. When in fact the event had already happened. A thousand times the event had already happened to her. And she hadn't realized it.

She unexpectedly remembered another man. So similar to the one from the bonfire, she was surprised to see. The events repeating and urging her on—and she blind hadn't noticed. "But I was always living!" She remembered that other boy who was playing ping pong and who'd repeated, for her, the existence of the boy from the bonfire. She'd seen him playing at the club where her father had taken her to distract her. Twenty years ago! Twenty years ago this had happened. Oh the richness of getting old, the older you got, the more unknown was the past. The woman blinked surprised: twenty years ago a boy had played ping pong agile and calm, and—while the world had kept moving on—she, Vitória, had stopped at the door of the lounge of the club and, twenty years ago, she'd looked at him. And while looking at him, she'd learned that that was how you could love: since she'd seen, for a minute and forever, that boy playing ping pong.

"And did he love you, ma'am?" Martim would ask if she'd told him that fact too, that fact that from now on, yes, from now on would be her future.

"How should I know?" she'd answer. Because just afterward she'd left the club brushing against the low plants. And bringing along the impression that today, now, in this moment, was finally revealing itself. As if she'd kept inside her whatever had no value. But had kept it for so long that the event was finally exhaling a ripe odor of fruit, and the wine that had been new was gaining thickness and that quality that brightens a glass.

The man who in that moment was waiting in the sun didn't understand a thing, she knew it. But Vitória didn't seem to need anything more of him—as if she'd chosen to live off the great freedom you can have regarding whatever already happened. She looked at Martim, in a deep, tired sigh. He hadn't understood a thing. But she couldn't even blame him. Since looking now absorbed all around her, not even she herself would have known how to make logical and rational the fact that her deep love was spread out, the fact that the mystery was locked up, the fact that every once in a while the sign of richness would take aim in a warning, the fact that she'd always sought, in her humble vocation, a certain intimate glory. And how to make rational the fact that all that mixed together was the source of the beauty and the austere goodness of a saint, and yet it was also the source of the suffering of a woman, and how to make rational the fact that a boy in front of the bonfire was warming her face today, and how to explain that she was waiting for something to conquer inside her just as one day St. George tread on the dragon, and how to explain that by herself on the ranch she was the queen of a world in which at night you could look at the entrails and no longer be surprised—oh no longer be surprised, because a person isn't she herself, a person is someone else; and how to make rational the fact that by herself she was heading toward that thought that a person must have at least once in her life, and how to explain that love isn't just love, love was all of that, and how heavy it was, ah how heavy it was. How could she blame Martim for not understanding, if she didn't understand either …

—Why didn't you ever get married, ma'am, said Martim without noticing that the conversation had ended.

—Because I never found an honest and sympathetic man, she replied simply. Everyone I've ever met to this very day, when I take a close look, I see that they're too free. I never met anyone who could live up to my need for order and respectability.

—How conventional you are, ma'am! he said almost flirtatiously, and, trying to praise her and her rectitude of character, he judged her in a quite conventional way, the way people expect to be judged, and toward which they work all their lives. How conventional you are, ma'am, he said with a certain respect.

—Conventional? she repeated. No, she explained to him slowly, it's that I always needed a form in which to live. Because I too am a person who is so free that I seek an order in which to apply my freedom.

In restriction, she thought, I am a saint. Which she didn't say to the man, because of the misunderstanding about saints.

Neither did Martim quite understand what she'd said—since not only did other lives still seem very abstract to him, but he was also more awake to his own thoughts than to other people's—nor did she herself totally understand what she'd said. But, if she hadn't told the truth in every single word of the truth, she'd said some recognizable thing. And the woman took on a vaguely satisfied mien. Both of them, moreover, had the tranquil impression of something justified at last.

The heat of the sun was unbearable, it was noon. The man was seeing with rippling eyes the woman's shirt drenched at the armpits. He wanted to avert his eyes but some thing in that dark moisture kept catching his stray gaze as if fascinating him. Vitória, without realizing that she'd fallen silent a while ago and that the greater confusion had taken place, actually, in her own thought—then closed her mouth, falling even more silent.

—So? said the tired man.

—So what? she asked awaking in a start.

As if she'd showed him in a jumble everything she had to show, the lady had nothing else for him. What had she wanted from Martim? Since everything she'd told him had nothing to do with the purified and useless life she'd chosen one day, everything she'd told him had nothing to do with the night of frogs she'd spent. And it had nothing to do with the fact that she'd just discovered that, without knowing it, she'd already lived. And if the knowledge of herself hadn't brought her anywhere up till now, except to a rocky bottom beyond which she couldn't go—now it was as if the rock had crumbled and was letting her through, at last a passage to a past. Oh, she owed herself that much: to experience at last her own experience. —And that man? what she'd wanted was from him? She looked at him without surprise, and he was a stranger. She'd even forgotten to tell him that she'd turned him in, once more she'd forgotten. Now that she had a whole past ahead of her, he was a familiar stranger.

And the stranger? The stranger was looking at her with a kind and curious attention. While looking at that woman, this is what he was thinking: bad people are so clever! Since Vitória's face was just soft and tired. Contradictorily, he was thinking: the danger is just in the acts of bad people since these have consequences, but they themselves aren't dangerous, they're childish, they're tired, they need to sleep a bit. And he looked at her curiously, with a smile of cordiality. That was when their gazes met—and there was no escape: we all know the same things. The man then was a bit touched and, in a flippancy of generalized love, said suddenly very young:

—To hell with it, madam, life isn't as serious as all that!

Vitória was a bit shocked. For an instant, it's true, an almost sly look passed over her face as if she'd glimpsed in this way of seeing, so new, unsuspected opportunities and non-dangerous freedoms. But it was just an instant, and right afterward she wandered off from whatever made sense and whatever Martim had meant to say. And all she had left was the man's smile.

He was smiling ... And—and she felt so understood that she jerked back rigidly as if the man had been obscene. She was startled. She, who was now wanting to be alone with her past, she was startled: any gesture of kindness toward him was still dangerous! she didn't want his smile! it was still very early to be tempted, she still hadn't aged enough! A quick rattle traversed her: "don't understand me because otherwise ... because otherwise I'll end up free once again." And, oh God, she didn't want to have once again the experience of the freedom that would lead her to seek once again and once again, and to shout that she didn't want just a past. The lady was frightened because she was aware that she was dangerously ripe in order to receive any compassion. "Don't break my power!", she thought—since she'd barely just finished constructing a whole life behind her—"don't be polite to me, don't smile at me, it was always dangerous to be nice to me!" That man who innocently was throwing her a bone. "Don't destroy me with understanding," she implored inside her—she knew that, forgetting her fear, she'd once again directly seek whatever belongs to a person, if that person ...

The lady looked at that man, that man who was crudely the day of today, the impossible day of today, and how to touch directly the day of today, we who are today? she felt horror of the man, just as she'd feared the great solitary beach shining in grace and the expectation of happiness, and all is thine if thou hast courage—but she only had courage to look straight ahead when it was already impossible to look straight ahead, and only now could she look at the disappeared boy by the bonfire, and the past must be full of things that she could finally look at without danger. But—but suddenly, in that man there, time had come from so far away in order to burst out into: today! the urgent instant of now. "Don't understand me," she thought already less convulsive and, luckily for her, a little sadder, "don't love me for even a second, I no longer know how to be loved, it's too late, farewell." She didn't know how to be loved. Being loved was so much graver than loving. That woman didn't know a thing. Out of a mistake of life—and a mistake was all it took, in that fragile thing that is direction, for a person not to arrive—out of a mistake in life she'd never used the silent request that we use and that makes others love us. And, dispossessed, she'd become so, so proud. And now—now she no longer knew how to be loved.

And yet—and yet, maybe if …?

Then Vitória averted her eyes from the smiling and kind eyes of the man. "No," her soul said once again, just as she'd said one night on the island. No.

And the contempt for herself left her hunchbacked and small among the great trees, because once again she had said no.

What did she feel then? This is what she felt: oh God, what do I do with this happiness around me that is eternal, eternal, eternal, and which will pass in an instant because the body only teaches us to be mortal? That's what the lady felt because, in saying "no" once again, she, wounded as she was, had seen the trees at the same time, and out of a pure recognition of beauty, she'd loved the beauty that was not her own, and loved the sadness that was, and, haughty as she was, had felt for an instant very, very happy, just out of pride, just out of insolence.

What Martim preserved of Vitória were overlapping and indecisive images. Now it was the image of a confused woman who was sweating under her arms—and then he wondered if he hadn't simply made up a danger concerning his own sojourn on the farm, since a sweaty woman wasn't dangerous. Now appeared to him, unconnected to anything else, the image of a face—and he could no longer say that he recognized it, bumping into the peculiar mystery of a face; and then the woman was becoming dangerously unpredictable, with her two hollow eyes. But then the image that he had of the woman was becoming somehow so familiar as if he'd touched her all over her body, or as if both of them in the sun hadn't realized that several years of intimacy had passed. But then, as if they'd really lived several years together in mutual love, inside familiarity, he suddenly once again didn't recognize her.

When, however, he remembered how she'd said she was a po-etess—then something like ridicule covered the memory of the bony woman, and the poetess became no longer dangerous, she with her four queens. Who, in fact, had told him that Vitória had turned him in? Nobody. What had happened, probably, is that the owner of the farm, intrigued, had mentioned his presence to the teacher since he, apparently, had made himself the spiritual guide of those uncertain and menstruated women. There was nothing, then, to be afraid of.

5

AND AS IF BEFORE THE APPOINTED HOUR EVERYTHING had ended, and as if everyone had got from the man whatever it was they'd wanted—suddenly they left him alone. The air was light and satiated, and in the morning the cow gave birth to a calf.

Ermelinda disappeared for long hours. Martim heard her tell the mulatta that she was going to cut a new dress. Francisco was working mutely, unhurried. As for Vitória, she was no longer chivvying him with orders: she no longer seemed to take pleasure in giving him tasks, or had unexpectedly admitted that he knew what to do all by himself. Simply curious, Martim saw her walk by with feminine dresses on now—clothes that seemed even stranger to him because, besides being unfashionable, re-called, with their wrinkles, the trunk from which they must have emerged. In this garb, she looked even less dangerous to him. One day he saw the most extraordinary thing: he saw her trying on a hat that was so old and dusty that only the unexpectedness of the situation kept him from smiling. And the woman was pay-ing such profound attention to the inside of the mirror in the parlor that she didn't even notice the man. He interpreted the fact that she didn't see him—she, who had always followed him with unmoving eyes—as a sign that he was at last free. Moreover, after the great rainfall, every tranquil thing was where it ought to be, and the hypothesis even seemed plausible to Martim that, instead of fleeing, he should simply tell Vitória that he was leaving. But he no longer even needed to leave.

A period of enormous calm followed. Life was revealing an obvious progress just as you suddenly realize that a child has grown. With the great rainfall nature, ripening, had headed for a high point, which you could feel in the leafier way the trees were swaying. And the few days that followed spliced on to one another without incident, like a single day.

They were bright and tall days, woven in the air by the little birds. Wings, stones, flowers and deep shadows were shaping the new humid heat. The clouds were piling up white in the sky and unravelling with grace, showing the immaterial depth that surrounded the house, each person's work, and the large nights. In the morning, in the wide-open sky the first shreds of clouds would let the gaze rest in order to carry on into the distance: early in the morning things would sparkle tranquilly. Yet, though it was far away, the sharp air would place the mountain at the distance of a single shout.

Some people had lost touch with others, each had retired to an individual life that was already preparing them for the life they'd have once the man left. Absorbed, they were already living lightly in the future like people reckoning on an extra room once the dying man was taken away. Even the woodshed was looking clean and well swept. And in the stables, since the calf's birth, there was serenity.

A bit disoriented by the peace, Martim sometimes would try to plan an escape. But the buzzing of the bees seemed more real than the future. And the man now had so much work ahead of him—a work no longer interrupted by Vitória's contradictory orders—that only his task seemed palpable. Nobody had ever said to him that there was a threat in the poor figure of the elementary school teacher. Eventually Martim could no longer exchange a simple suspicion for the reality that was emerging more and more: the ditches that were being opened by his hands, the golden heat full of short-lived mosquitoes, the wheel of the plow turning up a blacker earth. Only men could perhaps feel any sadness. But so tall and lovely was the sky that Martim, against himself, joined the light, going over at last to the side of the victor.

And harnessing the cresting movement of a wave in order to raise himself too, he allowed himself without concern be carried by the billow of abundance. Out of consideration and docility, he transformed himself into the instrument of his own work. Never, for example, would he dig a ditch at a place where the earth desired hardness. And when the cow would refuse, he would not milk her. This demanded a patient dedication from him, he was feeling the pleasure of someone who discovered a more delicate style.

The ranch benefited greatly from this new state as if upon it had been installed a long and productive Sunday. For there was a Sunday feeling in the indolence with which the countryside was fat. The corn was growing heavily, the apple tree was bursting out in sprigs as if the wound had awakened an urge inside it, the wind was rushing along the creek. That same wind would sometimes bring a heavy scent of fertilization and ripening—which Martim, breaking off his work with surprise, would recognize as if he'd already slept with wheat and corn, and could recognize from the depths of the centuries the scent of the movement of fecundation. The world had never been so large. Little birds active as children were partaking of the earth raked over for sowing: diving with closed wings into the waves of the air, and from the infinite returning in order to gaze with the ruffling of wings at the work of the seeds. With the drought disappeared, the now full trees were covering the house with shadows, giving its interior a freshness of afternoon dozing. In the pasture the cows were drooling. The world was thinking for Martim; and he was accepting it.

The women of the house too looked paler, calmer, carrying out their tasks. No longer in heat, the dogs were now thin and happy. They would bark at the clouds. And the mulatta was singing so loudly that even near the waterhole the odd sharper note would arrive by itself. The whole ranch was abuzz.

6

IT WAS JUST BEFORE THE INVESTIGATORS ARRIVED WITH the teacher and the mayor that Vitória had him summoned.

It was in the evening, and Francisco brought the message for Martim to the stables. Shortly thereafter he appeared in front of Vitória with the still concentrated face that he'd brought from work, his sleeves rolled up, his boots muddy.

The woman examined him in silence. She herself was once again wearing her black pants and her old shirt. Martim looked at her intrigued: he still had in his mind the image of the last few days—calm, dreamy, dressed like a woman. Now she looked to him somehow chilly. And he didn't like it. What could have happened? Had some important thread escaped him? Illogically it seemed to him that that woman had failed at something. And he didn't like it: he had the experience that, when a person failed, she became a threat to others; he feared the tyranny of those in need. And he didn't like what he saw at all.

But he was also used to women who "didn't know what to wear," and wondered if all that happened was that she couldn't find anything better to wear than those old pants; he even wondered if the situation of the ranch was so dire that the owner didn't have enough money to have any new clothes made, since she'd tried on her old clothes and they didn't fit. Who knows, maybe it was just a problem with her clothes? He recalled the tragic face of a woman who doesn't know what to wear. But, what he really didn't like, was the tired and chilly appearance of that woman who looked as if she'd returned from a long and fruitless journey.

—You called me, ma'am, he reminded her at last.

She remained quiet for a moment more as if she hadn't heard. Then she gave a sigh that was lighter than a breath. She closed her eyes, opened them once again. And said:

—Francisco gathered branches and leaves at the back of the yard, by the fence. They need to be burned.

That was the first order she'd given in those last few days, and he looked at her with a certain curiosity. He also felt vanity: so, somehow she'd gone back to needing him. He then looked at her contented, with contempt.

—Well? she said seeing him standing there.

—When I'm finished in the stables, he retorted with the calm insolence of a servant.

—No. Now!

—Now what? asked the surprised man.

—You have to burn it right now, she said more calmly.

The leaves were piled up between branches in a high heap that, to the man, seemed to have been prepared without any solidity: the power of the fire would instantly scatter the sticks. Martim shook his head, disagreeing with pleasure. He undid everything, and started to prepare with care a tripod made of short and thick branches. He took some time doing this.

Then he interspersed leaves and sticks with skill, set aside the green branches whose moisture wouldn't let the flame catch. And he lit the fire.

At first there rose a thread of yellow and dirty smoke, without a visible sign of flame. But soon tiny licks, quicker than vision, were escaping from the spaces between the branches, and popping out in a flashing eye among leaves. And right after the fire finally caught, the branches attacked by surprise were drawing back, the heated leaves quickly curling at the edges—and everything all of a sudden started to crackle as if at the same time branches and leaves had been hit.

And soon the air of the yard was unbreathable, with suffocating smokes and charred leaves dancing in the air—the man was moving securely and precisely with an ever more nimble trident that would push into the fire, at the exact instant, whatever was trying to escape the heat, pushing off any bark that wasn't burning. The scent was that of smoked spices, and his nostrils were smelling cinnamon and pepper, and at the same time there was the intimate smell of something animal that was burning, something like the smell of the feathers of a bird underneath the wings, but the most distinctive thing was a deep fragrance of hard burning husks. The smoke, because it was so compact, had acquired the thick shape of a bolt—though two meters above the fire the bolt spread out disoriented, hesitating pushed from side to side in the wind, the wind too disoriented by the urging of the smoke.

For a moment Martim turned his face away from the heat in order to wipe off the sweat—and saw Vitória among the thick smoke.

She was looking fixedly at the bonfire, her arms were crossed over her chest and her hands were grasping her shoulders with cold. It was a quick glance, the man's, and without expression. And right afterward he prodded the bonfire once again as if he hadn't noticed the woman. She was still standing there: he could almost infer her breathing. The evening was bright and without sun. But beside the bonfire it was as if night were being made, dark and reddish.

Now the activity of leaves and wood had become intense and, carried by the wind and by the frightened power of the fire, the scent of burning was rising beyond the tops of the trees. Now that the fire was totally open, the licks had the speed of joy and of fear, the coals were trembling alit. Martim was stirring the fire with the deft and speedy trident, and his skill was unquestionable, his firmness unrelenting. He was sweating, his reddened and watchful eyes weren't missing a single instant, the smoldering wasn't broken off. The flaring, which would sometimes arise in a sudden greater urging, was incinerating the air in the yard.

The woman was behind him, and he could feel her on his back, on his neck, on his legs, without an instant's respite, pushing him, pushing him, demanding more as in an arena—Martim was obeying in a concentration of violence, the fire was rising more and more cracking and obeying. Until the man unexpectedly turned around and faced her with fury.

She had her eyes wide open, panting as if she'd been running, looking horrified at the beauty of the world.

Then, without taking his eyes off her and without looking at the trident, the man threw it far away with a crude effortless gesture. And thus, with empty hands, with his arms drawn back from his body, it was as if he'd thrown away his last weapon and was ready to fight with his own hands. He would offer her his own death, as an insult. But he still wasn't moving and was looking at the woman, breathing with difficulty, with rage.

The woman didn't look at him, not even if someone shook her would she take her eyes off the fire.

But when the crude gaze of the man forced her to see him—not the other, but him—she took a step back as if finally realizing she'd gone too far. The man was wheezing with his body bent forward, his naked arms open in the air like a black and joyous monkey. She took another step back, terrorized.

As unexpectedly as he'd turned around to face her, he turned back to the bonfire—without even letting the woman figure out when exactly the transition had come. And with fury the man poked the fire, the undermost flames started to rise again—without fear of using up his own life, Martim created the fire, worked with those hands that had become faster than the challenged flame, and feeling the heat scorch the hairs on his arms.

Afterward, there was almost nothing more to do.

Like the first smoke, that last bit of smoke was nasty and thick and malign; and it was floating off in a sinuous thread. The coals were still blinking, short instants later they were still cleverly gilded. Afterward, you could feel that they were inflamed but they no longer had any light, and were tranquilly going black.

The man looked at them panting, his neck sparkling with sweat. His mouth, still grimacing with the effort, was open to show his teeth.

At last, forced to admit that there was nothing more he could do, he dropped his shoulders, relaxed the tension in his arms, and his eyebrows came down. Once again dissimulated by his eyelashes, his eyes became calm, intense. Without surprise, he saw that Vitória was no longer there. Then he looked cunningly around, as if he'd just shown what a man could do.

The evening was bright once again. The great softness of the air that surrounded his wet body made him scrutinize the sky with infantile surprise, his face puckered upwards as if they'd given him some thing. He stretched his burnt arms toward the breeze, touched his lips to his charred hands. Standing, full of himself, looking mysterious, magnanimous, bestial. Dealing with fire had been a man's task, and he was proud and calm. Everything was so rounded and polished that there was even a bit of dignified sadness in Martim. And the promise that was made to us—the promise was there. He was feeling it there—all he'd have to do was hold out the hand finally burnt in the exercise of his task as a man.

Although now, wiser and older, he wasn't holding it out.

But at least it was granted to him to look, without this implying a mutual insult. At least grandly he could look, and on equal footing. With hands nobly burnt in combat, Martim looked: the field had become vast and the light had the religious grace as for a man who no longer is ashamed of himself and looks face to face, human nature already redeemed inside himself.

Unexpectedly the first step of his great general reconstruction had taken place: if bit by bit he had been making himself, now he was inaugurating himself. He had finished reshaping the man. The world is wide but so am I. With the obscure satisfaction of having worked with fire and of having frightened whatever needs to be frightened in a woman, his first honor had been remade. It seemed to him that from now on he would no longer need to have a man's voice nor try to act like a man: he was one. His thought had never been so elevated as the work that he had just done.

And deeply inside him, he immediately started to despise people who didn't love what they did. Or who didn't have the courage to do what they loved. Forgetting that only a few minutes ago he'd found a symbol of work, and that he should pity those who hadn't found it—he, with fatuousness, was admiring himself. That man who for the first time was loving himself. Which meant that he was ready to love others, we who were given to ourselves as a sign of what the world can do; and he, who had just proved it.

"How could I have imagined that time had ended?", his heart beat with vigor. Since if he'd just, just started ... As if time were created by the deepest freedom, now suddenly the future was being reborn to him. And he—who had been sure that he had given up on his reconstruction—saw that he'd only had the great patience of the artisan, and was seeing gratefully that he'd known how to sleep, which is the hardest part of a work. Because—as if the pause had been just the preparation for a leap—unexpectedly his first objective step had ripened: for the first time Martim had advanced totally, the way that someone says a word. The word that he had expected hadn't come to him, then, in the form of a word. He had achieved it with the innocence of strength. Just like this: he had achieved it. And then, with the fatuousness necessary in order to create, the fullness of time was being reborn to him, and he knew that he had the strength to start again. Since— since having at last reached fully himself, he would reach men; and, tossing away the trident and working naked, exposed and naked—he had led himself to "transform men."

How he would transform men, Martim sagely didn't know. And sagely didn't question himself, since he was now a sage.

But not knowing didn't matter: now his future had become so immense that it was rising dizzily to his head. The time was ripe and the hour had come: that was all the calm heart and the patient breeze were saying to him, and the deep love that from him at last emanated tranquilly as if from something finally rooted. Because up till this moment he couldn't have done a thing—as long as he hadn't recovered inside himself the respect for his own body and for his own life, which was the first way to respect the life there was in others. But when a man respected himself, he then had finally created himself in his own image. And then he could look other people in the eye. Without the embarrassment of our great mistake, and without the mutual shame.

And as for not understanding others … Well, that no longer even mattered. Because there was a way of understanding that didn't lack an explanation. And that came from the final and irreducible fact of standing there, and from the fact that another man also had the possibility to stand there—since with that minimum of being alive you could already do anything. Nobody to this very day had ever had a greater advantage than that.

Moreover—thought Martim feeling that he was slightly overdoing it but no longer able to hold himself back—moreover it was silly not to understand. "You only don't understand if you don't want to!", he thought daringly. Because understanding is a way of looking. Because understanding, moreover, is an attitude. Martim, very satisfied, had that attitude. As if now, holding out his hand in the dark and grabbing an apple, he were to recognize with his fingers made so awkward by love an apple. Martim was no longer asking the name of things. It was enough for him to recognize them in the dark. And to rejoice, awkward.

And then? Then, when he went back out into the brightness, he'd see the things he'd foreseen with his hand, and would see those things with their false names. Yes, but he'd already have known them in the dark like a man who slept with a woman.

7

SHORTLY THEREAFTER MARTIM WAS SUMMONED.

The mayor of Vila Baixa was a small, clean man, with his hair smoothed by pomade and looking like an Argentine. The two investigators were short and calm. The teacher was moving around intensely, his thinned-out cheeks vibrating as if he had to deal with everything at the same time. Martim was the only tall one among them, as if a group of armed dwarves were surrounding him. He looked, dazed. Because there was not the slightest logic in what was happening to him. For starters, the fact of being tall amidst the short men had left him physically awkward, incomplete and at a disadvantage.

The others were waiting patiently: because you could see that that man still hadn't understood what was going on, and so they were giving him time. Vitória, very pale, had put on the dress she wore for company. The teacher was talking, talking. Martim nodded his head agreeing without hearing and smiling as if that might be what they were expecting from him; until he got his footing, the best thing might be to act cautiously in agreement with what the others were expecting.

— ... you must understand, sir! we must be punished, you know why? otherwise everything loses its point! the extremely agitated teacher was saying, and Martim, too addled to think about himself, lost precious time understanding at last why the two women called the teacher kindhearted; he was; even if he wasn't; a man who judges makes a sacrifice. —We must be punished! the teacher repeated plangently, you're intelligent, sir, you must understand! I'm appealing to an engineer! addressing a superior man, you must understand why I did this! and I swear that it's not for my sake that you must understand! because I, I understand what I did, God gave me the inspiration to understand myself! because if you don't understand, sir, you're lost! if you don't understand, sir, everything I did will be lost, and you won't complete, sir, the thing you started with the crime! Sir, you must understand that if there's no punishment the work of millions of people will be lost and rendered useless! he cried imploring. These are the stages of humanity that must …

—Yes, yes, said Martim dizzily, pacifying him.

—You are an engineer, sir, a superior man, you must understand, the teacher ordered.

—I'm not an engineer, Martim then said. I am a statistician, he said very distracted running his hand across his forehead and losing a valuable bit of time.

Nobody knew what to reply. The teacher, ill at ease, made a gesture of sudden annoyance as if that man really might have spared them that unpleasant information. But the tension had been broken. For an instant the situation had disconnected from its antecedents and from whatever was still going to happen. Which left everyone indecisive.

—What did he do? Vitória finally asked the investigator.

—I killed my wife, said Martim.

And he looked at her deeply surprised. Could he have forgotten?

—I killed my wife, he then repeated, trying out what he was saying with great care.

Was that all? That was all. But then why hadn't he said that long before? he blinked his eyes, dazzled. Vitória was looking at him openmouthed.

—But why? she finally shouted devastated, but why? why?! she grew enraged.

—Because I was almost sure that my wife had a lover, said Martim.

It was surprising how simple speaking had become, and it was surprising what he himself had said. The investigator with a black mourning ribbon in his lapel coughed:

—He'd come back from a poker game and did the deed.

There was a silence. Martim wasn't understanding a thing. He smiled silly, looking a little sheepish, "so much fuss," he thought, "about me." A crisis of shyness overtook him. He wasn't understanding a thing, only feeling that he was wasting time, which gave him an uncomfortable, physical urgency. If there was any recognizable feeling inside himself it was that of curiosity: he was looking with curiosity. That was all he recognized. For from the moment he'd said the surprising phrase to Vitória, he'd become a stranger to himself. He had nothing more in common with the man who'd just lit the bonfire. To the point of having the dizzying impression that before pronouncing the simple revealing phrase, he'd always been lying.

Always been lying? He then started to sweat a little. There he was with a crystallized smile. In a minute he'd recovered the politeness of a person among others, the civility of a man who transpires discreetly. But unease was giving him a weight on his chest. He started to sweat a bit more and wiped himself off with tact, with light little taps of his handkerchief to his forehead. Though now he could hardly breathe. The cold sweat once again moistened his face, he ran his trembling hand across his mouth. But the unease grew: he then smiled with care, with ironic impartiality. He still had nothing to do with whatever was happening to him. Until suddenly it seemed to him that the physical place of a soul was in the chest, imprisoned there the way a dog's soul is caught in a dog's body. He opened his smiling mouth, and he had that total muteness, if he wanted to speak his soul, he'd bark. He grew frightened, smiling.

But he'd spoken! He'd spoken at last. The phrase about his wife had been one of the most ancient ones of all, slowly recovered the way a paralyzed person takes a step. And there were still other words that were awaiting him, if language were recovered … he'd discovered it with curiosity when he'd said so simply that he'd suspected she had a lover. Which, if that wasn't the best of truths, was at least a truth that had some exchange value … With curiosity, with the weight on his chest, he was there exchanging once again, buying and selling. So that had been what happened to him: he'd suspected she had a lover. That's it? And all the rest that he'd claimed, thought, or wanted—all the rest started to become so unreal that he ran his delicate hand across his mouth, was a man's destiny invented? He ran his hand over his dry mouth, fascinated.

—Out of jealousy, said Vitória crushed. You loved her so much that you … —the woman fell silent dumbstruck, looking at that profound man.

Martim shivered quite shocked. "Loved her so much …", Vitória had said. Could that have been it! Intrigued, Martim looked at her.

And among the four men that he now examined one by one, suddenly the long interregnum of dream was being erased. "Loved her so much," Vitória had said by way of explanation. Maybe it didn't even matter that he hadn't ever really loved his wife. But, reduced to its own proportions, that's how he could understand: "loved her so much."

"Loved her so much?" he was startled again, still not quite

steady on the legs that were being given to him. He looked startled at the four men and the woman who were waiting: "it must,
then, be the truth." The truth of others had to be his truth, or
the work of millions would be lost. Couldn't that be the great
commonplace for everyone? His eyes blinked in cleverness and
subtlety and curiosity. Though he knew he hadn't loved her, he attempted with a certain caution to make other people's words his
own which after all couldn't be empty: "for a man loves his wife."

With a certain avidity, he was clinging to the wisdom of the
four small men—and suddenly, suddenly even though it wasn't
possible, he didn't want to flee.

And then, as if he hadn't seen people for a very long time, he
looked at the messengers with curiosity and a bit of emotion.
He'd forgotten what they were like.

"Had he loved her so much?" he insisted surprised once again,
forcing himself now with a certain impatience to recover the foreign truth. Yes, it had been for love, Martim still wanted to see if
it would work to establish a compromise between his own truth
and other people's, trying to make both of them the two sides
of a single truth: "yes, it had been for love, not for his wife, but
for love," he thought blinking, "a crime of love … for the world,"
he ventured embarrassed, awkwardly attempting this posturing.
"What's this nonsense I'm thinking?" he was startled, since the
ever more objective faces of the four men were now no longer
allowing him the slightest compromise, just demanding that he
make a tough choice: "A crime of love for the world?" Martim was
ashamed: those things don't exist! all that exists are acts! all that
exists are people's faces!

But once more he timidly tried the importunity of a bridge
between himself and the four men: "a crime of extreme love, yes,
which couldn't tolerate anything but perfection; a crime of compassion; of compassion and disillusionment? and of heroism; in

a gesture of rage, repugnance, contempt and love, he had committed the violence like a beauty."

Martim wanted to keep thinking that way since it was actually starting to work. But the men's faces were becoming a greater and greater obstacle. If he wanted to keep thinking that way, the thing to do would be to avoid those faces with their open eyes. So he averted his gaze, the way he'd once done when he was eating beef in a restaurant and a child had stood quietly contemplating him on the other side of the windowpane.

Disturbed, he averted his eyes: "Yes, a crime of love. In a world of silence, he had spoken." Oh, what nonsense was running through his head?, Martim was ashamed, though previously he hadn't been ashamed of far worse. But this time he was really embarrassed because, though he wasn't looking at the men, the four undeniable men were standing there. "What was my crime again?", he wondered, still stubbornly not looking at them, "what was my crime? I substituted the real, unknown and impossible act—by the cry of disavowal." That might have been the meaning of his crime.

"But of disavowal?" How to understand the meaning of this word, if disavowal—his strike—suddenly seemed to him now the most obstinate shiver of hope, and the hand most held out to the four men. "Had his crime been a cry of disavowal—or of appeal?" Answer.

—What was it again that you said that I loved, ma'am, what was it, he begged extremely confused, since that was a man who never ought to dig deeper, deep down he was someone meant to be led.

—I said ... —Vitória, after having started automatically to obey him, looked at him in silence, inexpressible. Now that she knew facts about Martim, now that she was finally looking at him with open eyes, now she didn't know him. And like a blind man who had recovered his vision and didn't recognize with his eyes those things that sensible hands know by heart, she then closed for an instant her eyelids, trying to recover the full previous knowledge; she opened them again and tried to make of the two images a single one. —I said … —once again she looked at him quietly; but since she no longer needed him for anything, she could also look at him with compassion and contempt. —I said, she repeated then bitter and untouchable, that you loved her so much that, out of jealousy …

—Yes, yes, now I remember! he interrupted hurriedly, his eyes touched by emotion.

Had he been jealous of her? Oh Lord, but I'd forgotten one of the capital truths!

The men were speaking softly amongst themselves.

—You might be sad to hear it, the investigator with the black mourning ribbon in his lapel said with irony, but she didn't die. First aid reached her in time, and managed to save your wife.

Everyone looked at Martim with curiosity.

—Great, Martim finally said, and his moist eyes sparkled for a second.

And so, she hadn't even died.

And so everything was erased. Not even the crime existed.

What had happened, then? Honestly a man ought to say: that he'd tried to kill his wife because he was jealous of her, since, as anyone might guess, he'd loved that drowsy wife so much. Then, immediately on that basis, Martim wondered with affliction: "Will she forgive me? How long will I go to jail? Will I still have time to start loving her, so that, whatever ends up happening, I'll always have loved her?" He was making an effort to construct a retrospective truth.

—And my son! he cried with a start, like a man who wakes up late. Using words once again, he shivered: "he'd always been mad about that boy of his"—and now those words belonged to him by right and he took them with eagerness. —And my son!

—Your wife, said the mayor with severity, deserved better than to be married to you, sir: she hid everything from the boy. Your son thinks that you're traveling.

And that, now? Martim's eyes sparkled with tears. And that, now? What to do, for example, with this? So that was his wife! A great woman. He saw her once more when she was yawning in front of the mirror while actively scratching her armpit. Courageous and good—everything he'd known about her was being erased now in front of the four men—and all that was left was that she was courageous and good. The other truth—an entirely useless truth amidst the four men whose power simplified them and gave them their size—the other truth had become as inexistent as the crime that hadn't come to be. Martim had an unexpected pleasure in using the words that have currency in the world: courageous and good. They were lovely words—since the existence of hollow words like those had saved the soul of his son!

The sentimentalization of decency overtook Martim with a painful assault.

—Courageous and good, he then said out loud so that the men would see that he was one of them.

The four quiet men looked at him. The four representatives. Representing, mute and unquestionable, the tough struggle that is undertaken every day against greatness, our mortal greatness; representing the struggle that we daily with courage undertake against our goodness, because real goodness is a violence; representing the daily struggle that we undertake against our own freedom, which is too great and which, with painstaking effort, we diminish; we, who are so objective that we end up being of ourselves only whatever has some use; with studiousness, we make of ourselves the man that another man can recognize and use; and out of discretion, we ignore the ferocity of our love; and out of delicacy, we give wide berth to the saint and the criminal; and when someone speaks of goodness and suffering, we lower ignorant eyes, without saying a word in our favor; we set ourselves to giving of ourselves whatever doesn't scare others off, and when someone mentions heroism we don't understand. The four men standing there, representing …

Then, suddenly—damn it, damn it!—suddenly, with a glance at the impassive face of men who had noses, mouths, eyes, identifying features and a forehead—Martim realized with a fright: they know! He realized: that everyone knows the truth. And that was the game: to act as if you didn't know … That was the rule of the game. How stupid he'd been! he thought terrified, shaking his head with incredulity. How ridiculous he'd been, trying to save a thing that was saving itself. Everyone knows the truth, nobody's unaware! Frightened by the noses and mouths with which we are born, Martim looked at the four men: they all knew the truth. And even if they didn't, people's faces knew. Moreover, everyone knows everything. And every once in a while someone rediscovers gunpowder, and the heart beats. Where people get caught up is when they want to speak, but everyone knows everything. That silent face with which we are stubbornly born.

The men were talking in low voices. And meanwhile, Martim was trying to feel through his mistake: his previous mistake had been trying to understand through thought. And when he'd tried to remake the construction, he'd fallen irremediably into the same mistake. But, if the intact person knew the truth. What a disgrace he'd been! he discovered ashamed and touched. As if he'd gone to tell a mother how to love her child, and the mother lowered her eyes and let him ramble on—and suddenly he'd understood that, without a word and without even understanding, the mother loved her child. And then, in humiliation—one of those embarrassments that very ardent people go through—he'd crept out on his tiptoes, promising himself never again, oh never again to make so much noise. Because millions of people were working without stopping, saving day and night. Only the impatient ones didn't understand the rules of the game. He'd thought the forests were sleeping untouched, and was discovering all of a sudden, through the face with noses that people have, discovering that silently the ants were gnawing at the whole forest, damn! we're interminable! What he hadn't understood is that there was a pact of silence. And ridiculously heroic he'd come with his words. Others, before him, had already tried to break the silence. Nobody had pulled it off. Because, much more than those who had the gift of the word, the four men and all the others knew.

Martim ran his hand across his forehead, confused. The men were speaking, studying the file. The truth is that, contaminated by the taciturn faces of the men who were speaking about the file, Martim now, as if he too were already losing the ability to speak, was no longer able to think in terms of words, he was metamorphosing into the four men, and transfiguring himself at last into himself—and penetrating into that surpassing whose summit is having a face that knows. And that was why he no longer knew how to express, not even to himself, this: that everything was right.

Miraculously right. Oh, Martim knew that if confronted with intelligence it would be very silly to say that. But it just so happened that, finally so supported by the four men, he wasn't afraid to be silly. Oh, how to explain that everything was right? Initiated now into silence—no longer the silence of plants, no longer the silence of cows, but into the silence of other men—he no longer knew how to explain himself, he only knew that he was feeling more and more a man, more and more he was feeling himself to be other people. Which, at the same time as it felt to him like the great decadence and the fall of an angel, also seemed to him to be an ascension. But the only ones who understand that are those who, with an impalpable effort, already metamorphized into themselves. Martim couldn't even manage to explain why a man would have as an ideal the urgency of being a man. Oh Martim at this point didn't know anything else. Except that mixture of fatigue, cowardice, and gratitude, where he finally stirred with the slightly ignoble and delicious flavor of a lizard in the mud. Oh, but some thing had been created.

Exhausted, but created.

More than anything Martim was very tired. A man by himself got so tired. He himself had wanted to carry a burden—"carry a burden" was one of those former symbols that he'd had to check out by himself, a remnant of the processions and the athletic matches he'd attended. He himself had wanted to carry the burden and pass it on. But the ones who were passing it on were the four tranquil men who were protecting with patience whatever it was that they were passing on. He himself, besides touching on symbols, hadn't been able to do anything else. But the four men were protecting the burden with ignorance. To hell with it, it wasn't quite a burden, it was "a torch" that in general you were supposed to carry! They were protecting the burden with ignorance, without opening their mystery, passing it on intact and so on and so forth, etc. Occasionally, then someone would invent a vaccine that cured. Occasionally the government would fall. Sometimes the woman would stop shouting and a child would be born. What the hell! thought Martim with a shiver, as if they'd hoisted the National Flag which he'd never been able to resist.

"Oh, but I too had the right to try!", he revolted suddenly, "I wanted the symbol because the symbol is the true reality! I had the right to be heroic! because it was the hero, in me, that made me a man!"

What was it exactly that that man was thinking?

Nothing. Transfigured remnants of public spirit and giving out grades, milkmen who don't let you down and deliver the milk every day, things like that that don't seem to instruct, but instruct so much, a letter that you never thought would come and that comes, processions that take a slow turn around the corner, military parades in which a whole crowd lives from the arrow that was shot—that man was getting everything back pell-mell. Memory ends up returning.

What was it exactly that he was thinking? Nothing, for that matter. The sun was still gilding, reddish, tranquil. The world was lovely, that's beyond dispute. Through the window the sun was gilding the file that the men were studying. Oh the world was so lovely! And everything was right. Futurely right.

"What is it exactly that's right?", Martim stumbled. His tired head got confused, he didn't know very well what it was that's right. He tried then, with superhuman effort, to go on. But it seems he couldn't.

It seems he couldn't, and that his goodwill wasn't enough; that's what the problem was. And now, as he found himself almost at the end of the road, having almost within reach a certain word or a certain feeling—now he didn't have the strength to reach out his tired arm and grasp. He had to stop right where he'd stopped, and transfer to others the construction of the course. And humbly remain there. And once again have guessing as his highest ideal.

Confused, in a manner of speaking, Martim was just guessing. But who knows, no power had ever managed to do more than to reach a man's arm all the way out—and then not grasp whatever it is that, with another tug, the final and impossible one, might fill with life a hand. Because the arm of a man has a correct measure. And it has a thing we'll never know. It has a thing we'll never know, you feel that, don't you? the man stumbled, moved as if that contradictorily meant venturing into the first step of a strange hope.

—She was courageous and good, he said interrupting the men in order to see their faces, for he felt that once again he was wandering away from them.

The men concentrated on the file raised their eyes, looked at him for a second and, beaten back, returned to the file.

—Courageous and good, repeated Martim interpreting their expressions as a sign that they hadn't heard him. And they needed to hear! He insisted on reducing everything that had happened to him to something comprehensible by the millions of men who live from the slow certainty that moves ahead, for those men risk themselves too. And they couldn't be disturbed in their sleeping work, and mustn't ever have their certainty shaken—without this constituting the greater crime.

Though Martim noticed that once again he was slipping back into discourse. And that the reality of the four men had nothing to do with that. So he felt a bit let down: nothing he had to offer seemed to be any use. He wanted to join the fun no matter what it cost, but all he was doing was just flaunting, no matter how discreet he was. He then felt a bit let down.

"Someday I want to find the man who's man enough to dare to tell me that I don't love my wife!", he said to himself suddenly pulling himself together. He was moved by his own generosity, he who was offering to sell his own soul, as long as someone wanted to buy it. It hurt him to lie, but the bravado did him a world of good, with coarse goodwill Martim wanted today to be the day that he was the one to buy everyone a round of drinks, and for everyone to drink as much as they wanted, and then he wouldn't at least confess that he'd ended up without any money—and then he too would have a secret sacrifice, as other people do. Martim wanted to make the sacrifice of his incredulity. And in that heroic amputation, he'd only accept in himself whatever men could understand without, because they'd understood, being shaken from their path: he was accepting that a crime of passion had happened to him.

He accepted that he'd committed a crime of passion, not only because, at that moment, recalling the breasts of his wife a retrospective rage overtook him, but also because it seemed that if he'd committed nothing more than a crime of passion he would have avoided the greater crime: of doubting. And after all, the truth is a secondary matter—if you want the symbol. And he now had a new symbol to pursue.

"I'm yours," he then thought, still with the remnants of a seriousness that was proud of itself. "I'm yours," he thought surrendered, attentive, aware. And the truth is that, by surrendering to them his own consciousness, he was finally surrendering nothing more than a consciousness that had failed; it wasn't much. A consciousness that had let itself be dragged along by beauty. "Is that really how I should perform the act of surrender?", he wondered, trying with concentration to get it as right as he could. And, surrendering the key to the small and strong men, he voluntarily was leaning up against the wall in order to be shot.

"Oh, could I be exaggerating my own importance, and the importance of whatever I was surrendering to them?" He was. But, without exaggerating, how was he supposed to live? How to attain anything, without exaggerating? Exaggerating was the only possible size for someone who was small; I have to exaggerate—otherwise what do I do with myself this small?

And that's how, no matter how great his goodwill, he still didn't know how to be another man. And he was surrendering enormous, awkward as a big rubber doll full of air. He noticed this; and tried to correct it or at least disguise it. For that way of surrendering was like insulting a poor person by showing him the charity of wealth, it was as if he were outraging the modesty of the four men. It was as if he'd thought that "the thing would be done quite correctly" if he showed himself suddenly naked— and the others would avert their eyes without at the very least reproaching him: just showing in silence that that's not how things work at all, and that nakedness is a purely personal matter.

Fine, I made a mistake, then. But then how can a man become the other man? How? Through an act of love, it vaguely occurred to Martim, which for the moment seemed really silly.

And since he was now at a dead end, he quickly tried to disguise his total lack of tact: "all right, that's enough! don't mention it again, all right? let's forget what happened, don't even mention it! I killed, didn't I? then I killed! anyway I didn't even really kill! but nobody needs to get upset with me, whatever happened, happened! let's move on!" His eyes were moist from the desire to be accepted.

The four men were still bent over the file.

They had the great practical advantage of being millions; for each million that erred, another million would arise. And some thing was happening through them—too slowly for impatience—but it was happening. Only the impatience of desire had given him the illusion that a lifetime was enough time. "For my personal life I'll ask for help from whatever already died and whatever will be born, only that way will I have a personal life," and only then the word time would have the meaning that one day he had guessed at.

"I am nothing," Martim then said to himself, this time out of naughtiness, blinking with pleasure. That's because, through some very complicated reasoning, he'd reached the conclusion that it had been a blessing to have erred, because, if he'd done things right, it would have been proven that the task of a life was for a lone man—which, contradictorily, would cause the task not to be carried out … A lone man would only reach a superficial beauty, like the beauty of a verse. Which, after all, isn't transmitted through the blood. (That's a lie! he knew that it came from much farther than that.) A lone man had the impatience of a child, and, like a child, would commit a crime, and then look at his hands and see that there wasn't even blood on his hands but only red ink, and then say: "I am nothing."

That's what he thought. And he also thought: I actually can rest—these men don't know that they know, that's all that's happening to them. The four small men carried on—dumb, small, stupid—dumb? I'm the dumb one!—they carried on. What? To hell with it, Martim thought very moved, it doesn't matter what. In the final analysis, they carry on. And in order to carry on, they were protecting themselves by being small and empty—they're not empty!—and stupid; and if they wavered in doubt, thousands of other little ones would sprout from the ground and continue the task of certitude.

It was then that Martim, for the first time, was sure.

Exhausted, as if he'd already been sure before, he recognized the feeling. The only way to discover was, moreover, to recognize. That's how it was.

And that's how it happened, just like that: he was sure. How? Oh, let's just say that a person might have a mathematical brain but not know that numbers existed—how then would that person think? by being sure! Oh, hope too is a leap. Martim then bet everything on sureness. And grew very still.

He grew quite still. From the place where he'd stood, life was very lovely. He'd reached an irreducible point, not divisible even by the number one. And then he grew still, tired. If he'd left home "to learn if it was true," he now knew that it was. Moreover, he knew the truth. Though he'd never planned to speak it, even when he was alone with himself, since, as has been said, he had become a sage—and the truth, when it was thought, is impossible. To hell with it! the truth was made in order to exist! and not for us to know it. For us, our only task is to invent it. The truth … —well, simply, the truth is what it is, thought Martim with a depth that placed him exactly into the void. The truth is never appalling, what's appalling is us. And also, since "the truth will happen." Let whoever doesn't believe that the truth happens see a hen walking powered by the unknown. "Moreover the truth has happened a lot"—by now Martim had already gotten lost in the depth that had always awaited him ironically. That depth from which—from which a great wave of love was born in his breast.

At first, not knowing what to do with love, his soul tottered a bit from so much crudity. Then he grew still, stoic, withstanding it firmly.

A few hours before, standing by the bonfire, he had reached an impersonality inside himself: he had been so deeply himself, that he had become the "himself" of any other person, in the way that the cow is the cow of all cows. But if by the fire he had made himself, right now he was wearing himself out: now he'd just reached the impersonality with which a man, by falling, a different man arises. The impersonality of dying while others are born. The altruism of other people's existing. We, who are all of you. What a strange thing: up till now I seemed to be wanting to reach with the final tip of my finger the very final tip of my finger—it's true that in this extreme effort, I grew; but the tip of my finger remained unreachable. I went as far as I could. But how did I not understand that whatever I can't reach in me … is already other people? Other people, who are our deepest plunge! We who are all of you as you yourselves are not yourselves. Thus, very concentrated on the birthing of others, in a task that only he could carry out, Martim was there trying to meld into those who will be born.

Slowly, he finally emerged from his stillness. "I'm counting on you all," he said to himself fumbling around, "I'm counting on you all," he thought gravely—and that was the most personal form for a person to exist. We who, like money, only have value as long as we are whole. Martim even felt ashamed to have been personal in any other way, that past of his was dirty, it had been an individual life, that life of his. But it also seemed to him, forgiving himself, that he hadn't had a choice: that that had been the only way he'd known how to be other people, since we are so similar and are children of the same mother.

Then, when he thought about "daughters of the same mother," he grew all sentimental, he got tender and soft—which from a practical perspective was bad because it diverted the course of his thoughts. "Now I have to start all over from the beginning," he thought very upset. But now it was too late to go back with any coolness, since he was all moved by problems of mother and love. It was then that—making inside his limits a perfect circle, and his luck was rare in that he could come back through obscure means to his own point of departure—in a perfect circle inside his own paltry limits, he then wanted to be good. Because, after all, putting off *sine die* the mystery, that was the immediate hour of a man. And above all because, after all, "the other man" is the most objective thought that a person can have! he who had so much wanted to be objective.

He looked. And without the slightest shadow of a doubt, he saw the four concrete men. They were undeniable. If Martim had one day desired objectivity, those men were the clearest thought Martim had ever had. And being "good" was at the end of the day the only way to be others.

Then, since many promises were made to us, one of them was kept right then and there: other people were existing. Existing as if he, Martim, were handing them over to themselves. Martim looked intrigued at the investigator with his black ribbon. "I return thee to thy greatness," he thought with effort and with a bit of solemnity. One of the promises was being kept: the four men.

And he, Martim, was ready to feel someone else's hunger as if his own stomach were transmitting to him the imperious absolute order to live. And if, like every person, he was a preconceived idea, and if he'd left home in order to learn whether whatever he'd preconceived was true—it was true, yes. Somehow, the world was saved. There was at least a fraction of a second in which everyone would save the world.

Martim's heart was confused. "The difference between them and me, is that they have a soul, and I had to create mine. I had to create for them and for me the place where they and I were stepping. Since the process is always mysterious, I don't know even at least how to say how I did it: but these men, I placed them standing up inside me. To tell the truth, I'm not in the least bit ashamed to, being nothing, be so powerful: because we are modestly our own process. I belonged to my steps, one by one, as these were moving ahead and constituting a way and constructing the world. It was a long way. And it's true that I lied a lot; I lied as much as I needed to: but perhaps lying might be our sharpest way of thinking; maybe lying is our way of grasping; and I grasped a lot; my hands have a past; it was a long way, and I had to invent the steps; but that innocence that I feel inside me is the goal; for I feel, also inside me! the innocence and the silence of others. Oh, it might be just for an instant! And then?—then it delivers us all to the task of living. We are our witnesses, there's no point in turning your head. The consolation is that not everyone must testify and stammer, and only a few feel the damnation of trying to understand understanding." With the grace of God, the world that he had been ready to construct would never have the strength to gravitate, and the man that he had invented fell short ... well, fell short of what he himself was!

Could he by chance be discovering gunpowder? But maybe that's the way it was: every man has to discover gunpowder one day. Or otherwise there was no experience. And his failure? how to reconcile with his own failure? Well, the story of every person is the story of his failure. Through which … He, moreover, hadn't failed totally. Because I made other people, he said to himself looking at the four men. And from the bottom of hell, love was rising. We who are sick from love. But would anyone ever accept the way he'd reached loving? oh people are so demanding! they eat bread and are disgusted by those who grab the raw dough, and devour meat but don't invite the butcher; people ask for the process to be hidden from them. Only God wouldn't be disgusted by his crooked love.

Moved and generous as he was, Martim would become even inconvenient in his luxury of goodness—like his own mother who, good and pestering, would insist with emotion that her visitors drink and eat. That's how, just like his mother, he looked at the four representatives. And without knowing what to give them, he hinted at a gesture of slapping the back of the investigator with the ribbon in his lapel, he opened his mouth to say to him in naughty complicity: "so, huh, you bastard?"—but he stumbled halfway, since his mother too had been a moderate woman.

Then, without realizing he'd thought of his darling mother, what happened to him, in a perfect circle, is that our parents weren't dead. At least not as dead as all that.

"What was it? what was it that I thought now," Martim astonished himself frightened. Once again that man had thought too quickly about his own slowness. Every time he got something right, he didn't understand himself, we are too intelligent for our slowness. That's how, without understanding why on earth he'd thought about his mother, he was now barely realizing that he'd thought; and grunted approving his filial feeling, with that tendency he had for rendering homage. He was a bit intrigued that he'd thought about his mother. Though he agreed; in a general way he agreed. He didn't know with what, but he was agreeing. What would become of us anyway if we didn't use, like God, the darkness? Then, without quite following the train of his thought, he discovered—all by himself and without anybody's help!—that God and people write with crooked lines! "If they write correctly, that's not for me to judge, who am I to judge," he conceded with magnanimity, "but with crooked lines." And that—that he discovered all by himself!

Another symbol had been, then, touched.

Excited by his success, Martim immediately got to work and thought: "the shoemaker's son goes barefoot!"—and stopped to see if that too might work. But it didn't make sense. Martim had fallen into pure blather, like a happy and tired man. From the time he was a boy, whenever he had a success, he ended up messing it up: when he'd play soccer and score a happy goal, his next joyous kick would always end up sending the ball into the foul zone: he was a man of good will. No, the shoemaker's son didn't take you anywhere—and the man felt in time that he was abusing his state of grace and pushing it a bit too far. Oh, how annoying everything is, he thought exhausted, bedazzled.

How many minutes had gone by? the kind of minutes had gone by in which thought is time.

—We've already wasted ten minutes with this file, said the investigator Martim had created and who was working for the first time since Martim had thought him up—and working perfectly right away. We're going to end up having to drive at night, said the disgusted investigator.

—Courageous and good, Martim said to him recovered, his former self, actually a bit too recovered and already in the Middle Ages; his armor was flashing.

He was eager to please them. Because for minutes and minutes he'd been burning to ask them if his wife really did have a lover. Now, for the first time, this was extremely important. And they ought to know, they were strong and good, he wanted to be judged by them who, secure and armed, also must be charitable—because in Martim's new system a person was unavoidably perfect since he'd reached the point of being alive, when a thing ends up being born it's because it was already complete. With moist eyes, he was wanting to ask them humbly like a child—wanting to be the men's child and learn everything all over again, and obey and be severely punished if he didn't obey, and wanting to enter that world that had the eminently practical advantage of existing, what am I saying?! an advantage that by the way is irreplaceable!—wanting to ask them: did my wife really have a lover, really? And if they said she didn't, he'd believe them: whatever they told him, he'd believe.

He remembered in time the contempt that people, especially those who are armed, had for a cuckold. He was a cuckold! Feeling himself classified filled him with emotion and gratitude.

—Did my wife really have a lover? he asked them with eyes blinking with greed, for Martim now wanted for everything that had happened to him to belong to him.

The two investigators saw his tears and exchanged an ironic glance.

—He's crying, said the man with the ribbon in his lapel pointing him out with his head. Besides being a … —he was going to say the word but recalled in time the presence of a lady—besides that, he's crying like a coward.

And that was how, with the new word of classification, Martim entered once more into the world of other people, which he had left in order to reconstruct. And he rediscovered with whiffing humility—like a dog without teeth but with an owner!—the old world, where he was finally some thing, we who need to be some thing that other people see, otherwise those same other people will run the risk of no longer being themselves, and how awkward that can get! He was the word that the investigator hadn't dared utter in front of Vitória, and a coward. They must be right, Martim thought with eagerness, leaping with generosity over his own disbelief, they must be right, they know what they're doing, he thought as contented as a woman. He was so moved by everyone's goodness. They were so good that they were taking him back, they even had a specific place for him and two names awaiting him. "Were they taking him back?", oh, but much more than that: actually they were demanding him back, they'd even come to get him! No man could be lost, the forward movement of millions needed every last man! And they were even ready to turn a blind eye—not to the crime, that fortunately never!—but to what he'd done that was worse: the attempt to break the silence those men needed in order to move forward while they slept.

—What's that music? he suddenly asked, he who'd never heard a gramophone in that house.

—Ermelinda didn't want to hear what was happening here and turned on the record player. But she wanted me to say that she's going to wave you goodbye through the window, said Vitória.

The unexpected interruption wrongfooted everyone a bit. For an instant they stood looking at each other, seeking in the fact of the gramophone its particular importance. Until that moment, one participant or another had been in charge of the situation. But now it was seeming to make itself all by itself, the session didn't have a president, events had taken on a life of their own.

—Right, said the mayor with insecurity but also with severity, since he was in his precinct and it was up to him to make sure everything was clear.

Because all of them, without realizing it, seemed to have forgotten some goal, or had for an instant gone astray from whatever it was they were symbolizing; things fall apart easily with a certain lazy goodness, with a certain empty meditation—which often ends up with everyone going home and, finally awakening from a mirage, starting once more to do what really matters. And what really matters? I don't know, maybe feeling with ironic goodness the way that the most real things and those we most want suddenly look like a dream, and that simply because we know very well that … that what?

—Is he going to be arrested? asked Vitória foolishly, running her hand across her dry mouth.

—But of course! Martim rushed to say looking at her resentfully as if she'd awkwardly offended the men. But of course! he said praising them; his voice was sweet and none too manly.

Vitória looked at him perplexed:

—Do you think he's all right, Mr. Mayor? she murmured as if in a sickroom.

With a hermaphrodite modesty, Martim lowered his eyes hiding the fact that he was so complete and perfect. Oh, he was realizing all sorts of things: that he certainly looked ludicrous in the eyes of other people; that he himself was voluntarily making himself ludicrous; that many of the emotions he was feeling weren't real; that he was faking the truth as a way of attaining it. And that he was on the verge of a disaster, and that he might suddenly start to shake with fever or otherwise feel in his own flesh the reality of what was happening to him. "You, please take no notice," he thought, "it's just that I'm exhausted."

The mayor shook his head while looking at him and speaking of him as if he wasn't there:

—That's how it goes, madam. When it happens people crack up. Until then they think they're really something, said the mayor checking him out with a curiosity already a bit fatigued by long experience, but when they're arrested they turn into women, they're afraid.

Afraid? oh no, thought Martim sincerely shocked and hurt, they don't understand me! They have the advantage of arresting me, and they don't even know for what! He lowered his head, annihilated, solitary. Would he be arrested in vain.

But since that man was awfully hard to knock over, he thought: it doesn't matter, maybe prison is exactly the place where I'll get what I want? Since, like a person who has already eaten the cake and nevertheless keeps looking for the cake, he was still stuck on the idea of "reform." It doesn't matter, he for example could in the tranquility of prison write his confused message. My own story, he thought already pulled back together in the fatuity he needed in order to have a minimum of personal dignity, the dignity the mayor had knocked over. Since there's still a lot I have to do! Because anyway, damn it!—he remembered suddenly—I've used up everything I could, except—except my imagination! I simply forgot! And imagining was a legitimate means of attaining oneself. Since there was no way to escape the truth, you could use the lie without scruples. Martim remembered how he'd tried, in the woodshed, to write; and how, out of narrow-mindedness, he hadn't used the lie; and how he'd been mediocrely honest about a thing that is too big for us to be honest about, we who have the idea about honesty that dishonest people make of it.

But with his imagination he'd write in prison the very crooked history of a man who had … Had what? Let's say: a pain and fright?

"Above all," he thought, "I swear that in my book I will have the courage to leave unexplained whatever is inexplicable."

Anyway—he then thought—the difficulty didn't matter in the least, since he'd used so many words because it was hard to sum up, so many that he'd strung together a book of words. Which pleased him, first off. Because he liked quantity too, not just quality, as they say about guava jam; and, if he was tired, he was also a glutton, because, after all, something bigger is always better than something smaller, though not always. A thick book, then. This is how he'd dedicate it: "In honor of our crimes." Or, maybe, what about: "To our inexplicable crimes."

Martim was pleased, attentive, imagining the story he'd write. "Somehow every one of us was offering his life to an impossibility. But it was also true that the impossibility ended up closer to our fingers than we were ourselves, since reality belongs to God." Martim thought afterward that we have a body and a soul and a wanting and our children—and yet what we truly are is whatever the impossible creates inside us. And, who knows, his story would be that of an impossibility that was touched. About the way it could be touched: when fingers feel in the silence of the wrist the vein. In that way, that man who one day didn't even know how to jot down the list of "things to know," wanted to write—his eyes closed halfway in a reverie like an old woman who, recalling the past, seems to transpose it in hope toward the future. And his armor flashed once more. He didn't know except roughly what that book would be that was dedicated to our crimes. Of one thing, though, he was serenely almost sure, though cautiously vague: he'd end the book with an apotheosis, since boyhood he'd always had a certain tendency toward celebration, which was the most generous part of his nature: that tendency toward the grandiose. But, after all, everything we attempt really is in order to prepare for a perfect "finale." In which, it's true, there's the danger of starting to talk out loud, and, after all, sweetness alone is power, Martim was starting to realize this. But the temptation of apotheosis was too strong: he'd always been a man who wanted to buy everyone a drink, he'd always been moved by being a dupe, and had never had the chance because of his cleverness and greed; he'd always longed for a generous apotheosis, without holding anything back, like at the end of a musical, when the whole cast comes onto the stage.

Oh God, God: he was exhausted. He didn't want any apotheosis.

Now serious, exhausted, he looked with fallen hands. He'd been playing around till now, out of pure excitement. But now what he wanted was poverty and sweetness. He was limp, tired, he wanted ... what was it that he wanted? What do I want? Oh God, help him, he doesn't know what he wants.

He didn't know. And in a superhuman effort to surrender, he made an expression with his face that if they knew how to read it they'd understand what he wanted, even if they couldn't say what. What was it again that he wanted? he didn't know, a person substitutes so much that he ends up not knowing.

Oh, but let's not make things too complicated. Since after all everything, in the final analysis, boils down to a yes or no. He wanted "yes." Which could be given indifferently with a lowered head or with the whole cast on stage, it's a little matter of personal preference, and there's no accounting for taste.

And the truth is that Martim was collapsing from fatigue. For months that man had been making an effort that was above his capacity, since he was a lesser person. His breath was short, his stomach's capacity small. The crime itself had been a draining performance. "In prison I just might take some vitamins," he thought vaguely, he who had always had the secret desire to be a fat man. His breath was short, and he was already nauseated by being people: he'd swallowed more than he could digest.

Out of fatigue, then, in a quick and soothing vision, he took shelter in the thick plants of his lot—who must now be tranquilly getting dark amidst the rats. "Go to hell," he then said to himself looking at the men, nauseated by being people. The tranquil plants were summoning him. "Not being," that's the vast night of a man. "It's not even with intelligence that you sleep with a woman," he thought hallucinating, and so deeply that he didn't quite understand what he meant by that. He thought with desire about the plants in the tertiary lot, missing the black rats. A limpness made of sensuality took away his fighting strength, gave him a nostalgic naughtiness, a pointless melancholy. Vaguely he still tried to stiffen his spine and pull himself back together: "after all I'm Brazilian, dammit!" But he couldn't. That man was sated, he wanted shelter and peace.

But in order to find that peace, he'd have to forget other people.

In order to find that shelter, he'd have to be himself: that self of his that had nothing to do with anyone. But I have a right to that!, he demanded tiredly, dammit! what do I have to do with anyone else! There's a place where, previous to the order and previous to the name, I am! and maybe that's the true common place I went out to seek? that place that is our shared and solitary earth, and where we only grope around like the blind—but isn't that all we want? I accept you, place of horror where cats meow contentedly, where angels have space in the night to beat wings of beauty, where the entrails of woman are the future child and where God rules in the grave disorder of which we are the happy children.

So why struggle. There was inside a person a place that was pure light, but didn't shimmer in the eyes nor cover them; it was a place where, all joking aside, one is; where, modesty apart, one is; and neither are we going to make, about the fact of being, a big deal! we're not going to complicate our lives: since we're entitled to this tranquil enjoyment! And it's not even something to discuss since, besides, we lack the power of argument—and, to tell the truth, long before we know it, dogs were already loving each other; anyway, we're entitled by birth, we're entitled to be what we are—so let's make the most of it, let's not overstate how important other people are! since there exists inside me a point that is as sacred as the existence of other people, let other people figure it out for themselves! a man is entitled because of his birth to sleep tranquilly—because things aren't as dangerous as all that and the world's not going to end tomorrow, fear confused reality with desire a bit, but the dog in us knows the way, dammit! you can't blame me for the silent faces of men, you have to trust a little bit, since we, thank God, have strong instincts and good teeth, not to mention intuition, and after all we have from birth that capacity to sit at night hushed at the door to the house. From which a few ideas are born ...

Yes, since that's how it had happened to him. A few ideas, and fright. Fright, rage, love, and then the door to the house becomes small, and none of these feelings and rights are enough, some other missing thing still needs to be born ... What's missing? When your own house becomes too small, the man leaves at dawn in order to bring some thing back.

Martim quickly pulled himself together. The limpness had passed. That was his chance! He couldn't miss it out of mere fatigue, he who had spent his whole life without knowing what to do with the fact of being small, and who now at last had found out what to do with himself, small as he was—join the small. He quickly pulled himself together—now that his turn had finally arrived for a little bitty apotheosis!

—All right, let's go, said the investigator closing up the file.

—I hope, madam, said the mayor, that he hasn't done you any harm. You were very courageous, ma'am, few women could have endured without fear the knowledge that they had a criminal in their house. Excuse me, few ladies, I mean. We, at City Hall, hope he hasn't done you any harm.

—No, no, said Vitória quickly, blushing in confusion.

Harm? no, no, she'd gotten what she wanted from him, hadn't she?

—Then let's go, said the investigator looking at Martim with a repugnance that was slightly feigned since in fact he was used to prisoners. You don't look like the type that runs away, but I'd better warn you that at the slightest movement, I'll fire.

Big and unarmed, Martim hastened:

—No, I'll behave very well! he said with pleasure and solicitude, trying with enjoyment to repeat some previous situation so that the current one might become comprehensible. And don't forget that I didn't resist, you hear? don't forget to say that to the judge: that I didn't resist! Don't you see that I actually could have fled? he said cunningly.

—Just you try it.

—Oh, I don't mean I could flee now! corrected Martim with respect. I mean I could have fled before! because before you gentlemen arrived, don't forget, I had months to flee!

Here's what had just quickly occurred to him: it would count in his favor if he lied by saying he hadn't fled because he'd planned to turn himself in ... Anyway—now that he thought about it, and in these new terms—how could he understand why he hadn't fled, except if he were planning to turn himself in? That he hadn't fled for other reasons, was a truth that no longer existed. For an instant Martim recalled the piece of paper where he'd written his plans, and recalled how he hadn't fled because he wanted to have time to carry them out—but that now had become so incomprehensible and somehow didn't fit into the system of the four men, that it only had a real and final value: that of having kept him from fleeing. Which would be called a lack of resistance. Which would be a mitigating circumstance. How perfect everything ended up being! he blinked.

—You couldn't have fled at all, the investigator replied. Ever since this lady mentioned her suspicions to the teacher, the investigations began and we've kept an eye on you. If we didn't pounce before that's because our method is to work with certainty, he added with dignity.

Martim nodded his head with surprise and curiosity: he'd completely forgotten how, generally speaking, stupid people are.

—But I couldn't know that I was being watched, could I? he argued patiently. I didn't know I was being watched, and I didn't try to flee, did I?

—No, that's true, the investigator agreed reluctantly, looking at him a bit fascinated: there was a mistake there but the investigator couldn't quite say what it was.

—He surely knew it was impossible to flee, ventured the man with the ribbon in his lapel who was one of the cleverest people Martim had created. He knew it was impossible to flee, he said trying to clear up the confusion in which the prisoner had thrown them—and knowing he was surrounded, he made up his mind not to flee in order to look like he was sorry and was turning himself in! he suggested with wisdom.

Martim looked at him surprise. He'd have to go through everything! Including innocence. Accused unjustly, for the first time Martim experienced innocence. His eyes blinked moist, grateful. Another symbol had been borne out.

And Martim now understood why his father, at the end of his life, would say stubborn: inexplicable: "I always got what I wanted." Yes, somehow you always did. And I, what did I get? I got experience, which is that thing for which we are born; and profound freedom is in experience. But experience of what? experience of that thing that we are and that you all are? It's true that most of our experience comes through pain, but it's also true that that's the inescapable way to reach the only summit, since everything has a single summit, and every thing has its time, and after we prepare ourselves for the next time which will be the first time—and if all that's confused, in all of this we are entirely supported by what we are, we who are desire.

"But anyway what did I get out of all that?" Lots. And lots of times our freedom is so intense that we turn away our face. Yes, but in all that I had, what to do about evil? Oh, but it's as if evil were the same thing as goodness, just with different practical results: but it comes from the same blind desire, as if evil were the lack of organization of goodness; often very intense goodness overflows into evil. Because evil, naturally, is faster as a means of communication. But from now on I will organize my evil into goodness, now that I no longer have the same greed to be good. Now that I'm ready for my own soul, now that I love others. "Could I really have got anything?" But I got to give existence to the world! Which means that I now would enter a war of vengeance or of goodness or of error or of glory, and that I'm ready to err or be right, now that I am common at last.

With a small start, Martim understood that he hadn't sought freedom. He'd sought to free himself, yes, but just in order to head without barriers toward the inevitable. He'd wanted to be unblocked—and in fact he'd unblocked himself with a crime— not in order to invent a destiny! but in order to copy some important thing, which was inevitable in the sense that it was a thing that already existed. And of whose existence that man had always been aware, like when you have a word at the tip of your tongue and can't remember it. He'd wanted to be free in order to go toward whatever existed. And which wasn't, just because it existed, easier to reach—it was as unreachable as inventing. No matter how much freedom he had, he could only create things that already existed. The great prison. The great prison! But it had the beauty of difficulty. After all I got what I wanted. I created something that already exists. And I'd added to what already exists, something more: the immaterial addition of oneself.

—Let's go, said Martim coming closer to the four men and the security they were offering him. Let's go, he said with the dignity of a fireman. Farewell, Miss Vitória—

Remembering with sudden pleasure a very old and humble phrase, gospel words, he then added almost amazed, slowly, bit by bit:

—"Forgive anything I may have done unintentionally."

What immediately bothered Martim is that he felt he hadn't repeated the phrase with precision. No, that wasn't the phrase he was vaguely remembering!—and it was important to him to reproduce it without the slightest mistake as if a simple modification of a syllable might already alter its former meaning, and take away the perfection of the perfect formula for farewells—any transformation in the rite makes a man individual, which endangers the whole construction and the labor of millions; any mistake in the phrase would make it personal. And, frankly, there was no need to be personal: if not for that stubbornness, the person would discover that there are already perfect formulas for everything you might want to say: everything you might want to see come into existence one day, in fact already existed, the word itself predated man—and those four representatives were aware of this: were aware that the whole question is in knowing profoundly how to imitate, since when the imitation is original it is our experience. Martim started to understand why people imitated.

And suddenly, just like that, Martim remembered the phrase!

—"Forgive any misspoken word!", he then corrected himself with vanity since that was the ritual phrase!

—Well, said Vitória turning red, averting her eyes.

—All of us, said Martim suddenly illogical, all of us were very happy!

—Well, repeated Vitória.

Martim held out an impulsive hand. But since the woman hadn't expected the gesture, she delayed in shock before holding out her own. In that fraction of a second, the man took back without offense his own hand—and Vitória, who had now held out hers, stood with her uselessly and painfully outstretched arm, as if it had been her own initiative to seek—in a gesture that suddenly became one of appeal—the hand of the man. Martim, noticing in time the skinny outstretched arm, hurried forward with emotion with two outheld hands, and warmly pressed the frozen fingers of the woman, who couldn't contain a movement of wincing and fear.

—Did I hurt you?! he cried.

—No, no! she protested terrified.

Then they fell silent. The woman didn't say anything else. Something had definitively ended. Martim looked at that empty and trembling woman face, that thing shapeless and human like two eyes.

And then the mercy for which he'd waited all his life broke his breast in heaviness and powerlessness, the heart of Jesus exposed, mercy assaulted him like a pain. The man's eyes went glassy, his features were clogged in a beauty for which only God feels no disgust, he looked like he was about to have an attack of paralysis. He babbled:

—Forgive me, madam, for not having … —and the worst thing that he said fortunately could no longer be heard as if the paralysis had already reached that mouth twisted by compassion.

Vitória raised her head. Her insulted features went white, tragic and hard. But her gaze didn't waver and her smacked face remained haughty and empty. Martim was aware that his own goodness was a cruel blow—did he have the right to be good?

—Forgive me for not having …, he murmured excusing himself like someone powerless.

But she'd never forgive. Because he'd asked for forgiveness, she'd never forgive him. If until now it had never occurred to her to accuse him, the moment he asked for forgiveness was opening an irreparable wound. And he saw it: that she'd never forgive. He saw it, though it wasn't something she'd thought or said. But he knew: she'd never forgive him. That wasn't the kind of thing you say, but it was the thing that was happening, and it wouldn't be the absence of words that would make what was existing cease to exist, and the plant feels when the wind is dark because it trembles, and the horse in the middle of the road seems to have had a thought, and when the branches of the tree swing there was nevertheless not a single word, and one day we have to discover what we are: he knew that she'd never forgive. Then Martim kneeled before her and said:

—Forgive me.

From the top of her lifted head, she looked down at him, not open to appeal, like a terrible queen, her severe wings open.

"What the hell am I doing?" the kneeling man wondered intrigued, and almost heard her telling someone years later: he even knelt.

But the woman suddenly clasped in an irrepressible movement her belly with her hands, right where a woman hurts, her mouth trembled stricken, the future was a difficult birth: in an animal movement she pressed her belly, where by force of destiny a woman hurts, and the joy was such misery, her mouth trembled poor, stricken.

—What are you doing, sir! she screamed at him.

But with his begging gaze he was waiting, he was insisting imploring, he now wanted more than the woman's gesture, that gesture with which she'd just allowed herself mercy at last—he was also wanting her to show him mercy too. And she, involuntarily, against her own strength, fleeing tortured as best she could—couldn't at last fail to obey, lowered her dry eyes, and, fascinated, dragged along, with a taste of blood filling her whole mouth, looked at him with hard goodness—tortured obeying, glorified obeying, with pains obeying. Oh it wasn't something you could escape—just as there had been sculpted images of men and women kneeling, there was a long past of forgiveness and love and sacrifice, it wasn't something you could escape. And if she'd been free, she'd obscurely hold out a hand and place it on the head of the kneeling man, there are gestures you can make, there are still gestures you can make:

—What are you doing, sir! she said to him as austere as if she were uplifting him.

The man got up, cleaned his trousers. The woman lifted her head higher still. And it was only then that they were surprised.

But then it was already fortunately too late: some essential thing had been done. What had really happened—nobody knows, especially neither of them knew, we substitute a lot. Something essential had happened that they didn't understand and that surprised them, and that possibly isn't meant to be understood, maybe whatever's essential wasn't destined to be understood, if we're blind why do we insist on seeing with our eyes, why don't we try to use our hands twisted by fingers? why do we try to hear with our ears things that aren't sounds? And why do we try, again and again, the door of understanding? the essential thing is merely destined to carry itself out, glory to God, glory to God, amen. And one of the indirect ways of understanding is to think something's pretty. From the place I'm standing, life is very pretty. A man, as impotent as a person, had knelt. A woman, offended in her destiny, had lifted a head sacrificed by forgiveness. And, by God, something had happened. Something had happened with care, in order not to wound our modesty.

They avoided looking at one another, touched by themselves, as if they finally belonged to that greater thing that sometimes managed to express itself in tragedy. As if there were acts that achieve everything that can't be done, and the act transposes the power; and when this is carried out, some thing is achieved that thought wasn't doing, we who are of an atrocious perfection—and the pain is that we're not up to our perfection; and as for our beauty, we can hardly stand it—Martim, for example, looked in that moment at his shoes, oh why do we disguise so much? sheepish in the hour of his death, he could disguise it by whistling. As if they'd just carried out once again the miracle of forgiveness, embarrassed by that miserable scene, they avoided looking at each other, annoyed, there's a lot that's inaesthetic that we have to forgive. But, even covered in ridicule and rags, the mimicry of the resurrection had been done. Those things that seem not to happen, but that happen.

Because otherwise how to explain—without the resurrection and its glory—that that woman right there had been born for daily life; that she, standing there, finally, finally born for the mystery of daily life, was the same one who tomorrow would give orders to Francisco; how to explain that that wounded woman, and maybe only because she had been mortally wounded, was the same one who tomorrow would turn to planting, once more whole like a woman who had a child and whose body closed back up? Otherwise how to explain that that man, tattered, helpless, would nonetheless keep on being that thing to look at and be recognized even by the eyes of children: a man, a man with a future. The resurrection, as had been promised, had happened. Unimportant like just another miracle. Carefully discreet in order not to shock us. Exactly the way we promised ourselves; and leave the task to us, and God is our task, we are not the task of God. You can leave life to us, oh we are well aware what we're doing! and with the same impassibility with which the recumbent dead know so well what they are doing.

The man cleaned his trousers once again, ran the back of his hand across his nose. He didn't look at the woman because he was ashamed by his own exhibitionism, that whole kneeling thing; yet it's also true that a person must express himself. His eyes blinked several times: also because he was realizing that in the whole scene something was escaping him. He felt a bit confused, he wasn't quite understanding and didn't have time or really the desire to understand more. But at least he sniveled again, and once again ran his hand across his wet nose. But he was feeling that, besides having "unveiled," he'd just carried out another commonplace he'd been chasing after since childhood: that whole thing about kneeling had always haunted him.

After all you could say that he was achieving everything he'd planned, even if he hadn't managed to write down on paper what he wanted. It's also true that often that man went too far. But he'd had to. He hadn't been able to be any other way. So, uncertain, anxious, helpless, he thought: I got what I wanted. It wasn't much. But in the end it was everything, right? Say that it is. Say it. Make that gesture, the one that costs the most, the hardest one, and say: yes.

Then, with superhuman effort, he said yes. And then—worn down, tired—the other promise was kept for him. Because "yes" is, finally, the content of "no." He'd just touched upon the objective part of the no. He'd just, at last, touched upon the content of his crime.

Nausea overtook him, that gentle taste as if he'd reached the other side of death, that minimal point which is the living point of living, the vein in the pulse. In agony, Martim averted his face from himself and sought the compensating face of other people.

The others were waiting curiously after having watched the melodrama of the genuflection. Martim blinked several times, indecisive, tired: those faces. Those faces. And looking at the four men and the woman, a hope enveloped him that was so absurd that it could only be a faith. And that had nothing do with what was happening to him, nor with the men who were waiting, nor with himself. Once again he'd had, for a nauseating flash, this: certainty. Which was a hope that was impersonal to a point of tears. As if hope didn't mean waiting, but attaining. With the absurd hope, Martim was thereby attaining like a man holding a child's hand.

Stunned, without knowing whom to address, dumbfounded by fatigue he looked at them one by one. And more and more he was approaching a truth that asserted itself so much that, even without his understanding it, it kept asserting itself. Not understanding it? But yes, somehow he understood! He got it the way you get a number: it's impossible to think of a number in terms of words, it's only possible to think of a number with the number itself. And it was in that inescapable way that he understood—and if he tried to know more, then—then the truth would become impossible.

"But for what? what did he have hope for?", he wondered, suddenly surprised once again. A certain pity for the world kept him from carrying his thought all the way through to the end.

So, without answering that question, since by doing so he'd make himself absurd, he didn't even try to respond, he thought: that it was for his own extreme neediness that he had hope. As if a man were so poor that—that "it couldn't be like that." There was a secret logic in that absurd thought, except he wasn't managing to feel around and locate that untouchable logic. If Martim knew he'd gotten it right, that's because it hurt. But he could never explain, and there's some thing we'll never know. But our neediness sustains us, he told himself, since he'd finally lost the limits of understanding and was admitting whatever you can't know.

It was then that the man suddenly grew truly excited, and sniffled. There's no doubt, I agree too: the thing is illogical, and having hope is illogical, he thought extremely excited, buying everyone a drink. It's as illogical, he thought slyly, as two-plus-two-make-four, which to this very day nobody has ever proven. But if on the foundation of two-plus-two-make-four you could construct reality itself, then, by God, why have scruples? Well, if that's how it is, let's enjoy it, people! since life is short!—Martim looked with a certain immorality at the men, cynicism was on his face. But he wasn't cynical, he was—he was trying to entertain them and cheer them up, and impossibility makes the clown—he was giving out of love, out of pure love—Love!—a somersault in order to entertain them, oh entertaining others is one of the most moving ways to exist, it's true that sometimes radio artists go too far and kill themselves, but that's because sometimes you make contact with the difficulty of love.

His cynicism, or whatever it was, didn't last long.

Oh God, how tired and unsure that man was, that man didn't know very well what hope was. Though he tried to rationalize hope, oh though he did try. But, instead of thinking about what he'd set out to think, he thought like a busy woman: "explaining never got anyone anywhere, and understanding is a futility," he said like a woman busy breastfeeding her child.

But no! but no! he had to think, he simply couldn't go off that way, just like that! Then, losing his footing, he argued with himself and justified himself: "Not having hope was the stupidest thing that could happen to a man." It would be the failure of the life in a man. Just as not loving was a sin of frivolity, not having hope was a superficiality. Not loving, was nature making a mistake. And as for the perversion there was in not having hope? well, that he understood with his body. Besides—in the name of others!—it's a sin not to have hope. You didn't have the right not to. Not having hope is a luxury. Oh, Martim knew that his hope would shock the optimists. He knew that the optimists would execute it if they heard him. Because hope is frightening. You have to be a man in order to have the courage to be struck down by hope.

And then Martim became actually frightened.

—Are you aware, my son, of what you're doing?

—I am, my father.

—Are you aware that, with hope, you'll never again have rest, my son?

—I am, my father.

—Are you aware that, with hope, you'll lose all your other weapons, my son?

—I am, my father.

—And that without cynicism you'll be naked?

—I am, my father.

—Do you know that hope is also accepting unbelief, my son?

—I know that, my father.

—Are you aware that believing is as hard to carry as a mother's curse?

—I know, my father.

—Do you know that our fellow creature is rubbish?

—I know that, my father.

—And you know that you're also rubbish?

—I know, my father.

—But you know that I'm not talking about the lowness that is so attractive to us and that we admire and desire, but to the fact that our fellow creature, besides the rest, is quite a bore?

—I know, my father.

—Do you know that hope sometimes consists in a question without an answer?

—I know, my father.

—Do you know that deep down all this is nothing more than love? than great love.

—I know, my father.

—But you know that a person can run aground on a word and lose years of life? And that hope can become word, dogma, and running aground and shamelessness? Are you ready to know that when seen from up close things have no shape, and that when seen from afar things aren't seen? and that for each thing there is but an instant? and that it's not easy to live just from the recollection of an instant?

—That instant …

—Shut up. Do you know what the muscle of life is? if you say that you know, you're evil; if you say that you don't know, you're evil. (The father was starting to go off the rails.)

—I don't know, he replied without conviction, but because he knew that that was the reply you're supposed to give.

—You've "unveiled" a lot lately, my son?

—I have, father, he said disconcerted by the intrusion of intimacy, every time the father had wanted to "understand him," he'd made him feel self-conscious.

—How are your sexual relations, my son?

—Very good, he replied wanting to tell the father to go back to the hell he'd dragged him out of.

—Do you know that love is blind, that whoever loves something ugly thinks it's pretty, and what would happen to yellow if it wasn't for bad taste? and that the shoemaker's son goes barefoot, and there's more than one way to skin a cat, and his-mouth-transgresseth-not? said the father going a bit more off the rails, it wouldn't be long before he started telling him what he did with women before I married your mother of course. You know that hope is a tough combat that wears down the weak, and the strong, etc.?

—I know, my father.

—My son. You are aware that from now on, wherever you go, you'll be stalked by hope?

—I am, my father.

—Are you ready to accept the heavy weight of joy?

—I am, my father.

—But, my son! you know that's almost impossible?

—I know, my father.

—You know at least that hope is the great absurdity, my son?

—I know, my father.

—You know that you have to be an adult to have hope!!!

—I know, I know, I know!

—Then go, my son. I command you to suffer hope.

But already in the first nostalgia, the final one as if just before never again, Martim cried for help:

—What's that light, papa? he cried already solitary in hope, walking on all fours in order to make his father laugh, asking a very old and silly little question in order to put off the moment in which he'd shoulder the world. What's that light, daddy! he asked mischievously, with his heart beating from solitude.

The father hesitated severe and sad inside his tomb.

—That's the light of the end of the day, he said merely out of pity.

And so it was.

It was almost night, and beauty was weighing down his breast. Martim disguised it as best he could, whistling vaguely without making a sound, looking at the ceiling.

From which, slowly and with care, he lowered his eyes toward the others—and looked at his fellows, one by one. Who are you? They were faces with noses. Should he invest all of his small fortune in a gesture of trust? Yet it was a life that wouldn't be repeated, that life of his, that life he would hand over to them. Who are you? It was difficult to give to them. Loving was a sacrifice. And even, and even there was the discontinuity: he'd hardly started, and there was already the discontinuity. Would he have to accept that too? the discontinuity with which he looked at them and—who were these men? who are you? what a dubious thing you are, as if I absurdly hadn't seen better days and known another type of people and couldn't accept you, but just love you? Really, are you? and to what extent? And—and could I love that thing that you are?

He looked at them, tired, incredulous. He didn't recognize them. A person was sporadic: he already didn't recognize them. Humble, he still wanted to force himself to accept that too: not recognizing them.

But he couldn't stand it, he couldn't stand it. How can I keep lying! I don't believe! I don't believe! And looking at the four men and the woman, he just wanted plants, the plants, the silence of the plants. But with his attention slightly awakened, he repeated slowly: I don't believe. Sleepily dazzled: I don't believe ... Dazzled, yes. Because, hallelujah, hallelujah, I'm hungry once again. So hungry that I need to be more than one, I need to be two, two? no! three, five, thirty, millions; one is hard to bear, I need millions of men and women, and the tragedy of the hallelujah. "I don't believe": the great coherence had been reborn. His extreme penury brought him to a dizziness of ecstasy. I don't believe, he said with hunger, seeking in the men's faces whatever it is that a man seeks. I'm hungry, he repeated helpless. Should he thank God for his hunger? since necessity was sustaining him.

Dumbfounded, without knowing whom to address, he examined them one by one. And he—he simply couldn't believe it. *Eppur, si muove*, he said with the stubbornness of a donkey.

Let's go, he then said approaching uncertainly the four small and confused men. Let's go, he said. Because they must know what they were doing. They surely knew what they were doing. In the name of God, I order you to be right. Because a whole precious and rotten freight was being placed in their hands, a freight to be thrown into the sea, and very heavy too, and the thing wasn't simple: because that freight of guilt had to be thrown in with mercy as well. Because after all we're not that guilty, we're more stupid than guilty. With mercy as well, then. In the name of God, I hope that you know what you're doing. Because I, my son, all I've got is hunger. And that unstable way of grasping an apple in the dark—without letting it fall.

WASHINGTON, MAY 1956

The Involuntary Eyewitness

WHEN I WAS THREE YEARS OLD, I WAS WITH MY MOTHER when she put the final period to *The Apple in the Dark*: it was in May 1956, in Washington, DC, and Clarice was, as always, working on the couch in the living room with the typewriter on her lap.

In her words:

> I remember very much the pleasure I felt writing *The Apple in the Dark*. Every morning I typed. I copied it eleven times to find out what I was trying to say, because I want to say something and I still don't know for sure what. By copying I will understand myself.

The book was only released in 1961, during the Brazilian Writers' Festival II, a very modest book fair compared to those of Rio de Janeiro and São Paulo nowadays, with their half a million visitors. At that time each writer had a "godfather," someone from another artistic area. And the godfather of Clarice was, somewhat haphazardly, the bossa nova composer Tom Jobim, already famous but not yet a legend. I was there, an eight-year-old. Having naive fun, Tom Jobim shouted "Buy the book, buy the book!" And I remember that Clarice was shocked that thanks to hyperinflation the book cost the very high price of ten cruzeiros.

For years now, I have read again and read again the first lines of *The Apple in the Dark*, always marveling at its mysterious poetry:

> *Esta história começa numa noite de março tão escura quanto é a noite enquanto se dorme. O modo como, tranquilo, o tempo decorria era a lua altíssima passando pelo céu. Até que mais profundamente tarde também a lua desapareceu.*

> [This story begins on a March night as dark as night gets while you sleep. The way that, peaceful, time was passing was the extremely high moon passing through the sky. Until much deeply later the moon disappeared too.]

I remember asking a literature professor about its strange construction, and he did explain it, but I prefer to remain astonished by her poetry.

The novel, with that formidable twist at its end, would have made a great Alfred Hitchcock film, and I hope someday it will make it to the screen. However, as some readers read the afterword before the book itself, I'll avoid any spoilers.

In any case, with *The Apple in the Dark*, my two memories (of my mother on the couch, of Tom Jobim hawking her new book at the fair) make me twice a witness—a different perspective from that of Clarice's excellent biographers, who unfortunately never got to meet her. (I guess a historian has a very different perspective about the Battle of Waterloo than the soldier fighting it.)

In 1961, *The Apple in the Dark* became for everyone Clarice's *obra prima*; for me, the book marks the passage between the more hermetic and innovative books from her initial career and the novels that followed it: the fully innovative, open-sky *The Passion According to G. H.*, *Água Viva*, and *The Hour of the Star*. I see the same trajectory with her short stories, which become markedly more experimental in the '60s and '70s, the stories which are my favorites.

In any case, *The Apple in the Dark*—a commercial and critical success in Brazil—was soon translated by Gregory Rabassa for Alfred A. Knopf; and there was also a German translation by Curt Meyer-Clason, and eventually a French translation by Violante do Canto for Editions Gallimard.

At that time, a Brazilian woman writer being translated abroad was still eccentric. And I was also a witness to the novel for a third time: I remember the famous Alfred Knopf, tall as the Empire State Building, in our small apartment in Rio de Janeiro, discussing the translation with my mother—and perhaps that was the first time I realized something really big was going on.

And last but not least—as New Directions publishes Benjamin Moser's brilliantly vivid new translation of *The Apple in the Dark*, the grand finale of its ambitious relaunch of all my mother's fiction in English versions true to Clarice's glorious and revelatory remaking of the possibilities of the Portuguese language—I am more than a witness. I'm also an enthusiastic champion of this campaign which, among other things, carries me back to that living room in the American chapter of my childhood.

PAULO GURGEL VALENTE,
RIO DE JANEIRO, JANUARY 2023